CASIDDIE WILLIAMS

Wynnie's Wishes

Dream big. Wish hard. Nothing is ever out of reach.

Contents

Preface

Content Warning:

Wynnie's Wishes in intended for adults 18+. There is explicit on page sexual activity.

Acknowledgement

Praise to my homies!!

I've published 4.5 books! Thank you once again for picking up another one of my wonderful, crazy ramblings of my mind. Seven months ago, when I saw an idea on *TikTok* with someone saying, "Write this book," I decided I could probably do that. Hazel and her men became real life on paper. I had no idea I was creating a world of people in my mind that would all have stories they wanted to tell. Hazel, Dellah, and Wynnie all hold a little piece of me in each of their personalities and traits.

A huge thank you to my Alpha K.K. Moore for always keeping me on my toes and pushing me past my boundaries. Sometimes I go down kicking and screaming when it comes to edits, but in the end, the best story comes out.

To my Beta N. Slater, who constantly makes me giggle with her commentary and, without even knowing it, pushes me to move forward in my writing. I aspire to be just like you!

As always, my ARC readers are the best. You've stuck with me through every story, and I love having my cheerleaders in my corner. Reviews are like gold to indie authors.

Thank you to every reader who's taken a chance to get to know and love these characters. Without you, there would be no book. Well, there might be books, but what good would they be without you reading and exploring their world!

THANK YOU!!!

Casiddie

1

Wynnie

Driving down the winding tree lined mountain with the windows down, hair blowing in the breeze, and the music blasting is my ideal way to spend an afternoon.

Well, my truly favorite way to enjoy the afternoon is on a long straight backroad, driving slightly too fast with my motorcycle between my legs. Unfortunately, I haven't had it at school with me the past four years, and I'm longing for the freedom of a ride.

I wish the drive back home was longer than an hour because I could get lost inside my head as the scenery whips by.

I'm officially a college graduate. Two days ago, I walked across the stage with a cheering section loud enough to rival a Super Bowl. I can't wait to see everyone again and spend time with them. I have my own-ish apartment, a great job, and money already in the bank. I'm killing this post-graduate thing already. I can't wait to start my new life.

My wandering thoughts are interrupted by the shrill sound

of my phone ringing through my car's Bluetooth speakers. Looking at the caller ID on the screen, I roll my eyes.

"How did I know you'd be calling already?"

"Because you were supposed to be home two hours ago. Where the hell are you? I'm dying over here." His exaggeration is comical.

"E, I promise you won't perish if you have to wait a little longer for me."

"You would take those chances? I thought I was your ride or die, Bitch! Apparently, you're leaning more towards the die side."

"Can you hear my eyes rolling through the phone?" He huffs at me.

"What's your ETA?" So pushy.

"Don't be a drama queen. I'll be home in twenty minutes."

"Make it snappy. I miss your face."

"Goodbye, Elliot. I miss your face, too." I hit the end button on the steering wheel before he can reply because he'll chat my ear off for the rest of the ride if I don't.

How I ended up with Elliot as my best friend is beyond me. At seventeen years old, when Elliot came to live with Aunt Dellah and Uncle Collin, I never thought I'd click with a thirteen year old boy. But we understood each other. What started out as making fun of our parents via text while at the dinner table has turned into a friendship that has blossomed and grown. At this point, I'd say we're more like weeds that have attached ourselves to the ground and refuse to go away, especially over the last several years.

He's so fucking brave. Elliot is my cousin for all intents and purposes, but we aren't related by blood. I remember when my mom told me about his mom, Aunt Zoey, dying right

2

after she gave birth to little Paige. Then, a few short years later, his dad, Uncle Griffin, died in a car accident. Elliot, Finn, and Paige were left orphans, but Uncle Collin and Aunt Dellah were named their guardians in their parent's Will and I had instant cousins by best friend relations.

Elliot became my soft spot, and I became his rock in those early days. Now he's my pain in the ass best friend who sits next to me and swipes left or right over guys on our phone screens. Maybe my soul knew he'd end up being my gay best friend who likes to steal my nail polish. *Asshat.* If only I could convince him that everyone loves him despite his sexual preferences.

Pulling into the driveway of my Aunt Dellah and Uncle Collin's house, I'm greeted with the fondest memories. My mom grew up in Mountain Pines, and it became my home when I was twelve years old and we moved back here for a job.

Peering out the front windshield at the two windows above the garage, I see my new, again, home. We lived in the apartment above the garage when we first moved back. Now, the apartment is all mine, and I'll live there and work with Aunt Dellah for her graphic design business. That was the deal we made when I asked her to help me pick a college all those years ago.

"Fuck." Rapid banging on my window pulls me out of my walk through memory lane, startling the shit out of me. "Dammit, Elliot, I think I just peed myself."

"Bitch, do some more kegels. You're too young for that to be happening. Get the fuck over here." He pulls open my door and drags me out of my car.

"Why are you so tall?" He crushes my head to his collarbone

because that's as tall as I am compared to him. "You're a fucking tree."

"Quit acting like you didn't just see me two days ago, woman." Is he serious? Not only did I see *him* two days ago, but he's been coming to visit me at college about once a month for the last two years since he got his license.

"Um, E. I could say the same thing to you."

"Shhh. Tiny creatures don't get opinions." He crushes me harder to his chest, and I flail my arms, trying to hit any part of his body that my hand will connect with. "Tiny, violent creatures. Ouch." He releases his death grip after my hand swats at his ear.

"This tiny violent *person* is a college graduate now, and you should respect her as such." I step back and plant my hands on my hips, giving him my most stern adult face. It takes him about .5 seconds before he erupts into a fit of giggles, followed immediately by my own.

Like an ass, he pats me on the head, and I swat at his hand again.

"Okay, I'll respect my elder,"—he winks, and I punch his arm—"and because I love you, I'm going to spoil the surprise. Wouldn't want you peeing your pants anymore and needing some adult diapers."

"Fuck off. You got jokes today, asshole. What's going on?"

"They're all inside." I look at the house and look back at him with a "duh" face.

"Of course they are. They live here."

"No. ALL of them are here." I don't like his emphasis on "all."

"Oh. So, are we talking about my seven in addition to your four?" Elliot's head shakes slowly and the corner of his lip tilts.

"Plus two more, *Pinky*. And there's some high school girls here, too."

Fuck. Of course, they're all here. It's not like everyone didn't see me two days ago. I take several cleansing breaths as Elliot wears a cheesy grin, watching me prepare myself.

"You're terrible at hiding your feelings. You wear them all over your face."

"Shut up. Let's get this over with."

2

Scotty

How did this happen? When did the angsty preteen turn into a gorgeous woman? Watching her walk across that stage and receive her diploma made me feel a sense of pride that I shouldn't have been feeling for my best friend's daughter.

I was honored when I received the invitation to her graduation. But I also wasn't surprised; I know it wasn't for me specifically. Wynnie has been Tori's nanny over the summers, during school breaks, and whenever she was home from college. She's helped raise my little girl almost as much as I have over the last five years. Tori loves her, and Wynnie loves her right back.

Watching Wynnie love my daughter has done terrible things to my heart. She may be a woman now, but I'm still not allowed to think about her in all the dirty ways my mind likes to wander.

I'm fifteen years older than her. Not to mention that any one of her three dads would have my absolute head if they even saw me give her a second glance. Except, I'm usually giving her a third, fourth, and fifth glance. How the fuck no one has caught me yet is beyond my comprehension.

Elliot let us know she was twenty minutes away, and we all prepared for her arrival. Dellah and Collin can't do anything small, and the house is packed to the brim with all of Wynnie's family and friends. I've become an extension of that family because of Wynnie's relationship with Tori.

Wynnie's dad, Phoenix and I have been friends for over two decades and I've become close with Mac and Jude, her other two dads, because of their relationship. Having Wynnie in Tori's life for the last five years has solidified my place in their friendship circle, something I both love and hate. Something that makes my dirty thoughts about the woman, who was a little girl I met at twelve years old, seem even more depraved.

I mingle and sip my beer as Elliot stalks the window, waiting for her arrival. He's like a kid on Christmas morning when she pulls in, and he disappears out the back door, bouncing as he goes.

Why is my pulse racing and my stomach doing backflips? *Fuck*. There's something wrong with me, and that brown-haired, gorgeous, blue-eyed siren is about to walk in the door.

"Surprise!" The exclamation is loud when she walks in. Her face shows shock at the outburst, but I know her. I can tell Elliot warned her before she came in. Wynnie startles easily and was too prepared not to have had a heads-up.

"Daddy." Tori bumps into my leg with her hands over her ears and big, fat alligator tears threatening to spill.

"Hey, Little Princess." I pick her up and rest her head on my chest, cupping her ear. "Was that too loud for you?" I feel her nod against my chest, and I rock her, kissing the top of her head.

When I look up, Wynnie scans the room, giving everyone waves and hellos. She meets my gaze, and our eyes lock. For a split second, her smile brightens, but when she sees the way Tori is curled into me, her face falls. Wynnie heads directly towards us, and my stupid heart tries to run down the block again. When she approaches us, her hand goes to Tori's back and glides down her yellow dress.

"Hey, Sunshine." Tori looks up and gives Wynnie a huge, toothy grin.

"Wynnie!" She practically leaps out of my arms and grabs onto her favorite nanny, cuddling into her neck. My fucking heart is gone. It's a puddle on the floor. How someone can love my daughter as much as I do is just incredible to me.

I never expected to be a single dad. Hell, I never expected to be a dad. When Becky showed up six years ago on my doorstep, seven months pregnant, it rocked my world. But not as much as the love I see shining between Tori and Wynnie.

"The shouting scared her. I probably should have expected it and prepared better." Wynnie gives me a half smile in understanding. "I'm sorry, sweet girl." I run my hand down Tori's back, and my pinky swipes over Wynnie's hand as I do.

I feel the bolt of electricity and wonder if she does, too. No, I have to stop fooling myself. She loves my daughter. Any affection Wynnie might have for me is because of Tori.

"Hey, Sunshine, want to know a secret?" Tori lifts her head and smiles through her tear-stained silver gray eyes.

"I like secrets." She's a great secret keeper. How a five year old knows not to blurt out everyone's personal information—and she hears a lot hanging out at the bar—is beyond me.

"I'm afraid of loud noises, too." She sweeps a piece of dark brown hair behind Tori's ear. "Elliot warned me before I came in. Otherwise, I'd probably be crying with you. I know Daddy is super sorry he didn't warn you. We'll make sure he doesn't forget next time. Right, Daddy?"

Fuck. Me. When she refers to me as Daddy, even though I know it's for Tori, it still does something to me.

"Of course, Little Princess. I'll make sure there isn't a next time that you don't know about." I kiss the top of her head, and the nearness to Wynnie allows me to smell her apple shampoo. The shampoo I know she uses because she accidentally left a bottle in my shower one weekend when she watched Tori while I was away.

"Congratulations, Pinky. How does it feel to be a college graduate?" As I had expected, a slight blush blooms on her cheeks from my use of her nickname. A nickname that started as innocent teasing.

I walked into her house one day to visit Phoenix and found a thirteen year old Wynnie sitting at her kitchen table drawing a bright pink cartoon character in her sketchbook. When I asked who it was, she went off on some juvenile tangent about anime, and the only thing that stuck with me was the name of the character, Pinky.

But now, in the last several years, as I've watched her grow into a beautiful, intelligent woman, I've noticed the pink tint to her cheeks whenever we're close. Maybe I'm not the only one who feels the attraction between us.

"It feels like a normal Monday."

"It's Sunday, Pinky."

"Oh, right." Her blush grows across her chest, above her pale blue v-neck t-shirt, and along the inch of cleavage peeking through. I should probably save her from her embarrassment, but I relish in her reaction for a few more selfish seconds before offering to take Tori from her.

"Let me take our Little Princess to get some juice and cookies. I'm sure you have plenty of mingling to do." I don't miss her smile when I said *our* Little Princess. I reach out my arms, and with mild protest, Tori lets me take her from Wynnie. "We won't leave without saying goodbye."

"Thank you." I watch as she walks away. Her long dark brown hair shines with the faintest streaks of auburn she inherited from her mother, Hazel. She turns back and looks over her shoulder, smiling that sweet smile, and her cornflower blue eyes, inherited from her father, Mac, sparkle at me.

"Hey Tori, can you keep a secret?" Tiny warm hands cover my cheeks and her sharp silver gray eyes look at me with amused interest.

"What is it, Daddy?"

"I really like Wynnie." She bounces in my arms, her smile so wide I can see all of her little teeth.

"I love her a lots!" *Dammit.* I think I might, too.

3

Wynnie

An arm hooks into mine, and a polite "excuse us" comes from my best friend as he helps pull me away from my torture.

"Thank you." I kiss Elliot on the cheek, well more like his lower jaw since he's obscenely tall, and he weaves us through the crowd towards the backyard. He stops when we've reached the coolers and pulls out two spiked seltzers. I look at him suspiciously.

"Do you expect me to double-fist these things, E?" He hands me one and cracks open the other, taking a long drink.

"Don't be ridiculous. Mom said I could have one with the graduate as long as I promised not to drive anywhere for the rest of the night. I asked Dad, and he gave me the same basic answer. So in my book, that means I can have two, as long as neither of them sees." He winks, and I can't help but love his logic. I also can't help the bloom of heat in my chest for his use of the terms Mom and Dad.

When Elliot's parents died, it was a huge life changing event for all of us. I quickly took Elliot under my wing, and here

I am, five years later, drinking in his backyard and hearing him call Aunt Dellah and Uncle Collin his Mom and Dad. It will never get old.

"Thanks for the rescue mission." I had been chatting with a few girls I graduated high school with and wasn't thrilled to be doing so. Of course, my best friend would understand my body language and sweep me away.

"That's what a best friend is for. Now, tell me about that interaction with Scotty Too Hottie, *Pinky*."

"Shut. Up." I push his shoulder and look around to make sure no one is within listening distance.

"What? You're a big girl now. All grown up and shit. It's more than a little schoolgirl crush at this point. Just man up and admit it to yourself." I can't help but burst into hysterical laughter.

"What's so funny, evil wench?"

"In this relationship,"—I point my finger between the two of us—"it's true. I'm more manly than you." It's his turn to look around and see if anyone is listening.

"I'll man up if you do," I dare him. Elliot hasn't come out as gay to anyone but me. I'm pretty sure everyone knows already, or at the very least assumes, but no one is going to encroach on his comfort. When he's ready, he'll tell them.

"Back to me calling you an evil wench, wench." I flutter my hands in front of his face.

"Yeah, yeah. Whatever. You love me." I make a few kissy motions in the air, and his eyes roll.

"I do. And I'm not the only one, Pinky."

"I'm his nanny and his best friend's daughter. He has to at least tolerate me."

"Rowyn Juniper—"

12

"Oh, we're getting serious now. Using government names. Okay, I'm listening." I cross my arms over my chest, careful not to spill my seltzer.

"As I was saying, Rowyn Juniper. I am a man—" I clear my throat and chuckle, which results in a serious stink eye. "I. Am. A. Man. That notices things about other males. And what I noticed, other than the puppy dog eyes he gave you and how hard he stared at your ass when you walked away, was the bulge in his pants while he was with you." My jaw drops.

"No way."

"Yes, way. And it was very impressive." He nudges me with his elbow.

"You're terrible and probably seeing things. We were comforting his daughter."

"And I'm sure he was thinking of comforting you…naked." I swipe the can from his hand.

"Holy shit. You're cut off." Elliot pouts, and then, with a taunting eye, reaches down, opens the cooler, and grabs another one. He pops the top and chugs down half the can before giving me his big cheesy smile.

"Guess I get to have two and a half since you took that one from me, so it doesn't count. Thanks." He raises his can in salute before taking another swig. I swear he's ridiculous and just the kind of person I need in my life.

"Okay, but seriously. What are you going to do? You're home now. No more quick Christmas breaks, long weekends, or summer nannying job. You're here to stay with a real job and an apartment. Are you going to add a hunky bar owner to that list?"

"First of all, being Tori's nanny was a real job too. And

13

second of all, my plan is to avoid my dad's best friend as much as I can. Because let's not forget, that's what he is. In no world would Mac, Jude, or Phoenix allow me to have any type of a relationship with Scotty, no matter how infatuated I am with him."

"Oh girl, look at that blush."

"Shut up. It's the alcohol." And the dirty thoughts of Scotty and me together.

"All 5% in the half a can of seltzer you drank? Tell it to someone under the age of five."

"Ugh, remind me again why you're my best friend?" Of course, there are a million reasons why.

"The list is too long, and you have a party to get back to." And knowing how long it is, is exactly why.

The afternoon quickly turns into evening, and the little kids start getting tired and cranky.

I watch my mom and dads collect my siblings, Dean, Alex, and Delilah Jane. Each of them come to say goodbye and congratulations again.

"Are you sure you don't want to spend one more night at home before going off alone into your own apartment?" My mom will miss me not being home, but I'm not that far away.

"Bestie, leave the poor girl alone and let her spread her wings. Besides, you know she won't be alone. I have a feeling that Elliot will quickly claim the second bedroom." Aunt Dellah to the rescue. My mom puts her hand over her heart and huffs.

"My daughter is too young to be shacking up with a boy." Three…two…one. Hysterical laughter from all three of us.

"Hazy, your place or mine next weekend?" Aunt Dellah has a devilish smile that I don't quite understand.

"How about Wynnie hosting us in her new apartment?" What am I hosting?

"What are you two trying to rope me into? And why is it happening at my place?" My mom eyes me suspiciously.

"If I remember correctly, you should be due for Aunt Flo on Thursday or Friday. Am I right?"

"Um, yes. It's odd you remember that, Mom."

"Nah." Aunt Dellah throws her arm around my shoulder. "We all cycle around the same time. It's pretty easy to remember. Your mom and I started getting together to commiserate the worst of it over wine and ice cream. Now that you're home, it's a party. A period party." My mom groans.

"Or just a weekend where the men have to take care of all the kids." My mom has three men to take care of my two brothers and sister. Poor Uncle Collin is just one man, but Elliot is a huge help. Except…

"You know Elliot is probably going to want to join."

"As long as that kid can keep a secret, he can join. Because it usually turns into a man bitching fest." Aunt Dellah knows Elliot is good at secrets.

"Trust me, my best friend can keep a secret."

They leave me to say goodbye to others heading home, when I feel his presence behind me.

"We're heading out." I turn to see a sleeping bundle of yellow dress and dark hair curled into Scotty's chest. "She's going to be sad that she fell asleep before saying goodbye to you." I run my hand through Tori's soft hair.

"It's a good thing I'm only ten minutes away now and not an hour. I can come by and see her tomorrow to make up for it."

15

"I'm going to miss not having you as my nanny." What is that look in his eyes?

"You are?" He clears his throat and looks away.

"I mean, of course. Tori loves you. You're going to be hard to replace." Oh, that makes sense.

"I can talk to Aunt Dellah about it. I know you need evening help, and I'm sure we could work something out. My job can be done anywhere I can take my laptop."

"Wynnie, I could never ask that of you. You just graduated, and I don't want to take you away from your new career for babysitting." His words say no, but I can see the hope in his brown eyes.

"You didn't ask, I offered, and taking care of Tori is more than just babysitting to me. Let me talk to Aunt Dellah before you replace me."

"I could never replace you." Did it just get hot in here, because I think my panties just melted.

"I should get Tori to bed. It was a nice party, and it was great to see you as always."

"Thank you for coming. I'll talk to Aunt Dellah and come by tomorrow to see her." I feel like I'm in a trance that I can't get out of. He's so fucking handsome. He personifies tall, dark and handsome.

"Have a good night, Pinky." He leans in and kisses my cheek. It's such an innocent gesture. The way you would kiss your grandmother as a greeting or a small child with a cut. But this feels like so much more. The heat from his lips lingers long after he walks out the back door.

Once everyone has left for the evening I say my goodbyes, I walk up the fourteen stairs to the red door of the garage apartment. An apartment that I moved into ten years ago

16

when my mom moved us back here to her hometown for a job. An apartment that led her to meet Jude and Phoenix. Roommates she didn't know she was dating, and when they found out, they didn't make her choose. They both chose her.

An apartment that led me to my dad. I'm the product of a drunken one night stand at a college party. And this apartment, in this small town, happened to be where my dad was a police officer. Once again, a man loved my mother, and she wasn't made to choose.

I have three dads, and I love every one of them. Without them, I wouldn't have my three incredible siblings. Without them, I wouldn't know and love Tori. And without Tori, there wouldn't be a Scotty.

A Scotty that kissed me on the cheek tonight. An innocent gesture that I can still feel as I lay in my bed, in my own apartment, as I drift off asleep with the sweetest of dreams dancing in my mind.

4

Scotty

"Victoria Lauren, no running in the house, please. If you can't follow the rules, there will be consequences. Do you understand?" I hate the thought of punishing her, but she needs to learn to follow the simple rules.

"N-no. What's consifences?" *Don't laugh. Don't fucking laugh, Scotty.*

"ConseQUENces. It means, if I give you a rule and you don't follow it you'll have to have a time out. Do you understand now?"

"Yes, Daddy. Sorry. I don't like timeouts." Her bottom lip juts out and I hate seeing her pout. Sometimes having to be the only disciplinarian is hard on me.

"It's okay, Little Princess. Daddy just doesn't want you to hurt yourself. Are you ready for some pancakes?"

"With chocolate chips?" There's the smile I love.

"They wouldn't be pancakes without chocolate chips."

My phone buzzes on the counter as I cut up Tori's pancakes and drizzle syrup on them. I help her onto the bar stool at the counter, and she dives right in.

Pinky: Show this to my Sunshine and let her know I'm thinking about her and can't wait to see her after lunch.

Attached is a selfie of a smiling Wynnie, taken at an above angle, looking fucking edible in an oversize t-shirt and barely there shorts. Next to her is a plate filled with pancakes smothered in syrup. I can't help but smile and chuckle at the absurdity of the picture.

"Why does your face look funny, Daddy?"

"Oh. Um. Wynnie sent a picture for you. She's having pancakes too. It's almost like we're all having breakfast together." I slide my phone to her so she can see the picture.

I hear her giggling, but I'm lost in the thought of how fucking incredible it would be to wake up to Wynnie in my arms and have coffee and pancakes together as a little family of three.

"Daddy, what's p-p-pin-key. Piiinnkey, Pinky. Right? Does it say Pinky?" *Shit.* I grab my phone and stuff it back in my pocket. Tori gives me a strange look for my quick reaction. Her sweet eyebrows knit together. I'm so screwed when she can fluently read.

"Yes, it does. You're so smart. Pinky is just a nickname, just like Little Princess. Now, eat your breakfast. Wynnie is going to come by after lunch. She was sad you fell asleep, and she didn't get to say goodbye."

"Yay! Can I draw her a picture?"

"Of course you can. I'm sure she'll like that."

"Can she take me to the park?" Her eyes suddenly roam around the room as if she's hiding something.

"If you ask her and she says yes, sure. But now I'm going to ask you why *you* look like that?" I wiggle my finger in her face and then boop her nose. She giggles but then looks serious.

"I don't want to make you sad, Daddy."

"Little Princess, as long as you're telling Daddy the truth, I won't be sad. Are you finished with your pancakes?" She nods, and I take her plate away and hand her a baby wipe to clean off her sticky mouth and syrupy fingers.

"I like going to the park better with Wynnie." I have to contain a laugh with a fake cough.

"Oh, and why is that?"

"Because she pushes me higher on the swing. And she picks flowers with me." She squints her eyes closed, which is something she does when she's scared or nervous.

I quietly round the island so she can't hear me, and when I reach her, I attack her stomach with tickles, making her giggle and almost fall off the stool. Scooping her up, we swing around the living room, giggling and laughing all the way to her bedroom. "Get dressed and brush your teeth. I have some errands to run before Wynnie comes over."

"Okay, Daddy. Will you braid my hair?"

"One or two?"

"Two, please."

"Wonderful manners, Tori. Bring me the brush when you finish, and I'll do your hair."

Braiding hair is another skill I never thought I'd have to learn. I make my way back to the kitchen, and as I clean up the pancake mess, I realize I never text Wynnie back.

Me: She's excited to see you. If you're up for it, you might get conned into taking her to the park. She said you push her higher than I do. I might be jealous. ;)

Pinky: I already knew she liked me better. ;oP The park sounds great.

Me: Make her ask nicely first. We're working hard on manners.

Pinky: Yes, Sir.

Well, *fuck me*. She needs to not say that again. My cock just twitched in my pants. An image of her—*No*. Get yourself together, Scotty. She's Phoenix's daughter. She's Jude's daughter. She's *Mac's* daughter. She's Mac's blood, and he can be a scary son of a bitch when he needs to be.

Running my hand down my face, I try to shake off the not-so-innocent image of Wynnie in my mind.

"Are you okay, Daddy?" I open my eyes to see Tori standing under me with her hairbrush in hand.

"I'm alright. Just thinking about all the things I need to do today." Wynnie *not* being one of them. "Let's get your hair done so we can get them started."

★ ★ ★ ★ ★

Wynnie showed up right at one o'clock with a lunch bag of snacks to take to the park. This is another reason Tori prefers Wynnie over me to take her to play. All. The. Snacks.

"Hey, Wynnie, would you mind if I ran some errands while the two of you are out? I have a few things to take care of at the bar."

"No problem at all. We'll probably be out for about two hours, but you don't need to rush. I'm free today. Aunt Dellah

21

doesn't have me starting until next week."

"You're the best." I walk over to the couch where they're sitting and lean over, kissing Tori on her head. Completely unconscious of my actions, I kiss Wynnie on the head as well.

I snap up, in shock at what I've just done. I didn't even think. It just happened. I look toward Wynnie; her cheeks are so bright it looks like she has sunburn. She's staring back at me in just as much shock as I feel.

"Um, you girls, be good. I'll be back later." I turn away and grab my keys off the kitchen counter.

"Bye, Daddy." The adorable jingle of Tori's voice floats through the air as I walk out the front door.

That was unexpected of me. My body went into autopilot as if it were the most natural thing to kiss her goodbye after Tori.

But it did feel natural, and that scares the shit out of me.

5

Wynnie

What. Was. That.

I'm not delusional enough to think that he actually planned to kiss me on the head. It was probably just a natural reaction since he kissed Tori first.

I saw the look of shock on his face. But what kind of shock? There was no guilt or horror, no instant regret. Was he shocked in general that he did it? Shocked that he allowed himself to do it?

I'm making way too much out of something so simple. I'm sure it was just some stupid mistake Scotty is mortified over. Similar to the kiss on the cheek yesterday. Although, that was a congratulations for graduating. That kiss served a purpose.

But just like yesterday's kiss, the heat of this one lingers on my skin or hair rather.

A delighted giggle pulls me out of my head as I push Tori on the swing. It's her favorite part of the park.

"Higher!" She's figured out by now how to pump her legs and swing on her own, but she doesn't quite have the strength to go as high as she likes by herself.

"Okay, Sunshine, but we need to leave in fifteen minutes."

"Aww, okay. Look at my braids floating in the air. I'm flying!"

"I see them." When she comes back down to me, I give a gentle tug on the braid over her right shoulder, and she giggles some more. "Daddy did a great job on your hair today."

"He's not as good as you, but he tries his bestest." Her hands grip tighter on the chains as I push her a little harder, and she goes higher in the air. A high-pitched "Whee" escapes her lips.

"You want to know another secret?" I know she does. Secrets make her feel special. When I see her braids nodding in the air, I know she's curious. "I taught Daddy how to make braids when you were littler. I let him practice on my hair because he knew it was something he needed to learn."

"I bet Daddy liked that. You have such pretty hair." A memory flashes through my mind, and I'm glad I'm behind Tori so she can't see my pink cheeks.

"As always, Wynnie, you're a lifesaver. I can't thank you enough for helping me out."

I'm home for Winter break of my first semester of college, and Scotty's usual babysitter isn't available. Someone called out at work, and he needed to go in and close the bar.

"It's no trouble. With everyone home for break, Aunt Dellah didn't need me to watch Finn or Paige. I'm glad to help out." And I am. Tori is an adorable one year old who toddles around the house and wants to cuddle all the time. Who wouldn't want to hang out with her?

"I'm sorry, but I probably won't be home until after three. You're

24

welcome to crash in the guest room and stay the night if your parents are okay with it. I know I'd feel more comfortable with you staying rather than driving that late at night. Also, I make some great pancakes." He smiles a syrupy, sweet smile. Probably as sweet as the pancakes he's promising.

"I already kind of planned to stay, if that's alright? And I don't need to ask my parents, I'm nineteen. I can just crash on the couch, though." Scotty puts his hand on my shoulder and looks at me sternly. My cheeks pinken at his touch.

"Sleep in the guest room. It's right next to Tori's. You can bring the baby monitor in with you. I'll grab it when I get home so she doesn't wake you in the morning. Just remember I'll be coming in so I don't startle you."

I've watched Tori plenty of times, but usually not past midnight, so spending the night has never been an issue. Scotty hired a manager to close the bar once Tori came along, but I understand tonight is an emergency situation.

"Got it. Plan for you to show up between the hour of three and three-thirty a.m.; any other time, it's an ax murderer." He rolls his eyes at me, and we laugh.

"I really appreciate this. I owe you one. Here's the baby monitor, but she shouldn't wake up. You have my number, remotes on the table, and the fridge is all yours. Except for the alcohol, of course." He points a finger at me in mock warning.

"Of course." I give him a curt nod and salute.

"Need anything else?"

"No, we'll be good. Have a good night."

"You, too. If you need anything, *you call me, Pinky." Before I can respond through the blush of my cheeks, he's out the door.*

I didn't stay up long. I retreated to the comfortable guest bed and read on my phone until I drifted off to sleep.

The next morning I'm woken up by tiny giggles and encouraging words from Scotty to "Go get Wynnie." I smile before I even open my eyes because I can hear the pitter-patter of Tori's feet.

"Tell Wynnie pancakes are done." When I hear her step up right next to my bed, I open my eyes, reach out, and grab her, pulling her into me while I sit up. Her giggles make me grin ear to ear.

"Morning, Sunshine." I kiss her on the forehead, and she giggles more. I turn to Scotty, who's smiling just as wide. "Sorry if I slept in."

"It's only seven-thirty. She's an early riser."

"Oh wow. Have you gotten any sleep? I can watch her today if you need to rest." He shakes his head.

"I'll nap when she does. Come on, breakfast is ready."

As promised, he makes the most delicious pancakes with chocolate chips and whipped cream.

After we eat, he takes Tori to her room to get ready for the day, and I gather my things to head home.

"Hey, before you leave, can I ask...an odd favor?" He rubs the back of his neck and I have to look away from his muscular forearm.

"Um, sure, I guess." He looks so apprehensive it makes me want to hug him. He's such a strong, confident man; seeing him look like this makes him look much younger.

"I was wondering if you could teach me things to do with Tori's hair. It's getting longer now, and it feels like a foreign language when I try to look it up online. Things like braiding and pigtails, which I still don't understand why they're called that. A pig only has one tail." I can't help but laugh at his ramblings. Being a single dad to a little girl can't be easy.

"I'd love to help. What would you like to learn first?"

"Uh, braiding seems the most complicated. Do you know how

to do that?"

"I do. And it's not as hard as it looks." I pull the hair tie out of my hair, and it cascades down my back. "Do you have a hairbrush and more hair ties? I can teach you using my hair."

We spent the next few hours that day braiding and unbraiding my hair while Tori hung out in my lap, and I read her books and sang her songs. Thinking back now to that memory, I believe that's when my nineteen year old self began having more than an innocent schoolgirl crush on Scotty.

"Time to go home. Daddy will be back soon, and I'm sure he misses you." I slow the swing so she can safely jump off. She lands and throws her hands up in the air like a little gymnast.

"A solid ten on the landing." I pretend to put an imaginary medal over her head, and she thanks me and waves to her adoring crowd. We've raised a little monster.

We? That's a weird feeling. Although, I guess I have had a big hand in raising her over these last five years.

When we approach the house, Scotty's truck is already in the driveway.

"Daddy's back!" Tori's excited shriek from my back seat makes me jump. At least she waited until I had the car in park.

"It looks like he beat us here." I climb out and unbuckle Tori from her car seat. She hops out of the car and runs ahead of me into the house. As she gets to the living room a loud, "Stop" booms from the kitchen.

I instantly freeze. My body reacting to the timber in Scotty's voice and the finality of his statement.

"Victoria, you know Daddy doesn't like you running

through the house. I warned you there would be a consequence if you did it again. Do you remember?" She nods.

"Yes, Daddy."

"And do you remember why we don't run in the house?"

"Because you don't want me to get hurt?"

"That's exactly right, Little Princess. It's important that you follow the rules so you don't get hurt. Go sit in your room and think about your actions."

"But—"

"Victoria, don't argue with me. You were warned." Her lip pokes out and she looks to the ground.

"Yes, Daddy." He kisses her on the head, and she quietly walks down the hall to her room with her head hung.

"You okay, Wynnie?" I inhale sharply at his nearness. How did he get so close without me realizing?

"Sorry, you startled me." My heart hammers in my chest. I can't do anything but stare into his brown eyes.

"I see that. I didn't mean to. I've been working on Tori following directions. Do you think you could help me reinforce it when you're with her?"

"Yes, Daddy." I see his pupils dilate, and heat flashes in his eyes before I realize what I've said. "I...I didn't... I mean—"

Scotty brushes a stray strand of hair behind my ear, stopping my rambling. As he leans into my ear, his scent engulfs me. It's rich and earthy, almost like maple syrup and the fresh scent of the air during a long motorcycle ride. Hidden underneath is the faintest smell of lemon lingering on his hands, most likely from the cleaner he uses at the bar.

"It's okay, Pinky. I kind of liked it, too." We stare at each other for a long moment. Our eyes shift back and forth between each other. Does he wear contacts? I've never been this close to him to notice.

As quick as the moment came, it's gone. Scotty steps away from me as if nothing happened.

"Are you staying for dinner? I need to go talk to Tori about her running, but you're welcome to join us."

Words, form words, Wynnie. "I should go home. But thank you."

I quickly retreat to my car, taking the first deep breath in what feels like hours.

He was just being funny.

He was making fun of you for your slip-up.

He didn't mean anything sexual by it.

Despite my little anti-pep talk, my mind is reeling with what the brush of his hand meant. What did he exactly like? And did he like it as much as I did?

6

Wynnie

I give up. Every interaction I have lately with Scotty is more hormone-inducing than the last. So, tell me why I find myself giving in to a girl's night at his bar, Tipsy Penny.

Oh, right. Because I have an obnoxious aunt for an employer who decided we *needed* to celebrate my first official day of work with one of Scotty's famous blue fish bowl drinks.

I was practically manhandled into her car and told I had no choice. My stomach flutters with nerves and excitement.

"Aunt Dellah, it's a Monday."

"And?" She gives me such an incredulous look as if I dared to question her judgment and choice of drinking days.

"I'm just saying, we barely did anything today, and it seems a little strange to be celebrating." She pulls into the parking lot of the bar, puts the car in park, and turns it off. Her body shifts towards mine, and I can tell by her exaggerated sigh how ridiculous she thinks I'm being.

"I'm sorry, little niece, but did you wake up this morning?"

Despite being twenty-two and a college graduate, she still insists on calling me little. And is this a real question?

"Yeeees?" I stretch out the word because I'm clueless about where she's going with her question.

"Then it's a good day for a fish bowl." That's it? That's her entire logic. She flings her door open and steps out, peering back into the car when I don't immediately move. "Young lady, you're barely legal to drink. Could you stop being so responsible for once and let loose a little bit? Sometimes, I think Hazel raised a nun." I reluctantly leave the car.

"Don't let my mom hear you say that." Aunt Dellah suddenly burst out into laughter so loud she's coughing. I open the door to the bar, and she walks in almost doubled over. It's a good thing there are only a few people in here, or she would be causing a scene.

"Uh, is she alright?" Scotty walks over to greet us from behind the bar, looking between Aunt Dellah and me.

"Honestly, I'm not sure. She called me a nun, and then this happened." I motion at her as if I'm on a game show presenting a prize. At the word 'nun,' she laughs impossibly harder.

"While she's having her midlife crisis, I guess we're here for two fish bowls." Scotty arches a brow at me.

"Fish bowls, huh? What are we celebrating?" *Shit.* I groan because, at this point, I don't even think Aunt Dellah is breathing.

"I'll go make your drinks and let her calm down."

It takes her several minutes and some deep breaths before she finally composes herself enough to speak, just in time for Scotty to return with our drinks.

"You good now?" He slides our fish bowls to us.

"Yeah. Okay. Whew. So, I compared Wynnie to a nun. Her mother is…" Oh no. She's giggling again. "…in a committed relationship and has children with three different men. *Three.* There's no way she's a nun. And… and then, I was just telling her we were celebrating because she was young, and we can. Then you came over here and asked what we were celebrating. It was priceless." And we've lost her again to a fit of giggles.

I slowly reach out and slide her fishbowl closer to me. "I think maybe you've already been drinking, Aunt Dellah."

"Unless you want to lose a hand, little niece, I suggest you not try to steal my alcohol."

For whatever reason, her use of the term 'little niece' has me look towards Scotty, who's wearing a smirk. I take a few large gulps of my blue drink. I wonder if he's thinking about the Daddy slip-up like I am?

Shit. And now I can feel my cheeks heating. I hope he doesn't notice.

"Are you okay, Pinky?" I guess he noticed.

"Yep, all good. The drink's good. I'm good. Thanks." Shut up, you stammering idiot.

"Mhmm. I'll leave you ladies to your drinks. Let me know if you need anything." I try to keep my head down and follow his sexy retreating form with my eyes, but my body betrays me, and my head tilts in his direction once he's farther than my eyes allow.

"Interesting." *Double shit.* Play dumb. Play dumb.

"What's interesting, Aunt Dells?"

"Your little schoolgirl crush isn't so much a crush anymore, is it?" I almost spit out my drink and instead end up choking, causing a scene and Scotty to come check on me. Cue the embarrassment.

"Hey. Hey, you okay, Wynnie?" Aunt Dellah is patting me on the back, and Scotty grabs my hand with concern in his eyes.

"Yep." I manage to croak out between sputters. "Wrong pipe." I should pull my hand out from under Scotty's, but it's so warm and rough. It makes butterflies erupt in my stomach.

"Let me get you some water." He walks away, and I can feel Aunt Dellah staring a hole into the side of my head.

"That bad, huh?" I know she's referring to my not-so-little crush. I drop my head to the bar top with an audible thud.

"Aunt Dellah, you're my mom's best friend. You aren't allowed to see what you just saw." I roll my forehead so I'm looking at her. "Please."

"You know you're a grown-ass adult, Rowyn Juniper." I lift my head up and turn towards her. She used my actual name, not my nickname. She's being serious.

"And you know who he is, right?"

"You mean the yummy, tattooed, single dad who very clearly has the hots for you, too? The same one with the adorable daughter who loves you to the moon and back?" I shove my hand over her mouth and quickly look around to make sure Scotty isn't lurking somewhere. She licks my hand, and I pull it away.

"Eww. Gross. And, no." I reach over and wipe my hand on her jeans, causing her to shift away and almost fall off her chair.

"No, you don't think he's hot, or you don't think Tori loves you?"

"You know I absolutely adore Tori as if she were my own, but—"

33

"Well, I thought I liked this where this conversation was going until I heard the word, but. Do I want to know what comes after that?" No, no. *Fuck no.*

I slowly turn on my bar stool to see the hot single dad in question towering over me with his arms folded across his chest. His right arm, which is at eye level with me, is corded with muscle, and I feel my cheeks darken with heat.

His left arm is decorated in hollow shapes and outlines of flowers and basic animals. I smirk at the reasoning behind them when Scotty clears his throat.

"My eyes are up here, Pinky." I snap up to meet his. And good god, that nickname. I know it started as a tease for my drawings, but it's become so much more. I feel like I'm in a constant state of blushing when he's around.

"You adore Tori, but?" He's really not going to let me off the hook.

"I...I..." His arms unfold, and I feel his warmth as he cups my cheeks and bends to my level.

Did the temperature in here just rise to a hundred? His hands are rough, but his touch is gentle. I must feel like an inferno under them.

"Is something wrong, Wynnie?" My brain is mush. Someone call 9-1-1. I think I'm having a Stroke. I can't be this close to him. He can't be this close to me.

"She was just asking me if we could adjust her schedule to help you out, Scotty." Aunt Dellah places a hand on his forearm. He looks to her, then back to me before lowering his hands.

Thank you, Aunt Dellah, for rescuing me from my own funeral. I spoke to her over the weekend about potentially helping Scotty with Tori. She obviously thinks quicker on her feet than I do when alcohol or Scotty are involved.

"I told you that you didn't have to do that. You're just starting your career, and that's important. I don't want to interfere with that." He looks so sincere but also hopeful.

"And I told her there are perks to nepotism. She can work for both of us if she wants. Right, Wynnie?" I'm still stunned in silence, so Aunt Dellah kicks my foot.

"Oh, yes. I mean, right. I'm happy to help you both."

"You're sure?" His touch may have elevated my temperature, but the smile he's wearing right now just melted my panties.

"I'd love to spend more time with you…I mean Tori by helping you." I spin back around in my seat and try to grab my drink but I'm so over eager that my chair keeps going in a circle. On my way back around I knock knees with Scotty and almost fall off my chair.

Almost, because he catches me and pulls me towards his chest so I don't faceplant on the ground.

"You alright, Pinky?" I moan into his chest at the nickname, and without realizing I'm doing it, I take a deep breath, inhaling his sweet, earthy scent. My hands grip a little tighter to his shirt that I must have grabbed during my almost fall.

"Hey, Pinky?" His breath is at my ear. His words meant only for me. "While I wish we could stay like this all day,"—so do fucking I—"I have to get back to work, or your moaning is going to put me in a position where I may need to take a break before it's decent for me to be around customers again."

"Shit, I…" I release my death grip on his shirt, smooth out the wrinkles it caused, and step back, bumping into the bar. My eyes quickly dart to his pants, where a slight bulge forms, then to his face, where his smile is as bright as the sun. I can feel the crimson that's taken over my entire body.

I fumble back into my seat and close my eyes, wishing I could melt into the seat and disappear. This is the epitome of embarrassment.

"I'm grateful to you, Dellah, for allowing Wynnie the flexibility to help me with Tori. I've got this week covered, so she's all yours, but I'll gladly take her off your hands come next Monday."

"Next Monday is perfect, Scotty. Maybe we should order some chicken nachos and another round of fish bowls. I have a feeling this first round will go down quickly." Right on an embarrassing cue, my straw slurps as I hit the bottom of my drink. Great. Now, you can add lush to my list of embarrassing qualities.

Bumbling idiot—check. Lack of ability to be in the presence of a Scotty Too Hottie—check. No, uncheck. The lack of ability to be around Scotty, the hot single, tattooed dad—check.

A lush who is drowning in her bumbling, lack of self-control self to a stupor—check, check, and triple check.

I don't have to see or hear to know that Scotty walked away. I can feel it. The air is thinner. The electric charge that seems to hang around when he's near has fizzled out. My hormones, which were jumping frantically on a trampoline only moments ago, are now taking a much needed nap.

All of this brings me back to Aunt Dellah's original question.

I turn to look at her and flatly say, "Yeah, THAT bad."

7

Scotty

Wynnie is intoxicating, and I own a bar, so I think that gives me a unique perspective of the word. I had her in my arms. I called her Pinky, and she moaned. I'm not sure she realized, but I watched as she inhaled my scent, and a small sound rumbled through her chest. That vibration went straight to my cock and stirred things it's not allowed to be stirring.

I couldn't help but give her a bit of information about what it was doing to me. I know it was wrong, but god fucking dammit if the color on her entire body wasn't gorgeous. And as asshole-ish as it was, I know it was all for me.

It wasn't enough that she showed up in a pair of too-short denim shorts and an old band tee that she had no business knowing about since she wasn't even alive when they were famous. I've endured many summers of her in tiny clothes as she's watched Tori over the years.

She came home the first summer after college, and something had changed. I had never given Phoenix's daughter a second glance. He's one of my best friends.

Wynnie has always been a little shy. She opened up when Elliot came into her life, but she came home from college that first year with the confidence of a woman. Breaking out on her own let her bloom, and fucking bloom she did.

She caught my attention, and I was completely off guard when I saw her that summer at her house for the beginning of summer BBQ. I almost didn't recognize her from behind and found myself checking her out until someone walked into the room and called her by name.

She was wearing a pale pink floral sundress that stopped mid-thigh with tiny straps and a shape that accentuated her waist. It felt like she had filled out while in college and come back mirroring my every wet dream.

Long, dark hair, a waist that dipped, and hips that curved accented her long, tanned legs. When she turned around at the mention of her name and smiled, I took a stumbling step back as if someone had pushed me.

The commotion I caused made her glance my way, and her eyes, paired with her smile, her fucking smile, grounded me into the floor. I've been a goner ever since.

It was easy back then, knowing she'd be gone after each summer and only home on breaks, but she's graduated now and is here to stay.

I'm going straight to hell. Murdered by any one of, or all three of her dads. I bet Mac knows where to dispose of a body, so it never gets found. Why does Hazel have to have three men in her life whom I respect more than anything and also a daughter who stars in all of my nastiest fantasies? Maybe I should update my will soon?

Monday nights are usually slow, and today is no different. There are only two tables of patrons and just the girls at the bar. I'm trying not to pay attention after putting their order in, but every time I turn around to grab a new liquor for their drinks, I find myself looking at them through the mirror. Let's be honest. I'm looking at her.

Wynnie's skin has turned back to her normal shade, and I find myself wondering what I can do to change that. I fucking love how she reacts to me.

I hear the speakers stutter and look around the room, wondering if I'm having internet problems.

"I can see her hand moving between her slick lips."

What the fuck? What happened to the music? And what is this?

"Tell me what to do. Imagine it's your hand around my cock. What would you be doing? If that were my hand on your pussy, I'd be gathering the wetness from your entrance and gliding it toward your aching clit. Swirling around it but not touching it yet."

Whatever is happening through my speakers sounds like someone is speed-reading through the sex scene of a book.

I see Dellah and Wynnie fumbling over a phone, both with frantic looks on their faces. Leaning back against the shelf, I watch in amusement. Wynnie's phone must have accidentally connected to my Bluetooth and they're trying to stop it.

"I'd want to drive you wild so you're aching for me. Are you aching?"
   "Yes." Her answer comes out as a moan.
   "Tell me what to do. I want your commands." I know I'm

practically begging, but I yearn for the loss of control. For her control over me.

The bar suddenly goes silent as they turn off the book.

"Well damn, that was just getting good."

"Oh shit, Scotty. I'm so sorry." Wynnie's blush is back in full force. "I was just opening my phone to pull up a song, and I guess my Bluetooth connected to yours and started playing my... um... book that I'm listening to."

I add the gummy fish to their new drinks and bring them over. "So I was right, it was a book. Sounds like something I might enjoy."

"Do you have time to read anything that isn't One Fish, Blue Fish, or a liquor order?" Dellah thinks she's funny sassing me.

"I will, now that Wynnie is helping me with Tori."

"Right now, Wynnie needs a cold shower and a hole to climb into." I hear her sarcasm, but I can't help but snort at Wynnie's third-person commentary of herself.

"No, I mean, I need a cold shower because I'm dying of embarrassment and blushing so hard. Not because of the same reason that guys usually need one." She's rambling, and it's the cutest fucking thing I've ever seen. "Like, I'm not turned on or anything. Oh god, seriously. Just make me another drink. I'm going to inhale this one. Maybe I can forget tonight ever happened." Tonight's a night I'll definitely never forget.

"Sure thing, Pinky. Write the name of that book down for me while I make you another, and I'll check on your food." I tap the bar top twice with my knuckles and wink before walking towards the kitchen.

I watch as Dellah and Wynnie enjoy the rest of their evening. I convince them to drink water and eat their nachos before indulging in another fish bowl, but they're pretty toasty.

Me: You might need to come retrieve your wife and niece.

Collin: Oh no, that bad, huh? They're drinking your blue drinks, aren't they?

Me: Sorry, man. What the women want, the women get.

Collin: Are they ready now?

Me: For your sake, let me get some more water and food in their stomachs. Try and even them out a little bit.

Collin: Thanks, Scotty. I'll let Elliot know he's going to be on sibling duty, and I'll head out soon.

Me: I've got their keys. They aren't going anywhere.

Collin: You're a good man.

If only he knew the dirty thoughts I have about his niece, he wouldn't think I was such a good man. My death certificate is signed and dated. Now I have to make her mine.

A little while later, Collin comes in, and Dellah greets him with an exuberant kiss.

"VIPER! What are you doing here?" She looks around him. "Where are our babies?" I smile at her use of the term babies. Elliot is now eighteen, Finn is twelve, and Paige is nine. It's been a while since they've been babies.

Five years ago, I found myself in a similar situation to Collin and Dellah, suddenly becoming a parent. It was the most unexpected and life-changing thing for all of us. But I couldn't think of better people to be parents to those three, and I wouldn't change being Tori's father for anything.

Hmm, I wonder if they could handle adding Tori to their herd when I go missing because of my want and need for Wynnie?

"Scotty, my white knight is here."

"Oh no, Bunny, we aren't playing this game again." I watch her pout at him. "I'm sorry, Dellah, but I need to get you and Wynnie home. We have adult responsibilities now, remember? We have kids and a niece. No knight and princess talk." Ah, I think I get it now.

"Kids. Where are our kids?" I hear giggling, and it seems Wynnie finds their interaction as entertaining as I do.

"Hey Collin, do you need a hand with the little one?" I tilt my head in Wynnie's direction, and she narrows her eyes and scrunches her nose at me. I knew that would get to her.

Sliding off the bar stool and taking a moment to catch her balance, she crosses her arms over her chest.

"Excuse me. I'm going to take a page from Paige. I... oh, that's funny. A page from Paige." She starts giggling uncontrollably, mumbling "Page from Paige" over and over.

"Hey, Pinky. Did you have something to say?" Her giggles are getting to me and I want to scoop her up caveman style and beat my chest.

"Huh, what?" She tilts her head at me and taps her pointer finger on her pouty pink lips a few times, deep in thought.

I hear Collin and Dellah not-so-whispering behind me, and he asks her what's going on.

"Shhh. Just watch." Dellah cups her ear and leans in farther towards us. Collin has to hold her up so she doesn't faceplant on the floor.

"Was I about to yell at you for something?" I chuckle, her face looking very fucking kissable right now.

"I think you were about to yell at me for calling you little." She shoves her pointer finger in the air.

"Ah ha! I am not little, mister." I take a few steps forward until I'm right in front of her, towering at least eight inches over her. She bites her lower lip as she slowly trails her eyes up my body until her blues meet my browns.

"You were saying?" Her mouth opens and closes a few times before she huffs, admitting defeat. I turn back to Collin with a smirk. "So, need help getting this one to the car?"

"Um, yeah. That's probably a good idea. Thanks." Dellah bounces around with a goofy smile, chanting, "See, see, see."

"Alrighty, Pinky, let's get you secured and ready to go home.

"Home is boring and lonely." I grab her purse and sling it over her head, across her body. "Oh, I have an idea. You should come with me. Then I won't be lonely."

"Pinky," I warn her because she has no idea what she's saying now, and we're entering into dangerous territory.

"What? But you're—WOAH! Holy cannoli. I'm upside down. Aunt Dellah, are you upside down, too?" I had to stop her from talking before she got herself in trouble. Throwing her over my shoulder seemed like a good distraction.

"No, niece-ey wee-cey. I'm not, but you definitely are. How's the view?" We walk out the front door into the warm night air as the girls chat.

"Hey, Aunt Dells. Scotty Too Hottie has a nice ass."

"Pinky." This time I growl as she grabs two handfuls of my butt. Thank fuck we reach Collin's car, and I'm able to put her down into the back seat and get her securely buckled before she has time to roam her hands any farther.

"Pinky."

"Dadd—" I hastily put a finger over her mouth, stopping

her from completing that word.

"Don't call me that." I realize I've just played right into her hands as I use my dads voice to reprimand her. "Hey!" I pull my finger away as I feel her lick it with her tongue. This fucking siren. I can give her something to wrap her tongue around.

"But I thought you liked it?" She pouts, and I close my eyes and place my forehead on hers. I don't care that Collin and Dellah are seeing this. They're bound to have questions already based on our behavior tonight.

"Wynnie, I need you to let Collin take you home, and I want you to text me once you've taken some pain medicine and drank a big glass of water. Do you understand me?"

"I'm not—" I pull my forehead away and look into her eyes.

"Rowyn. Do. You. Understand. Me? There's no room for more questions right now. It requires a simple yes or no." Just yes or no is all I need her to say.

"Yes, Sir." I close my eyes and sigh.

"You're going to be the death of me, Pinky." I kiss her forehead and stand up. "Text me. Don't forget, or I'll show up at your apartment to make sure you're okay."

She salutes me and rests her head back on the headrest. I have a feeling she's going to forget.

"Everything good, Scotty?" I nod. Out of the three of them, Collin is going to have the most questions, but I don't have any fucking answers. I can't pine over my best friend's daughter.

Except I fucking am.

8

Wynnie

One, two, three…twelve, thirteen, fourteen!

"I made it, Uncle Collin." I raise my hands in the air, excited that I made it up the fourteen stairs to the red door of my apartment.

"Good job. Now go inside, lock the door, and call me if you need anything."

"I'll be A-Ok." I give him two thumbs up and unlock the door, stepping into my apartment above his garage.

I lock the door as instructed and wonder why I feel like there's something else I should be doing. Peeing. I have to pee. That must be it.

Once I'm done in the bathroom I sit on the couch and decide it's the most comfiest couch in the whole wide world. And this throw pillow is the softest pillow in the whole big universe…

I'm floating, except the cloud isn't very soft and fluffy like I'd expect. It's a little hard and smells like…maple syrup.

"What have I told you about sniffing me, Pinky?" My eyes pop open to a very hunky Scotty carrying me. I wrap my arms around his neck for fear of falling, and he chuckles.

"Wait, what's going on?"

"I warned you if you didn't text me, I'd show up. So here I am." I snuggle into his chest. Here he is. All big and sexy. My Scotty Too Hottie. My—*no.*

"Not mine."

"What's that, Pinky?" He gently places my feet on the ground but doesn't let go. "Sit. I'll be right back." I sit on my bed and watch him walk into the en suite bathroom.

This was my mom's room when we lived here, but since it's just me, I decided to take her old room and utilize the larger bathroom.

"Where do you keep your acetaminophen?"

"In the kitchen cabinet above the slove. The stobe. The… uh…STOVE. Man that's a hard word." He walks out chuckling, turns off the light, and heads for the kitchen. A few moments later, he returns with a bottle of water, a bottle of pills, and a sandwich.

"Drink." He hands me the water as he opens the pill bottle. "Swallow." He smirks as he offers me an open palm with two little white pills, and I take them. "Eat." My brow arches in confusion, and he huffs. "It's a PB&J. Protein, sugar, and carbs will help with the hangover." I take it and eat. When I finish the sandwich, he smiles at me.

"Good girl."

"Not nice." I pout at him.

"What's not nice?"

"You can't call me a good girl. It makes me feel all tingly inside. I'm not allowed to feel all tingly for you."

"Oh, you're not?" Scotty kneels on the floor at my feet and slowly unclips my sandal, sliding it off my foot. A light finger trails up my inner calf, stopping at my knee, switching sides and trailing down to my other sandal, removing it as well.

All I can do is shake my head no because the sight of this man on his knees in front of me has turned every bone in my body to jelly. He stands and looks down at me. "Where do you keep your pajamas?"

"Nightstand." He walks to the table and reaches for the top drawer. Panicking, I lunge across the bed. "Bottom drawer!" I grab my head as the room starts to spin and groan. "That was a bad idea."

"What's in the top drawer you don't want me to see?"

"Just my vibrators." *Shit.* I cover my mouth with both hands and roll to my back. Why did I say that out loud?

"Plural. Interesting. Hmm, maybe I'll save those for another day. Today, we'll just start with pajamas." He reaches into the drawer and takes out a blue tank and shorts set with yellow ducks on them.

"Uh oh. You picked my sexiest pair. Those help catch me all the boys." I think I just heard him growl, and not in a sexy way. In the way I imagine one of my possessive Alpha book boyfriend's would growl in my smutty books.

"Shh. Growling makes the fireworks bigger."

"Oh, so we went from tingles to fireworks? I like that progression." No, he can't like that. I really need to stop talking.

"You keep tricking me into saying things that I shouldn't." He stands in front of me and places the pajamas on the bed. Taking both of my hands in his, he helps me stand.

"Do I? Like what?" His fingers graze the hem of my shirt, slowly bunching it and lifting.

"Like, I shouldn't let you take my shirt off right now, but

I'm going to."

"Yes, you are." I lift my arms, and my band shirt messes up my hair when my head pops out. As he lowers his hand, his finger grazes down my arm, leaving a line of fire behind. Once my shirt is on the floor, he takes his fingers and brushes the hair out of my face.

"Hi." Fuck. Me. He's wearing his panty-melting smile. "What else?" His hands are already on the button fly of my shorts. *Pop* goes the first button. His gaze hasn't left mine. I'm standing in front of him in a bra, and he hasn't looked.

Pop goes another button. "The fireworks are turning into electricity."

"Are they?" *Pop.* I nod, staring back at him. Two more buttons. "Are you going to let me take these off of you?" *Pop.* I nod. "Can I hear your words, Rowyn?" Why does my name sound so sexy on his lips? *Pop.* No more buttons.

"Yes. Take them off." My words are breathy, almost pleading. His thumbs hook into the back of my shorts and slide along the edge. He skims my lower back, hips, and stomach before pushing down until they slip off.

My breath hitches as I realize I'm standing in front of Scotty in nothing but my black bra and underwear.

"More electricity?"

"No, I'm just a melted puddle now. Are… you going to take more off?"

"No." He must see the disappointment written all over my face. His hand raises, and a thumb rubs tenderly along my cheek.

"You've been drinking, and I would never take advantage of you like that."

"But—"

"No. Not tonight. But, may I look as I help you get dressed?

"Please." He leans over, grabs my sleep shorts, and kneels back on the ground before me. For the first time, his eyes wander down my body. My neck, which I know is pink with blush. My chest, the swells of my breasts that he lingers on for a moment before he continues down my stomach to the top of my lacy black boyshorts.

"Hands on my shoulders, Rowyn." He's so tall I don't even have to lean over. "Lift your leg, now the other." He takes his time pulling up the shorts, and it feels like forever as his hands brush my skin.

As he rises he picks up my top along the way. "Arms up." He slowly lowers it over my arms, head, shoulder, chest and lands on top of my shorts.

His large arms reach around and unclasp my bra. With a finger, he pulls off one strap and then the other. Reaching up under my shirt, he hooks a finger around the middle of my bra between my breasts, and pulls it down my stomach.

"Breathe, Pinky." Shit. Was I holding my breath? I inhale a stuttering breath.

"Scotty."

"Rowyn."

"Thank you." For being a gentleman. For not taking advantage of me. For taking care of me.

"You're welcome." His hand cups the side of my neck, his thumb caressing my jaw. There's a moment when we look into each other's eyes, and the whole world stops. The air thins and I swear the room sways.

"Whoa there. Let's get you to bed before you fall over." *Oh.* Maybe it wasn't the room swaying. Maybe it was me.

He pulls back my yellow and navy comforter, takes the

medicine bottle from his pocket, and sets it on the nightstand.

"Take two more in the morning and drink plenty of water. You call me if you need anything, alright?"

"I understand." Once I'm in bed, he pulls the comforter up to my chest and brushes the hair from my forehead.

"You're a handful, you know that?" I can't help but smile because I've heard him use those exact words about Tori.

"Do...do you want to stay?" I don't even know where I got the courage to ask that question.

"Do I? Yes. But I have to get back to Tori and relieve the babysitter. Another time, and maybe when you're sober. I promise."

"Okay." I can feel my eyelids getting heavy. "Thank you, Scotty Too Hottie." He laughs at me.

"Always, Pinky. Get some sleep." He leans down, and I think he's going to kiss my forehead, but he hesitates, and I feel the faintest brush of his lips on mine. Before I can register the sensation and try to take more, he's standing and turning towards the door.

"But—"

"Next time, Rowyn. Be patient with me. Sleep well." With those final words, he walks out my bedroom door, and I listen as I hear the front door click, close and lock.

I wait and listen to his truck start up and leave the driveway before I text him.

Me: You're my favorite hottie

Me: I mean Scotty

Me: Well you ARE my favorite hottie Scotty ;)

Me: You saw my boobies. In my bra. You should have been more naughty. Next time be more naughty.

9

Wynnie

My head is pounding.

I have to pee, but that would require moving my body, and I don't think I can do that. I can't even manage to open my eyes because I know as soon as I do, the light is going to make my head hurt even more.

What the hell happened last night?

Pulling the blanket up over my head, I blindly reach around my nightstand for my phone. I knock over what sounds like a bottle of pills before my hand finds my cell.

It's only six-thirty. I should still be sleeping, but I notice I already have several missed texts.

Elliot: I need ALL the details!!

Scotty: Rowyn, naughty girls get punished. You were told to go to sleep. Don't make me have to come back there.

Panic races through me. What is Scotty talking about? What does Elliot want details from? Why do I feel like absolute shit?

51

Uncle Collin: Come on over when you're up. Coffee and breakfast will be waiting.

He sent that five minutes ago. That might be what woke me up. I wonder how Aunt Dellah is feeling? I unlock my phone and look at the rest of the messages.

Scotty: Take the pills before you get out of bed. Drink lots of water today. Your duck PJs are adorable. Thank you for trusting me last night.

What! I shoot up in bed, immediately regretting the quick movement. I reread his text, trying to remember what happened after we left the bar.

Uncle Collin picked us up.

I counted all fourteen stairs until I got to the top.

I locked the door as Uncle Collin told me to do.

I look down and see I'm wearing my favorite duck pajama set. How did he know? Think, think.

I see a bottle of water on my nightstand and peer over the edge of my bed to find the container that caused the sound when I knocked it over. Acetaminophen.

He was here. When? Oh god. What did I trust him to do? What did *we* do?

Me: What do you know?

Elliot: I was hoping you'd tell me. I saw Mister Hottie leaving your apartment.

Me: Elliot! I don't remember.

Elliot: Don't move. I'm bringing coffee and breakfast. Be there in 5.

Five minutes later, there's a steaming mug of creamy hazelnut-flavored coffee in my hand and a breakfast burrito on my nightstand next to the bottle of water that's taunting me.

"He was here." I can't believe it.

"You really don't remember anything?"

"I don't, but I wish I did. What do you think I did?" I show him the texts, including the mortifying ones I sent in the middle of the night, and we try to jog my memory.

"Do you feel…sore…anywhere?"

"Ugh. I hate that I have to even think about that. I know Scotty wouldn't have taken advantage of me. He's a great guy. Although someone changed my clothes. It may have been me."

"You're so disappointing, Wyn. I came for details, not a game of *Clue*." I'd love details myself. Something obviously happened; I just need to figure out what.

"I'm just going to text him and ask. What other options do I have?" I pick up my phone, and Elliot swipes it out of my hand.

"You can't text him. Do you want him to think you're a little girl who can't hold her liquor?"

"No. But I can't sit here and wonder if something happened between us that I can't remember."

"Fine. But can we play pretend for a few more minutes?" Elliot gives me a playful grin. Rolling my eyes back at him, I shove his shoulder.

"Thanks for the breakfast. How's Aunt Dellah?"

"Oh, she's the reason the house is up so early." He sees my confused expression and continues. "She was up puking and moaning about blue fish, I think. I'm not sure. It was hard to tell from the echo of the toilet." I burst out laughing at the thought.

"I had an entire fishbowl more than her." He shrugs and takes another bite of his breakfast. I pick up my phone and consider what I should send.

Me: Can I come by today before opening and talk?

Scotty: Of course, Pinky. How are you feeling?

How am I feeling? Lonely. Confused. Turned on. Embarrassed.

Me: Good. Thanks to you, I think. I'll come by around 1:30 if that's okay.

Scotty: See you then.

10

Scotty

"Thank you, Mrs. Peterson. I'll be back around ten." I wave to my neighbor, who keeps Tori for me while I'm at work.

She's a sweet elderly lady who also watches her grandchildren. When I suddenly found myself a single dad after only three months of knowing I would be a father, she offered her help and has been a grandmother to Tori ever since.

Her proximity of living right next door has saved me on more than one occasion. On the nights that I have to work late, Tori sleeps over there, and I get her as soon as she wakes up.

Having Wynnie help out on school holidays over the past several years gave Mrs. Peterson a break from Tori's constant care. This year also eased things with her starting Kindergarten full-time.

Between Dellah and Hazel having kids at the same school and Elliot having his license, we all help each other with childcare.

Tori is excited to have Wynnie watching her again soon.

My Little Princess is obsessed with her.

Wynnie.

Last night.

I wonder if that's what she wants to talk to me about. I used all of my willpower not to cross any boundaries. She was so drunk and pliable. It would have been so easy to take her any way I wanted. Based on how she was acting, she would have let me.

And then those texts she sent me after I left. I almost turned my truck around. "Next time be more naughty." Even thinking about that has me adjusting myself in my pants.

But I'm not that kind of man. She was heavily intoxicated. No matter how badly I want her, she needs to be completely coherent if or when it happens.

She wanted me last night. She wanted me to see her—all of her. I've seen her in a bikini before, which is why I allowed myself to look at her body, in just her bra and underwear.

She was as stunning as I expected her to be. Probably even more so.

I told her I would come over if she didn't text me. I had no intention of actually going, but as the minutes ticked by, and I still hadn't gotten a call or text, this intense need to protect and care for her took over.

The moment I was able to leave, I did. My night manager comes in at eight, and I usually stay until ten to help with the rush. She was running late last night, and it was already ten-thirty when I was able to leave. I told Mrs. Peterson I would be late and headed straight for Wynnie's apartment.

I've had a key for a few years since that's where Tori would end up most nights in the summers. If I were picking her up after a late shift, I'd let myself in and take Tori home. The apartment above the garage almost became a little daycare for all the kids.

Wynnie looked so serene when I found her on the couch. I considered just covering her up and letting her sleep, but I knew how much she had to drink and how terrible she would feel in the morning if I didn't get her to hydrate and eat a little.

★ ★ ★ ★ ★

Promptly at one-thirty, Wynnie knocks on the glass door to Tipsy Penny. I was taking inventory and put my clipboard down to let her in.

"Hey, Pinky." I smile as she walks past me, holding the door open for her.

"Hey, Scotty." I don't like that timid tone she just used. I quickly lock the door behind her and take a few long strides until I'm standing in front of her. Placing a crooked finger under her chin, I tilt her head until she's forced to look into my eyes.

"What's going on?" I rub her cheek with my thumb and see some of the tension melt away. Lines form on her forehead as she overthinks whatever she came here to talk to me about.

"What's going on in that pretty little head of yours?" Her eyes close.

"You came over last night." A statement, not a question. So she remembers.

"I did."

"Did we… Did you… My clothes were changed." She seems even more concerned, and then it dawns on me.

Walking her backward until her legs bump against a chair,

I guide her down and pull up a seat right in front of her. I take both of her hands in mine and dip my head until I can look directly into her eyes.

"Do you not remember me coming over?" She quickly jerks her head side to side, embarrassment pouring off her, and her skin starts to pinken.

"Are you worried that you, we, did something that you might not remember?" She nods, and I squeeze her hands.

"Wynnie. Please tell me you don't think I would have taken advantage of you. Please tell me you know me better than that." She must see the hurt in my eyes.

"I—no, never. I don't think you would. I don't remember anything after getting upstairs. I didn't even know you were there. Elliot saw you leaving, and I saw your text. And the texts I sent you." She flushes with embarrassment. "What did I trust you with?"

"I'm sorry. I had no idea you were that intoxicated. I really should set a two fishbowl limit." We both laugh a little. "I came by when you didn't text me. I found you asleep on the couch. I gave you water and medicine and had you eat a sandwich. Do you remember any of that?"

Her brows pinch, and she stares at the ground, trying to piece together the evening.

"Was it… peanut butter and jelly?" I see the hope in her eyes as she remembers a small detail of the night and smiles.

"It was. Wynnie, I did help you undress and put your pajamas on, and you might have said some things that you ordinarily wouldn't have, but I respect you. I would never, and I mean never, do anything to take advantage of you. Drunk or sober."

"My duck pajamas." She releases my hands and covers her

58

chest as if she's remembering something else. "I, um… I didn't have a bra on this morning. Did you do that?"

"I did. But only after you had your top on. I didn't see any part of you naked." I gently remove her hands from her chest, careful not to touch anything I shouldn't be. "You wanted me to. You asked and pouted at me when I told you no." I cup her cheek and run my thumb along her bottom lip. I need to stop touching her, but fuck, it's all I want to do.

Her face is a blaze of self consciousness.

"I…I'm sorry. I'm so embarrassed." She tries to dip her head, but it's still in my hand.

"Don't be. I'm not oblivious to the way you react around me, Wynnie. It's written all over your face."

"Oh, god." She closes her eyes. I lean my forehead against hers, and we sit silently and breathe each other's air for a long moment.

"Do you understand why anything between us is a bad idea?" She shocks me by standing, almost knocking the chair out behind her.

"I'm sorry. I'm young, and dumb, and stupid. I don't know why I would even think—I'm so sorry." She's spiraling, and I'm not sure why. She tries to walk past me toward the door, and I grab her wrist, stopping her.

"What just happened?" She turns to look at me—fierce determination in her eyes.

"I get it. You're fifteen years older than me. I'm just a naive little girl with a puppy dog crush. I know that's how you see me."

I growl and stand, intentionally using our height difference to my advantage. She may be mad now, but I'm furious.

"Do you really think so little of me?" I bark at her and rub my hands over my face. How can she not see? "Rowyn, you are a gorgeous, mature woman. I watched it happen before my eyes. I see it. Believe me, I fucking see it. And I see you."

She puffs out her chest in defiance, trying to make herself taller. "Then why the hell do you still call me Pinky? A nickname that you gave me when I was thirteen."

She's completely clueless to how she affects me. I thought I was doing a lousy job of hiding my lust for her—all the stolen or lingering glances. I know Dellah has seen it. After last night, I'm sure Collin has seen it, too.

I take my index finger and run it across her exposed collarbone, up the side of her neck, and across her cheek. My temper is down to a simmer.

"Pinky, it may have started over a drawing, but this…" My finger continues across the bridge of her nose and follows the opposite path back to her collarbone. "This is the reason I continue to use it. Your body reacts to me every time you see me. I can tell what you're feeling based on the shade of pink you've turned. It's like my own personal mood ring. You don't seem to do it towards anyone else."

"I…don't know what you're talking about. You have no effect on me." Did she issue me a challenge?

"No?" I lean down close to her ear, whispering. "Are you sure?" Her body shudders at my closeness, and I look down to see her nipples pebbling under her thin yellow tank top. "Your body would disagree. Your blush just darkened, and your nipples hardened." I lean closer and brush my lips across the racing pulse in her neck. "And your heartbeat is trying to leap out of your neck."

She crosses her arms to cover her nipples, and her arms brush my chest.

"It's cold in here. And I'm mad, so of course my pulse is racing, and my temperature is rising, causing my face to flush."

"Mhmm." My nose and lips continue to lightly brush her neck. I pull away, and she sighs. Placing both of my hands on her cheeks, I make sure she's looking at me.

"You have it all wrong, Pinky. I *want* you. But I can't have you." I kiss her forehead, then her nose. "Do you understand that your fathers would have my head if they found out how I feel?" I kiss her left cheek, then her right.

"I've known you since you were twelve. That may have been ten years ago, and you are most definitely a woman now, but you're still their little girl. And I'm still Phoenix's friend." I gently kiss the corner of her left eye, then the right.

"So *they* are the problem?" Her question is so innocent. They are the *entire* problem.

"Yes, Rowyn. *They* are the problem. *They* are what's stopping me from taking you home right now and making you mine." My confession causes a pin-sized leak to form in my heart. A leak that she's drinking into her essence.

"But—"

"Pinky, there's so many 'buts' in this situation. *But* we are adults. *But* we can make our own decisions. *But* their opinions shouldn't matter. *But* I'm about to do something I know I shouldn't. *But* right now, I don't care."

I close the small gap that's left between us. Sliding my hand into her hair and wrapping my other arm around her waist, I lower my lips to hers.

For a moment, they just touch. No other movement as I let her shock wear off. I want to give her the opportunity to pull away. To see if I've read the signs wrong. When she doesn't, I run my tongue along the seam of her lips, testing to see if she'll let me in.

Her arms wrap around my waist, and her lips part. I pull her closer to me so our bodies are flush.

Slowly, I move my lips, and our tongues begin to explore each other. Hesitant at first.

I have no idea what kind of experience she has. But I've never seen her with anyone of the opposite sex other than Elliot.

As her confidence rises her tongue becomes more demanding, darting and licking into my mouth. She pulls away, and I think she's going to end the kiss when I feel a slight sting of pain on my bottom lip. *Damn, she just bit me.* She sucks my lower lip into her mouth, soothing it with her tongue.

An involuntary growl escapes the back of my throat, and I pull her even closer, fisting her hair in my hands.

Our kissing becomes frantic. I suck her tongue into my mouth, and she moans. She tastes sweet, like cherry soda. I happen to know that's her favorite.

Her arms move from around my waist to my shoulders, and she plays with the hairs on the nape of my neck. Little moans slip from between her lips, driving me insane. She's making me feral for something I know I can't have.

If this is the only chance I get to kiss her, I'm going to savor it. I back her up slowly to a wall and lean her flush against it.

Without warning, she jumps up, wrapping her legs around me like a koala. I grab the back of her thighs for support and realize what a terrible idea this is. Her core is on my stomach, and I can feel the heat radiating from her. If I lowered her a few inches, she would feel my erection trying to burst through my jeans.

She bites my lip again, and as my mind wanders to how good that little nip would feel on my cock, I pull away, leaning my forehead against hers.

"Fuck, Wynnie. We have to stop. We can't do this." I'm panting as she tilts her head and nibbles at my neck. "Rowyn." Her name is a warning growl. I release her thighs, and she hangs on for a moment longer before letting them slide down my body.

She's still pinned between the wall and me, and I don't want to move. Her body feels so soft and pliable under mine, as if I could mold her into the perfect version of a Wynnie, just for me. But I don't have to because she already is.

She peers up at me through dark eyelashes with lust and stars in her eyes.

"Fucking christ, Wynnie, we can't." I'm trying hard to convince myself, but even I don't believe me. The words sound flat.

She needs to stop touching me. Her hands have been roaming my chest since she slid down.

"You need to go. I need you to go." She pouts, and I want to bite that pink plump lip. It's swollen from our kisses, and that sparks a hunger in my chest, knowing I did that.

"Are you kicking me out?" Her tone is low and sultry.

"If I have to. I'm at the end of my rope, Pinky. I have a daughter, and I value my life—"

"I love your daughter."

"I know you do, and that's part of what makes it harder to stay away from you. You're so fucking amazing with her. She loves you so much."

I somehow find the last ounce of my willpower and step back from her. I see her lip start to poke out again.

"Please, don't. I don't *want* to stop. But we have to. There are too many major speed bumps to contend with." I run my hands through my hair, pulling at the strands.

"Fuck, Pinky. You're my own personal heaven and hell, having to watch you and not touch you. And now this. I won't be able to get your lips out of my mind." She rubs her fingers over her swollen lips.

"I don't want to get you out of mine," she confesses. I reach down and grab her hand.

"Let me walk you to the door." She hesitates. "Please. This isn't easy." She gives in and lets me lead her.

I box her in when we get there. Hands on either side of her head. "Can I kiss you one last time before you go?"

"You didn't ask the first time. Why ask now?"

"You're so much fucking trouble." I crush my lips to hers. This has to be a goodbye kiss. I can't let this happen again. She tastes so fucking good. Her lips are soft and plump and the perfect shape to fit mine. But she can't be mine.

I reluctantly pull away, and she keeps her eyes closed for a few more seconds.

"You okay, Pinky?"

"No, but I don't have a choice in the matter. Do I?" She opens her eyes, and I'm pierced all the way to my soul by the blue staring back at me.

"No, and I don't either." Please understand.

"Fine. But I don't agree with you. My dads want nothing more than for me to be happy."

"I know, Wynnie. But that happiness doesn't include me. Trust me." I reach behind her and unlock the door. "I'll see you Monday at noon if I don't see you before then." I give a lingering kiss on her forehead, then pull her away from the

64

door to open it.

"Thank you." I think I see a glimmer of a tear in the corner of her eye, but she turns her back and leaves.

Locking the door, I drop my forehead to the glass with a thud and watch her walk to her car. I'm the biggest fucking idiot known to man, and the most perfect woman just walked out of my bar.

What the fuck did I just do?

11

Wynnie

Me: S.O.S

Elliot: I'll meet you at your apartment as soon as I see your car pull in.

I don't know what I look like, but Elliot's blue eyes are laced with pure concern as I step out of my car. He crushes me to his chest, his frame only slightly shorter than Scotty's.

"Wynnie, if you're about to tell me he did something to you last night, I'll—"

"No. Scotty was a perfect gentleman." Without letting me go, he closes my car door, and walks me towards the side of the garage to my apartment.

It's midday, and the sun has crested over the front of the garage and started to dip below the trees. As I walk into the apartment, I stop and close my eyes tight when I see them.

Elliot understands and doesn't question me as I bury my face into his chest.

I wish I could have everything I want with Scotty without any outside interference.

66

"I don't know why you torture yourself like this." Elliot looks around the room and smiles at the rainbows dancing on the walls.

After I make my wish and peel myself away from Elliot, I head to the kitchen for snacks and sodas.

"Because sometimes the simple things in life can be the most impactful. Do I believe that a fairy is dancing off to grant my wishes? Of course not. Can manifesting what I want make my wishes come true?" I shrug. "Who knows."

"Alright. So what's our vice of choice?"

"Ice cream floats?" I grab the freezer handle, knowing I have a fresh tub of vanilla ice cream for just this occasion.

Well, not the occasion where I expected to have my first real kiss with a guy completely out of my league that I've been pining over for at least five years. Or the occasion that he crushes me after said kiss. That's a lot to ask of a four dollar tub of ice cream.

But the occasion where I'm sad and need a pick-me-up more than a good book or a coffee can do.

"It sounds like heartbreak. Is that what we're commiserating?" I shrug one shoulder because I don't really know the answer.

Can I be heartbroken over something that never was? But that kiss—it just WAS. I've never been kissed like that before.

"Okay, so I need to know what just caused your cheeks to flame red like that."

"What?" I touch my cheek, and sure enough, they're on fire. My fingers absentmindedly trail to my lips.

"You kissed. Oh my god, you kissed. I need all the details. And if you kissed, why are we sad? Oh no. Was it bad? Did you bump noses? Did you accidentally bite him?"

"Oh, there was biting, but it wasn't bad or accidental. Ouch." I clamp my hands over my ears as Elliot squeals.

"Jesus, you're as bouncy as Aunt Dellah and as ear-piercing. You're going to break my couch if you don't calm down." I can hear the springs creaking under his bouncing.

"Give. Me. All. The. Details."

I explain the last hour of my life to my over-eager, fabulous best friend. He oohs and ahhs at all the appropriate places. He gets mad when I get mad.

"I just knew that man could kiss. Please tell me he has a younger brother, older brother, a sister. Something." He grabs my forearm and bats his puppy dog eyes at me.

"Only child. Sorry." He pouts and sits back on the couch.

"So what are you going to do?" I open my mouth to respond, and my phone chimes with an incoming text. Elliot grabs it before I can, and his eyes become as wide as saucers. "It's him." He swipes open the text and tries to read it out loud before I get a chance to snatch it from him. I don't make it easy when I tackle him to the couch.

"Pinky... please forgive me..."

"Give it back, Elliot." He's holding his hand out farther than my reach, and it's so unfair. We're both giggling as we wrestle for control of the phone.

"I don't... regret our kiss, but..." I stop, sitting up straight to listen.

"But? But what? What does it say?"

"I don't regret our kiss, but I hope you understand it can't happen again. There are things outside of our desires that need to take precedence."

I huff, and I flop back onto the couch, letting my head rest on the back of the sofa, my heart bleeding out into my lap.

"There's more."

"More? Oh god, do I even want to hear it?" I pretend to pull a dagger out of my heart and hand it to Elliot. "Make it quick."

"Please believe me when I tell you I've wanted to kiss you. What happened today wasn't a spur-of-the-moment decision. I have no regrets other than wishing I didn't now know what you taste like because I won't be able to get it out of my head. I hope this doesn't ruin anything between us."

"Is that all of it?" He nods and hands me my phone. I reread the text and feel Elliot swipe a thumb across my cheek as he gathers my tears.

"None of that, Wynnie. We don't cry over boys."

"How about men? Can we cry over men?" He sighs.

"Okay. Maybe a little for men."

"Wait. Pause my pity party. How's Aunt Dellah? Did she survive her puke fest this morning?" He laughs.

"Mom's... alive. I heard her mumbling about forty not being the new thirty. She also cursed your name when she saw you leave the house looking like a normal human being."

"I should go over and check on her, shouldn't I?"

"It might be fun to rub it in her face." Now we're both laughing at her expense.

Scotty: I have a favor to ask, but I understand if you want to say no.

Scotty: If it makes a difference, it's for Tori more than for me.

I've been staring at my phone for the last ten minutes, not knowing how to respond.

I haven't heard from him since the text after our kiss. That was four days ago.

I'm supposed to start watching Tori in two days. What could he need me for now that can't wait until then? But he said it's for Tori, and I'll do anything for that little girl. Reluctantly, I respond.

Me: Sure. What does Tori need?

Establish right away that this favor is for her, not him. That should lay down some ground rules.

Scotty: Can I call you? It'll be easier to explain.

Why does this have to be awkward? I need our easy friendship back. He's never asked to call me before; he just does. I hate that he feels like he has to ask. I decide to call him myself and put the phone to my ear.

"Hey, Pinky. How are you?"

"Hey, Scotty. I'm good. What's up?" No small talk. Right to the point.

"So Mrs. Peterson said Tori's been acting funny, but she won't talk to her about it, and she isn't acting any different around the house for me. I thought maybe I could fund an ice cream trip, and you could see if she'll open up to you." Oh no. What's wrong with my Sunshine?

"Absolutely. When should I come over?"

"Your mom is keeping her tonight. She's having a sleepover with Delilah Jane, so whatever works for you. And then

70

maybe you could take her there once you're done?"

"That sounds good. Are you home now?" I look at the time on my phone, and it's almost eleven o'clock. He should be at the bar getting ready since they open at noon on Saturdays.

"No. Tori is here with me at the bar. Hazel was going to come get her, unless you want to."

"I'll be there soon, and I'll text my mom."

"Thank you, Wynnie. This means a lot to me."

"Anytime. See you soon."

This could work out perfectly. I've been wanting to get my bike from my parent's house since I got home. I can have someone drive my car back tomorrow and ride back tonight.

12

Wynnie

Taking a deep breath, I steel my emotions as I prepare to walk into Tipsy Penny. I haven't seen him since our kiss right in this building. I'm terrible at 'keeping it cool,' and I know this will be torture.

It's not quite noon, so I have to knock. A blur of colors and giggles bounces to the door. I crouch down, wave at Tori through the glass, and see Scotty walking across the bar behind her.

I stand and take a step back so he can open the door for me. Tori attacks me when there's enough space for her to slip through."

"Wynnie!" I pick her up before she has a chance to climb me.

"Hey, Sunshine. What are you wearing?" She leans back in my arms so I can get a better look at her outfit. She has on rainbow-striped leggings and a bright pink shirt with a sequinunicorn on it. Her hair is adorned with a huge rainbow bow over her braided ponytail.

"You're taking me to my sleepover, right? After ice cream?"

"I am."

"Delilah Jane loves rainbows. I wanted to wear all of her favorite things." She rubs her hand over the sequin on her shirt, changing the unicorn from solid silver to rainbow. "See."

"I see. Do you want to know a secret?" Her face lights up. She loves secrets.

"DJ loves rainbows because they are *my* favorite, too." She gasps.

"So you love my clothes?"

"I do. And do you want to know one more secret?" She nods vigorously, full of excitement. I point to a spot in front of the window. "Do you see that crystal hanging there?"

"That's my favorite!" I look up to Scotty, who's smiling. He knows what I'm about to tell her. "Your Daddy hung that up there because of me. One year for Christmas, I gave everyone I loved a crystal to make their own rainbows whenever they wanted to."

"Oh my gosh." Her little hands cover her mouth. She's stunned.

"Do you know what I do when I see a rainbow?" Her head shakes. "I make a wish. When I was your age, my mom and I would make wishes, and the rainbow fairies would take them away to be granted."

One of the first things I did in the apartment was hang up a small chandelier in front of my window. On sunny days, for about an hour, the rainbow fairies dance in my space, and it always makes me smile, no matter what mood I'm in.

Her face is awash of pure joy as she stares at the hanging crystal. It was the Christmas when I was fourteen. I had earned some babysitting money watching Dean and I wanted to give out my own presents. I spoke to Jude about what I wanted, and he helped me buy and wrap all the crystals. Each one is a little different from the rest. I picked out the perfect shape and size for each person in my life.

Oh, god. I just told Scotty that he was a person I loved at fourteen. He probably didn't catch it since it was an offhand remark. I hope.

"Are you ready to get ice cream? Do you have a bag?"

"It's in Daddy's office. I'll get it." She skips away, leaving Scotty and me alone.

"Pinky."

"Scotty, we don't need to talk about it. I understand."

"You don't, or you wouldn't be giving me the cold shoulder." Am I? I guess I am. I just don't know how I'm supposed to act.

His hand comes up and pushes a stray hair behind my ear that fell from my ponytail. Our eyes lock, his hand lingering on my cheek, not knowing what else to say. Scotty opens his mouth to speak again but Tori's arrival interrupts him.

"I'm ready," she announces coming back down the hall, and Scotty drops his hand.

"Let me know if she says anything to you, please." His eyes are pleading. I know his little girl is his entire world. She's hiding something, and it's eating him up inside that she won't share it.

They say their goodbyes, and we make our way to the local mom-and-pop ice cream parlor that boasts over 30 homemade flavors daily.

To no surprise, Tori gets a birthday flavored ice cream with tons of rainbow sprinkles, and I keep it relatively simple with cookies and cream.

74

We sit outside at the light blue umbrellaed picnic table—her choice—and dig in before our ice cream melts in the summer heat.

"Alright, my little Sunshine. Daddy said we needed to talk. What's going on with you? Is something going on at Mrs. Peterson's house? At school?" I see her little body tense up when I mention school.

"Okay, something at school. Is someone bothering you?" She nods, and it's so sad. "Hey, pretty girl. What's going on at school? You can tell me anything." She hesitates for a moment and her eyes dart around. She's trying to decide if she should tell me. "It's okay, Tori. I want to help." I run a soothing hand down her arm.

"Brayden said my mommy hated me, and she ran away. That's why I only have a daddy and no mommy." Her voice cracks and big fat tears stream down her face. I pick her up and place her in my lap.

"Victoria, no. That's not true at all."

"Did you know my mommy?" I nod.

"I met her once." She came to my parent's house one night with Scotty for dinner just before she had Tori. I only knew her for those few hours, but it was enough to know that leaving Tori in Scotty's care was the best thing she could have done.

"Did she hate me? Why would she leave me?" I pick her up again and sit her on the table in front of me so we're almost at eye level. Swiping my thumbs across her cheeks, I wipe away her tears.

"Sunshine, sometimes people aren't ready to be mommies and daddies. Sometimes, people are sick and can't be. I didn't know her well, but you have an entire family of people who love you. I love you."

"You do?" Her little heartbreak is killing me.

"Of course I do. With all of my heart, Tori." I pull her into my chest and feel her body shake as she takes in a deep breath. She pulls away and looks at me with a quivering lip.

"Can you be my mommy since you love me so much? You love me just like Daddy loves me. Aunt Hazel and Aunt Dellah are already mommies. You don't have anyone to be a mommy for, so can you be mine?" Oh god. Abort mission. Abort mission. This is way bigger than ice cream. What should I do?

"Um. It doesn't exactly work like that, Sunshine." Her lip trembles, and the tears start rolling faster. She's abandoned her ice cream for her emotions. I feel like I'm out of my league and free falling.

"You don't want me either." It's not a question. Her little heart believes that I just rejected her. I pull her to my chest again and wrap my arms around her tightly.

"Oh, Sunshine, I will always want you." I let her cry into my shoulder while I send a text to Scotty.

Me: She just asked me to be her mommy. Someone at school has been picking on her for not having one.

Scotty: Fuck. I'm sorry. I had no idea. Do you need me?

More than anything. But that's not what he's asking me about.

Me: I'll take her to my Mom's, and the kids will help distract her.

Scotty: Okay. Come by when you're done?

76

Me: Sure.

If I drive my bike there, I won't drink, and I can keep my head on straight. If there's one thing my dad has taught me, it's the responsibility of driving a motorcycle.

★ ★ ★ ★ ★

"Hey, Mom, we're here." Her house seems too quiet to have a nine, seven and four year old running around somewhere.

My siblings aren't known for their ability to be calm or still. But then again, neither are my dads.

Tori skips off in search of DJ when I see Phoenix crawling on the floor behind the couch.

"What are—" He jumps up to place a finger over his lips, telling me to be quiet. I look at him in confusion until I see the neon green foam gun in his hands and he drops back to the floor. It appears I walked into the middle of a war zone.

As I'm watching the absurdity of a grown man crawl on the floor, an arm wraps around my waist, and a hand cups my mouth, pulling me out the backdoor.

Mild panic fills me as someone drags me outside. When they let me go, I turn around swinging.

"What the fu—" I turn to see Elliot as my fist connects with his shoulder.

"Damn, girl. That hurt." He rubs his arm and I give him an accusatory look.

"What the hell are you doing here, E?"

"Dad got a text from Phoenix about some manhunt, foam gun fight. He's in there somewhere with Finn and your dads and brothers. We drove together, and Mom, Aunt Hazel, and

Paige went to get their nails done."

"This is perfect." Sometimes things work to my advantage.

"Which part of what I said is perfect to you?" I laugh.

"I guess context would be good. I want to grab my bike while I'm here. Since you came with three drivers, one of you can drive my car back to the house, and I won't have to figure it out later." I drop my keys in his hand and smile.

"Glad to be of service." His tone is laced with sarcasm.

"So what now?" I don't feel like playing war games.

"Well, I certainly don't want to deal with all that testosterone, do you?" How no one has called him out on his lack of masculinity is beyond me. Truthfully, I think everyone knows, and no one cares. We'll all love him no matter who he chooses to love. I wish he would talk to Phoenix and Jude so they can help him feel more comfortable in his own skin.

"Gossip and ice cream in the pool house?" Elliot's face lights up.

"Girl, you're speaking my language. Lead the way."

Elliot and I spend the next few hours gossiping and gorging. I tell him about the conversation I had with Tori, and although he was much older than her, and his circumstances were different, he has a unique understanding of what it feels like to lose a parent.

Even though she never knew her mother, like I didn't know my father at her age, I never felt like I wasn't wanted. I think I need to talk to Scotty about that.

"Wynnie, it makes complete sense that she would try to attach herself to the most influential female figure in her life. You've been amazing for her and to her."

"You should have seen her face. She was so hopeful but also broken. I can't imagine, at only five, feeling like someone didn't want me."

Elliot and I hang out until the sun begins to dip behind the trees. I want to watch the sunset with the wind in my hair. After changing from shorts and a tank top to jeans and a leather jacket, I pack my extra clothes into a bag and say my goodbyes to everyone. With an extra safety inspection of my bike from my dad, I take off.

I don't actually mean the wind in my hair. Even if Georgia didn't have a helmet law, there's no possible way any of my family would let me ride without one.

Feeling the power between my legs and the hum of adrenaline in my veins gives me a natural high, both physically and mentally. My mind is empty and full at the same time. Constantly searching for any dangers around me but allowing the nothingness to take over.

My immediate answer was no when my dad asked me if I wanted to learn. I'm a small person, and the thought of this intimidating machine between my legs scared the shit out of me.

My dad was persistent. He took me on rides and got me used to the idea, and eventually, I found enough courage to learn. For my twenty-first birthday, I got a Harley of my own and a lecture about never drinking and driving, especially while on a motorcycle.

As I get closer to town, my anxiety starts to peak. I have to talk to Scotty about everything Tori confessed to me. He's an amazing single dad and does everything for that little girl, but some things can't be replaced simply with the love of a father.

Tipsy Penny is open until two a.m. on the weekends, and at nearly eleven, it looks packed when I pull into the parking lot.

"You can do this, Wynnie." I don't think my little pep talk will do anything, but I at least have to try.

Walking through the door, I see two people behind the bar, neither of them Scotty. His manager and another bartender are serving drinks, and I see his waitress on the floor taking orders. It's not the usual weekend sight.

I scan the room and see Scotty sitting on a corner bar stool with a tumbler of amber liquid in front of him. He doesn't drink when he works. Is he off the clock? I recheck my watch. He usually works until midnight on the weekends and lets his manager close the last two hours unless they're busy.

I walk up behind him and touch his shoulder.

"Hey, everything okay?" When he spins on the stool, I can instantly tell he's not okay. His eyes are slightly glazed over, making it evident he's been drinking for a while.

"Hey, Pinky." His smile is half-hearted as he looks me up and down. There's a sadness to it. "Have a seat." He waves his hand in the air. "Kristina, bring Wynnie whatever she wants on me."

"Just a cherry coke is fine. I'm driving." She nods and grabs a glass. I take off my jacket and place it on the back of the chair next to him.

"You're not going to join me to celebrate?"

"What are you celebrating, Scotty?" He reaches for his drink and I grab his forearm to stop him.

"I'm celebrating being a shitty Dad and ruining my kid's life because I slept with a stupid crackhead who decided her life was more important than her daughter's."

"Oh, Scotty. I'm so sorry." I lean my head on his shoulder because I know in some way my text to him about what Tori said caused this.

13

Scotty

This week has been a particularly evil brand of hell. I had a beer distributor come a day late, a cook called out sick for several days, and Mrs. Peterson said Tori seems to be going through something, but she doesn't want to talk to anyone.

I hate to send this text, but it'll be easier than starting with a phone call. Sometimes, being a Dad to a little girl has its disadvantages. Mostly because I'm not a girl.

Me: I have a favor to ask, but I understand if you want to say no.

Me: If it makes a difference, it's for Tori more than for me.

I know things are weird between Wynnie and me right now; who could blame her? But she'd never say no to Tori. Thankfully, she agreed to take her out for ice cream and then to her parent's house for the sleepover planned with DJ. I hope Tori will open up for Wynnie.

I can't get our kiss out of my head. Why did I do it? Because

I'm a fucking idiot, and I let my dick lead my brain when it shouldn't have, that's why.

Getting the text from Wynnie, telling me Tori asked her to be her mom, absolutely gutted me. I can be a lot of things for her. I'll move mountains for my little girl, but a mother is something I can't replace.

I try to ensure she has plenty of time with Dellah and Hazel. I want her to know what a mother figure can be like, but maybe that was the wrong approach.

Fuck. Of course, Tori would ask Wynnie that question. She's practically been the most constant woman in Tori's life since birth.

I open the doors to the bar at noon, and one by one, an adult kickball team comes in post-game to fill the seats. They're loud and rowdy, but nothing that Kristina and I can't handle. My server doesn't come in until four because we usually don't have a crowd like this until we're closer to dinner.

At four, both Aimee, my server, and Rachel, my other bartender show up. Except Rachel isn't scheduled to work tonight, I am. Seeing as I'm having a shit day, and I know my girls can always use the extra money, I make the decision I'm going to take the night off.

Getting everything settled, I hand my bar keys over to Kristina, officially making her in charge for the rest of the night, and order myself a bourbon on the rocks. And then another. And another.

And then, my sexy, naughty, little secret walks in the door wearing tight jeans and a leather jacket. I don't like the look she's giving me. But I like how she looks as she comes to talk to me. I watch her set a bookbag on the floor, remove her jacket, and sit beside me. She's wearing a tiny black tank top, and with my height advantage, I have a great view of her cleavage.

"What are you celebrating?" She's so fucking beautiful.

"I'm celebrating being a shitty dad and ruining my kid's life because I slept with a stupid crackhead who decided her life was more important than her daughter's."

"Oh, Scotty. I'm so sorry." Pity. The tone in her voice is pity as she puts her head on my shoulder. What does she have to pity me for? I'm the one doing all the screwing up.

"If you won't drink with me, will you at least keep me company and tell me about what happened this afternoon?"

"Of course." She climbs onto the bar stool next to me, and our knees rub together as she settles. That casual touch sends a jolt straight to my cock. Does this woman have any idea what she does to me?

Wynnie is so incredible to look at that sometimes, it hurts my chest. Honestly, what makes her the most beautiful and captivating is how she loves my daughter.

She really does treat Tori as if she belongs to her. She's told me stories over the years of people telling her that her daughter is beautiful or well-behaved. Eventually, she realized being polite and smiling rather than correcting people was easier.

"So, Tori told me—"

"I think you should see less of Tori," I blurt out. Yes. That seems like the perfect solution.

"What? Scotty I…" She trails off. Tears start to flood the corners of her eyes and I slam my head into my hands.

"What the fuck is wrong with me?" I turn in my seat to face her and brace my knees on the outside of hers. Grabbing her hands I pull her in close to me.

"That was stupid of me to say, and I didn't mean it. I'm so sorry. I-I have no lame excuse. It was a dick statement. I didn't mean it."

"There must be some truth to your words if you said them."

"No. No, Pinky. Listen to me. You are the best thing to have ever happened to Tori. She loves you. She looks up to you. You fill a hole in her life that without you would be gaping. The truth is it scares me how much of a mother figure you are to her. You have no reason to stay in her life. But you give her something I can't, and it scares me that you could take it away and crush her." Fuck. It would crush *me*.

"Scotty, I would never—"

"Intentionally hurt her? I know that. But…" I look into her bright blue eyes and get lost.

"But?" She places her hand on my cheek and I lean into it. It's warm and soft and everything that I want and can't have.

"But you hold all the cards and that's a really fucking scary thing for me and my daughter." What's wrong with me? It's the fucking bourbon. I'm splitting myself open for this woman in the middle of my bar.

"I've never tried to be a mother to her. I just love her for who she is. For the relationship that Tori and I have."

"Wynnie, you don't have to try. Your heart is kind and loving. You make it so easy to love you." *Easy there killer.* Dial it back a notch. You don't need to word vomit all your emotional crap into her lap. I haven't had *that* much to drink. Or maybe I have?

I pull her hand down from my cheek, the heat becoming unbearable between us.

"She loves you, Wynnie." I think I do too. I turn back towards the bar, letting those words hang in the air. I don't know what more to say. I feel raw from everything I've already confessed.

"Rachel, can I have another drink?" She nods. Wynnie stares at me, boring a hole in the side of my head with her eyes. "It's been a rough day. I'm sorry. I hate feeling inadequate." Closing my eyes, I run my fingers through my hair, pulling at the roots to ground myself.

"I love her too, Scotty. You know that. And you aren't inadequate. You give her everything."

"Everything but a mother." I hear her sigh next to me.

"Here you go, Wynnie." I hear Rachel's voice, followed by the soft thud of two glasses. Then a jingle of something metal hits the bar top.

"What's this," she says.

"Scotty's keys. He's going to need a ride home."

I open my mouth to object to Rachel, and she shoves her finger in my face. "Your rules, Boss. More than two drinks and you get a ride."

"Fuck. Yeah, you're right." I hadn't even thought about it as I was wallowing in my self-pity. "Wynnie, do you mind?"

"Not at all. Whenever you're ready, I'll take you." Of course, she will. And not just because that's the type of person she is but because we all changed our habits after Griffin died. And because I have a little girl that needs me.

"Well, shit." She suddenly looks nervous.

"What's wrong? I can get a ride from someone else if you don't want to drive me." I'd rather not, though.

"No, it's not a problem. I just drove my bike here and I can't exactly ride us together. We have a bit of a size difference." And it's fucking perfect. Her head tucks right into my neck when we hug. On the rare occasions over the last few years when I've had the opportunity to fully embrace her, the way we fit perfectly together hasn't gone unnoticed.

She's right, though. Our size difference on a motorcycle wouldn't work. I'd throw off her center of gravity. But I have an idea. A smirk tips the corner of my lips.

"Can you handle my big truck, Pinky?" I drive a lifted pickup truck. Tori loves it because it's so high she can see all the cars out her window. I love it because I'm not a small man and it fits me well.

"You trust me to drive your truck?" That's a valid question. I don't usually allow anyone else to drive it.

"I trust *you*." Mmm. There's the blush I love so much. My hand itches to reach out and brush my fingers across her cheek, but I ball it up in a fist instead.

She smiles and lightly tosses my keys in the air. When they come back down she misses and they fall to the floor.

"On second thought…" I slide her glass of soda across the bar top. "Maybe you're cut off and I should drive after all." She pushes my shoulder at my teasing tone.

"Finish your drink and let's go."

"Yes, ma'am." I raise my glass to her and swallow the last gulp, winking. Her blush creeps lower and I have to stop my eyes from wandering down her neck to see just how far it does.

"I'm out, Rachel. Call me if you need anything, Kristina. Have a good night, Aimee." The girls say their goodbyes as I slide off the stool.

"Ladies first." I extend my arm for Wynnie to walk in front of me. She grabs her bag and we head towards the back of the bar where I park. I really just want to watch her ass as it sways in front of me in her tight jeans. Fuck, they should be illegal.

Walking out the back door she stops and I almost run into her.

"Everything okay?"

"I forgot how tall your truck is." She's eyeing it like it's going to bite her.

"Alright, let's go." She squeals as I pick her up bridal style and carry her to the driver's door. "Push the button, Pinky. We can't get in unless you unlock it."

"Oh, yeah." She's giggling in my arms, and I force myself to let go once she's safely in the driver's seat. "Um, Scotty. We have a little problem." She looks down at her feet and she wiggles them. They're nowhere close to touching the pedals.

"Pinky, I think *you* are the little problem." I push the button on the side of the seat and it creeps forward until she can reach. "Do you need me to buckle you or can you manage that yourself?"

"I can buckle myself. Thanks, *Daddy*." She rolls her eyes through her sarcasm.

God fucking dammit. I shut the door before she hears me growl at her. I take several deep breaths as I round the front of the truck, willing my dick to stay the fuck down.

The ride to my house is quiet, and I'm impressed with how well she handles my truck. Two of her dads, Mac and Phoenix, drive pickups, so I'm sure it's not a foreign vehicle for her. After all, Mac is the one who taught her to ride motorcycles, I'm sure he's made sure she can drive almost anything. They also own a fifteen-passenger van that I've seen her drive.

When she parks the truck, she pulls out her phone and starts scrolling.

"What are you doing over there, Pinky?"

"I'm texting Elliot to come and get me." I reach over and grab her phone from her hands. "Hey!"

"Come in first. You can take my truck home or take my bike. You don't need to call for a ride." I step out of the truck, pocketing her phone so she has no choice but to follow me inside.

"Um. I could use some help. I'd rather not break my ankle." I stop and turn to see Wynnie hanging out of the driver side door, looking at the distance to the ground.

I chuckle to myself and walk around to her side. Grabbing her waist I pull her into me and like an asshole, slowly slide her down my body until her feet hit the ground. I can't control myself around her.

We stare at each other for a moment before I let her go and step back so she can grab her bag, and I close the door.

Once inside, the atmosphere between us feels different. I don't think I've ever been in my house alone with Wynnie before. Tori is always here. But not tonight. It's just Wynnie and me. Me and Wynnie and fuck I need to stop.

"Want some coffee? I'm gonna make a pot. I should probably sober up some before heading to bed or tomorrow is going to suck." I didn't drink too much. I'm a big guy, and I'm already feeling more fuzzy and less foggy.

"Sure. Coffee sounds good." She walks over to the refrigerator and takes out her hazelnut creamer. Hers. The creamer I buy specifically for her because I drink my coffee black. I bought it when she returned home from college last week and it's been waiting for her to come use it.

Does she know how much of my random everyday life she consumes? Coffee creamer in my fridge, cinnamon cereal in my pantry because it's her favorite and she got Tori hooked on it. The crystal hanging in my bar that she told Tori about. Hell, I even use apple scented plug in warmers around the house because it reminds me of her shampoo.

Alright Scotty. You're starting to sound a little stalkerish. Maybe your obsession is a bit extreme.

"Are you okay?" Okay? What did my face look like that she asked if I'm okay?

"Yeah. I'm good. Just lost in thought." She sits on a stool at the counter while I gather all the coffee supplies. I have to make some kind of small talk before my mind starts wandering again. "Are you all set for next week? Is there anything I need to get for you and Tori?"

14

Wynnie

This is awkward. Why is this so awkward? Things have always been easy between Scotty and me. Has that kiss really changed everything?

He's making random small talk. He knows Tori and I don't ever need anything. There's more than enough here to entertain us; if not, we'll go out and get whatever we need. We always have.

"Nope. I'm all good." He's tense. I can see the muscles in his back moving as he scoops the coffee grounds into the filter.

Scotty is big and broad. He has a home gym that I know he uses regularly. His t-shirt strains at the sleeves around his biceps. His forearms, covered in tattoos, still show the veins running down his wrists.

Pulling me out of his truck was as easy for him as it is to lift Tori. The slide down the front of his body, though? That was anything but innocent. I could feel his hard muscles caressing against me, and I almost moaned at the feel of him.

He seems so unaffected by me, by the kiss we shared.

Sometimes, I feel like a dog in heat around him, and he goes about his day, probably thinking I'm the same obnoxious preteen he saw drawing pictures in my kitchen. Just the teenage girl who nannies for his daughter when I'm home on school holidays.

I need to get over this stupid little crush. But it feels like so much more now. Aunt Dellah tried to ask me about it, and I averted the topic by grabbing Paige as she walked by. She was a quick and easy distraction to my prying, nosy aunt.

"Fuck." I see Scotty leaning over the counter, gripping the edge, knuckles turning white. His back is still to me, and I can't see a reason for his outburst.

"Is everything okay?" He doesn't respond. I see his fingers flex and his shoulder muscles tighten. "Scotty?"

"Pinky." He almost growls my name. "Tell me no."

"No? No to what?" I don't understand what he's asking me.

"Please." He looks over his shoulder at me with one eye, and I can't understand the look I see on his face. He almost looks like he's in pain.

I stand from my seat and walk up next to him, placing my hand on his back. His muscles tense under my palm.

"Scotty, what's wrong?" I hear him growl, and as quick as I can blink, he has me pinned, my back against the kitchen wall, hands above my head. His elbows are leaning next to me; his face, inches from mine. "Scotty," I whisper.

"What are you doing to me? Why do you make it so hard to stop constantly thinking about you?" My hands start to tremble. There's a hint of fear but mostly a spike of adrenaline from his closeness and his words.

"I..." My voice shakes, and I try again in a whisper. "I think

92

about you too."

"Fuck." He dips his forehead to mine, connecting us with another point on our bodies. I close my eyes and gather all of my courage into one breath.

"Kiss me, Scotty." He mutters another curse under his breath.

"You don't understand what you're asking of me, Pinky." I open my eyes to see the war raging in his.

"Kiss me, Scotty." I feel his fingers flex around my wrist. He licks his lips, and I think he's going to lean in and do it, but he lets go of my hands instead.

He moves to take a step away, and I use my new freedom to grab his shirt. Before I can talk myself out of it I lean up on my toes, and kiss him. For a few seconds, there's no movement. Our lips are locked, frozen in the moment.

Maybe this isn't what he wanted. I read the situation completely wrong. His hands hang at his sides. He could be kissing his grandmother.

I pull away defeated, and he lets me. But only for a heartbeat. His mouth crashes into mine. His tongue doesn't wait for permission before it invades my mouth and explores. I moan with a sigh and his restraint snaps. Scotty lifts me off the floor and places me on the counter without releasing my lips. His fingers lace through my hair, and he pulls my head away.

"Tell me to stop, Rowyn. I can't do it myself. I can't stop unless you tell me to." I hear his words, but his eyes plead with me not to stop.

"I can't. Kiss me. Please."

"Fuck," he hisses. "Last chance, Pinky. I won't ask again." Fisting his shirt in my hands, I pull him close and whisper into his ear.

"Don't. Stop." His hands leave my hair and scoop me up under my ass. I'm lifted from the counter as his lips descend on me again. Wrapping my arms around his neck, I deepen the kiss and feel us moving from the kitchen.

My senses are misfiring. He's so close. I smell his woody scent; his hair is soft and thick in my hands. His body is hard against mine, and I can still taste a hint of the bourbon on his tongue.

I trail my lips along his jawline and feel his stubble under my tongue. I don't want to bump into any walls as he walks us to his room, so I continue sucking and nipping on his neck.

We pass Tori's room, and I know his is the next door. I can smell the moment we walk in. The scent of him thickens. I've never really been in here before. It's always been off-limits, which has never been an issue.

Scotty kneels on the bed and crawls us up to the pillows before laying me on his comforter. He straddles my hips, kneeling over me.

With one hand, he reaches behind him and pulls off his shirt. I've seen him shirtless plenty of times over the years, but nothing compares to this view right now. My fingers instinctively trace the planes of his abs and the light trail of hair that disappears into his jeans. He shivers from my touch, and I can't help but smile.

His hungry eyes roam over me. I reach between us to remove my tank top, and he stops my hands.

"Let me." I nod, and he grabs the hem of my shirt, slowly lifting it over my head. He tosses it to the floor, and his fingers trace the line of the top of my white lacy bra.

94

"How far do you want this to go, Rowyn? You're the sober one. I don't want to take advantage of the situation." I'm having trouble forming words as his finger runs a line of fire starting at the pulse point of my neck, down between my breasts, and stops at the top of my jeans.

"I-I..." I don't know. This has never been anything more than a fantasy. How do I voice what I want?

He leans down and traces my collarbone with his tongue, and I arch into him. I feel his smile against my skin. He pauses for a moment and sits up, looking into my eyes.

"Pinky." His tone has changed. "Please tell me you aren't a virgin."

"Yes, I mean no. I'm not a virgin." He doesn't believe me. I can see it in his eyes and feel my skin heating up, knowing my entire body is blushing. His fingers trail all over my exposed skin. He's cataloging my blush.

"Tell me. There's more in that pretty little head of yours based on this gorgeous pink tone to your skin. Tell me."

"I've had sex...once. Barely." This is it. He's about to reject me. I'm the child that he thinks I am. I have no experience, and he has an entire kid with another woman. He's experienced beyond anything I can imagine.

"Hey, open your eyes." I hadn't realized I'd closed them. "It's okay. We don't have to do anything." He cups my cheek, rubbing his thumb across my lips.

I shock him when I suck his finger into my mouth and swirl my tongue around it. He inhales sharply and groans when I run my teeth along his thumb.

"Rowyn. What do you want?"

"You. I want you. Just...show me. Tell me."

"Are you sure? What does 'barely' mean?" I'm embarrassed

to admit this next part.

"Barely means it...went in, and it hurt. There was some blood, and he freaked out. It was his first time, too. It was my freshman year of college, and it was awkward and didn't feel all that great." He sighs and leans down to kiss me again. This kiss is different than any of the previous ones. It's soft and tender. His tongue caresses and teases playfully.

"This is a big step. I can't deny I want you, but I'm not sure this is the right time." He's rejecting me.

"I'll still be barely not a virgin tomorrow, next week, next month."

"But I've been drinking, and you deserve better."

"Scotty, if you're sober enough to recognize that you've been drinking, and your head's on straight enough to consider that this may not be the right time, then you're sober enough to make the right decision. I'm saying yes. I'm telling you I want you. The decision is yours, but I'm saying yes."

"You're a huge test of my sanity. Do you understand that, Rowyn?" His head tips back and he stares at the ceiling, contemplating. "There are so many reasons why I should get up and walk out of this room, right now." Here it comes. "But they can all fuck off."

He rolls us to our sides, twisting our legs together. Large hands wander the center of my back, and his fingers make work on the clasp of my bra.

"I want you to talk to me, Pinky. Tell me what you like and don't. I'll take the reins, but you're in control."

"Do you think we need a safeword or something?" He laughs, and I feel silly for asking.

"Maybe another time, but there's nothing to worry about right now. I'll go as slow or as fast as you want. If you say stop, we stop. Nothing crazy is going to happen except me pleasuring you. Okay?"

"Okay." He pulls my bra strap off my shoulder and weaves the other side from under us. His calloused hands engulfs my breasts, kneading the flesh. Every touch and caress feels better than the next. When he leans up and takes my nipple into his mouth, my entire body feels like it's on fire, and my core clenches.

"Was there any foreplay involved with your lackluster sex experience?" Am I being that obvious?

"Not really. Mostly just kissing…on the lips." I hear him mumble "fucking amateur" under his breath. He's tenderly kissing and licking my neck and chest. I can almost hear the gears turning in his head.

"So this is all new for you? It's all your first time?"

"Please don't reject me for my inexperience." He firmly grabs my chin, making sure he has my full attention.

"Rowyn. I would never reject you. I'm just trying to determine your boundaries." I breathe a sigh of relief. "Since you don't know what you do like, is there anything you think you might not like? I want to make sure you enjoy everything."

"I, um, nothing with my butt." He laughs.

"Anal play is an advanced skill. We are working on a beginner's level. What else?" He's returned to nipping and licking various parts of my upper body again. I feel like I'm on fire, and my clit is throbbing as if it has its own heartbeat.

"W-whips, chains, beatings." He laughs again before swirling his tongue around my nipple.

"I have no whips or chains. As for beatings, how do you feel about spankings?" Spankings. How *do* I feel about spankings?

I've read enough smutty books to know that spankings can be erotic and pleasurable if done right.

"Would you want to spank me? Is that something that turns you on?"

"Fuck, Pinky. YOU turn me on. You don't have to know what you like or don't like tonight. Just let me make you feel good. How does that sound?" He's kissed down my body and is teasing me along the waist of my jeans as I nod.

He unbuttons them and pulls down the zipper. Standing, Scotty undoes his pants before letting them drop to the floor. He's wearing nothing but his light gray boxer briefs that leave little to the imagination. My breath hitches in my throat at his size and he smirks when he sees where my eyes are focused.

"Is there a problem, Rowyn?"

"You're...you're..." I can't find the words. He's hard and long.

"I'm a man."

"But it's so..." He dips down and takes off his boxers, rendering me speechless. He's naked. Completely naked and more mouth-watering than any man I've ever seen.

"We might as well get all the stammering out of the way at once." He's smiling, and I can imagine the lovely shade of tomato that I am right now.

"Scotty, that's not gonna—"

"It will. I promise. And you'll enjoy it." He extends his hand for me to stand. "How about we even things out a little bit? I'm at a disadvantage." He smiles and looks down at my jeans and then at his nakedness.

I raise my arms in silent permission to help me up. The movement lifts my breasts, and he grabs both of them, squeezing firmly once I'm upright. My arms hook on his shoulders when his thumbs graze my nipples.

"Fuck."

"I love it when you curse. You do it so sparingly that it must mean you like the feel of my hands on your bare skin. Or was it your nipples specifically that made you curse?" He pinches my nipple between his fingers, and I arch into his hands.

"Holy fuck."

"There it is, Rowyn. Don't stop letting me know what you like. I'm not quiet in bed, and I don't expect you to be either. There's no one here but us."

I feel his thumbs swipe my hips as he tucks them inside my jeans and underwear. He slides them down together until they hit the floor, and we're both standing naked.

Taking a true look at his bare chest for the first time, I see more of the empty shapes similar to the ones on his left arm.

"These are new." My fingers trace the outline of a rainbow with clouds that span across his shoulder and a few fairy outlines.

"Tori told me she was getting bored coloring the same ones over and over."

"You're such an amazing father." I kiss the tattoos along his shoulder and chest. His entire left arm and now half of his shoulder and upper chest are covered in blank tattoos for Tori to color. It kept her occupied when she was younger, and he's been building her a canvas ever since.

"Would you let me color them one day?"

"I'd love it if you did." He tips my chin up and kisses me slowly and passionately. "Lay down on the bed."

I crawl up to the headboard and lay my head on the pillows like our earlier position. Scotty crawls up the middle of the bed with a devilish glint in his eyes.

"Hey, Rowyn?"

"Yes."

"Please tell me you haven't lived twenty-two years without an orgasm." He kisses my ankle, my calf, my knee.

"N-no. I have a drawer full of vibrators, remember." My mind is turning to mush.

"Ah. Right. How could I forget that?" Kisses pepper just above my knee. He pushes my legs apart, and I feel exposed and a little embarrassed.

"Scotty?" He hmmm at me, and his lips trail higher.

"I've never…uuuh. That feels so good. Never been touched—" He pops up on his elbows.

"Rowyn, has no one ever touched this sweet pussy?" His hand dances along my pubic bone through the short strip of hair that I keep neat and trimmed.

"Just B.O.B.," I chuckle an uneasy laugh.

"Who's Bob?" Hmm. He sounds a little jealous. I can't help but laugh now.

"B.O.B. You know—my Battery Operated Boyfriend." I see the confusion on his face as he rolls the words around in his mind.

"Wait. Your vibrator?" Now I'm giggling at him. A giggle that quickly turns into a gasp as his finger takes its first stroke over my clit. It's already sensitive from everything that's happened so far, and I have a feeling this is just the tip of the iceberg.

He's lying between my legs, watching his fingers as they run up and down, gathering my arousal and spreading it around. My breath increasing with each swipe over my clit.

"Rowyn, can I taste you? I want to devour this pussy with

my tongue and clean you up when you come on it. Let me show you what real pleasure is."

"I-I…"

"If you're uncomfortable, you can say no."

"No. Yes. Please. My brain…is mush." I can't even form coherent sentences between his languid finger strokes and all of the mental images he's giving of what he wants to do to me; I'm a goner.

He props himself up on his elbows again and pushes my thighs farther apart to gain better access. I watch his head sink lower until I can feel his hot breath on my already heated core.

His tongue flicks out and swirls around my clit, and I nearly jolt off the bed.

"Shh. Relax." I feel his large hand cover my lower stomach to keep me in place. "Feel and enjoy." That's exactly what I do.

I melt into the bed as his tongue twists and licks, nips and sucks. It doesn't take long before I feel the telltale signs of an orgasm beginning to build. Except this feels different. This feels like more. Bigger. The sensation is spreading farther than usual. I feel a build-up in my belly and my spine.

Scotty shifts around, and I feel his finger at my entrance. I know I'm wet, and I feel it slide inside of me. It almost feels intrusive. The pressure isn't something I'm used to. He pulls out and easily slides in a second finger. He moans into my pussy, causing the vibration to tip me closer to the edge of my impending orgasm.

When his fingers inside me start to move, I gasp.

"Scotty, what—oh god. That feels. I'm, holy shit." I don't know what I'm feeling. Well, I do. It's intense. I almost feel like I'm going to pee, and that's not a pleasurable feeling.

"Shhh. Do you trust me, Rowyn?" I stare at him, unsure of what to say. Of course, I trust him, but I don't trust this feeling taking over my body.

"I-I don't. It feels…"

"I promise you aren't going to pee on me." He softly laughs at the shock on my face. How does he know what I was feeling? "You're so fucking perfect." His fingers inside me stroke again, and I'm zapped with lightning. "This is your G-spot, Wynnie. Do you have any toys that go inside?"

"No. Only outside. Uuh." He's brushing inside me again.

"These are more nerves, like your clit." He quickly sucks my clit into his mouth to emphasize his point. "They can cause a different type of orgasm. Will you trust me? You just have to ride the sensation, and I promise you'll feel more pleasure than you've ever felt before.

"Okay. Okay, god. I fucking trust you." I lay back down, and almost instantly, I'm overwhelmed with feelings inside and out. His tongue sucks, and his fingers rub. I feel like a balloon filled with too much air. One wrong bounce, and I'll explode.

"Scotty." I moan his name, and my hands pull at his hair.

"I know. I can feel it. Just relax and let go. Don't think." Don't think? My mind is a tornado of thoughts and emotions all swirling around. My entire body is tingling. I'm on fire with a blush that I can feel all over my body.

"Scotty. Oh fuck. Scotty. Scotty!"

Stars.

Fireworks.

A whiteout.

A blackout.

There are a million pinpricks of feelings. I can't breathe because all the air has left my lungs refusing to return. Tidal wave after tidal wave of pleasure flows through my body.

"Fuck, Scotty. Oh, my fuck." The bastard smiles while continuing to flick my clit with his tongue. I didn't realize that I shoved his head further into me as my body convulsed around him.

I release his hair as my soul slowly floats back to my body. That was…what? I have no words to describe what just happened to earth.

He finally stops and pulls his fingers out, sitting up between my legs. My jaw drops as I watch him suck his fingers into his mouth and clean me off of him. He crawls up my body, hovering over me, holding himself up.

"My god, Pinky. That was the most beautiful fucking thing I've ever seen. The way you fell apart for me. Fuck."

I pull him towards me. He groans into my mouth. I can taste myself. It's a little salty, but it's almost intoxicating mixed with him.

"How was that?"

15

Scotty

I don't know what good karma I've done lately to deserve this goddess under me right now, but I don't fucking care.

She just fucking shattered for me. It was incredible to watch. I had to keep reminding myself not to stop and watch her. I wanted her to feel every ounce of pleasure I could give.

"How was it?" I don't even need to ask. Her eyes are glazed. She kissed me, not caring that her come was smeared all over my face.

"It was...decent." Her lip twitches in her attempt to keep a straight face.

"Decent? Your dirty mouth said otherwise." I shift my hips so my cock slides between her legs, teasing her. Teasing us both. "Your dripping pussy says otherwise. You know, Rowyn, brats get spankings. Are you being a brat?" Her head shakes, but her eyes tell a different story. Curiosity and excitement are shining through them. I hope I get a chance to explore that with her.

What now? Do we continue tonight? I'm willing to go as

104

far as she is, but I don't want to rush her into anything. Her orgasm was intense, and I wouldn't blame her if she wanted to roll over and sleep.

Sleep. In my bed. I like the idea of that way too much. I'm completely sober now and know all my thoughts are rational. Well, as rational as they can be around Wynnie.

She drives me crazy. I look into her eyes and brush a stray hair off her forehead.

"What do you want to do now, gorgeous? It's your call. Your show, remember."

"Please." She flexes her hips into mine. I know what she wants but I'm not letting her off the hook that easily.

"Please, what?"

"Do you have...condoms?" I can't help but smile at her. She's the perfect mix of innocence and siren.

"Do you want me inside you, Rowyn? Do you want to feel my cock stretching you out to fit me?" My hips rock against her. I can tell it's driving her wild, but it's having the same effect on me. I'm only containing my need to thrust deep inside her because we need protection.

Her face is flushed, partly from her orgasm and partly because of the direction of our conversation.

"I do. I want you inside me. I'm on the pill, but..."

"There's no but, Wynnie. I have no problem wearing a condom. If it makes you comfortable, I'll wear one. I had every intention to." I lean over her and open the top drawer of my nightstand. Smiling, I realize we both keep our dirty things in our top drawers.

"Do you want to help me?"

"Help you put the condom on?" Her eyes widen as she considers my offer.

105

"It might help you not be so afraid of the size of my cock."

"I'm not afraid…" I tilt my head to the side, daring her to object any further. "Okay, it's a little intimidating."

"I promise there's nothing little about it." I kiss the tip of her nose and sit up on my knees motioning for her to join me.

I open the package with my teeth and show her how to put the tip on and let her roll it down my shaft. Every brush of her fingers is the sweetest torture. She giggles when I involuntarily twitch under her fingers.

"Are you sure that's going to fit?"

"Say cock, Rowyn."

"What?" She looks at me confused.

"Say. Cock. I've heard fuck come from these pretty lips several times already tonight." I lick her bottom lip and suck it into my mouth before popping off. "Say cock for me?"

"You're ridiculous, Scotty." She pushes my shoulder and I grab her wrist.

"If you want it, say it. Cock. It's just a word, Pinky, but I need to hear it pass through your sinful lips. Cock. Scotty, I want your cock. Scotty, your cock is huge. Scotty, fuck me with your cock. Pick one."

She's not one to back down from a challenge, and I know I'll win. I want to see her sweet mouth say such a filthy word.

"You're serious?" Her blue eyes bounce between mine.

"Absolutely serious. Say cock, and it's all yours."

"Cock." She barely whispers the word under her breath.

"You have to mean it if you want it. Don't be shy. You talked about anal, whips, and chains. Where's that dirty girl from earlier?" I see the determination cross her face. I'm challenging her just outside her comfort zone. Not too far. Just far enough to make her think about what she really wants.

She may not be a virgin, but she's about to give me something she can't take back, and I need her to be confident and sure.

"Cock." She rolls her eyes. "Cock, cock, cock. Dick, penis, schlong, wiener, sausage, eggplant. Happy now?"

"Fucking ecstatic." I tip us over so we're lying side by side on the bed and kiss her. Pulling back, I caress her cheek. "You're so unbelievably beautiful. Inside and out."

"How about we test that inside theory?" She's being sassy. I growl and roll us again until I'm on top of her.

"Sassy, aren't we? The girl says cock a few times and grows a pair of balls."

"Are you stalling, Mr. Langford?"

"Not at all, Ms. Harmon." I line up with her entrance, knowing I need to be slow and gentle. She was tight with my two fingers, and I'm much thicker. "I want you to talk to me and let me know if anything doesn't feel good."

I take her nipple into my mouth to distract her and push my hips forward. She inhales but doesn't ask me to stop. I make slow, rhythmic thrusts, sinking deeper each time.

When our hips meet, and I'm entirely in, I have to take a few deep breaths to not come on the spot. She's so tight. She's hugging my cock with her heat.

"How are you, Pinky?" She's holding her breath.

"I'm…" She exhales her breath and thinks. "I'm full, but you feel so good." I pull out halfway and push back in. We both moan at the feeling of our connection.

"Scotty?"

"What do you need from me?" I can tell she wants

107

something.

"Will you *not* be so sweet and nice? Will you take me how you want me, and I'll let you know if I can't handle it?"

"Fuck. I want nothing more, but are you sure?" She nods and thrusts her hips into mine.

"I'm positive. Fuck me. Please." Pulling out, I shift her legs up. When I sink back in, I'm deeper than before. I set a pace I'm comfortable with while battling the war inside me.

I have to find the balance between losing control and making this pleasurable for her. She told me to fuck her because that's what she thinks I want, but it's not. I want to take my time and worship her. She's not a random woman who's going to crawl out of my bed after sex and never be seen again. And she needs to know that.

"Rowyn, I want to give you what you want, but will you trust me to know what you need? I want to make this experience better than your first."

"It already is. And I trust you." Releasing her legs, I lay my body entirely on top of her, wanting to feel as much of her skin on mine as I can. I kiss her neck and shoulders while continuing my pace.

"Next time, I'll bring out the whips and chains for you." She huffs a laugh in between her moans. "Tonight, right now, I want you to know what it feels like to be someone's priority. To have all of their attention focused on you and your pleasure alone."

"Keep talking. You feel so good." Her hands roam over my shoulders and back. Reaching down, I grab one knee, wrap it around my hip, and then the other. Her breathing increases at the new, tighter angle.

"Do you like praise, Rowyn? Do you want me to tell you

how sexy you look right now with your mouth parted and those moans and whimpers of pleasure escaping you? How about if I tell you what a good girl you are for taking all of my hard cock into your tight pussy."

"Fuck, Scotty." Mmm. There it is. She does like praise.

"Or do you want to hear what a dirty little slut you are for opening your legs for me?"

"Oh god, yes." My pace increases with every noise she's making. Let's try one more thing.

"Tell me Rowyn. Do you want to know what a good little slut you are for me? How filthy this pussy is. How good you are for taking me so deep." There it is. Her inner walls clench around me. Her nails dig into my shoulders. "Is that it? You like a little degradation with your praise? You want to hear all the nasty things you do to me, but you can't fully put down those good girl walls you've built can you?"

"Fuck, Scotty. Oh Fuck." Her eyes are closed, and her head turns side to side, chasing. She's chasing another orgasm, but she isn't quite sure how.

"Shh, Rowyn. Let go. Don't think. Just feel. Feel how hard my cock is sliding in and out of you. You made me this hard. Your sweet fucking moans sound so innocent, but your pussy sucking me in tells me you're anything but."

"Please. Fuck, please." Mmmm. Listen to her beg.

"What do you need, Pinky? Do you want to come? Are you going to come for me like a good fucking girl?"

"Yes, yes, yes." Leaning further into her, I growl in her ear.

"Then. Fucking. Do it." As if her body was waiting for permission, she explodes. Her little moans from a moment ago turn into loud, wild, unabandoned screams. Her nails dig into my shoulder so hard she's sure to break the skin.

"Give it all to me. You're such a good girl for me." I pump feverishly, chasing my own orgasm. Burying my head into her neck, I inhale the fresh scent of her apple shampoo, and it tips me over. My orgasm rips through me as fiercely as hers does. I continue to pulse into her until we're both spent.

We lay there panting, slicked in sweat, and I feel her shake. I slowly pull out, not wanting to leave the warmth of her body, and see she's crying. I take her cheeks in my hands and look into her eyes. "Hey, hey, are you okay? Was it too much?"

"No. No, it was…beyond words. Thank you. Thank you, Scotty." I kiss each of her cheeks, tasting her salty tears.

"Don't scare me like that. Let me get cleaned up, and I'll grab a cloth to clean you up. I'll be right back."

"Mmm, okay." She's tired. I wore her out. Walk into the bathroom I dispose of the condom in the trash can feeling a sense of pride. I clean myself off and run a washcloth under warm water to do the same for her.

She's asleep when I walk back into the room. I look at her momentarily, wondering if we've just made a huge mistake. If *I've* made the mistake because ultimately it's mine. I wasn't lying any number of times I told her this was a bad idea. She's their family. If anything goes wrong, I'm going to be the one to lose her. And them in the process.

"Hey, Pinky. Let's get you cleaned up, and you can sleep." I run a finger up and down her arm, trying to wake her gently.

"Hmm. Oh, okay. I should get home." She tries to sit up, half awake, but I stop her.

"Stay, please. Let me take care of you. Roll for me."

"Okay." She's barely awake. I get her cleaned up and toss the washcloth back into the bathroom. Climbing into bed next to her, I pull her body into mine and tuck her to my chest. Fuck spooning. I want to feel her breath on my chest. Hold her under my chin where she fits perfectly.

I kiss her on the head—a gesture almost as tender and passionate as the sex we just had.

"Goodnight, Rowyn." But she doesn't answer. She's already blissfully asleep.

16

Wynnie

Something smells delicious and feels just as good. Warm and comfortable. Like a weighted blanket.

I don't own a weighted blanket. My eyes slowly crack open to a room that's...not mine.

The blanket, that's actually an arm, pulls me closer.

"Morning, Pinky. You're still at my house. Don't freak out." That's Scotty's voice. I'm at his house. Okay. Except, that's not okay.

"Rowyn, stop. I can hear you overthinking. It's alright." I take a deep breath and exhale with a whoosh. "Tori is at your mom's house. It's just you and me here. And whatever you're thinking about last night is okay. We can talk about everything after I get some more snuggles." He nuzzles into my hair, inhaling deeply.

That sounds reasonable. Except, did he say he wanted to snuggle?

"Snuggle?"

"Yes, snuggle. You got a problem with that?" He gives me his faux stern dad voice.

"Not if you're a five year old." He rolls me over onto my back and buries his head beneath my chin, laying his cheek on my chest.

"It's a good thing I *have* a five year old. She likes to snuggle with me. Do you want to snuggle with me, Rowyn?" I feel his finger trail the entire left side of my body, from my breast to my hip and back again. "Unless you'd like to do more than snuggle?"

My legs shift on the bed, and I feel his erection digging into my thigh.

"It seems like someone wants to do more than snuggle, Scotty."

"Ignore him. It's morning, and I'm lying next to an exquisitely naked woman." I decide to be brave and snake my hand down his body until I reach the part that he told me to ignore.

"Whatcha doing, Pinky?"

"Exploring." I trace the length of him with my finger. He's getting harder with each pass I make. He's velvety soft. Who knew a dick was soft when it was hard. That makes me giggle.

"Something funny about your hand on my cock?" He's smiling at me as he trails kisses across my collarbone.

"I was just thinking how soft you are when you're so hard." I wrap my hand around the base of his cock and squeeze. He groans from deep in his throat as I stroke my clenched hand to his tip.

"Fuck. You cruel little thing. Are you trying to kill me first thing in the morning?" I sure hope not. I'm not entirely sure what I'm doing, but his moans tell me he's enjoying my hand on him.

"I like the noises you make. I like knowing I'm making you

feel good."

"I like a vocal partner, Rowyn. I wouldn't expect them to accept it if I weren't as well. But you're making it easy. You're hand on my—fuck." I squeezed the tip and I think he likes it.

I don't have much experience, but I went to college. I had chatty roommates who would gossip about their conquests. They would talk about tips and techniques, and I soaked it all in. I've also read my fair share of romance books. I've never been shy around Scotty, but knowing he's so much older and more experienced, I need to keep my best foot forward at every turn.

He's lying next to me, eyes closed and his breathing heavy. Knowing how much control I have in just one hand is empowering.

"I want to give you a blow job." Scotty's eyes pop open, and he chokes on air. I release my hold on him and roll to my stomach to make sure he's alright.

"Are you okay?" He pounds his chest a few times to compose himself, blinking rapidly.

"Yeah," he croaks out. "I wasn't expecting such filthy words to come out of such a pretty mouth."

"Filthy? I could have told you I wanted to suck on your cock." His mouth drops open. He makes me feel bold and courageous. Smiling, I shrug and he gives me a mischievous smile back.

"Why, Rowyn. Have I corrupted you after a single night with me? What will you be like after several more nights?" More? He wants more?

I assumed last night's actions were fueled by bourbon. I knew I would probably feel guilty, but I couldn't bring myself to care. I wanted him, and he wanted me, and I let it happen.

Hell, I practically made it happen.

"You want to do this again?" He sighs and pulls me into his chest.

"I don't think I have the willpower to fight my desire for you anymore, especially not after last night. If you want this to be a one time thing, I'll understand and respect it. But know that I don't." He runs his fingers through my hair, and a shiver runs down my spine.

"But how?"

"Well, I think that's what we need to figure out. As I mentioned last night, I have everything to lose in this situation. You scare the shit out of me, Pinky. I'm a joker in your deck of cards, and you're the Queen. Tell me what you want."

"Ugh, Scotty. This is a really heavy conversation to have before coffee. Can we go back to the snuggling and blow jobs?" He laughs and rolls to his back, grabbing the blanket and flinging it off himself. With a cocky smile, he watches me as he rests his hands behind his head. "Take whatever you want, Rowyn. I'm all yours."

He's gorgeous, and my bravery slips momentarily as I look over his body. I want to make this good for him. My soul left my body with the orgasm he gave me last night. I won't fool myself that I can be as good as him, but I can try my best.

He's already hard and waiting for me as I crawl down the bed. Having only seen one in real life, I admire it as I situate myself between his legs. He's right about what he said last night. I was with a boy before, and he's a man. Scotty is all man.

"Enjoying the view down there?" His cocky smile is still in place as he leans forward to tease me. The act makes his abs constrict, and now I'm distracted by another part of his body.

"How are you so beautiful?"

"I could ask you the same question." Before he can get any more gushy on me, I take his cock in my hand and stroke it. I'm starting to like that word. Cock. Cock, cock, cock.

Now, I must look crazy because I know I'm smiling and blushing.

"What's going on in that silly little head of yours? You've done a lot of laughing while my cock is in your hands. You're gonna give me a complex, Pinky." I erupt into laughter because he just used my new favorite word.

"Sorry. I was just thinking how much I liked the word cock. It isn't a word I've ever used before, but I like the way it sounds. Cock. Cock."

"Oh, really. Well, how about you put that sweet mouth of yours on my cock and give me the blow job you keep teasing me with. Otherwise, I have some alternative ideas on how to use my cock that aren't so wholesome, my dear little Wynnie." Oh, that sounds like a challenge and also a complete turn-on.

I love the things he says to me, but maybe I shouldn't. Either way, I want to hear him moan because of me.

Opening my mouth with my eyes locked on Scotty, I lower myself to his tip and swirl my tongue around it. He's leaking in anticipation, and I taste the saltiness of his pre-cum.

He growls, and I like that even more than the word cock. It's time to search the depths of my mind and remember all those *Cosmo* magazines I read in college about how to give the best head. I knew one day they would come in handy.

I keep my hand on the lower part of his shaft in a firm grip. There's no way I can take him all. Pulling him into my mouth, I hollow my cheeks and suck and pull at the same time. Scotty's entire body contracts, and I hear him mutter "fuck."

Brownie points for me. I continue the sucking, and Scotty's hand tangles into my hair while he groans in pleasure.

It's time to level up. I graze my lower teeth up the bottom of his shaft, and just before I pop off, I flick my tongue in the slit at the head of his cock.

"What the jesus fuck, Rowyn. God fucking dammit. I'm already so close to blowing. Your fucking mouth should be registered as a deadly weapon."

I'm already back on his cock, sucking and licking. I gently cup his balls, letting them roll in my hands. I hum around his head when he pulls on my hair.

"I'm gonna come soon. Are you going to let me come down your throat?" His hips are pumping, and I can tell he's holding himself back. I answer him by squeezing his base harder and nipping at his tip.

"Fuck, Rowyn. You better be my good girl and swallow it all down. Don't disappoint me, or I won't let you indulge again." I don't plan to disappoint him. Not at all.

I pick up my pace, simultaneously pumping my hand and mouth, and he sits on his elbow to watch me. It doesn't take long before he throws his head back on a long, loud moan, and I feel the first jet of his hot come in my mouth.

Eagerly, I swallow everything he gives me. His hand flexes in my hair like a scalp massage, and he pulls away when he can't take anymore. I look at his semi-hard cock and pout. I was enjoying myself. He plops back on the bed, laughing, and stares at the ceiling.

"What...I... How." The stuttering is hilarious. His chest

117

glistens with sweat, and he's trying to catch his breath while poorly attempting to form words.

As I kiss up his body, he grabs me under the arms and hauls me to his chest, smashing his mouth to mine. His kiss is hungry, and he devours me.

I try to pull away because he must be able to taste the remnants of himself in my mouth, but he growls and pulls me closer.

When he finally releases me, he locks our foreheads together, and now we're both panting.

"Where the fuck did you come from? Fuck, Pinky. You just sucked my soul straight through my cock."

"Funny, that's how I felt last night. Only you sucked mine out of my pussy."

"We need to get out of this bed right now, or I'm keeping you locked up here naked for the rest of the day. And as incredible as that sounds, there's a little girl that needs to be picked up, and life kind of goes on, and we need to participate in it."

"Outside life gets zero stars. Staying in bed gets five stars. I choose option B." I feel his rumble of laughter under me and it's soothing. He kisses my forehead, making me smile.

"Have you ever done that before?" He's running his hand up and down my spine, and my brain has trouble concentrating on anything but his touch.

"Nope." I pop the P, and he chuckles.

"There's no way you are that good on your first try." He's in awe but a little skeptical.

"The internet is a wonderful place."

"Oh man, Pinky. I bet your personal FBI agent must love your browser history."

"You should see what my e-reader reading list looks like."

"I heard some of it, remember?" Oh shit, I had forgotten about the Bluetooth incident. I need a quick subject change, or we really aren't going to get out of bed anytime soon.

"What time do you need to pick up Tori?" There's nothing like a kid to decrease your libido. Scotty rolls and flips me onto my back, hovering over me.

"I don't have to pick her up until eleven. We need to get your bike from the bar. Wanna go for a ride beforehand?"

"Together?" I've only ever ridden with my dad before.

"Yes, together. Unless you wanted to sit around and drink coffee while I go alone? I don't get out as much as I like to because of Tori. Hopefully, she can ride with me soon. But I'd like to go for a ride with you if you're willing."

It's a wonder that Scotty and I haven't ridden together before. My dad taught me the respect I needed for motorcycles and the trust required to get on the back of someone else's bike. I know him and Scotty have gone on rides together, so I know my dad trusts and respects him.

"Okay. Let's go. But I need coffee first." He chuckles to himself.

"How do you feel about iced coffee?"

"What do you mean?"

"We made coffee last night and never got to it." He's right. We got a little preoccupied.

"Okay. How about a shower and then the coffee shop? We can go to the Book Beanery."

"Alright, Pinky. That sounds like a plan. I'll let you shower first. Towels are in the closet in the bathroom, and spare toothbrushes are under the sink. Let me know if you need anything else." He kisses me on the forehead and crawls off the bed.

I watch as he grabs a pair of black lounge pants from a drawer and walks into the bathroom. He returns with his pants on and a few things in his hands.

"The bathroom is all yours. I'll use the other one."

17

Scotty

Keep your composure, asshole. I may be acting cool and collected on the outside, but inside, I'm like a teenage boy. My heart is pounding as fast as a hummingbird's wings.

I walk into the bathroom that's primarily used by Tori and reach for the toothpaste. I didn't think about this when I took my toothbrush out of my bathroom for Wynnie to use. It seems I'm brushing my teeth with sparkly pink bubblegum-flavored toothpaste today.

As I brush, I open the cabinet under the sink to grab saline solution and a contact container. I keep several of these in various places around the house. It became a habit when I had an infant, and I never knew when or where I would have a chance to take them out.

I didn't take out my contacts last night; my eyes could use a little break before I put new ones back in. I grabbed my glasses from my bathroom before I left it to Wynnie.

This seems surreal. Wynnie was in my bed. She's currently in my shower. I was inside her last night, kissing and touching. She was mine.

Her being here is terrifying. She's always been an unobtainable fantasy. The precious gem behind the glass wall to be admired but not touched. I broke those rules last night. I obtained, and I touched. I coveted, and I took.

But I didn't take more than she wanted to give. I was the one drinking last night. She was sober and utterly aware of all of her decisions. And then this morning happened. She was completely uninhibited.

Is this something we can make work? Is it sustainable? There are so many roadblocks for us.

I hear the shower turn off and remember she had a bag with her last night. I retrieve it and stop in the doorway when I reach my room. My bathroom door is open, and she's standing at the sink in a towel.

Her brown hair is wet and slicked to almost the middle of her back. Her exposed body is glistening with the dew from the shower. I watch a drop fall from her temple, trail down the side of her face, and fall onto her collarbone. It continues down and disappears, soaking into the towel.

"I grabbed your bag for you." She jumps, not expecting my voice.

"Thank you. Hey, you wear glasses? I had no ide-Scotty." Why does she look so shocked?

Wynnie walks up to me and touches my face. She gently removes my glasses. They're thick black plastic frames, more for function than style. I learned the hard way that babies and glasses don't mix well.

"Scotty, your eyes." She sees my heterochromia. Now I understand her expression. My left eye is three-fourths silver like Tori's and a quarter brown to match the brown of my right eye. I wear brown contacts to cover the color difference because I don't like the attention.

"I'm sorry. I didn't think about it when I took my contacts out. It's weird, I know. I just needed to give my eyes a rest because I forgot to take out my contacts last night." Her fingers lightly brush the skin under my eyes.

"They're beautiful. Why do you hide it?" I grab her wrists and put them over my shoulder, pulling her close to me. I kiss her softly, allowing our lips to graze each other.

"I don't want to feel like a circus freak, constantly answering questions. I had contacts by the time I started high school. I'm not even sure Phoenix knows."

That hurt. Being reminded of her dads while I have her in my arms in only a towel turns my stomach. We have a lot to discuss if anything is going to go on between us beyond this moment.

"I don't think you're a freak. They're mesmerizing." I pull her in for another kiss, ignoring the outside world while we still can.

"My turn to shower." I kiss her forehead and leave her to get dressed while I finish preparing for the day.

I shower quickly and when I leave the bathroom, Wynnie sits on my bed, laughing at her phone.

"What's so funny over there?" I approach my dresser and pull out clothes for myself.

"Elliot is freaking out. He's spam-texting me, wanting all the details of where I am and why I didn't come home last night." I freeze, thinking of what she might tell him. How much does he already know? They may be cousins, but they're also best friends.

"Scotty, are you alright? You look like you've seen a ghost."

Shit. I guess I got a little too lost in thought.

"I'm good. We should probably talk about things. But I definitely shouldn't be naked when we do it." I peek over my shoulder at her and smile. "I know how your hands like to roam. Wouldn't want to give you easy access." I wink and turn my back to her, dropping my towel to give her a show. I hear giggling and a thump on my back when she throws a pillow at me.

Turning, I squint my eyes at her and stalk forward, abandoning my clothes on the floor.

"You're asking for trouble, Pinky." She scurries off the side of the bed, putting a barrier between us. I grab a pillow and sling it in her direction.

"Truce. Truce. I haven't had coffee yet. I can't be held responsible for my actions." She throws her hands up in surrender, and I watch as her eyes trail down my body. I see her smirk when they drift to my growing naked cock, since I had dropped the towel. She licks her lips and I can see in her eyes she's remembering how our morning started.

"Can I help you, perv?" She blinks and snaps her eyes to my face, obviously startled that I caught her staring.

"I-it's still impressive. Sorry." I love the blush creeping across her cheeks.

"It's okay to look. I don't mind." Her eyes start to drift down again, and she catches herself, turning around.

"I'll wait in the living room and let you finish getting ready." She's suddenly turned shy on me, and I find it endearing.

"How desperate is your need for coffee? Are we going straight to the Book Beanery, or can we cruise around first?" Wynnie walks alongside me as I back my motorcycle out of the garage.

"Hmm, I think coffee is imperative after everything already this morning."

"Okay, coffee first. Hop on, Backpack."

"What?" She cocks her head to the side, laughing at me. "Did you just call me a backpack?"

"Yeah. Isn't that what all the cool kids are calling it these days? You'll be hanging off my back, so you're my Backpack."

"Um, maybe I'm not part of the cool kid crowd, but that's hilarious."

I get our helmets set up with my communication devices, a microphone that connects between the two of us, and a camera that attaches to me, and Wynnie climbs on.

My dick instantly reacts as her body flushes against mine. Despite our leather jackets, I can still feel the swells of her breasts against my back, the heat of her body connecting with mine.

I confirm the bike is in neutral and press the start button. Wynnie tentatively puts her arms on my sides, and I want them closer.

I release the clutch and jerk the bike forward, causing her arms to wrap further around me. Before she has a chance to move them back to my side, I lay my arms over hers and squeeze.

"Be a good Backpack and stay." She jumps, not expecting to hear me so clearly in her helmet.

"Ugh, fine." When I'm confident she isn't going to move, I reach back and rub my hand up and down her thigh. "Good girl." I put both hands on the grips, and we take off towards town.

18

Wynnie

Scotty's abdominal muscles flex under his jacket as he expertly maneuvers his motorcycle through town. He thought he was funny with his little bike trick, getting me to wrap my arms around his waist. I had every intention of holding onto him. I wasn't passing up the opportunity. He was just impatient.

Scotty pulls up in front of the Book Beanery and parks us in a motorcycle space. Mountain Pines is very accommodating to alternative vehicles. There are bicycle racks and EV plugs scattered around town as well. While I didn't grow up here, I've been in this town for the last ten years, minus college. It's large enough to have all of the luxuries of the big department stores but small enough to have adorable shops like the Book Beanery.

As we walk inside, Scotty almost crashes into me when I pause. It's what I do every time I come here and a hazard for anyone behind me. Coffee, sugar, and paper invade my senses.

This amazing little coffee shop still sells homemade pastries, a wide variety of coffees to your left, and bookshelves lined with every book imaginable to your right. But the middle of the store is my favorite part.

Once you pick your coffee or book, you choose your seat. Mismatched tables, chairs, and couches crowd the middle of the store. Every style and color imaginable tempts you, from metal to floral to pleather. It reminds me of my prism rainbows and always brings a smile to my face.

"Are we going in, or are you hoping to get your caffeine high through osmosis?" I shudder at Scotty's warm breath on my ear and walk toward the coffee counter.

We get pastries and coffee and sit on a loveseat tucked beside a bookshelf. I prop my leg up on the couch so I'm facing Scotty, and we can talk easier.

"This place is interesting. I've never been here before. I bet Tori would love some of those cookies in the display case."

"You've never been? It's adorable. I love coming here to relax and read. In high school, when I needed some quiet from the little kids at home or the overbearing testosterone of three dads, I'd sneak out and come." I laugh, but he looks a bit uneasy.

"I'm usually a travel mug coffee guy. I don't stop often; if I do, it's typically a diner. I don't need all the fancy stuff since I drink it black. But damn if this muffin isn't fantastic." I tip the paper cup to my lips and savor my caramel latte with extra whipped cream and cinnamon.

"Black? Don't you always have hazelnut creamer in the fridge?" Scotty's smile starts small and grows to light up his entire face.

"That was never for me, Pinky." I don't understand. If he doesn't buy the creamer for himself, who is he buying it for?

127

I always thought we both enjoyed the same style of coffee. "You don't have any idea, do you?" He takes one of my hands from my coffee cup and laces our fingers together, kissing my knuckles before bringing them to his lap.

"I guess I don't." I see a spark in his eyes.

"Wynnie, I—"

"Hey, you two!" I quickly pull my hand out of Scotty's lap and turn to see Aunt Dellah standing in front of us with a knowing smile on her face. "I guess this answers why you weren't home this morning." She smirks at Scotty.

"Hey, Aunt Dellah. What are you doing here?" That was a dumb question. Why else would she be here? I'm lucky it was Aunt Dellah and not my mom, who just found me holding hands with Scotty. The three of us love this place.

"I came by to grab some treats for Paige and me. We're having a girl's day. I knocked on your door to see if you wanted to join us, but it seems you already have plans."

"Dellah—" She holds her hand up to stop Scotty from speaking.

"Nope. I've learned my lesson about keeping secrets from my best friend. I've seen nothing." She covers half her face so Scotty isn't in her vision. "Wynnie, the boys brought your car home last night. I didn't see your motorcycle outside, but I assume you have a ride." She quickly moves her hand to give Scotty a stern look before covering him again. She motions for me to stand and pulls me in for a hug. She whispers into my ear so he can't hear us.

"You're all grown up now. I'm going to assume you know what you're doing. Hazel might be my best friend, but I'm happy to be yours too. If you need to talk, I can keep your secrets. I love you, little niece."

"Thank you, Aunt Dellah, I love you too." She releases me and turns back to Scotty.

"Person that I'm not officially acknowledging, you know who this wonderful young woman is to me. Whatever may or may not be going on here, do it right. Don't hurt her, or I'll be the least of your worries."

"Understood. Thank you. She's special to me as well." Scotty looks at me and smiles the sweetest smile, and I return the sentiment. He didn't back down from Aunt Dellah's threat, and I know what she's referring to. We need to talk about what's going on between us. My dads will have a lot to say if and when they find out.

"Have fun, you two." She wiggles her fingers at us over her shoulder and heads to the coffee counter.

"That was..." Scotty trails off.

"Interesting. Terrifying. Eye-opening." I express my current feelings about this situation.

"Yeah. All of those work. What now?" Scotty has finished with his muffin, and I've drank over half my coffee and lost my appetite for the Danish I got at the counter.

"Did you still want to go for that ride before we get your bike? Or we can go right to the bar, and you can head home. Whichever you prefer." His eyes look hopeful.

"Let's go for the ride. After that surprise guest, I could use some fresh air to clear my head."

"Alright, Pinky. Let's ride." I itch to take his hand, but Aunt Dellah is still here, and she keeps not so subtly looking over her shoulder at us. I wave as we walk out the door and she waves back.

When I mount the seat behind him, I wrap my arms around his waist without playing around this time. He starts her up, and the rumble underneath me instantly soothes my nerves. We need to talk. I want to talk. But not right now. Now, I want to free my mind and watch the world fly by me.

We amble through the streets of town until we get close to the mountain. Scotty reaches behind him and rubs his hand on my thigh again.

"You ready, Pinky?" His voice reverberates through the helmet. I rest my head on his back and squeeze tighter as my silent response. He rounds the corner and opens the throttle as we weave through the mountain turns.

"Thank you."

Our ride ends sooner than I would have liked, and we pull up in front of Tipsy Penny. The parking lot is empty except for my motorcycle and a few cars on the other end of the lot. Scotty puts down the kickstand, and when he dismounts, he pulls me into him and kisses me.

"I love how you feel against me on the back of my bike. I've been wanting to kiss you since we left the house." I melt into his arms, and for a moment, I don't care that despite not being able to see anyone, we're out in the open and may not be alone.

Scotty removes his gloves and reaches for my hands to remove mine. He slowly unzips my leather jacket and moves his hands under the hem of my shirt, rubbing my stomach and sides. Leaning forward, I rest my head on his chest and listen to his heartbeat through his jacket.

"What does this mean? We should figure things out. There are a lot more people involved than just you and me, Scotty."

He sighs, and I feel it in my bones. I wish we could live in our little bubble. There's even room in here for Tori, but everyone else...

"I know we should. Do we have to do it now, though? Everything feels so perfect. How about Monday night when I get home from work? Can we have a late dinner? Or just some drinks and talk. We don't have to decide anything right this second. Let's enjoy these last few moments and take the rest of the weekend to really think about what we want." I like his idea.

Think about what we want. I know what I want. It's what I've wanted for years and feels like it's finally within reach. But Scotty has already expressed his valid fears. He needs to think about Tori. I'm only twenty-two years old. He's thirty-seven with a daughter who has a heart in his relationship, too. I'd hate to do anything to jeopardize the relationship I have with Tori.

"That sounds perfect. I'll have a light dinner with Tori, and we can have something when you get back. I'll cook so you don't have to worry about it.

"Are you sure? I can bring something back."

"Positive. I'd like to cook for you." He kisses my forehead, and I want to stay here forever, but life and responsibilities call to both of us.

I get on my motorcycle after a not so G-rated makeout session and reluctantly start the ride back to my house. My mind wanders to last night, and I begin to hum *Kings of Leon's. Your sex is on fire.*

"You have a beautiful voice, Pinky."

"Shit, Scotty!" I hear him chuckling in the earpiece. "How long of a range do these things have?"

131

"It advertises up to two miles. Want to see how long it goes?"

"That depends. Do you promise not to talk dirty to me so I don't crash?"

"I hate to make that promise, but I'd hate you crashing even more. I suppose we can just talk about the weather." I hear the sarcasm laced in his tone. "I had an amazing time last night, Wynnie. Thank you for making sure I got home safely. I really appreciate it."

"No thanks needed, Scotty. I'll always be there to help you. But…I was hoping you were thanking me for something else."

"Oh really? Little Miss, didn't you just tell me no dirty talk? It sounds like that's what you're asking for. I'm more than happy to oblige if it is. I could talk all day about how I'm practically drooling to get my face in that amazing pussy of yours again."

"Scotty!"

"How sweet it felt to slide into you. How hot and wet you were."

"You know two can play at that game. I bet I have better concentration than you do." I've perfected the art of a straight face in public while listening to the raunchiest audiobooks. I can handle anything he can throw at me and dish it out just as thick.

"Try me." His tone is challenging, and I wholeheartedly accept it.

"Do you want to hear about how I've fantasized about what it would be like to have your cock in my mouth? To be on my knees in front of you, looking up into your eyes while I make you moan." I hear his breathing increase and his groan through the earpiece. "Yeah, just like that, Scotty."

"Fuck, you evil temptress. I was worried about making you crash. I now have to figure out how to adjust myself without everyone around me seeing." I have no idea where this bravery is coming from to say these things to him out loud. Maybe it's knowing that he's on the other end of the speaker and can't do anything about what I say.

"Aww. You poor thing." I giggle at my teasing words.

"Rowyn, you aren't that far away. Don't make me come and find you. I'll put you on your knees right where you want to be."

"Uh oh, I made Daddy mad." I hear him growl.

"I don't know if I love or hate you calling me Daddy because the things I want to do to you are *not* appropriate."

I said it to him as a tease, but I don't think I have a Daddy kink. Actually, I know I don't. It's not something that gets me hot and bothered in my smutty books.

"Let's go with hate because I think I'd like to try whatever inappropriate things that you're thinking, and I definitely don't want to think of you as my daddy while you do them."

"Agreed. You already have enough of them." He chuckles but I can hear the undertone of his discomfort. "Now that that's settled, Pinky, I'm almost home and shocked we're still connected. But I have to go pick up Tori. I had an incredible evening. I'll see you Monday afternoon?"

"You will. And I had a mind-blowing evening. Thank you, Scotty." The reception finally starts to crackle and I'm impressed with their range.

"Dr-v…s-f…Pi-y." He may have broken up, but I still understood him. I hope the rest of his drive home is safe, too.

19

Scotty

What an incredible weekend. After I picked up Tori from Hazel's house, we went to the bar to work on inventory. Tori loves to help me count, and the girls love to see her. I don't work a shift on Sundays, so that's when I usually do my counting.

"What's wrong with you, Bossman?" Kristina walks into the supply closet and grabs a container of salt while I'm counting, giving me a funny look.

"Wrong? What do you mean?"

"You're acting weird. You're too...smiley," she says, pointing at my face.

"Yep. She's right, Daddy. Your face is smiling a lots." It seems to be gang up on Scotty day.

"Can't a guy just be happy?" I throw my hands up in the air in mock exasperation. I turn to Tori and scrunch up my face. Lowering my voice, I stalk towards her. "Would you rather I be grumpy? Mr. Grumpy Daddy tickle monster?" I scoop her up and tickle her as she giggles and kicks her feet while I growl like a monster. I hear Kristina laughing behind us.

"Scotty, have you been involved in any extracurricular activities to be in such a good mood? Maybe with your chauffeur?" I appreciate the code she's trying to speak with Tori in the room, but I won't answer her question.

I decide to play dirty and whisper into Tori's ear. She jumps from my arms and runs over to Kristina.

"Can I have some cherries? Please, please. Pretty please." Kristina smiles and looks at me.

"Well played, Boss. Come on, little miss. Let's get you some cherries." I quickly finish my counting while she's distracted, so Tori and I can leave.

On the ride home, she tells me about her night with Delilah Jane and the wars the boys played around them. When we stop at a traffic light, she makes sure I see the sparkly purple nails that Aunt Hazel painted on her.

"Hey, Daddy?"

"Yeah, Little Princess?"

"Can you and Wynnie get married so Delilah Jane can be my sister too?" I choke on air at her question and slam on my brakes, almost running through a stop sign.

"Whoa, Daddy. You stopped hard." Yeah, well, you shocked the fuck out of me, kid.

"Tori, that's not exactly how that would work. If Daddy married Wynnie, DJ would be your cousin and Wynnie would be your stepmom."

"Oh. I like that better! I like that plan. Let's do that."

"Tori, I don't think—" In my rearview mirror, I see flashing red and blue lights and pull to the side of the road to let the police car pass. Instead, it pulls up behind me. "Shit."

"What's wrong, Daddy?" Her little face is laced with worry.

"Nothing, baby. It's okay. Daddy just pulled over to talk

to a police officer. Everything is okay." As I'm pulling my information out of my wallet, I hear Tori squeal with delight.

"Uncle Mac!" Oh, thank fuck. Mac leans into my open window.

"Hey, Tori. Everything okay, Scotty? You almost blew through that stop sign back there. I would have just called you to yell at your ass, but the other guy at the stop sign across from you saw me and threw his hand up in a 'What are you going to do about that' gesture. I had to save face and light you up."

"It's all good, Mac. I'm fine. Tori caught me off guard with some of her funny jokes and—"

"Daddy, it wasn't a joke. You and Wynnie are gonna get married so she can be my stairmom and Delilah Jane can be my sister."

"It's STEPmom, not stair mom."

"I'm sorry, what is she talking about?" Mac just went from friendly to deadly in a few words from Tori. I nervously chuckle and turn to Mac.

"It's not what it sounds like. Tori has a big imagination." I lean in closer to Mac to try and avoid Tori from hearing. "She's been asking a lot of questions about her mother lately and you know how much she adores Wynnie. She even asked Wynnie if she would be her mom." His face softens, and I try not to exhale in relief.

"I get it." Of course, he would. Wynnie went the first twelve years of her life not knowing Mac and him not knowing her. He can understand a little girl wanting both parents. Mac steps back to the rear window to talk to Tori directly.

"Hey, sweetheart. You can come over and play with Delilah Jane anytime you want. We would love to have you."

136

"What about Wynnie? Can she come too?" Mac and I both laugh. His is in humor, and mine is all nerves.

"Of course, Wynnie can come. You know I'm her Dad, right? Do you remember her bedroom at my house? It's the one next to DJ's." Tori's face lights up. She probably doesn't remember. Wynnie has been away at college, and it's been awhile since she's taken Tori there. Most of her breaks were spent at the apartment with Wynnie and I know they don't allow anyone in Wynnie's room at their house. Mac is making her day.

"Daddy, when can I go back to Aunt Hazel's house? I want to see Wynnie's room again."

"You can ask her on Monday when you see her." Mac walks back to my window and puts his hand out for me to shake.

"These little girls are a handful, aren't they? They speak their minds and say the darndest things. She's welcome any time."

I thank him and watch as he walks back to his police cruiser. I finally let out the sigh of relief I'd been holding in.

"Alright, Little Princess, what's for dinner?"

"Mac and cheese, mac and cheese. Mac. And. Cheeeeeese." Her voice sings from the back seat. I don't know why I even asked. That's always her answer.

"How about chicken nuggets *with* mac and cheese? And maybe even some strawberries on the side?" I have to at least try to throw in some healthy food.

"O-sky Dos-sky, Daddy. I like strawberries. Is tomorrow Monday? I want to ask Wynnie if I can see her room. I wonder if it's pink like mine?"

"Yes. Tomorrow is Monday. She'll be over around lunchtime. You can ask her then." I glance at her in the rearview, and she's already lost interest in our conversation. Probably tuning me out after I confirmed tomorrow is Monday.

Tomorrow afternoon, Wynnie is Tori's, but tomorrow night, she's ALL mine.

20

Wynnie

"Tell me." I don't know who's the worst gossip, Elliot or Aunt Dellah. They both rushed out the back door when they heard me pull into the driveway. I barely have time to turn off my bike in the garage before a bottle of wine is shoved in my face.

"Details, Bitch. All. The. Details."

"Tell me why you're my best friend again?" I remove my helmet and hang it on the handlebar, smiling at the intercom system still connected inside.

"Mom, do you see that? Look how pink her cheeks are turning." I shove Elliot's shoulder.

"Seriously. You two are terrible. Can I at least get upstairs before you interrogate me?"

"Yes, sure, of course." I roll my eyes at Aunt Dellah's rushed response. They want details. How much am I willing to share? Probably less with Aunt Dellah being here than I'd be willing to if it was just Elliot.

But she was completely cool this morning when she saw us holding hands. Maybe it wouldn't be the worst thing to get her opinion.

I look at the bottle of white wine as we walk up the stairs. Maybe after a glass or two, I won't care who's listening as long as they give good advice.

They follow me through my red apartment door at the top of the fourteen stairs like two obnoxious shadows, and Aunt Dellah walks straight to the cabinet with the wine glasses.

"Three?" Elliot looks a bit shocked when she hands him a glass.

"I have a feeling we're all going to need it." She lowers her tone. "Don't tell your father, and don't get sloppy." *Father.* Seeing how their relationship has grown since I was away at college warms my heart.

Aunt Dellah opens the bottle and pours three generous glasses of wine. She turns and looks around the apartment, assessing the beachy theme that she decorated the space with.

It's been over a decade since my mom and I moved back to Mountain Pines, and Aunt Dellah created this space for us. We didn't stay long before moving in with Mac, Phoenix, and Jude, but I have fond memories here.

"I want you to change it. All of it." She turns back to me and I'm confused by her statement.

"Change what exactly?"

"The apartment. Your apartment. You need to start a portfolio. I had a small sticker business in college that I had created during my freshman year. By the time I graduated, I was making book covers and window designs, and it snowballed for me." She turns back to the room and sweeps her hand in game show hostess-style, presenting a prize package. "Make this your portfolio. I'm hiring you to redesign the space and funding it. I'll be your first client."

"I-I don't know what to say. I can't take your money and redesign your apartment. That seems ridiculous." She shrugs and takes a sip of her wine.

"What do you think of this room, Elliot?" She gestures into the room again. The apartment is an open floor plan. On the left side, from the front door, through the living and dining room, and straight back to the kitchen we're standing in. The right side has three doors. The master bedroom with an en suite bathroom is the first door. The next is the bathroom for the apartment, and the third is my old bedroom, now more Elliot's room.

"I think the beach theme is nice but old and outdated. And we are nowhere near the ocean, so it's a little depressing." He gives her a small smile, but I can see the haze of memory clouding his vision.

His father died in a car accident, coming back from a lunch celebration, landing a new big account. With the bonus he earned, he was excited to take Elliot and his siblings on a beach vacation that Elliot had been asking for.

We've taken a few beach trips since he moved here, and he's always been fine. But in this moment, he's getting lost in his memories.

"Want to help me shop? If I'm going to do this for the first time officially, I might need an assistant. You know, to hold my purse while I spend all of Aunt Dellah's money." I watch his smile grow, and the light comes back into his eyes. I glance at Aunt Dellah, who mouths "thank you" to me over her wine glass. She saw it, too.

"Can I?" I'm not sure who he's asking, but Aunt Dellah answers.

"I don't have a death wish trying to keep you two apart. I

would be more shocked if you didn't help her. But we can talk about redecorating later. Right now, I need to hear about Scotty."

Looks like I've avoided the topic for as long as I can.

Two bottles of wine later, and I've told them mostly everything. I left out more of the explicit details; too embarrassed to share those. I'm sure Elliot will pull them out of me later. We don't have any secrets that I know of.

Aunt Dellah started this conversation, telling me it was a judgment-free zone and a firm "Your mom isn't my best friend tonight" speech. I appreciated it even though it wasn't necessary. She's obviously been aware of my crush. It was just a matter of time before we collided.

"So what now?"

"Aunt Dellah, I have no idea. We're going to talk about things tomorrow night after he gets home from work.

"Okay, I'm about to be very mom-ish on you right now, and I know you're a fully grown woman but I still love and worry about you. Could you do me the smallest favor? If you know you aren't coming home at night, let Elliot or me know." I open my mouth to protest, but she says one more thing to drive the stake in and stop any negative words I might have on the subject.

"I lost you once when you were under my care. I don't ever want to worry like that again." I was twelve. I ran away for less than twelve hours when I found out my mom was dating not only one of my softball coaches but both of them and also my dad. Three men.

It wasn't the number of men she was dating but the men themselves and what they each represented in my life at that time. I didn't even know my dad yet, and I was shocked to find out my mom was dating him. It wasn't my finest moment.

I love my three Dads and I have three new siblings because of them. I wouldn't change it for the world. But that night, when I found out from texts on my mom's phone that she had forgotten at home, I freaked out and ran.

"Okay, Aunt Dellah. I'll do my best to text one of you if I'm not coming home."

"Thank you. I'll leave you two to gossip. I'm sure you have more to spill that this old lady probably doesn't want to think about her niece doing." She hugs me and goes back to her house.

Elliot is practically vibrating with excitement to get the juicy details.

"Oh my god, girl! He is so into you. How does it feel to finally catch the man of your wet dreams?"

"I don't know if I've caught him yet, but this weekend felt like a fairy tale."

"That wasn't a fairy tale, my dear Wynnie; that was a porno."

"Good god, El." I flop back on the couch. He's not wrong. What we did wasn't necessarily crazy or kinky, but compared to my previous experience, it was wild.

"Have you thought about the ramifications of the two of you being together? What will your dads' say? Uncle Phoenix has known him the longest."

"I haven't decided if their relationship is a good thing or a bad thing. At least Scotty isn't some random guy fifteen years older than me, but also one of my dads has known him for… ugh math. Since they were in high school and now they're in their late thirties." Elliot laughs at me.

"So, like thirty-seven minus fourteen. That's basic math. But also, they've known each other for longer than you've been alive."

"Eww. That's it. There's the red flag. It's waving high and proud…and I'm going to ignore it completely."

"As you should, woman. But I have a more serious question. How did you get your Graphics Design degree if you can't do basic math?" Reaching next to me, I grab a white throw pillow with a blue anchor and smash it across his face.

"I've had like three glasses of Aunt Dellah poured wine, which is basically an entire bottle. I can do basic math when I'm not floating on wine. And that pillow is the first thing I'm replacing. Grab my laptop, and let's brainstorm how to improve this place." He laughs at me as he walks across the room.

"Are you sure you should design and drink?"

"It's how I got through college. Don't underestimate me. You're about to watch me in action."

Elliot and I spend the next several hours, another bottle of wine and a large sausage pizza, going through design ideas for my apartment. The longer we talk, the more excited I get.

21

Wynnie

"Wakie, wakie, my little worker bees." I peek through my eyes to see it's morning. I quickly close them again and reach my arms above my head to stretch and fall off the couch.

"What the hell!" Aunt Dellah tries her best not to laugh, while Elliot sits on the loveseat, not even attempting to contain his full-on belly cackling.

I groan. My entire body is sore, and that tumble didn't help anything. The wine must have knocked me out, and I slept like shit on the couch.

Without moving from my horizontal position, I stick my hand in the air and motion the "gimme" sign with my hand. Like magic, a travel mug of coffee appears, and I hum my thanks to Aunt Dellah. Rearranging my position so I sit with my back leaning on the couch, I pop open the spout on the mug and take a sip of the hot hazelnut-flavored coffee.

"She brought donuts too." Aunt Dellah sits on the couch beside me and dangles a sprinkled donut in my face. I lean forward and grab it with my teeth, mumbling "Thank you" with my mouth full.

"You're such a lady, Wynnie." I glare at Elliot as he giggles behind his mug. I stick my sprinkled-covered tongue out at him, and the three of us erupt in laughter.

Aunt Dellah looks over the coffee table at the papers we printed last night and the sketches I drew.

"This all looks amazing. Are you ready to pitch it to me yet?" Is she serious? I barely remember half of what I did in my drunken stupor. She chuckles to herself, obviously seeing the panic on my face.

"Relax. I'm kidding. But you have some killer ideas right now, and I can't wait to hear what you come up with." I sigh in relief, dropping my head back onto the couch.

"You don't have any ideas you want to throw out to me for design choices?"

"None at all. This is entirely your project. I want you to present to me as your boss, not as your client. I'll assess your design as such." I have so many ideas. Now, to tie them down to one specific design.

"Thank you again, Aunt Dellah. This is a huge opportunity." She leans down and kisses the top of my head.

"I have to get back. I have a breakfast casserole in the oven if you want to put some food in your stomach besides sugar and caffeine." She points to Elliot. "You're coming with me. She can make her own poor food choices; I still have control over your nutrition."

"Yes, Mom." His eye roll is thick with sarcasm.

"You're heading to Scotty's at twelve, right? That gives you almost five hours to work more on your design. You can bring it to breakfast if you want to bounce some ideas off me." I smile and thank her. She grabs Elliot's shirt sleeve as she walks by, forcing him to follow.

146

"Bye, Bitch." It's my turn to roll my eyes. I blow a kiss at Elliot, and he exaggerates catching it and smacking it on his cheek. He's too much sometimes.

Breakfast sounds good, but a hot shower to relax my stiff muscles sounds better. I walk into my en suite and turn on the shower to give it time to heat up.

I didn't even remove my makeup last night, and my face is a mess. Oh well, the shower will do that for me.

I know it's time to get in when the mirror is sufficiently steamed. The heat of the water licks my skin and instantly turns it pink. Being wrapped in the thickness of the steam feels comforting. Tilting my head back to wet my hair, the steamy water flows down my chest.

I hiss at the sting the hot water causes on my nipples. They must be a little raw from the extra attention that Scotty gave them. I grab my apple-scented shampoo, realizing I saw this product in Scotty's shower. I'll have to ask him about it.

When I rinse my hair, the soapy bubbles slide over my now hard nipples, causing a new sensation. It feels like a light caress, and I find myself unconsciously moaning.

Crap. What's wrong with me? Did my weekend with Scotty jump-start my libido? I guess it wouldn't be the worst thing.

I can't help but slide my soapy loofah down my chest and over my peaks. I feel the spark of desire in my clit from the touch, and I do it again. Closing my eyes, I pretend it's not me doing the swiping. I feel my arousal start to quicken.

Fuck it. I keep a waterproof vibrator in here for a reason. I might as well give it some use. I pull back the curtain and reach into the top drawer of the vanity. Hidden in the back is a clit sucking vibrator.

It's sleek, black, and no bigger than my hand, but it packs

a punch sporting twelve different settings. I stick my finger over the cylindrical hole near the top and turn it on, testing the battery life. Nice and strong. I set the vibrator on the ledge and finish rinsing and shaving while occasionally teasing my nipples or lingering a little longer between my legs. I want to enjoy myself, then lay on my bed like jelly for a few minutes before going next door.

Picking up the toy, I turn it to low and tease myself back and forth with the vibrations. I'm amped up, and I don't think it will take me long, even if I leave it on this low setting.

I set the cylinder over my clit and allow it to suction for a few pulls to adjust the angle to where I need it. Clicking the button a few times it sets a rhythm.

Suck, suck, pause. Suck, suck, suck, pause. Repeat. I lean my forehead against the cool tile wall, letting myself relax and be swept away by the sensation.

My breathing increases as the tingle begins low in my belly, spreading outward. I click the button as I get closer, and the rhythm changes to a constant sucking motion. Gliding my hand up my body, I roll a nipple between my fingers, teasing myself further.

Picturing Scotty between my legs, coaxing me into my first explosive orgasm, helps pull me over the edge, and I have to sit on the floor when my legs go weak.

"Fuck. Fuck." My moans echo off the ceiling, and I pull the toy away, turning it off. I'll have to remember how much this room echoes and not do anything like that when Elliot's here. Not that he'd care, but he also wouldn't ever let me live it down.

★ ★ ★ ★ ★

148

"Did you just knock?" Scotty looks at me with a blank expression and steps back to let me in. I never knock. At least, I haven't in years. I have a key to his house.

"I wasn't sure what the etiquette was after…" He looks behind him. I assume he's looking for Tori, who isn't in the room as far as I can see. He steps forward and I take a step back. We do it again, and I'm against the wall next to the front door. He looks into my eyes, and his voice is low and husky when he speaks.

"After what, Rowyn? After our kiss? After I was between your legs, drowning in your orgasm? Or after I was deep inside your hungry fucking pussy?"

"Y-yes. All of that." My voice is breathy and full of lust. I can smell his sweet, woodsy scent.

"The etiquette is whatever we want it to be, and we can discuss it tonight over dinner." He brushes a piece of hair behind my ear, and my mind fizzes out. I have no idea why that simple act gets me every time.

"Can I kiss you, Pinky?" As I look into his eyes, I can see the outline of the contacts that I never noticed before. I guess I have spent a lot more time lately being in extremely close proximity to this man.

"I don't know why you ask every time." His eyes squint at me as if he's going to say something about my sass. Instead, he leans down and grazes his lips over mine.

I don't know what comes over me. Maybe it's the residual hormones from my shower orgasm or his nearness, but I grab his shirt and pull him into me.

He doesn't hesitate, weaving his hands into my hair at the nape of my neck. Eliminating any distance left between us, he pulls me in by the waist.

149

Our kiss is frenzied and I know it's because we have limited time. Scotty has to get to work, and there's a curious five year old wandering somewhere around the house that could pop up at any moment.

He pulls away, and I'm thankful. I don't think I could have found the willpower to do it myself. Our foreheads lean together, and he stares at me.

"You're such fucking trouble, Pinky. I'm not sure how I'm supposed to survive you." Smiling up at him, I have the same feeling.

"We should…" Before I finish saying it, he understands what I mean and kisses my forehead, stepping back. I watch him adjust himself in his pants, and give him a knowing smirk.

"Tori is playing in her room. She had lunch about an hour ago, and I told her it was quiet time until you arrived.

"Nice artwork." I take a closer look at his arm and see the glitter pen coloring his tattoos.

"Yeah, not my brightest idea. I know how much she loves sparkles, and the pens came with a princess coloring book. She took one look at the flowers on my arm and ditched the book for me. I guess it temporarily solved the boredom problem."

"It looks like it." I laugh as I trace my fingers over his multicolored-glittery flowers.

"I'll wash it off when I get to the bar. Otherwise, she'll be upset that I ruined her artwork." He looks down at my fingers caressing his arm, closes his eyes, and hums.

"That feels so good." I trail farther up his arm until I hit the hem of his sleeve and trail back to his wrist.

"You're too easy." I giggle at the bulge in his pants, and

his eyes darken with lust. I don't even see his hand move, but I feel his thumb slide across my nipple, and it becomes instantly hard.

"It seems like I'm not the only one." He moves his hand to the other nipple and swipes a few times. Our eyes are locked on each other when I hear a squeal from behind Scotty.

"You're here! Did you see Daddy's arm? It's so sparkly." Scotty steps to the side to adjust himself again, and I quickly cross my arms over my chest. I don't need to have an awkward conversation about nipples with a five year old.

"I did. It's so pretty. Your best work. I can't wait to try out those pens on some paper and coloring books." Her brow scrunches, and she frowns.

"Coloring books are boring." I can't help but laugh, thinking that not long ago, she said the exact same thing about Scotty's arm.

"I'm sure you'll have fun doing whatever Wynnie has planned, Little Princess." He scoops her up, and she gives him the cutest grumpy face as she crosses her arms. "You better be good for Wynnie. She's doing us a huge favor watching you. She has a big girl job now, and she's taking time away from that to be here with you. Isn't that so nice of her?"

"I guess." She looks at me, and her face softens.

"Do you want to see what I've been working on? I'm changing my apartment to make it fun and fancy, not the boring blue and orange that Aunt Dellah chose. Maybe you can help me pick out some colors." Now, her face lights up.

"Can your walls be glittery?" I reach out and take her from Scotty.

"You know, I've heard about people painting glittery walls. We can look on my laptop and see what we can find. You might have a great idea, Sunshine."

Scotty smiles at me and walks closer. He kisses Tori on the forehead, says his goodbyes, and then does the same to me. This time, when the butterflies swarm in my stomach from his kiss, I know he feels it, too.

22

Wynnie

I don't know how a forehead kiss can be just as memorable as some of the dirtier things we did this past weekend, but it's been lingering in my mind all evening.

Tori and I had a fun-filled afternoon of coloring, hide and seek, and picking out sparkly paint. I might try to incorporate a glitter wall. It makes a big statement with little effort.

She helped me make homemade mac and cheese for dinner, and since I already had some leftovers as a side, I decided to make meatloaf for my dinner with Scotty. Tori helped me mix the meat and promised she'd try some of the leftovers tomorrow for lunch, as long as I saved her some mac and cheese.

The house smells amazing as I pull the meatloaf out of the oven to rest before Scotty gets home. He should be home in the next fifteen minutes, which gives me enough time to saute the broccoli.

I'm lost listening to my audiobook and scooping the broccoli into a casserole dish when I think I see something pass out of the corner of my eye. I pull out an earbud and look around.

"Sunshine, are you up?" Silence answers me. My mind must be playing tricks on me. I check the time on the microwave and see Scotty should be walking in the door any minute.

I turn the faucet on and soap up the sponge to clean the dishes I've made. A tingly feeling spreads across the back of my neck, and I turn my head to look into the empty room. The air feels different, thicker.

"Tori?" The house is still silent except for the narrator in my ear. I really must be going crazy. I pick up the pan I used for the broccoli and start scrubbing. I can't shake this weird feeling.

"Boo!"

Several things happen at once. My sides are grabbed from behind as "boo" is whisper-shouted into my ear without the earbud. I scream and swing around in a circle, yielding the soapy frying pan as a weapon.

"Oh fuck, Pinky." The pan clatters to the floor as I barely miss hitting Scotty across the nose with it. My hands fly to my face when I realize what I almost did, and instant tears spring to my eyes.

"I'm so sorry, Scotty. Oh my god, I'm so sorry. I almost…" He pulls me into his chest, cradling me in his arms.

"Shh, it's okay. I'm sorry. I should have known better. I forgot for a minute how easily you scare." I groan into his chest as my heart calms from its breakneck speed.

"That was completely unfair. I almost hit you. Are you okay?" He laughs, and I almost want to hit him again.

"Yeah, Pinky. I'm good. It smells amazing in here." I slip

my hands out from between us and wrap them around his waist, embracing his warmth.

"Meatloaf, broccoli, and mac and cheese. It's all finished if you're ready to eat?"

"I'm starving. I haven't eaten since lunch. I didn't want to ruin my appetite." He kisses the top of my head, releases me and steps to the side to get us plates from the cabinet.

"This looks so good. Who taught you to cook? This isn't boxed mac n cheese."

"My mom some, but Jude loves to cook and made sure I helped whenever possible."

"Ah, Jude. I'm not surprised." We pile our plates with food and sit at the counter together, knee to knee. I watch as he takes his first bite, and his eyes close as he enjoys the flavor.

"This is incredible." He moans around his food as he takes another bite. We sit in companionable silence as we eat. The only noise is the scraping of our forks and the occasional moan of satisfaction from Scotty.

"You keep moaning like that, and I might think you're replacing me, Scotty." He drops his fork and growls at me. Spinning in his seat, he cages my legs between his and grabs my chin.

"Rowyn, you're irreplaceable. Don't you ever fucking forget that." There goes my panties. Shit, how does he do that?

"So, I guess we should talk about this, huh?" I might as well get this started. He takes my hand and smiles.

"What do you want, Pinky? Where do you want this to go?" Me? Well, damn, I didn't think this through well enough.

"I…" I have no idea how to answer that. He gives me another moment to continue before putting me out of my misery.

"How about we look at all of the facts first?" I nod in response.

"This past weekend was pleasurable. Agree?" I nod again. "We have great chemistry, and I don't want this weekend to be a one-time thing. Do you?"

"No. I feel it, too." He squeezes my hands.

"Good. That's the easy part. Now, the obstacles."

"Obstacles?"

"Yeah, Pinky. Obstacles. Tori, your dads, our age difference, Phoenix specifically. Actually, Mac might be a bigger obstacle. They are all potential roadblocks. Do you have any thoughts on any of those?" I have lots of thoughts on all of those.

"How is Tori an obstacle?"

"Tori has the biggest part to lose in this. You. Her's is the biggest heart to break if anything goes bad between us. She loves you. You're the closest thing she has ever had to a mother figure. I don't say that to put any pressure on you. I'd never want you to feel obligated to fill that role for her. *Especially* that one."

"Scotty, I would never. I know what she asked me the other day, and I've put a lot of thought into it. I didn't have a dad for twelve years. It's a hard thing for a child to be missing a parent. Even harder when you have no idea who they are and why they aren't here. I love the snot out of your little girl, and nothing can change that. Not even my relationship with you."

"Do you want that, Wynnie? A relationship with me. Despite all of the obstacles."

"A relationship is between two people—"

"Well…" he cocks his head and gives me a knowing smile.

156

I roll my eyes and correct my sentence.

"Excusing my mother, who has her cake and eats them too, relationships are *usually* between two people. There's nothing wrong with you for them to object to, other than our age gap. You're a good guy. A great one, actually. You're an incredible father—a business owner. Honestly, you're everything a girl could want in a partner. And everything my dads should want for me. But my mom…" Oh god, my mom.

Scotty looks at me like I've lost my damn mind as I laugh hysterically.

"Pinky?" I hold up my finger, asking him to give me a minute to compose myself from the thought I've just connected.

"Oh my god, Scotty. I just had the most absurd realization. You went to high school with Phoenix. You graduated together."

"Yeah. That isn't new information. What makes it so funny?"

"Who is Phoenix engaged to?"

"Your mom." He isn't putting it together.

"I'll wait." I can almost see the gears turning in his head as he tries to figure out what I would find so funny.

"I'm lost. Can you explain more?"

"You and Phoenix are the same age." He slowly nods. "And Jude. All the same age." I guess I need to spell it out for him. "Scotty, my mother and I are dating men the exact same age, and she's eighteen years older than me." His eyes widen as he puts the math together.

"That's…yeah, okay. I can see how that can be funny. But does that bother you?"

"Your age doesn't bother me. When I was seventeen, yeah.

But not now." He releases one of my hands to rub the back of his neck.

"Yeah, seventeen was a little young. I didn't notice you noticing me until you went off to college. But Dellah did." Aunt Dellah noticed me watching Scotty?

His hand comes up to brush my cheeks. "What's got you blushing, Pinky?" I put my hand over his to keep it on my cheek. I want to feel his touch.

"How do you know she saw me watching you?"

"She told me. Well, it was more of a warning. Do you remember Finn's birthday party when they first got here? It was foam gun themed." I nod, remembering how crazy the guys got with the obstacle course Uncle Collin set up in their backyard. "She said something to me during the party."

"No way. What did she say?" He shrugs as if it's no big deal that seventeen year old me was caught giving goo goo eyes to a thirty-two year old him.

"She just wanted me to be aware of it and warned me to watch out for your puppy love crush. Teenage girls can get clingy." He winks and glances at my hand, covering his. I quickly let go, feeling embarrassed. He grabs my hand and laces our fingers together.

"Don't do that. You aren't that seventeen year old girl anymore. You're a charming, intelligent woman."

"So you just want me for my brains? I see how it is." That sparks something inside him. Scotty slides off the stool, so he's towering over me. His hand slides up my side until it cups my breast. With precise accuracy, he swipes his thumb across my nipple. How does he do that every time?

"I most definitely want you for more than just your brains." His lips find their way to the top of my shoulder, and he trails

158

kisses across my neck and up to my ear. "Are you going to take a chance with me, Pinky?"

"Yes. Please. Don't stop."

"There's that eager teenager." I slap his chest playfully.

"Are you trying to kill the mood?"

"Pinky, you could walk in here wearing a trash bag after rolling around in the mud, and I'd take you to the shower and worship you like the fucking Queen that you are."

"Did my clothes just combust?"

"What?" he says through a chuckle.

"My clothes? Your dirty talk has me on fire. I feel like I just went up in flames."

"God, I love how easily you react to me. What else gets you hot? Is it my touch?" He trails kisses from my ear, across my jaw, and ends at the dip in my neck. "How about my voice? Does that do it for you? What if I tell you I want to bend you over this counter and fuck you until my fingerprints leave marks on your hips."

"Please." My voice is so full of lust it comes out in a whisper.

"Does it even matter what I'm saying or how I say it?" He gets close to my ear and, in a deep, raspy voice, starts saying random words. "Avocado. Elevator. Purple Nurple. Whippersnapper." He stretches out each word in an attempt to make it sound sexier. I'm giggling, but also, why am I getting turned on?

"You had me at elevator." His hands find their way under my shirt and unclasp my bra.

23

Scotty

This woman turns me on like a fucking teenager. I just spouted random words, and her moans made me hard. Well, I was already hard, but now my dick wants to bust out of my jeans.

Fucking avocado. How is that seductive? Elevator isn't any better, but my hands unclipping her bra? That's fucking hot.

"My little Pinky. Do you have an elevator kink that I need to know about? Does a little voyeurism make you wet?" Fuck. Now, I want to figure out where the closest elevator is and take her for a ride. My hands skim the hem of her shirt, and I lift, needing to remove it and see her.

"Wait, wait." I drop my hands and take a small step back.

"I'm sorry. We can stop."

"No. It's not that. We haven't come to any conclusions." Fuck. She's right.

"Okay." I pull her in close so I can invade her space. I just want to be touching. Her hands find the hem of my shirt and I feel her smooth skin glide across my lower back. It seems she doesn't mind the invasion. "I think we agree that we both want this. The question is, how open are we going to be about it?"

"Scotty…" Her blush creeps across her chest. "Can we not be? Can we keep it between us for a while? Like you said, there are obstacles that are going to want us to *not* be together. Let's just be us and see where it goes in our own little bubble before we let everyone come and pop it. Would that be okay with you?" Her blue eyes pierce me with the anticipation of my answer.

"You're asking me to stay in hiding and sneak around with you behind everyone's backs? You want to keep me your dirty little secret?" The light dims in her eyes as she thinks I'm going to reject her. "You're a naughty girl, Rowyn. Naughty girls get punished. Should I punish you?"

"I-Is that a yes?" I give her a devilish smile in response to her question. Slowly, so I don't scare her, I raise my hand and cup her throat. I feel her gulp under my palm, but I watch her pupils dilate with lust.

"That's a yes, Rowyn. I'll be your dirty fucking secret if you'll be my dirty little slut." Her eyes glaze over, and I know she's right where she wants to be.

Her head nods the slightest nod. "Words, Rowyn. This is when we learn the rules. Rule number one: the nonverbal answers aren't going to fly. You use your words and tell me exactly what you do and don't like. What you want and what you don't want. Do you understand?"

"Y-yes."

"Good girl. Do you like my hand around your neck?" I feel her swallow again as I add more pressure to my fingers.

"Yes." Her answer is more confident than the last.

"Rule number two: you need a safeword. Something that

you wouldn't normally say during sexual activity. A word that will immediately stop anything we're doing if you don't like it or are uncomfortable." I watch her lips twitch as she tries not to smile. "Words, Rowyn." No one calls her Rowyn anymore, but it sounds so beautiful. It feels perfect to have her under my hand with such an exquisite name.

"Avocado." Of course.

"Fucking avocado. Really? You want avocado to be your safeword?" She shrugs.

"I'm not a fan of them, so it seems appropriate." She continues to amaze me.

"Okay, avocado it is." I look over at the microwave and see it's almost midnight. Using my grip on her neck, I pull her flush to my body. She's practically vibrating with adrenaline. "Stay with me tonight." It's not a question, but I'd love for her to defy me.

"What about Tori?" Always thinking about my little girl. She's fucking perfect.

"We can just tell Tori we had a sleepover. It wouldn't be the first time you've spent the night."

"What if she sees me in your room?"

"Tori and DJ sleep in the same bed when they have sleep-overs. She won't think anything of it. I'll make sure you get back home in time for work with Dellah. Stay. With. Me." She starts to nod but then realizes her error by my face and says yes.

"Good girl," I purr as my other hand slides up the back of her neck into her hair. I make a fist, forcing her head to tilt up. Her tongue glides across her bottom lip, and I crash my mouth to hers, sucking her tongue into my mouth. I moan as I savor her taste. Sweet from the wine she was drinking but savory from the fantastic meal she cooked.

She pulls away and reaches into her back pocket, retrieving her phone.

"What are you doing?"

"I promised Aunt Dellah that if I planned to not come home, I would text her or Elliot so they don't worry. I know I'm an adult, but she guilt-tripped me with the runaway thing." I release my hand from her neck and hair.

"Give it to me." I take it from her without any objection. I swipe her phone open, interested that she's comfortable enough not to have a lock code on it.

"Which one?" She looks at me curiously. "Who am I texting?"

"Elliot."

She grabs my wrist, not holding her phone, and places it back on her neck. She wants me to squeeze her again. Abso-fucking-lutely. I put my hand around her neck and pull her in for a kiss. When I pull away, I add downward pressure on my hand, and she understands me without words. Slowly, she descends until she's on her knees.

"Fucking perfect. Now show me how good you can be and suck my cock while I text Elliot." I reluctantly remove my hand from her neck and hear the slight whimper that escapes her.

Without hesitation, her hands undo my belt and then my jeans. She makes quick work of opening them and pulling me out of my boxers. "You're fucking gorgeous on your knees, Rowyn." She mewls from my praise, and my cock jumps in her hand. I send a quick text and put the phone down on the counter.

She lifts my shaft, and I watch as she licks a line from my

base to my tip and sucks me in at the head. I have to grab the counter to steady myself as my knees threaten to give out.

"Fuck, Rowyn. You suck me like a champ." I can't help myself and reach down, grabbing a fistful of her hair at the back of her head. She moans when I tug at her roots.

Note to self: test pain play with my Pinky.

"Fuck. Okay. Okay. Stop." I step back, and my cock makes a popping sound when I pull it out of her mouth. "I want to have more fun with you than a blowjob in my kitchen." I tuck myself back in my pants and extend my hand to help her up.

"Let's clean up the kitchen, and I can show some attention to your pussy that I'm sure is dripping for me."

"Okay." I wrap my arms around her back and palm her ass, taking another kiss before we quickly clean up.

"Scotty? How do we do this with Tori in the house?" She sounds apprehensive as I close the bedroom door behind me.

"You're going to have to learn how to be quiet. Rule number three: You only get to be loud when I say you can be loud." I caress her cheek with my thumb and run it over her top lip and around to the bottom. "Your noises are mine."

"I've never had to be quiet before. Well, I've never actually had a reason to make any noise until this weekend."

"Perfect. Another lesson for you to learn. The anticipation of having to be quiet, of potentially getting caught, will heighten your arousal."

"Shit." I can't look away as she finally removes her shirt, and her already unclipped bra falls to the floor, exposing her creamy white breasts. Her nipples are hard and a beautiful pink color that's almost rivaled by the color of the blush creeping down her neck.

164

She's watching me watch her, but I can't pull my eyes away. Wynnie is giving me a show as she slowly undresses. Her shorts easily pop open and she lets them fall to the floor. Stepping out of them, she walks up to me in just her navy blue lace panties. She pulls at my shirt with her fingers.

"Off."

"Hmm. You're not the one giving orders here, Pinky."

"Please." Her eyes turn wide and doe-like. I swipe my finger across the top of her panties.

"Since you asked so nicely." I reach behind my head and pull my shirt off. My pants are still open, and she works them off my hips. We stand in just our underwear, drinking in each other's bodies.

"I thought about you this morning…in the shower." I like the sound of that.

"Were you touching yourself?" She shakes her head, and I wait patiently until she realizes she didn't answer my question with words.

"No."

"That's upsetting." She grabs my wrist and slides it into her panties, guiding my fingers where she wants them. I swipe my middle finger over her already swollen clit. She gasps, and I do it again.

"I used my vibrator."

"Oh, you naughty fucking girl." I remove my hand, and she pouts. "On the bed. Show me what you should have done instead of using that toy."

"You want me to-to touch myself while you watch?"

"I do." There's question in her words, but she's climbing onto the bed anyway. "I want to see how you pleasure yourself. I want to learn what you like. If you're uncomfortable, use your safeword. Otherwise, open those legs and touch that pussy. Show me how wet I make you."

She crawls to the top of the bed and gets comfortable sitting halfway on the headboard. Looking at me seductively, she slowly spreads her legs.

"Take them off." The navy lace shimmies down her thighs, and she uses her legs to finish removing them. Each movement gives me a tease at what I want to see. When she finally opens for me, I have to stop myself from drooling when I see her wet cunt.

"Show me. I want to see your fingers glistening with your arousal." She swirls two fingers around her entrance, and when she removes her hand, I see the pearlescent strings between them.

I feel feral. My boxers drop to the floor, and I stroke my cock walking towards her. The bed dips under my weight as I position myself between her legs to watch the show.

"Don't keep me waiting, Pinky." Her eyes shift around the room as embarrassment washes over her face. I reach out and caress her spread calves. "What is it?"

"I don't usually do this myself."

"This?"

"Touch myself. I...always use a toy." She doesn't know how to pleasure herself without outside stimulation? We need to fix that.

"I'm happy to help teach you how to self-pleasure, Rowyn. A woman should know what she likes first before seeking pleasure from another person. Give me your hand." I crawl up closer and pin her legs under me, forcing them open wider.

"What type of toy do you use? Does it vibrate, suck, or rotate? What gets you off?" The blush on her cheeks darkens.

"You have them *all,* don't you?" Her head tips down for the start of a nod before she catches herself.

"Yes. My mom and I have always had a healthy relationship when it comes to our openness to share things. I don't ask her specific details because…eww. But we talk about other things like toys and such. She bought me my first bullet when I was sixteen after she caught me in the bathroom using the removable shower head." Interesting. She has no shame in sharing that information with me. I like that she isn't embarrassed about that part of her sexuality.

"Well, good. Do you have a favorite one? Tell me which one you used in the shower today."

"I used one that suctions. It's waterproof, so it stays in the bathroom."

"Well, that's something *I* could duplicate, but not so much solo. Back to your favorite one." She thinks for a moment, and I draw circles in the palm of the hand that I took from her.

"That. I like that." She nods towards our hands. "Slow and steady unless I'm in a rush. I enjoy the buildup."

"Do you edge yourself?" The confused look that crosses her face is adorable. "Edging is when you bring yourself close to orgasm but back off before you tip over the edge. You do it over and over, building the anticipation until you finally give in, and it produces a more intense orgasm."

"More intense? More than what we did yesterday?" My naughty girl perks up with the thought of her orgasms yesterday.

"Yes, more. Different. It depends on the mode of the edging. Sometimes, it can even be a little painful before you get to the true pleasure. But it's always enjoyable."

There's a myriad of emotions flashing on her face. I can tell she's curious but also apprehensive.

"Is that something you'd like to try? It doesn't have to be tonight." She opens her mouth to speak, and I raise a hand to stop her. "But, before you decide, if it's something you want to try, you have to be able to relinquish control to me. You'll want to stop, but I won't let you. You'll get mad and might cry, but I *promise* the end result will be worth it."

"I do. I do want to try. But based on that description, maybe it should be on a night when Tori isn't just down the hall."

"That's a valid, fair point and probably a good idea. Once I get my hands on you, I won't be willing to stop. Not until you use your safeword, or I feel you've earned your orgasm." She almost looks a little relieved. I wonder if it's relief that it won't be tonight or relief that I didn't object to her wanting to wait.

She squeezes the hand I'm holding. "So, maybe just the original lesson for tonight?" Together, she guides our hands to her wanting pussy that I can see has gotten wetter since our conversation started.

"Is this all for me?" I swipe our joined fingers through her arousal and run the wetness up to her clit.

"All because of you." She moans as I make circles around the swollen nub. Her finger rests on top of mine, feeling what I'm doing. Learning.

I lift my finger so hers falls to her clit, and guide her to continue the circles I was just making. Adding pressure to her finger, I can tell she feels the pleasure she can give herself. It's a different feeling than a vibrator can create.

I shift our fingers again, and hers are back on top, following mine. My previous slow circles turn into a faster finger curl, rubbing directly atop her clit rather than around it like the circles were doing.

When she moans, her hips start involuntarily moving, and I switch our fingers once again. I add pressure and pull away completely, letting her do all the work.

"Both of those movements will get you to an orgasm. Find a rhythm and pressure that will work for you, and let me watch you shatter."

It doesn't take her long. She was halfway there using both our hands. I could tell by her breathing and the blush on her chest.

I cup her breast in my hand, kneading the flesh.

"Don't forget you need to keep quiet, Rowyn." Pinching her nipple gives the last stimulation she needs for her orgasm to crest.

"Oh god, Scotty. Fuck, Scotty." Her voice is straining in her attempt not to shout. My name on her lips as she throws her head back and orgasms is a sight I want to see repeated every day. Several times a day.

I untangle our legs and reach into the nightstand for a condom while her orgasm is still rolling through her. I have it on in record time and push her fingers away, burying my cock deep inside her in one quick thrust. Her inner walls are still spasming as I pump in and out. She's slick with her hot arousal, and I lean down to kiss her, swallowing her moans.

I pull away and prop up on my elbows, getting lost in her blue eyes. My pace slows. I want to savor and worship her this time. There's no need to rush.

"What are you thinking, Scotty?" Her fingers lightly dance on my chest.

"I'm thinking about how fucking perfect you feel under me.

I could live inside this pussy." I take her mouth again, licking and nipping.

I'm hungry for her. Not in a way that I want to devour, but I want to savor. Enjoy every touch of her skin on mine, the taste of her tongue in my mouth. I want every noise she makes to be my own personal symphony.

Reaching between us, I find her swollen clit and give it a few languid swipes.

"Can you give me another one?" She nods.

"I think so. Will you do it?"

"I'm already there, Rowyn. I'm claiming the next one."

I contain my own release until I hear her sweet moans increase, and her eyes roll back into her head. I let go, and we both orgasm. It's slow and worshiping. I crush our bodies together, and we kiss, dampening the sounds of our moans. Being quiet is something we will both need to work on. I haven't had a woman in my bed since before Tori.

When we come down from our orgasm high, I roll off the bed, remove the condom, and get us a warm washcloth to clean up. She hums when I wipe between her legs.

"This is almost as enjoyable as the sex." She giggles and winks at me.

"You're a pain in my ass, Pinky."

24

Wynnie

The sound of giggling wakes me up, and I look around the room, forgetting for a moment where I am.

Scotty's house, in his bed. The giggling that woke me is Tori. And the delicious smell...coffee and vanilla? Something sweet. Pancakes I bet. I know how much she loves her pancakes.

As I sit up in bed, my body aches from another evening of sex. I feel like I should go to the gym more. Although, if this is how my body feels after sex, it's obvious I'm already getting a workout.

I wonder if Tori knows I'm here? I hope Scotty has said something to her because if I show up in their kitchen, she'll have a million questions.

The doorknob jiggles, and I panic, sinking further into the bed and covering up my naked body with the blanket. I hear a deep laugh and peek one eye out to see Scotty holding a steaming cup of coffee. At this moment, I love the man in front of me. But holy shit, I can't be having these kinds of thoughts, so I quickly sit up on the bed and shove my hands out with the 'gimme' motion.

"How did you know I was up?" Scotty sits on the bed beside me and rubs my thigh over the blanket. I inhale the rich scent of the hazelnut creamer and wait for his answer.

"I didn't, but I know you have to get home to start work soon. I was coming to wake you." I close my eyes and moan as I take the first sip of coffee. Why are food or drinks always better when someone else makes it for you? Love. It's the love that they pour into it for you. Dammit, there's that word again. It's the generosity. That must be it. *Generosity.*

"Does she know I'm here?"

"She does, and she's excited to see you." I sigh, closing my eyes.

"How do we do this? What did you tell her?" Scotty pulls me in for a tender kiss, and my stress melts away.

"It's okay. Tori saw your car was still here, and I told her you were too tired to drive last night, so you decided to be safe and stay here."

"Okay. That makes sense to a five year old."

"Why do you look so worried? It's not like this exact situation hasn't happened before."

"But I'm in your bed, Scotty. That's the difference." How can he think this is the same thing?

"And she thinks you're in the guest room. I closed the door before she got up." Oh. That was smart. Now I can understand why he isn't freaking out like me.

I lean into him, careful not to spill my coffee. He takes it from my hands and places it on the nightstand. A devilish smile appears, and he tackles me onto the bed, quickly putting a hand over my mouth to muffle my squeal of surprise.

"Shhh. You need to be quiet." His voice is low and husky

in my ear. "If you can be my good girl and be quiet, Tori just got a huge stack of pancakes drowned in syrup. I can make your morning start out right with a quick orgasm."

"A morgasm?" His hand muffles my voice, and he laughs, removing it from my mouth.

"Yes, Pinky. An orgasm. Would you like that?"

"Who would say no to that?" He pulls the pillow out from under my head, and it bounces on the mattress before he plops it on my face. He slowly makes his way down my body, trailing teasing kisses and spreading my legs as he goes.

The moment his mouth surrounds my center, I gasp and understand the need for the pillow. He somehow knows my body entirely too well for such a short amount of time. His tongue flicks, and teeth nip all the places I need to make me orgasm. Scotty uses nothing but his tongue, his expert, fucking tongue. Within a few minutes, I'm sweating, trying to control the sounds that want to fly from my mouth.

I orgasm with a long, low groan into the pillow and hope I managed to stay as quiet as I think I was.

Crawling back up my body, he uses the back of his hand to wipe his mouth. Kissing the top of my head, he inhales deeply.

"Thank you." He hums with a smile.

"Me? Why are you thanking me? What did I do to be thanked?"

"I enjoyed my breakfast. I could start every day between your legs if you'd let me and never get tired of it." Rolling my eyes at his ridiculousness, I look around the room for my clothes. Scotty grabs a neatly folded pile from the top of his dresser.

"If you'd like to shower, your shampoo and conditioner are

in there."

"My?"

"You left your shampoo once, and I went and bought the matching conditioner in case you ever needed it again while you were here." Holy shit. He did that for me.

"A shower would be nice, but—"

"I'll let Tori know I woke you, and you are using my shower because it has grown up hair stuff, unlike her bubble gum scented shampoo. She won't question it. You worry too much."

"Yeah, yeah. A shower would be nice. Will I have a stack of pancakes waiting for me when I get out?"

"Only if you hurry and Tori doesn't eat them all." Laughing, I understand, she's a pancake fiend.

"Okay, I'll hurry." I give him a quick peck on the lips and head to the bathroom.

★ ★ ★ ★ ★

I hear the cartoons playing as I walk into the living room, freshly showered.

"Wynnie!" Tori hops up off the floor and slams into my legs, almost knocking me down.

"Calm down, Little Princess. Let Wynnie walk in the room."

"Sorries." She steps back from my legs and I give her a big smile.

"How about a hug." I squat down and open my arms wide. I make a show of toppling to the ground and taking her with me. "You're so strong, Sunshine. It must be all those pancakes that you eat. Did you save any for me?"

"Hmm. Daddy can make you some. I ate all mine, so I

don't have any to share." She rubs her belly, showing me how full she is. "Daddy makes the best pancakes in the whole big world." She crawls off me and skips towards the kitchen.

Scotty walks over, laughing, and extends his hand to help me up.

"I made you a fresh cup of coffee and saved you some pancakes from the pancake monster."

"I appreciate you." He pulls me close to whisper in my ear.

"You definitely sounded like you did when you were coming all over my face this morning." He steps back and smiles. "There's the blush I love so much." And there's that pesky "L" word again.

"I'll take those pancakes now, Scotty," I step around him before more than my blush starts reacting to him.

"Can I sit with you, Wynnie?"

"Of course, Sunshine. Will you color me a picture while I eat?"

"I'd rather color Daddy." I can't help but laugh because, of course, she does. Scotty sighs.

"Fine, but no glitter pens. Only washable marker that I'll wash off before work, okay?"

"Fiiiiine. But I want to color the new ones." Oh, those are under his shirt. He'd have to take it off, and I would have an excuse to stare at his cut chest.

"I agree. The new ones are more fun." Scotty stares at me as his hand dips behind his head, and he pulls his black t-shirt off with a knowing smirk. That's so fucking sexy.

"Let me get the markers while you ladies sit." He takes a plate out of the microwave, sets it on the counter, then adds syrup and my coffee next to it.

The food smells delicious, and I dive right in. Scotty

returns with a container full of markers, and the three of us talk, color, and eat. I can't help but be in awe at how natural this feels.

25

Scotty

It feels so weird to drive such a tiny car. I've had my lifted truck for well over a decade. This little sardine can feels like it's one pothole away from falling to China. How does Wynnie drive this, and why did I agree to let her borrow my truck?

I know exactly why. I'm pussy whipped. Pinky is no longer just a nickname for the blush that creeps on her face. That woman has me wrapped around her damn pinky.

She mentioned a few days ago that she had purchased some new furniture pieces for the apartment remodel. The furniture company wanted to charge an obscene delivery fee, which would take two weeks unless she wanted to pick them up herself.

She was planning to rent a box truck to get them, but after showing me the pieces, I knew they would fit in the back of my truck. I insisted that we trade vehicles for the day so she could save money. I know she's driven her dad's truck, so I have confidence she could drive mine a longer distance than just the trip to my house from the bar.

I wish I could have gone with her to pick them up, but I already had several suppliers scheduled for drop off today that I couldn't reschedule. She took Elliot with her and was told there would be employees to help load the furniture into my truck.

The early afternoon goes smoothly and all of my deliveries are on time. I'm restocking paper products in the supply closet when my phone rings, and I see Wynnie is calling.

"Hey, Pinky. How's your pick up going?"

"It went great. I'm heading back with all of it now, but I wanted to let you know I'm putting gas in your truck. This thing is a gas guzzler, and I just want to make sure I at least paid you back with a full tank. *And* don't worry, I put the fancy gas in your baby." *Oh, no.*

"Wynnie, what do you mean by fancy gas?"

"Well, I always put the regular stuff in mine because I'm cheap, but I know you like to take good care of your truck, so I'm putting the ninety...one or is it three?" I hear her muffle the phone as my blood starts to boil. "Elliot, what's the number on the push button? Ninety-one or ninety-three?"

"Three. It's ninety-three."

"Wynnie." It's taking every ounce of patience I've ever had in my entire life not to scream right now.

"Yeah, Scotty? What's up? It's really no big deal. You don't need to thank me or anything."

"Where are you?" If it was real, I know steam would be pouring out of my ears like a damn cartoon.

"Oh, um? We're still about thirty minutes outside of town, so less than an hour away. Don't worry. I'm taking really good care of her, and I'll make sure you get your baby back in perfect shape."

178

"Wynnie."

"Hey, are you okay? You sound tense. Did something happen at work?" Something is about to happen. I'm going to have an aneurysm from the stress my body is currently under.

"I'm coming to you. Don't move from that gas station; tell me your location." If I can get to her and drain the gas tank, we shouldn't have any issues. Why did I not think to tell her it took diesel? Or that she didn't have to put gas in it at all.

"We're okay. You don't need to come to us. Elliot's pumping the gas, and I feel like a badass in this driver's seat. I'm plotting world domination from this height. Of course, Elliot has to help me get out, which totally kills my street cred, but—"

"Wynnie, my truck takes diesel." My voice rises with each word, and I'm losing my cool. "You can't put regular gas in it, or you'll kill the engine."

"But I'm putting the fancy stuff in. Doesn't that count for anything?"

"DIESEL, WYNNIE. That's not regular gas!" My outburst turns some heads, and I close the door to the supply closet, shutting myself in.

"Oh." That's all she has to say?

"Tell me where you are, and I'll come to you right now and get the correct gas in it. Don't. Move. The. Truck. If the gas station gives you any problems, I'd rather have it towed than—" Why is Wynnie laughing? Why is she fucking laughing? Does she think this is funny?

"What the fuck is so funny?" I can hear she's practically hyperventilating with laughter. "Wynnie? Rowyn Juniper Harmon."

"Oh shit." That voice was Elliot's.

179

"Elliot, what the fuck is going on?"

"Hold on, Scotty, I don't think she's breathing." Not breathing? Oh, fuck.

"Elliot, what do you mean? Is she okay? Is she choking on something? What's going on?" Panic replaces my anger. I have to get to her. Where are my keys? Shit, she has them. I have her car. I have a general idea of the direction they're in and can start heading that way.

"Scotty." Wynnie. I freeze, let my panic pause, and wait for her to say more words.

"Oh god, Wynnie. Are you okay, Pinky? Please tell me you're okay." Fuck please be okay.

"I-I...I'm about to pee my pants." What the fuck is happening? She's laughing again. "Joke. It's...a joke."

"What's a joke? I need to know what's going on, right now. Someone tell me if she's okay."

"Scotty, we're fine. She's fine. We filled your truck with diesel. Wynnie thought it would be funny to call you and play dumb." *A joke*. Elliot said it's a joke.

My body instantly drains of its adrenaline. Wynnie is fine. My truck is fine.

"Put her on the phone." I hear rustling and panting. She's trying to compose herself before speaking to me. Smart girl.

"I'm so sorry. I thought it would be funny. I didn't expect such an extreme reaction from you. Please forgive me."

"Pinky. Tell Elliot you won't be home tonight. I'll ask Mrs. Peterson to keep Tori, and you are spending the night with me. This stunt deserves a punishment. I'll let you choose spankings or orgasms."

"Wait. What?" All of the humor is gone from her voice.

"You heard me. A stunt like this deserves punishment."

"But how are orgasms a punishment?" Sometimes, her naivety is so adorable.

"Choose that option and find out. You can think about it and get back to me, but I expect you to be at my house when I get home around ten thirty with your choice."

"Um. Okay. Hey El, I won't be home tonight. I'm in trouble." I smile when I hear "Oh shit" in the background.

"Good girl. Now, Pinky?"

"Yes."

"Drive safe, and I'll see you soon."

I hang up before she can say anything else. As much of an emotional rollercoaster as the last few minutes have been, that actually was a pretty funny joke in hindsight.

Now, I have several hours to plot her punishment based on both possible options. Either way, it's going to be a fun evening.

26

Wynnie

That did not go as planned. Scotty's reaction was so genuine I couldn't stop going along with it. And then he started panicking, and I was already laughing so hard I couldn't tell him it was a joke.

"What do you think is going to happen?"

"I have no idea, El. He didn't sound mad or upset. I'm not even sure how to describe it. Maybe stoic. I have no idea."

"What are you going to choose? Because honestly, both options sound hot to me." Ugh.

"Of course they would. I don't know how I feel about spankings. I don't think I want to be abused."

"Oh, Wynnie. That's your first problem. Wipe that thought right out of your head. A spanking is for pleasure, not pain." His head cocks, and thinks for a moment. "Well, it can be painful, but it's a pleasurable pain."

"Oh, now I understand. Thanks for clearing that up for me. Let's revisit this after my dads are gone, please."

As we pull into the driveway, I see the shock on my dad's face when he sees me open the door to Scotty's truck.

"Hey, Sweetheart. Why are you behind the wheel of this tank? I thought you were renting a box truck." Crap, I never did come up with a good cover story. Let's go with the truth-ish.

"Oh, I was, but Scotty insisted I use his truck and save the money."

"If I had known that, you could have borrowed mine or Phoenix's." He extends his hand to help me out. It's a little less embarrassing than when Elliot helps.

"Thank you, Dad." Despite this man missing the first twelve years of my life, I wouldn't change a thing. I wished for a dad whenever I blew out my birthday candles or saw a shooting star. Every penny thrown in a fountain, all I ever wanted was a dad. My wishes came true in their own time. Now, I have three younger siblings that I wouldn't change for the world and three dads who each hold a piece of my heart.

"Are you alright, Sweetheart? You look like you have something on your mind."

"There's my girl." Phoenix walks out of the garage, saving me from having to come up with a lie. Strong arms wrap around my shoulders as Phoenix hugs me. He pulls away and tilts his head, looking at the vehicle behind me.

"Isn't this Scotty's truck? He never lets anyone drive it. I don't think I want to know what you had to promise him, to let you drive his baby." The blowjob I gave was sure persuasive...fuck. Change the subject, Wynnie.

"What do you think of the furniture?"

"Everything looks great. You picked some very sophisticated pieces. It's all going in the garage for now, right?

"Yep. My apartment is a mess and isn't ready for the furniture, but I couldn't pass on these."

183

"Alright, let's get this unloaded. You know your little brothers and sister miss you. You should come by the house soon and more often."

"We all miss you, Wynnie." My dad is trying to lay on the guilt. Elliot walks past me and whispers, "So do we," as he carries a dresser drawer. All of them miss me for entirely different reasons.

I'm trying not to spend too many nights at Scotty's house. Tori is starting to get suspicious. But he drives a hard bargain and bribes me with orgasms. It's really hard to say no to orgasms.

Maybe that should be my choice for tonight. Orgasms sound much more pleasurable than spankings, despite Elliot trying to convince me otherwise.

To keep my mind off my impending punishment, I decide to make cookies. I know Scotty keeps chocolate chips in the house for pancakes, so making chocolate chip cookies seems the most reasonable option.

The house feels eerie being here alone at night. It doesn't help that I have the distinct memory of Scotty scaring me in the kitchen and almost hitting him with a frying pan.

He should be home soon, although he hasn't sent me a text yet letting me know. I can't shake the eerie feeling of being watched.

Picking up my phone, I consider whether I should call or text Scotty and decide hearing his voice would settle my nerves a bit.

"Hey, Pinky." I can hear the commotion of the bar in the

background, which tells me where he is.

"Are you coming back soon?" He laughs, and it doesn't soothe my nerves any.

"Are you eager for my punishment?"

"It feels weird being alone in your house, and I have that creepy feeling like someone is watching me. I'm sure I'm just being paranoid."

"I'm wrapping up here and heading out in about five minutes. We had a late pop, and I didn't want to leave Kristina by herself. Do you want me to stay on the phone with you?" He's so thoughtful.

"No. I'll be fine. I just wanted to check in since I hadn't heard from you yet."

"Are you sure?" I can hear the hesitation in his voice.

"Yeah, I'll call Elliot and annoy him. Just do me a favor and text me when you pull into the driveway so I don't get startled when you walk in. Wouldn't want any more close calls with frying pans."

"Of course. I'll text you when I get in my truck. I'll be about fifteen minutes, and when I pull in, I'll text again."

"Thanks, Scotty."

"And Pinky, if Elliot doesn't pick up, I'm happy to talk to you on the ride home, okay?"

"Okay. I'll be fine. I have to put on my big girl panties. I'm twenty-two and shouldn't be scared to be home alone."

"I much prefer you with no panties at all."

"If you were here, you'd see my eye roll. See you soon."

"Have you picked your punishment?"

"Orgasms."

"You sound awfully confident in that decision, Rowyn." His voice has gone husky, and the background noise fades as I

185

hear a door shut. He must have walked into the office.

"Spankings still make me nervous." They really do. Pain in place of pleasure doesn't sound exciting to me.

"Okay. We can leave that as a limit for you…for now. I'd like you to consider trusting me one day to show you how pleasurable it can be. But we can do it on your time." I like the sound of that. I like his understanding of my limits.

"I do trust you. And I'll let you know when and if I'm ready to explore that."

"I'm walking out of my office now, so here's my text letting you know I'll be there in about eighteen minutes."

"Okay. See you soon. Drive safe."

We hang up, and I call Elliot. He picks up on the first ring.

"What's wrong? Do I have a body to hide? Shouldn't you be tied up getting your ass spanked by now?"

"Elliot! No one is getting tied up. And no one is getting spanked. I chose orgasms."

"No. Girl, you chose wrong. Is there time to change your mind? Have you ever heard of a pleasure Dom? I hope you know what you've gotten yourself into."

"El, that's a lot of information all at once. What are you talking about?"

"Oh, no. I'm not telling you anymore. You'll have to figure it out for yourself, my little naive Wynnie."

"Thanks, Asshole."

"Anytime, Bitch. Now, I suppose you called me for a reason?" Oh yeah.

"Yes. It feels funny being here alone, and I just wanted some company. Scotty is on his way home now. And…" I look around the house, making sure all the blinds are closed.

"And?"

"Do you ever get the feeling you're being watched? I just have a funny feeling tonight."

"Did something happen? What's going on, Wynnie?" Now I've worried him.

"Nothing happened. I don't know. It's just a feeling. I'm sure it's only my imagination. Aunt Dellah corrupted my juvenile mind with all of her horror movies." Elliot laughs a full belly laugh.

"I definitely know that."

"So, was anything said about me back at your house? My dad was a tiny bit suspicious, which basically means he secretly went into cop mode, and his gears were turning."

"Almost. Your dad mentioned that it was 'nice' of him to let you borrow his truck, but the word nice was laced with suspicion. Then Phoenix grumbled something about never being allowed to drive Scotty's truck. My mom played it off, saying how much Scotty appreciated you watching Tori and that it was no big deal."

"Did they buy it?" Oh shit. I could never keep secrets from my dad. I swear having a cop for a father is a curse as much as a blessing.

"You know Uncle Mac, he's hard to read when he wants to hide things and Uncle Phoenix seemed unphased."

My phone dings just as I see lights cross the front window.

Scotty: I'm here. Get naked in my bed now, Rowyn.

"Oh shit."

"I'm sure it's okay, Wyn—"

"No, Scotty is home and just text me to be naked in his bed."

187

"Well, shit. You better go and do what you're told. Drink lots of water, and I'll see you on the other side. Good luck." He laughs maniacally as he hangs up.

27

Wynnie

S hit. Shit. Shit. I wasn't prepared for Scotty to give me instructions. I have to put the cookies away before I forget about them. I'm glad I cleaned up my mess already. I quickly find a container to put them in, and I'm closing the lid as the front door opens. *Shit.*

Ducking down, I squat on the floor, hiding like I just got caught *stealing* a cookie from the cookie jar instead of putting them away. Why am I being so stupid? What the hell am I hiding for? *Because you're already afraid of your punishment, and now you've disobeyed an order.*

Scotty walks through the kitchen straight to the bedroom and pauses at the doorway when he doesn't see me. He walks into the room assumingly to see if I'm in the bathroom and steps back into the hallway.

"Piiiinky. Are we playing a game of hide and seek? I'm a master seeker. I have a five year old who's an excellent hider and she keeps me on my toes." I quietly sit on my butt and scoot into the corner of the "L" shaped island.

"It smells good in here. Did you bake for me? I smell

chocolate. Did you make a cake or cookies?" *Crap.* He's heading toward the kitchen now. Think. Think.

I have to distract him. I peek around the island, but I can't see him. Where did he go? I take a chance and look a little farther, and I still can't see him anywhere in the living room.

Do I tempt fate and try to get to the bedroom without him seeing me? It seems like the only logical thing to do.

Okay, here I go. I crawl a few feet away from the island and still don't see him. I think I'm in the clear. I just need to make it to the back of the couch and then to the hallway.

"Gotcha!" Scotty grabs my ankle. Where the hell did he come from?

"Fuck." I scream, and I'm glad that Tori isn't here because I would have just scared the shit out of her.

"Did you think you could disobey me and I'd let it slide? Why aren't you naked?"

I roll over to sit, and he releases my ankle. "Where were you?"

"On the other side of the island. You never looked up. Now, why aren't you naked?"

"I got your text and hadn't put the cookies away yet. I tried to be quick, but they were still warm, and some stuck to the drying rack." He looks behind him and sees the cookie container and the crumb-filled drying rack.

"What kind?"

"Chocolate chip." He suddenly looks deep in thought.

"I'll give you the count of ten. Nine."

"What? For what?"

"Eight. Seven. You better hurry. Six. I won't give you another chance. Five." I scramble off the floor, stripping clothes, and run to Scotty's room. I'm kicking away my shorts and panties at the same time when he stands in the doorway.

He grips the top of the doorframe in the sexy way they talk about in my smut books. I've never seen it in real life, but holy shit, do I understand why the women in those books lose their shit over a move like this.

"Will you remove your shirt and put your hands back on the door like that?"

"You don't get to make demands, Rowyn."

"Please?" He cocks his head, considering.

"Why?" I can't tell him why. It's embarrassing that I even asked in the first place.

"Nevermind. No reason." He reaches behind his head and takes his shirt off. Fuck. Yeah that's even hotter.

"Why, Rowyn? You asked me for a reason. I'm just asking what the reason is?"

"It's, um...it's silly." He puts one arm on the doorframe, and I can feel the flush growing on my face.

"Interesting. Tell me. Now I need to know. You're gloriously pink, Pinky."

"In the um, books I read. It's something that they always describe the hunky guys doing. I've never seen it before, and when you just did it, it was hot, and I wanted to see you doing it without your shirt on. Like I said, it's silly."

"You wanting to admire my body isn't silly." He does it. He puts his other hand on the doorframe and leans into his arms. His biceps and abs pop, and I think I might drool. I wonder if I asked him, if he would do it again, but oiled up.

"Is this what you wanted, Rowyn? Come closer." I hesitate momentarily before standing from the bed and sauntering towards him. I stop about a foot away, and he smiles down at me. "Admire away."

I lift a finger to his abs and trace the dips and valleys. My finger follows the top of his V before it disappears into his jeans. He's so fucking gorgeous.

Closing his eyes, he stands in the door as I trail his torso and upper arms with my fingers. His breathing is ragged, and I can see his muscles straining from exertion. Are his arms getting tired from being up in the air, or is he struggling to hold himself back?

I let my fingers roam lower until I'm tracing the outline of his already hard cock.

"Do you like being admired?" He drops his hands and steps back.

"Get on the bed. You have a punishment to receive." Right. Punishment by orgasms: I'm soooo worried.

Crawling on the bed, I rest against the headboard, wondering what he'll do.

"Pick a number from five to ten, and don't tell me. Got it?" I nod, thinking of the number eight. "Good, now add two and tell me what number you got."

"Ten."

"Ten it is."

"Wait. Ten what is? What did I just give you a number for?" Crawling up my body, he runs his tongue along my hip, up to my belly button, between my breasts, and finally, he kisses my lips.

"Ten orgasms," he whispers into my mouth.

I must have misheard him. Ten orgasms isn't feasible, is it?

"Is it negotiable? That's a lot of orgasms."

"No." And I guess that's my answer. "Let's start right now. Open these legs for me." He taps my thigh with his hand, and I spread as wide as my knees allow.

Scotty slides down my body and dives into my pussy without hesitation. I'm already wet, and he moans in appreciation as I moan in pleasure. He sucks my clit between his lips and uses his teeth to nip as it swells. I can already feel the orgasm tingling in my stomach.

"Oh fuck, Scotty." I fist my hands in his hair, and he groans again. "Oh my god." The vibrations from his groan sends a shockwave through my body. He reaches his arm up between my legs and flicks my nipple a few times before grabbing and pinching it. I'm overstimulated, and the anticipation of the impending orgasm has me panting with need.

He must be able to tell that I'm close because he increases the suction on my clit and pinches my nipple harder. I almost wince in pain from the sting of the pinch when my orgasm shoots off like a firework.

Not firework, fire*works*. They continue to explode all around my body and his tongue seems to be moving faster, not slower, as my orgasm subsides.

"Scotty." I tap on his head as his tongue continues to make circles around my clit. "Scotty."

"Another."

"A-another?" He slips two fingers into me and lifts his head to meet by eyes.

"Ten orgasms, Rowyn. That's one. Give me another. And rule number two, Pinky. I want to hear you. All of you. We're alone tonight, don't hold back." He curls his fingers inside me and grazes my G-spot. It feels so good, but my body is still buzzing from the first one. How am I going to survive nine more of these?

His fingers inside me pick up pace as he scissors them back and forth. Lowering his mouth back down to my clit, I hiss at the slight sting the feeling of his tongue brings.

"Your walls are fluttering for me. How close are you?" I can't believe he's gotten me there again so quickly.

"Close. So. Close." He flicks my clit with his tongue, and I come all over his fingers with a long high pitched moan. I'm struggling to understand the sounds coming out of my mouth, but I feel so fucking incredible I don't even care.

As I come down from another orgasm, he climbs up next to me on the bed, brushing hair away from my damp forehead.

"You're so fucking beautiful when you come. How do you feel?"

"I feel floaty." I giggle because I wonder if I sound as drunk as I feel.

"Floaty is good. But I want you to feel like you're no longer in your own body. I want you to be a bystander as you let me take every ounce of pleasure that you can give. And then? Then I'll fuck you until your so exhausted you can't even keep your eyes open." I moan and smile at him. "It seems like you approve of that idea?"

"I like the idea of sleep?" I'm already tired. My body is satisfied and relaxed.

"That's enough break." I feel his thick fingers slide down my body and push my leg aside. He massages lazy circles around my clit, sending jolts of electricity every time he gets too close.

"I want you to remember your safeword, Rowyn. Do you remember it?"

"Can you…can you stop so we can have this conversation? You're making it hard to think." My mind can't handle so many feelings at once. He slides a finger inside me and chuckles deep into my neck.

"Am I a distraction to your thoughts?" His finger glides gently in and out of my soaked pussy. I giggle when he nips at my neck and he pulls out. I know I asked him to stop, but I wish he didn't.

He brings his finger to my lips and stops hovering over them.

"Do you want to taste yourself?"

"Um, I don't know." He gives me his half smile that I usually see him give Tori when she's being silly. "Don't look at me like that." His smile grows wider.

"Like what?" He sucks the finger he offered me into his mouth, and I can't help but stare at him. "Like what, Pinky?"

"Like I'm a naive little kid who doesn't know anything." He kisses me and traces his tongue over my lip. When I open up for him, I realize what he's done. I taste it. I taste *me.* He's sneaky. It's not the first time he's kissed me after going down on me but he was intentional with this kiss. I smile into our kiss, and he smiles back, knowing I figured him out.

When he pulls away, he brushes his nose against mine. "I don't think that at all. The look is wonderment. You're experiencing things for the first time, and I love seeing it. I love being able to experience it with you. To be able to *be* that experience for you. And to be so many of your firsts."

"You don't need to sugarcoat it for me. I know I'm inexperienced. I'm probably so boring for you."

"Don't do that. I'll happily go through every new experience with you. It means I get to mold you however I like." He shifts his hips and his thigh settles between my legs. His rough jeans press firm into my core. He looks down at me, contemplating something.

"What?"

195

"How about I reduce your punishment to five since I unfairly made you pick a number without knowing why?" It's not that easy.

"What's the catch?"

"Smart girl." I gasp as he takes my nipple into his mouth. "You let me spank you. I'll trade you three for three." He wants to spank me three times in exchange for three less orgasms. I open my mouth to protest and he puts his lips to mine before I can speak. "Before you say no, did you like when I pinched your nipple?" What a strange question.

"Of course I did."

"Even when I pinched hard?" Was that his intention? Was he testing me to see if I liked the pain?

"Were you...y-yes."

"You won't know what you don't like if you never try it. Let's explore together. Let's learn your body together." He leans down and takes a nipple into his mouth. My back arches off the bed.

"I bet I could make you orgasm just by playing with your nipples." I bet he could. My core is already spasming, wanting him to fill me. His fingers tweak the nipple that his tongue isn't teasing.

"Oh, Scotty." I grab his head and push him further into my chest. How is this man's tongue so talented? He switches his hand and tongue, and sparks shoot straight to my clit.

"Are you trying to cheat, Pinky?" I feel pressure on my core and realize that I was grinding on his leg between my thighs. "Take it. Fuck yourself on my leg while I taste and tease your breasts." I do what he tells me, and he adds more pressure to my core.

Every part of my body is overstimulated as I grind myself

to completion on his leg, screaming out my pleasure.

28

Scotty

I need to do a better job of praising Wynnie if she thinks I find her boring. Everything about her is fascinating to me. Her amount of sexual experience, or lack thereof, doesn't make a difference to me. I greatly enjoy watching her learn new things about herself and her body.

I knew I was testing my luck when I added the extra pressure to her nipple. I would have backed off instantly if she had an adverse reaction to it. Instead, it pushed her over the edge, and she came undone so beautifully for me. Three orgasms down and four more to go if she takes my deal. Will she let me spank her? My hand twitches, thinking about spanking her. Will she go for my new deal?

"Can we explore and learn together, Rowyn? I promise you will always be safe with me." Staring down into her gorgeous blue eyes, her cheeks still flushed from her leg-grinding orgasm, I get lost in their unique color.

"I trust you. Will you go slow with me?"

"What's your safeword?"

"Avocado." I chuckle and rest my forehead against her.

"You're incredible." I kiss the tip of her nose, and she giggles. "We can go slow, but tonight, you owe me a punishment. Do we have a deal? Now four more orgasms and three spanks for your punishment?" She's so intrigued but equally as nervous.

"And avocado stops everything, no matter what?" She wants to say yes. It's on the tip of her tongue.

"No matter what, Rowyn. Even a punishment. Everything is for your pleasure."

"What about your pleasure?"

"*You*, my sweet Pinky, are my pleasure. Every moan or whimper, every twitch of your muscles. Every smile, every kiss…" I lean down and kiss her neck, "lick…" I swirl my tongue along her shoulder, "and suck." I pull her flesh into my mouth. I want to mark her as mine, but I know I can't. "It's all my pleasure. Every bit of it."

"I'm going to channel my inner Elliot and say yes." I can't help but laugh.

"Is he your conscience? Does a little Elliot sit on each shoulder, tempting you in either direction?"

"Hell, no. Could you imagine? I'd definitely have two devils on my shoulders." Oh, I can imagine, and she's absolutely right. It's funny because he's younger, but he's a bad influence on her. "He's the one that likes to take risks, does things with his heart, and worries about his mind later. I'm going to go with my libido and worry about my mind later."

My thigh shifts between her legs, and I should probably take my jeans off since she's naked, but she hums when I put pressure on her pussy, and I don't think she cares how much clothing I have on.

"Are you ready for your next orgasm, or did you want to try out those spankings first?"

"I want…" Her indecision is always my favorite. I can see her thoughts running through her head, trying to make the right decision. "I'd like another orgasm first, then maybe the spanking."

I'm already sliding down her body, eager to taste her again, to hear her scream. She's had enough time for her body to relax from her heightened state. I internally debate with myself to make her next orgasm quick so I can get to the spanking, or make it slow, torturing her because she knows what's coming next. Or, I can just ask and heighten her anticipation.

"Hey Pinky. Fast or slow?" I look at her up the length of her body. Her nipples are hard, and there's a light pink blush across her chest. Her brows pinch in question. "Do you want a fast orgasm or a slow one? How long until we get to the spanking?" My fingers massage her lips and circle her entrance. I'm distracting her from answering.

"Hmm. I'm going to take your lack of a response as you don't care. Fast it is." My fingers make entrance and her mouth drops open in a silent moan.

I watch the blush on her chest deepen and rise to her neck. Lowering my mouth, I flick her clit back and forth. I'm still learning what truly drives her crazy. She reacts to everything I do with moans, whines, and whimpers. Her biggest tell is when she grabs my hair. That's when I know I've found a spot she enjoys most.

My cock aches in my pants, wanting to be let free. Soon. I plan to give her a very enjoyable evening once she gets through her punishment.

Her breath hitches, and her inner walls begin to flutter. I hear her moving, and when I look up, her eyes are closed, and she's pinching her nipples. I can see the tensing and loosening of her finger. She's testing her pain tolerance, but I know she can take more than she realizes, and it's going to be fun to learn what she likes.

"Ah, ah. Scotty. Fuck, Scotty." My name on her lips as she comes is fucking heaven. I lick at her wet pussy until she pushes me away.

"Flip over. Chest on the bed, ass in the air." I see the corner of her lip twitch before she rolls over. Once on her knees, I have the most perfect view of her pussy. Glistening from her arousal, I lick a line from her clit to her virgin puckered hole. She gasps and tenses up.

"Shh, I know your limits. I'm just having a little fun. I didn't want to waste anything."

"I don't know if I'm more turned on or grossed out by that thought." Sitting up, I run my palms smoothly around the globes of her ass cheeks. I briefly step back off the bed to remove the rest of my clothing.

Settling back down, I position myself between her thighs.

"Do you want me to warn you or just do it?"

"Just do it." She's panting with anticipation. I rub her left cheek a few more times and swiftly smack her ass. The sound rings through the room. I make sure that my slap is controlled with just enough pain to sting. I immediately flick her clit with one hand and rub her ass cheek with the other.

"Breathe, Rowyn." Her back rises and sinks with relief. It must not have been as bad as she expected.

A growl escapes my throat as I watch my handprint bloom into a perfect red spot on her ass. Running a hand down her spine, she relaxes even further.

"Could you, maybe, try it harder?" *Fuck yes.*

"Anything for you. Play with your clit. Make yourself come while you accept your spanking." This time, when the sound cracks through the air, I don't need to touch her, other than my hand rubbing to absorb the sting.

"Talk to me, Rowyn. Can you take your final punishment?" There's a long pause, and I'm worried she's going to use her safeword, but the most delicious word comes from her lips.

"Harder." *Holy fucking shit. She likes it.* Her fingers move at a frantic pace.

"I'll give you what you want, but not until you're coming. Make yourself come again, and after this one, I'm taking your dripping cunt and making your last two orgasms count. Be warned." Her ass wiggles, and fuck, I need to have her.

I continue to rub her ass as she flicks at her swollen clit. Her breathing and moans falter, and her orgasm rips through her body.

I smack her pink ass one more time, and before she can react, my hands encircle her hips, and I slam my cock into her. Harder and faster, with each thrust, her moans intensify. She's soaking my cock with her arousal. She fucking loved it. Time to finish her punishment. I slow my relentless thrusts and lean over her body.

"Rowyn, check in with me. How are you?"

"So...deep." Peppering kisses along her shoulder, I laugh.

"Yes, I am, but that's not an answer to my question." This isn't a position we've tried before. I sit back up on my knees and admire her. Taking her from behind gives me a perfect view of her body, and I can see the markings of my handprints on her ass.

Slowing my pace even farther, I knead her ass cheeks, and she whines.

"Your body took my spanking so fucking well, but I need your words to know your mind is alright, too. Talk to me, Rowyn."

"Please don't stop. It feels so fucking incredible."

"I don't want to stop. I don't ever want to fucking stop. But Wynnie, I didn't put a condom on. I didn't even think about it. I'm sorry. I know you said you were on the pill. What do you want me to do?"

"I'm…fuck. I'm so good, Scotty. It's okay. Please keep going." Thank fuck. She feels so fucking incredible raw. Her pussy is hot and tight and her arousal is soaking me.

"That's my good girl. Play with your clit again. Make yourself come on my cock." She shifts under me until I hear her sigh as she begins playing with herself.

Grabbing her hips to help stabilize her, I resume my vigorous motions slamming into her pussy over and over.

"I feel it, Rowyn. Give me that orgasm. Squeeze my cock." Her body rocks back into mine, meeting me thrust for thrust.

"Oh god. Fuck." She turns her head and screams into the comforter as her orgasm overtakes her.

"Fuck. You're so fucking tight right now. You have a vice grip on my cock, baby." A sheen of sweat glistens off her back and I kiss down her spine tasting her salty skin.

As her orgasm subsides, her body relaxes, and I almost want to let her off the hook. My own orgasm wants to be released, but I can't let this first time slide. I've already changed the rules once. "Don't get too comfortable. You still owe me one more, Pinky."

She moans in exhaustion and pleasure, and I'm satisfied that I've done both of those things for her.

"One more, Rowyn. That's all you need to give me, and

then I'll run you a hot bath." I hear her mumble into the comforter, and I think she says, "sounds nice."

She's done so well. I had no expectations for tonight other than her pleasure. While I told her this was a punishment, it was all for the thrill and anticipation of tonight's events. Her gas prank was a good one, and I'll get her back soon.

Lifting my leg up and planting my foot flat on the bed changes our angle, making me impossibly deeper. Judging by the colorful expletives pouring from Wynnie's mouth, she's enjoying it as much as I am.

She begins to squirm under me, and I soothe a hand down her back.

"Shhh. I know it's still a new sensation. Work through it." I quicken my pace, rubbing harder on her G-spot. My palms are tingling to smack her ass again, but I don't want to overwhelm her.

"Scotty. Oh fuck, Scotty."

"Be my good fucking girl. Come, Rowyn."

"I can't. Oh god. Fuck. Fuck."

"You can. Let go." She's shaking her head into the bed, mumbling unintelligible curses. "Don't be a brat. Give me what I want." I give in and smack her ass as hard as the third blow earlier, and she screams. And screams. And screams.

I release my orgasm and fill her pussy with my come. Her legs give out from under her when I loosen my grip on her hips. Her head falls to the side, and she's open mouth panting with her eyes squinting.

I pull out and lay next to her side. "Are you alright?" She wiggles her hips.

"I feel so…sloppy." I run a flat hand between her legs, smearing our arousals together.

"You were beautifully perfect, Rowyn. How about the bath I promised you?" Her head vigorously nods, and I chuckle. I lightly pat her butt. "Don't move, I'll be right back."

"I couldn't even if I wanted to." I kiss her forehead and walk to the bathroom, starting the bath with some Epsom salt. I don't have anything to make it smell pretty and I'll have to rectify that soon. But I know the salt will help with her muscles. I'm sure she'll be sore tomorrow.

When I walked back into the room, Wynnie hasn't moved. I sit beside her on the bed and move her hair from her face.

"Are you awake?"

"No. I'm dead. Death by orgasms."

"Hmm. Sounds like a great way to die. Come on. Let's get you in the bathtub." She grumbles but rolls to her back anyway. As she moves to sit up a rippling sound fills the air. Wynnie freezes and instantly turns bright red.

"I didn't…That was…I don't. Oh my god." I've never seen her so red. She sits forward farther to bury her face in her hands, and more noise escapes her. "Oh my god. Holy shit."

I can't help but chuckle at her mortification, which only makes things worse.

"Hey. Relax, Wynnie."

"But I…I mean, I didn't actually, but…"

29

Wynnie

H oly.
  Fucking.
  Shit.

I'm dead. My life as I know it is over. I need to crawl out of this room and disappear.

I've run away once before, kind of. I can do it again. This time more successfully. I have a car and a job that I can do remotely. I have my own money. I can do this.

Mortified.

Embarrassed.

Humiliated.

Appalled.

Where's a thesaurus so I can look up more words to describe how I'm feeling right now?

I just…I have no idea what that was. Did I fart? No. It didn't come from there. It came from my vajayjay.

If I sit here long enough without moving, maybe I'll cease to exist.

"Pinky, look at me." I'm afraid to move a muscle. The

noises I made. Oh god, the freaking noises. From THERE.

"Rowyn." My eyes snap to Scotty at his stern tone. I can't imagine what I look like right now. I feel wrung out, which I absolutely hate because two minutes ago, I was blissed out from incredible sex and way too many orgasms.

"What's wrong?" I slowly turn my head to look at him. I barely manage to whisper out my issue.

"Didn't you hear that? I swear it wasn't a…" I mouth the word "fart" without making a sound.

A full-belly laugh roars from Scotty. I don't think there's any blood left in my body. It's all in my face that feels like it's at the bottom of an erupting volcano.

"I'm so sorry. I'll leave. That was—"

"Stop." Scotty's face is stern and commanding, and it makes me flinch.

"That was your Dad voice." He freezes and wipes his hand over his face, sighing.

"Wynnie, I'm sorry. Please, just listen to me. Pause and take a deep breath." I inhale, expanding my lungs, and slowly let it out. "Good girl. First of all, don't be embarrassed by what you just did." I huff a laugh. "Pinky, you queefed."

"I what'ed?"

"You queefed. It's actually my fault."

"Ugh. Now I'm embarrassed *and* confused."

"Come here." He reaches out a hand for me to come closer, and I shake my head.

"I'm too afraid to move." I watch the corner of his lip twitch. He wants to laugh at me again.

"Would you like me to help you with that?" My face twists in horror.

"Help me with what?"

"To get rid of the air. That's all it is. Our position pushed extra air into your vagina. I can help you relieve any that's left."

"I think I…"

"Lay back. Don't argue, please." I'm going to have to do this. I reach my hands behind me and slide them backward, doing everything in my power not to use a single abdominal muscle. Somehow, I manage to make it to my back without humiliating myself any further. Scotty lays his hand along my pubic bone.

"Take a deep breath."

"What are you doing?"

"Staring at a brat. Do as you're told." What is he doing? I take a deep breath because, at this point, I don't think things could get any worse. He pushes down as I inhale, and I'm fucking dead. A long, loud ripple pierces the air. I close my eyes, grab a pillow above my head, and bury my face in it, hoping to figuratively suffocate myself.

"Rowyn, are you ready for your bath now?" What? I just did all of…*that*, and he's just going to pretend it didn't happen.

Scotty climbs off the bed and offers me his hand. He must see the concerned look on my face because he smiles at me.

"It shouldn't happen again." Nervously, I rest my hand in his, and he pulls me up from the bed and into his arms without incident. I nuzzle my head into his chest, still trying to hide from the entire situation. He laces a finger under my chin and lifts it, forcing me to look into his eyes.

"What your body just did is natural, and you shouldn't be embarrassed about it. In fact, I'm a little proud of it. Your vagina just told me thank you. It was a job well done. I'll expect that every time I take you from behind from now on. And, of course, any other time you feel so inclined." He releases my chin, and I drop my head into his chest with a groan.

"So that's a normal thing?"

"It can be. Depending on the position, the angle, and the speed. But it's not anything that I care about, and you shouldn't either. We can laugh about it next time together."

I grumble under my breath, "I hope there isn't a next time." Apparently, I didn't say it low enough.

"Oh, I'm sure there will be. And Rowyn, I want you to remember something. Boys may care about things like that, but a real man knows how to treat a woman before and after he gives her pleasure. Now get your ass in that bath."

30

Scotty

You're invited to:
Muffins with Moms
Please join us for a special treat to celebrate You.
Thursday in the Cafeteria.
9AM for girls & 10AM for boys.
Coffee, Milk, and Juice will be provided.

I love my daughter. I love my daughter. I. Love. My. Daughter. The only way I know I can endure this archaic torture is the thought that Hazel and Dellah will be here to rescue me. Why can't they call this Pastries with Parents? Or even better, Smoothies with Someone Special. Anything other than Muffins with MOMS.

Tori has already been struggling at school with the kids teasing her about not having a mom. This drives that fact home even harder.

As I sit in the elementary school's parking lot, impatiently waiting for nine a.m. to arrive, I can see Hazel's passenger van on the other side of the playground. I can't help but laugh at the fact that she needs a small bus to haul around her small circus of people.

All of our elementary school kids are taking a two-week summer art course inside. This was another one of Hazel's bright ideas. Tori begged me to attend when she found out Delilah Jane and Paige were going. I was forewarned that they have the muffins thing with the kids but planned to just skip out on it. Hazel convinced me it would be better for Tori if I came rather than not. I wanted her and Dellah to enjoy this activity with Tori. I know she would still have fun without me there, but you can't tell Hazel no once she's set her mind to something.

Rechecking my watch for the hundredth time, it's finally eight fifty-six. I've been watching women walk in the front door, one after another, bright-eyed and cheery, to have muffins that I'm sure will be dry and bland with their daughters.

I wanted to wait until the last possible moment to go in when I knew the tiny cafeteria would be crowded, and hopefully, I could blend in. Well, as much as a man with a penis can blend into a room filled with estrogen.

"Oh, Mr. Langford. What can I do for you?" I'm pretty sure by the unease on the front desk receptionist's face she knows why I'm here.

"I'm here to join Tori for Muffins with Moms." I hand her my license to sign in and she reluctantly takes it.

"I see." She looks around the room uneasily, probably hoping someone will stop me.

"Tori doesn't have a mother, and you don't do anything special for dads. So here I am, Mr. Mom."

"Yes. Of course, Mr. Langford. We should definitely look

into incorporating more occasions for the children's fathers. I'll be sure to mention that to the principal."

She returns my ID and the little computer prints out my sticker ID tag.

"It's right through those doors and down the hall—"

"I know where the cafeteria is. Thanks." I walk to the interior door and wait to hear the buzzing sound so I can enter the school. Not only have I been here before, but this is the same elementary school I grew up in.

I pause when I approach the cafeteria doors and take a deep breath. I can hear the commotion inside and silently curse Hazel for talking me into this. I hear chatty voices coming down the hall and realize the kids are coming, and I have no other choice but to go inside.

Opening the door just enough to slip inside, I stay to the wall and walk deeper into the room. I scan for Hazel or Dellah and don't see either of them. I know they're here somewhere, and I'd feel a hell of a lot better if I had safety in numbers.

The cafeteria door opens, and the room roars with high-pitched squeals as kids find their mothers. I see Paige come in, and somehow, in the sea of women, she spots Dellah and goes running.

I sigh with relief as I try to make my way towards them. I see Tori pop up in the crowd, and luckily, she sees me without having to call out her name and cause attention to myself.

"Daddy!" Tori jumps into my arms and gives me a big hug around the neck.

"Hey, Little Princess. Long time no see."

"You're so silly, Daddy. You just dropped me off."

"I know, but I missed you so much it feels like I haven't

seen you in forever."

"Did you see Delilah Jane or Paige yet?" She wiggles in my arms, and I put her down.

"I saw Aunt Dellah and Paige." She grabs my hands and starts tugging.

"Let's go see them. Come on Daddy, why are you soooo slow." I laugh as she tugs me along through the crowd of people, seeming to know exactly where she's going.

When we reach Dellah and Paige, she lets go of my hand and practically tackles Paige.

"Hey, Scotty." Dellah's smile is warm, but there's a hint of sadness in her eyes. I know she tried to get Hazel to let me off the hook, but even she's no match for her determined best friend.

"Aunt Dellah, have you seen Delilah Jane?"

"I have, Little Miss. Aunt Hazel is helping with the muffins, so they are just over there by the kitchen." Dellah points in the direction of the kitchen bay doors, and I see Hazel.

"Let's go, Daddy!" She grabs my hand again, and I swear the room parts to let us through. When we reach them, she gives DJ a big hug and then turns to Hazel, doing the same. Her head moves back and forth, looking for something, and I watch her smiling face fall.

"Aunt Hazel, where's Wynnie?" Wynnie? Why is she asking for Wynnie?

"Um…" Hazel looks as confused as I feel.

"She's at her apartment working." Dellah and Paige walk up behind me, and Tori's face falls even further at Dellah's answer.

"But…buuuuut…" Huge alligator tears start pouring down her face as she whines.

"Tori, what's—"

"No! Where's Wynnie? Why isn't Wynnie here?"

"Little Princess, Wynnie is working."

"No." She drops to the floor at my feet and starts hysterically crying. Tori is throwing a full-blown tantrum, crying
and yelling. She isn't usually the type of child who throws
tantrums, and this is very out of character for her. "I want
Wynnie. I want to share a muffin with Wynnie."

Dellah gives me a look that tells me she knows more than
I'd like her to know. Hazel looks completely confused as
to what's going on. At least she's still in the dark about my
relationship with Wynnie. I can't say the same about Tori,
judging by the way she's acting.

"Tori, I need you to get up. Paige and DJ are here and Aunt
Hazel and Aunt Dellah. They all want to share muffins with
you."

"I. Want. Wynnie." She's flailing her feet on the floor, and
the moms and kids around us are starting to stare.

"Do you want me to call her?" Dellah asks in a whisper so
only I can hear. "She isn't busy, and it wouldn't take her long
to get here." My eyes drift to Hazel as I consider Dellah's
offer. What will Hazel think if Wynnie shows up for Tori?
As if reading my mind, Dellah eases my conscience.

"Hazel knows how much Tori and Wynnie love each other.
She wouldn't think it's odd." I nod.

"Please. And thank you." Dellah squeezes my forearm and
leans down to whisper something in Tori's ear. I'm shocked
she can hear anything over the fit she's throwing, but she
almost instantly calms down. Dellah smiles at me and walks
to a corner of the room, pulling out her phone to call Wynnie.

"What's going on?" Hazel's confusion has changed into

concern. Tori rises from the floor and hugs Hazel's legs while stuttering a sigh.

"You're the bestest Mommy, Aunt Hazel." Tori's voice cracks as she gets over her crying. Hazel looks between Tori and me and smooths her hand down her hair, attempting to further calm her.

Hazel looks at me with confusion in her eyes. All I can do is shrug and play dumb.

"She's a little attached to your daughter. I guess she expected her to be here with us." She nods in understanding, and I'm so grateful she doesn't ask any more questions.

Dellah returns and crouches next to Tori.

"Wynnie will be here in less than ten minutes, and she's so excited to see you. Why don't we all find a seat together and wait for her? What kind of muffin do you think she will like?"

"I'll take them to pick out muffins if you two want to go find us a seat for...seven, I suppose." Thank goodness they broke this muffin thing into two parts. Girls first and then boys, or Dean and Alex would have witnessed all of this craziness.

Dellah and I agree, and Hazel walks to the end of the line while Dellah and I walk in search of a table for us all.

"What's going on, Scotty? Did you know she was expecting Wynnie?"

"I had no idea. I don't think Tori even mentioned it to her. I know I didn't. I was too worried about coming here myself. I wouldn't have even thought to ask." We stop at a table with enough seating for everyone and Dellah turns to me.

"Scotty—"

"How much do you know, Dellah?" I close my eyes and brace myself for her answer, or criticism, or I don't know what. All I know is whatever she says is about to change things.

"I know everything but the *finer* details. And before you freak out..." My eyes pop open, and she must see the instant panic on my face. She looks to see where Hazel and the girls are before continuing. "I approve, Scotty. You'd already know if I didn't. I made a promise to my niece before she was even born that I would always protect her. And I made a promise to you one drunken night to keep all of your secrets." She smiles at me, and I know she's being genuine.

"Thank you, Dellah."

"Don't thank me yet. You have an issue on your hands. With the way Tori just reacted, I'm not sure how long you two will be able to keep things a secret. I assume that's what you're trying to do?"

"I'm not ashamed of being with her or for the feelings I have for her. I'm fucking terrified of Mac and Phoenix. And Hazel, honestly." She tilts her head to the side.

"Not Jude? Interesting."

"Jude is the level-headed one, like you. I also think he sees more than the average person does. I have a feeling he knows more than he's letting on. Or at least might have an inkling."

A high-pitched shriek pierces the already loud room, and I whip my head in the direction of the sound, knowing it's Tori.

"Yeah, you definitely have a problem." I can't agree more with Dellah as Tori races across the room, having seen Wynnie enter the cafeteria. She jumps into her arms and clings to Wynnie's neck, much the same as she did when she first saw me. My heart melts at the sight of them. I fucking love those girls. *Wow.* Okay, that's a realization that I can't unpack right now.

"You better be sure?" Dellah places a hand on my shoulder.

"What?"

"If you love her, you better be sure because there's a lot of heart right there to break if you aren't." Did I...?

"Did I say that out loud?"

"You did, and I see it. Just be careful. I love her, too. Both of them. And you too, when you make me your Scotty Special blue drinks." I stand in awe for a moment and watch as they approach Hazel, and Wynnie says hi to her mother and sister.

Fuck. Wynnie's mother and sister. Her sister who's the same age as my daughter, and her mother who's only a few years older than me.

"Are you okay? A moment ago, you had hearts in your eyes, and now you look like someone ran over your puppy." Do I really look that bad? Shit.

"Dellah, am I doing the right thing? Do you honestly approve? I'm fifteen years older than her. I'm a single dad, and I run a bar. Doesn't she deserve better than that?"

"Scotty. First, stop spiraling. Sit." We sit on the bench, and she turns to me. "I already told you I approve. And you don't just *run* a bar; you own it. And you're the best fucking single dad I know." She looks over at Wynnie, who's gushing at Tori. My little girl's face is smiling so bright. "Look at them. You brought Wynnie into Tori's life, and they are thriving together. You need to decide if you can handle Mac and Phoenix because when they find out, and they will, it won't be pretty. That's probably something the two of you should discuss. But if you really love her, and I believe you do, don't let others' opinions matter. You're both good for each other, and I know you wouldn't intentionally hurt her."

"You're awfully insightful for nine a.m."

"Elliot keeps me on my toes." We laugh, and I feel a little lighter. Wynnie and I, yet again, need to have another discussion. It feels like we do a lot of talking…and fucking… and love making.

31

Wynnie

The apartment renovation is coming along wonderfully. It's been helpful spending some nights at Scotty's house because I've been able to work on my bedroom without feeling like I'm sleeping in chaos.

Falling asleep after a series of orgasms and lovemaking is also massively helpful. Tori seems to get more and more excited every morning that she sees me there. Although, it might be the pancakes that Scotty always makes when I'm over. It's how she knows I'm there before she sees me.

I've tried successfully and unsuccessfully to wake up before Scotty so I can make us breakfast, but no matter who wakes up first, pancakes are eaten.

This morning, she was extra excited for something at art camp and barely ate. She told me she wanted to save room in her tummy for the special event at school.

She excitedly announced to me that she picked out her dress all by herself because she knew it's my favorite colors. Her dress is rainbow stripes because she knows I love rainbows.

I let Scotty sleep in this morning, but I had a few errands to run, so when he joined us for breakfast, I was already in a hurry and quickly finished my coffee. He kissed me while we hid inside the pantry before I went home.

As I sit on my couch drinking my third cup of coffee for the day, surfing the internet for the perfect wall tapestry to hang up, my phone rings on the kitchen counter. I silently curse myself for leaving it so far away and set my laptop on the couch to head for the kitchen.

"Hey, Aunt Dellah. Everything alright? You should be ankle-deep in muffins right now."

"What have you done, Wynnie?"

"Um. Nothing?" What am I being accused of?

"Your little girl is here throwing an absolute meltdown tantrum in the middle of the cafeteria because she expected you here to eat muffins with her." *My* little girl?

"Wait. DJ?"

"Your sister is perfectly fine. Your mom is here. Your *other* little girl."

"Shit. What's wrong with Tori?"

"Woman, get in your car and get your ass here. Tori thought you were coming to Muffins with Moms. She's on the floor screaming because you aren't here. Scotty is at his wit's end."

"Okay. Okay. I'm coming. I had no idea. I would have been there in a heartbeat. Tori didn't say anything this morning—oooh." I mentally chastise myself. The dress. It makes sense now. I feel like such an idiot.

"I'll tell her you're on your way. Hopefully, it will calm her down. She's making a big scene. Hurry."

My heart breaks for Tori as I carefully run down the stairs and into my car. Luckily we aren't far from the school.

I'm dancing back and forth on my feet as it feels like the receptionist takes her sweet time to print out my sticker ID. When I finally have it I race down the hall and into the cafeteria. It only takes a moment for Tori to spot me, but when she does, she squeals and comes running.

Knowing her as well as I do, I brace myself and crouch down so she can easily jump into my arms. The rainbow blur does just that, and I cling to her, whispering apologies in her ear when she buries her face into my neck.

"I didn't know, Sunshine. Why didn't you say anything this morning? I didn't mean to make you upset. You know I would have been here if I knew. I'm so sorry, sweet girl."

She pulls away, and her face is pure joy.

"You're here. I knew you'd come. I got you a chocolate chip muffin just how we like our pancakes." *We. Our.* I almost crushed her poor little heart. Why didn't Scotty say anything to me? It's muffins with moms. She knows how I like my pancakes because of all the time I've been spending at her house. Are we confusing her?

I look around the room, knowing that my mom and Aunt Dellah are here somewhere, and obviously Scotty. Tori sees me looking and points toward a table, and I see Scotty and Aunt Dellah talking. He looks nervous.

"Shall we go eat?" Her smile widens as she nods her head. I carry her over to the table and join the group. There's a slight hint of interest in my mom's eyes, and I wonder if a reason was given as to why Tori insisted I be here.

This is the first interaction we've all had together since Scotty and I became...what? We're obviously dating, right? It's been over a month, and I'm at his house at least three nights a week. Oh god. Are we even exclusive? We haven't had that kind of talk.

"Hey, Pinky. Thank you so much for coming. I had no idea she thought you would be here." Scotty startles me out of my intrusive thoughts.

After we finished our muffins, the three girls went off to color a special picture at the coloring table, and my mom went back into the kitchen, helping set up for the next round of muffins with the boys.

"It's alright. I would have been here if I had known. Tori told me about her special dress this morning and how she picked it because rainbows are my favorite. I didn't even think about it. I feel terrible." A hand appears on both our shoulders.

"You two need to figure your shit out because that little girl is more than attached." Aunt Dellah points her finger at us like we're petulant children. "She already loved you as her nanny, but it's obvious she can tell something more is going on with you two for her to act the way she did."

"I know." Scotty and I both say in unison.

"You can't hide forever." Aunt Dellah has a point. As much as I'd love to continue to live in our bubble, it's not feasible.

"Do you think she knows?" I look at Scotty, wondering what he thinks.

"She hasn't said anything to me. You've been spending more time at the house. All the sleepovers and breakfasts."

Aunt Dellah hums. "You know, little kids are more perceptive than you think. Trust me. I'm speaking from experience." Her face momentarily falls, and I know she's remembering when Elliot, Finn, and Paige first came to live with her and she was in the middle of a big fight with Uncle Collin.

222

"We need to sit down and talk with her." Scotty's hand twitches like he wants to reach over and take mine.

"Yeah. You two are so obvious. The only reason no one has noticed yet is because you haven't left your little bubble. Please be careful."

A bell rings, signaling the event is over, and the girls run back to us with their pictures. Tori happily presents me with a picture full of people.

"It's beautiful. Will you tell me who everyone is?"

"Sure. This is Aunt Hazel and Delilah Jane." She points at two people. One is supposed to be my mom with hair made from red and brown crayons, standing next to a smaller figure with dark brown hair and big green eyes.

"This is Aunt Dellah and Paige." The taller figure has yellow hair and blue eyes, and the smaller one has black wavy hair and blue eyes.

She points to the final three figures. "This is Daddy." He's the tallest person on the page with black hair and brown eyes. I see a tiny spot of gray where she tried to color his heterochromia. "Here's me." The small figure has gray eyes, a colorful dress, and dark brown hair. "And this is you." She proudly points to a figure standing close to the representation of Scotty. My hair is brown, and there are several different swirls of blue for my eyes. It looks like she was trying to find the perfect color. "Do you like it?"

I stare at the picture and take a moment to compose myself. I can feel the tingling in my eyes as tears try to make their way to the front.

"It's beautiful, Sunshine. Can I take it home and hang it on my refrigerator?" Her face lights up, and she bounces as she nods her head.

"Or you can hang it on my refrigermator. You'd probly get to see it more."

Tori's teacher calls her class to the door and I'm glad I don't have to dive any further into her comment. She gives everyone hugs before running off to get in line.

"That was a close one." Scotty gives me a knowing smile.

"Yeah. Do you need to get back to work, or would you like to grab a coffee?" I look around for my mom, who's still in the kitchen.

"Coffee sounds great."

Pulling into the driveway behind Scotty, I wonder where this conversation will go. A lot went on in the cafeteria less than an hour ago. No matter what happens between Scotty and me, Tori needs to be our number one priority.

Aunt Dellah called her *my* girl, and while I've always regarded Tori as someone special in my life, I feel a fierce protectiveness that goes beyond nanny and charge. I'm not sure how to put into words what's changed, but I can feel it.

Scotty walks up to my car door and opens it for me. It's a sweet gesture that he does all the time. He opens doors, pulls out chairs, and is always a gentleman. Even the simple act of knowing how I like my coffee seems more significant.

"Thanks for coming over."

"Of course. No need to be so formal." I step out, and he closes the door behind me, caging me against my car.

"Believe me, I want to be anything but formal with you, but I think we have some things to discuss first." His thumb caresses my cheek, and his lips brush my forehead before he

224

takes my hand and leads us inside.

I sit at the counter and watch as he expertly prepares our coffees, and we exist in companionable silence.

"I never got to tell you why I keep hazelnut creamer in my fridge, did I?" Scotty slides a perfectly made coffee in front of me, and I wrap my hands around the warmth.

"I don't think you did." He turns and grabs his cup, taking a sip of his black coffee.

"You're everywhere, Pinky. You've been everywhere for a while. The creamer in the refrigerator, the cereal in my pantry, it's all because of you. Little pieces of your personality and your likes have made their way into our lives."

"Like the shampoo?"

"Like the conditioner. You left the shampoo." I guess I did.

"I knew I couldn't have you, but seeing you smile from something I did made me feel good. Even if you didn't realize why I had done it."

"Scotty, that's—"

"Weird, creepy, stalkerish. I know."

"It's sweet and thoughtful."

I look at him tenderly and lift my coffee to my lips. When I look at the mug, my heart warms. On the ceramic is a cartoon sunshine with a big smile. Written in rainbow text are the words "You Are My Sunshine."

"She picked it out for you. Don't tell her you saw it before she has a chance to show you. She'll be upset."

"I wouldn't dream of upsetting her." Scotty reaches over the counter and grabs my hand.

"I know. And that's why we're here having this conversation. Today was…God, Wynnie. I've never felt so inferior as a parent. No, as a single parent. A single Dad." Squeezing his

225

hand for reassurance, I can't imagine how he's feeling.

"You're an amazing father."

"But she wanted you. I wasn't enough for her."

"Scotty, you know I'd never step on your toes. I didn't do anything to encourage her this morning." He releases my hand and rounds the counter to come to me. My chair spins, and he captures my legs between his, standing over me.

"Don't stop what you're doing. She loves you. She needs you." He hangs his head. "I just didn't realize how much until this morning." I reach up and cup his face so he looks at me.

"Scotty, I can see the concern in your eyes. I'm all in with her in whatever capacity you'll allow me to be."

"And me? What about me?" I drop my hands, and his face falls.

"No, no. It's not like that." I rush out my words so he doesn't think any negative thoughts. "There are still a lot of obstacles between us. We need to figure out *us* and decide what the next step is." He leans forward and rests his forehead on mine.

"Wynnie, that's something you need to figure out for yourself. I'm a grown man with a bar and a baby. You're fresh out of college with the entire world in front of you. I don't want to tie you down." I sit back on the stool, a little shocked and hurt by his statement.

"Have I given you the impression that I don't want to be here? Scotty, I'm not trying to play house with you. I love Tori. Fuck, I love that little girl so much. And I love making her pancakes in the morning or watching her eat the ones you've made for her. I love taking her to the park. I love that Tori wanted me there this morning so bad that she threw a colossal tantrum until she knew I was coming. I. Love. Her."

"Wynnie, she's a package deal. I think that's the biggest issue here. I have no doubt about the love you have for my daughter. I never have. But it's not just her in this relationship. She comes with a pretty sexy as fuck dad." He smirks at me, easing some of the tension slowly rising in the room.

"I'm pretty partial to the package." I raise my knee and brush along the inside of his thigh.

"Talk first. Play later, brat." I huff and lower my leg.

"Scotty, I know I'm young compared to you. Believe me, that thought crosses my mind on a regular basis. But I want this. My mom has always told me I'm an old soul. I never needed the partying scene in college. I'm happy to stay in and watch movies on the couch with good company. Elliot picks on me all the time for it. I want to be with you. I think it's…more than just puppy love." Okay, I just said that. It wasn't exactly a confession of love, but it wasn't *not* one either.

"I think it's more than just puppy love for me, too, Pinky." Wait, he just *not* not confessed too. "We need to figure out how to tell your parents about us, though. All of them. Some worry me more than others."

"So, are you like my boyfriend now? Are we going steady?" I giggle as I fiddle with the collar of his shirt.

He nips at my ear and growls. "There's nothing about me that's a boy. Do you need to be reminded?"

"Yes. No. Maybe. Gah! What's the right answer to that?" He huffs a laugh in my ear. "Before we go any further, we need to settle one more thing. We need to tell Tori first." He pulls away from me squinting his eyes.

"As in first, right now? Or first, before we tell anyone else?

Because I can go to the school right now and let her know, and I'm sure she'll be thrilled."

Smacking his chest, I give him my best "you're being ridiculous" look.

"I just want to make sure I know what I need to do in order to get you in my bed right now. I'm not passing up this opportunity when I have you alone with me and you don't have to be quiet."

"Are you sure there's nothing about you that's boyish? You have the hormones of a horny teenager." Scotty sucks on my neck, making me moan.

"You make me horny like a teenager. Just you. And I've never heard you complain."

"Take me to bed, manchild." My ass is suddenly in the air, and the world is upside down.

"I prefer caveman to manchild. Me take my woman to bed." Like a goofball, he beats on his chest.

I know we have some scary conversations coming up, but I want to live in our bubble for a little longer.

32

Scotty

Wynnie's skin is damp under mine. A thin layer of sweat glosses over her chest after the orgasm I just gave her.

I edged her until she was begging. Until my cock was so hard I thought I would combust before she did. I watch as her swollen cunt parts for my cock to make entrance. She glistens with come from her orgasm, and I slide right in without any resistance.

She's tight. She's always tight. The walls of her pussy squeeze me as little aftershocks from her orgasm go off around my cock.

"Scotty?" I hear knocking. "Earth to Scotty. Hey." I'm brought back into the present when Dellah grabs my arm. "You really need to cut that out. You should be glad it was me that found you lost in your sex-crazed mind, and eww... I don't want to think of you having sex with my niece. She's still a twelve year old girl sitting at my kitchen counter drawing pictures of cartoon girls wearing cat ears and tails."

"Pinky." I remember those days fondly.

"Yep, and eww, get that image out of your head because she's not twelve. She's about to be twenty-three. You're more than welcome to have sex with my twenty-three year old niece. Oh my god. I need to stop and quit while I'm ahead. Wynnie's surprise party. That's what we're here for, remember?" I laugh at her word vomit.

"Are you reminding me or yourself of that fact?"

"Ugh. Less sex talk, more birthday talk."

"Dellah, you're the only one here talking about sex."

"Oh, whose sex life are we talking about?" *Fuck.* Hazel. How did we not hear her? Dellah suddenly looks like a deer in headlights. She spins around to Hazel with a huge, fake grin.

"Hey, Bestie, you sneaky Bitch. Where did you come from?" She points behind her to a giant cluster of rainbow-colored balloons.

"Did you not hear the bell when I came in?"

"Nope. Sure didn't. Let me help you with that." Dellah runs away like a scared dog with its tail between its legs. Hazel gives me a confused look and I shrug.

"You know Dellah." I let that statement hang in the air. Hazel finally rolls her eyes and walks off after her.

Wynnie's birthday is this week, and the girls asked if they could throw her a surprise party at the bar like they did for Dellah. Of course, I said yes, but I'd be lying if I said I wasn't nervous. We haven't been around her dads together since we started our relationship.

The state that Dellah just found me in, my mind wandering back to moments alone with Wynnie, seems to happen more often. My staff knows about Wynnie, but I trust them with my secrets.

The other day, Aimee found me frozen in motion while cleaning a glass behind the bar. I was remembering Wynnie on her knees in the shower that morning and how beautiful she looked while sucking my cock deep down her throat.

My staff all picks on me, and I couldn't care less. But Dellah is right. I need to get my head on straight for tonight. Mac may be showing up as Wynnie's Dad, but he's always in cop mode in the background.

"Elliot, are you sure she doesn't know?" Hazel has done her best to make this a surprise for Wynnie. He's been her spy in the background.

Wynnie thinks she's watching Tori tonight like any other night. My job is to call her around noon and tell her Mrs. Peterson asked if Tori could spend the night to play with her granddaughter and to let her know she can have the night off.

Dellah's part is to convince her to take advantage of the evening off. She's going to take Wynnie birthday shopping and end up at the bar for drinks around eight tonight.

I hate having to lie to her, even for something as simple as a surprise party. But I know she's going to love the party, after hating the surprise part.

At noon, I do my part and call Wynnie. We make plans for her to come over tonight since I'll be kid-free, and I feel guilty because I'm not sure if we'll be able to see each other. Tori won't actually be spending the night away and that might be hard with everyone here and how much they convince her to drink since I've been required to have my Scotty Special fishbowls ready.

The bar is beautifully decorated with balloons and streamers of every color. It looks more like a party for Tori's age

231

than an almost twenty-three year old but that's what I love most about Wynnie. She's unashamedly her, colors and all.

I don't think I can hold that word back anymore. I love her. I want to tell her but don't know if now is the right time. I think we need to tell her parents first. I would hope that Tori would give me that respect when she's older.

Wynnie's friends and family start to trickle in around seven p.m., and I hang out behind the bar serving all of them. Around seven-thirty, Mrs. Peterson drops off Tori, dressed again in her favorite rainbow dress just for Wynnie. I hand her off to Hazel to keep an eye out for me.

"Have we heard from Dellah?" Hazel smiles at me as we watch Tori runoff to find Delilah Jane.

"She just texted me. They should be right on time." Of course, I already know this because Wynnie has been texting me all afternoon. She's been sending me pictures of the dresses Dellah has been making her try on, and each one is more stunning on her than the last. She warned me that Dellah convinced her to come, so she didn't show me the final dress she's picked out.

I can't wait to see her tonight. Keeping this secret has been torture. I know how much she hates surprises, but she loves her family and will love them for this.

"Hey, Scotty. Thanks for letting my girl use your truck the other week. It was nice of you." Mac walks up to Hazel and puts his arm around her shoulder, pulling her in for a quick kiss.

"Oh. It was no trouble. Did Wynnie tell you how she pranked me?"

"No, but I'm interested to hear." I tell them about the gas debacle she tried to pull on me and Mac roars with laughter.

232

"I see I've taught her well. She knows damn well that those trucks take diesel. Have the two of you gone out riding yet? I know she has her bike at her apartment now."

"We've taken a few short rides. We kind of work on opposite schedules." I smile, and he laughs back in return.

"Yeah, I guess you do when she's your nanny. You and I should go riding together soon. It's been a while."

"We definitely should. You want a beer?" Riding with Mac is always a good time. Riding with Wynnie's father sounds terrifying.

"Yeah, I'll take one. Wine, Alice?"

"Sure. If that's okay with you, Scotty? I know I'm helping watch Tori."

"Of course. We're all watching her and all the other kids. She can't get into too much trouble with all eyes on her. And you know, once Wynnie gets here, she probably won't leave her side." Hazel's eyes twitch at my last statement, and I think maybe I've gone too far. Mother's always see more than they let on. Does she know? Is she suspicious?

Hazel's cell phone dings at the same time I feel mine vibrate in my back pocket.

"They'll be here in five minutes. Everyone get ready." I'm sure my text is from Wynnie saying the same.

Hazel walks around to make sure everyone knows she's almost here, and I see Tori pop up on the other side of the counter in front of me.

"Hey, Little Princess. Are you ready to surprise Wynnie?" She frowns.

"She doesn't like loud shouting like me." I walk around the counter and scoop her up.

"I know, but this is a fun surprise, and hopefully, she won't

233

be too upset. Want me to hold your ears when she comes in?" Her nose scrunches in deep thought.

"No. I want to be brave like Wynnie. I can be a big girl. Did you bring my present?" Brave like Wynnie. They are both so fucking brave.

"I did. It's in the office. I wanted it to be safe."

A hush falls over the crowd, and I know they must be here.

"Alright, my brave Little Princess. Get ready. She's here." Her face lights up with excitement, and she wiggles for me to put her down.

The bell chimes above the door in the silent bar, and there's a moment of pause before a loud "SURPRISE" rings through the room.

Wynnie screams. Then curses. Then, to add insult to injury, Tori slams into her legs, knocking her back into Dellah.

"Sunshine. Did you do this?" Wynnie clutches onto my daughter, and the sight almost brings a tear to my eyes.

"Happy Birthday, Wynnie. Do you like all of the rainbow stuff? I told your mommy rainbows were your favorite and you should have your favorites on your birthday party day. Do you love it?"

"Not as much as I love you, Sunshine. But it's all perfect. Thank you for making sure I had all of my favorite colors." Everyone starts to crowd around Wynnie, wishing her a happy birthday. I walk back behind the bar, and Kristina and Aimee stare at me.

"What?"

"It's bad," Aimee says to Kristina.

"So fucking bad. He's a goner." Kristina shakes her head and smiles.

"You're both fired." I roll my eyes at them and grab a clean glass rack to empty and stack.

I try not to pay attention to the sexy as sin brunette with blue eyes in a devilishly red dress that hugs her every curve, with matching strappy red heels. No surprise, I'm failing miserably. Thank fuck she isn't wearing lipstick because the second I get a chance, I'm kissing those lips. It takes her a while to make her way to the bar, but when she does, she's wearing a big smile.

"You aren't my favorite right now. How could you let me walk into this?" I finish making her fishbowl before she asks for one and slide it across the bar top to her. I lean in close enough for her to hear me but leave enough distance so it doesn't look inappropriate.

"You're always my favorite, Pinky, but seeing you in this fuck-me dress makes me want to start calling you Red. Even if it isn't tonight, I *will* see this dress on my bedroom floor." She frowns.

"Not tonight?"

"We'll see. Tori isn't really spending the night with Mrs. Peterson. That was part of the ploy to get you here."

"Oh." Her frown deepens.

"Pinky, don't pout. If we can make it happen with all of these prying eyes around, we will. God, you look so fucking sexy. Red is your color. I'm buying you a drawer full of red lingerie, and you're never allowed to wear anything else."

"I like the sound of that." Her eyes sparkle with mischief.

"Hey, birthday girl. You're hard to get alone." Phoenix walks up, bursting our bubble, but it's probably for the best.

"Hey Dad P." Dad. Phoenix isn't just my best friend anymore. He's the Dad of the girl I love, and he doesn't know it yet.

235

"Hey, Scotty. Can I get a beer? I see you're already taking care of my girl."

"What?" *Oh fuck. What?* My head snaps up to Phoenix's, and I choke on air.

"Shit, you okay?" I nod and compose myself. "I see Wynnie has her drink already. Make sure it ends up on our tab." *Thank fuck.* Wynnie looks relieved as well.

"Don't worry. The birthday girl is drinking on the house. I wouldn't dream of charging her tonight." Or any night, for that matter. Wynnie has a standing open tab, and my staff knows it.

Wynnie mingles with her friends and family. It's fascinating to watch. She's in a weird in-between age where she's the oldest of all the kids but younger than all the parents. You wouldn't know it, though, with how seamlessly she blends with whoever is around. She's goofy and playful or serious and conversational.

I continue to catch her eyes roaming in my direction, which doesn't bode well for me because it means I'm looking at her just as much.

"You're drooling," Kristina whispers in my ear as she walks past me and laughs. She's probably right, and I can't even be mad about it.

I see Wynnie excuse herself and head toward the hallway where the bathrooms are.

"Kristina, I'll be right back." She replies with a sarcastic "uh huh," and I walk in Wynnie's direction, knowing I can cut her off before she gets there.

33

Wynnie

As I walk down the hallway toward the bathroom, I'm relieved to have a few moments of peace. I've been overwhelmed since I got here.

I reach out for the handle to open the bathroom door, and I'm pulled into the bar office directly behind me. The door closes, and I find my back up against it, tattooed forearms caging me in.

"You need to stop that." Scotty stares into my eyes. His hand comes down, and fingers caress my cheeks.

"Stop what?"

"Every time you look at me, your face turns the most beautiful shade of pink. I'm already having enough trouble on a daily basis not thinking about your legs wrapped around my head, and then you show up looking like,"—his eyes roam up and down my body—"Fuck like *this*. Are you intentionally trying to torture me?"

"I…I'm not…" I'm not what? I knew exactly what this dress would do to him, and so did Aunt Dellah when she told me this was the one.

"Your lust is written all over your face, Pinky. My staff has been picking on me all night because I can't take my goddamn eyes off of you. Let me have you. Right here, right now."

"Here?" In his office, in the middle of my surprise party?

"I'll make it quick. I'm so fucking turned on you could probably look at me and make me come. I bet you're wet for me. If I touch your cunt right now, will you be dripping for me?" His voice is gravelly with his lust. I swallow hard and take a deep breath. His sweet, woodsy scent engulfs me. Scotty's nose nuzzles the shell of my ear.

"Tell me, Rowyn. Are you wet for me? Are you going to let me take you on the couch with all of your friends and family right on the other side of the door? I want you to sit on my cock and ride me hard and fast. All you have to do is slide this tiny dress up your creamy thighs and sit." His hand plays with the hem on the bottom of my dress.

"Fuck it." I jump, and he catches the back of my thighs with a chuckle. He walks us backward until I feel him bump the couch. Carefully, we get into a seated position, and he slides me to the middle of his lap to undo his pants. I shimmy my hips to pull my dress to my waist.

"Are you fucking kidding me?" He freezes when he sees my bare pussy sitting on his lap. "You've been fucking commando this whole time?" I give him a mischievous smile. His hands become frantic, and he pulls his pants and boxers down at the same time. His hard cock bounces off his abs, and there's already pre-cum beading at his tip. "You really are trying to fucking torture me tonight. Lift your ass right now and sit on my dick."

I happily comply and lift myself, grabbing his cock and aiming it at my entrance. When I sit and he slides inside me,

238

we both moan in relief.

"Hard and fast, Pinky. We need to get the birthday girl back out there. Play with your clit, and I'll control the pace."

"Hard and fast. Got it." I flick my clit between us and use his movement to determine the speed of my fingers. He's right. I'll be missed if I'm gone for too long.

Scotty's hands dig into my hips, and he thrusts me up and down on his cock. I brace my free hand on the couch beside his head, and he kisses my forearm.

"You're so fucking beautiful. You ride my cock like a fucking goddess. I want you to come all over my cock. I want to think about this for the rest of the night. My come dripping from your bare pussy. You're a naughty fucking girl."

His words are my undoing. I bury my face in his neck as my breathing becomes labored.

"Scotty, I'm so close."

"Me too, Pinky. Milk my fucking cock with your orgasm. Give it to me."

"Fuck. Fuck. Oh god, yes." His shirt muffles some of my sounds. As my orgasm hits its peak, I bite down on his shoulder to contain as much of my moans as I can.

He grunts at the pain from my bite, but it quickly turns into his pleasure when he comes inside me. His groans are long and deep as he tries to contain his noise.

"God fucking dammit, Rowyn. What are you doing to me? I definitely more than puppy love you." I giggle at him, knowing what he means because I feel the same. But those are hard words to say out loud.

"I more than puppy love you, too." We kiss a sweet, tender, loving kiss that expresses beyond words how we truly feel.

"Let's get you cleaned up in the bathroom." He points to a door attached to his office, and I breathe a sigh of relief that I don't have to use the public restroom.

We clean up and make ourselves look presentable again. As we're about to head back to the party, there's a knock on the door, and it opens. To my shock, Jude walks in.

"Hey, there you are. We've been looking for you." I look over my shoulder at Scotty, who looks calm and relaxed.

"Hey, Dad J. Sorry we were just—"

"Coming to get Tori's special present for Wynnie, I know all the little kids are getting tired. I saw her walking back this way and remembered I had put the present in my office." He makes a show of looking around and grabs an envelope off the top of a filing cabinet. "Ah, here it is, Wynnie." He hands it to me and I give him a tight smile.

"Oh, thanks."

Jude doesn't look like he's buying it. I want to tell him. I want to tell someone. Jude seems like the right *someone* to start with when it comes to my family. But I chicken out, and Jude doesn't push it. There's an awkward pause before Scotty speaks again.

"Let's get the birthday girl back to the party."

As the three of us walk into the crowded bar, a few heads turn our way. Aunt Dellah has a shit-eating grin and gives me a thumbs up. She's clearly proud of herself that the dress she picked did the job she wanted it to do. But her face quickly falls when she sees Jude step out from behind me. Her eyes widen and she turns her back away from us.

Bitch. I'm gonna get her later. She owes me tacos and margaritas.

"Hey, kiddo. Where have you been." I hold up my alibi to

my mom, wondering if it's actually what Scotty said it was.

"Tori's present to me was in Scotty's office. We went and got it."

"Awe. That's adorable. All of the littles are getting grumpy, so we need to head out. You look gorgeous. Are you still coming for dinner on Sunday for your birthday? Jude said he'd cook you anything you'd like."

"I wouldn't miss it for the world." Just then, Tori comes slamming into my legs. This time, it's from exhaustion, not excitement.

"Daddy gave it to you. Did you open it without me?" Her brows scrunch together as she assesses the envelope in my hand but perks up when she sees it's still closed. This also confirms the lie isn't actually a lie. There was a reason for being in Scotty's office.

"I would never open it without you. Should I do it now or wait until my actual birthday? It's on Tuesday, which is four days away." I hold up four fingers, and she counts each one a few times before coming to a conclusion. She takes the envelope from my hand and points it in Scotty's direction.

"Take this back, Daddy. We can give it to her again in four days. She holds up four fingers and yawns.

"Hey Scotty, is Mrs. Peterson coming back for Tori?" My mom brushes a hand over one of Tori's pigtails.

"No, she's gonna hang out here until I'm done."

"Let us take her for you." Phoenix walks up behind Hazel and puts an arm around Jude's shoulder and one around my mom's waist.

"Phoenix, you don't have to do that. It's not her first rodeo."

"It's not a problem at all." Jude kisses Phoenix on the cheek. "They're all going to be asleep before we even get home. We have clothes she can borrow. Sleep in and come get her when you're up. No rush." Jude looks at me and winks. What the hell was that about?

"You're sure?" Scotty crouches in front of Tori, and I can see his eyes trying not to wander up my legs.

"Little Princess, do you want to spend the night at Aunt Hazel's house?" He knows as well as I do that Tori will automatically say yes. She looks up at me.

"Can Wynnie come too?" *Oh shit.*

"Tori, Wynnie has been drinking adult drinks and probably wants to sleep in her own bed tonight. But I bet she would love to schedule a sleepover with you and DJ sometime soon." Scotty took the words right out of my mouth.

"Daddy's right, but you should go hang out with DJ and Aunt Hazel if you want to." Tori smiles and throws her arms around Scotty's neck and my leg, hugging us both.

"I love you, Daddy. I love you, Wynnie. I can't wait to have pancakes with you again for breakfast soon." We have to get his kid out of here before she starts spilling secrets.

"I love you too, Sunshine. I love having pancakes with you any time of the day." Please don't correct me. Please don't correct me.

Scotty picks her up to distract her from her current conversation and kisses her on the cheek.

"You be good for everyone, okay?" She wraps her arms around his neck.

"I'm always good, Daddy." He puts her down and she takes Jude's hand, clearly on a mission to look for Delilah Jane. I see my dad standing near the doorway with DJ asleep in his arms. He blows me a kiss, and I smile back and mouth, "Love you."

Without the pressure of my parents' watchful eyes, the rest of the evening goes by smoothly. I avoid Aunt Dellah, but she keeps throwing me goofy smiles every time our eyes meet. I think she's had at least two fish bowls.

"You can't avoid her forever."

"Uncle Collin. I feel like I haven't seen you in forever." I give him a quick hug and smile.

"The feeling's mutual." I can feel my cheeks heat, and my eyes involuntarily drift to Scotty, who's behind the bar serving drinks.

"You know I know, right? Dellah tells me almost everything." While I'm not surprised, it's still scary that more and more people seem to know. I need to tell my parents soon.

"And? Do you have any thoughts? Comments, questions, or concerns?" He bumps my shoulder and laughs.

"Does he treat you well?"

"So well."

"Are you happy?"

"Ridiculously."

"Then what more could I have to say?" He shrugs.

"You could have a lot to say, Uncle Collin. A lecture for our age gap. He's a single dad. I have my entire life ahead of me."

"Eh."

"Eh? Really?"

"Really. Who cares about that stuff? That man is head over heels for you. And…"

"And?"

"And he's really good friends with Mac and Phoenix and is taking a risk with you every day and doing it with a smile. He's partly crazy and fully in love." Love?

"Don't look at me like *I'm* crazy. I met Aunt Dellah while

243

she was bartending. Well, actually, I almost ran her over in the parking lot of the bar she was working at, but I know love when I see it. She tried to deny me, but love won over fear."

"I know we need to tell them. Jude almost caught us tonight, but he's not the one that I'm most worried about. I have a feeling my mom will be okay. Eventually. But Mac. *And Phoenix.* They went to high school together." Uncle Collin puts his arm around my shoulders.

"I don't have any advice about them other than they love you, and he loves you. It's obvious. I know Scotty will be good to you." My straw slurps as I reach the bottom of my second fishbowl.

"Thank you, Uncle Collin."

"Viiiiiper?"

"Oh shit, that's my cue." I glance down to see the half-empty beer in his hand.

"Is Elliot driving you guys home?"

"Yeah. Having a driving teenager is awesome." He smiles, and his eyes fade off for a moment. It's been over five years since they lost Uncle Griffin due to driving while intoxicated. There are still hard days for all of them.

I touch his hand, and he blinks several times, coming back from whatever memory he got lost in. "Sorry. Hazel's crew took Paige and Finn. I saw they took Tori, too. Does that mean you have a ride home?" His eyes drift to Scotty behind the bar. It's close to one a.m., and he's cleaning up while Kristina takes care of customers.

"I do."

"There's an overnight bag in Dellah's trunk. She packed it while you were in the shower this afternoon. She wasn't sure if you'd need it." I love that woman. Only she would think to pack a bag for the potential of me going home with my secret lover. I huff a laugh at that thought, and Uncle Collin gives me a strange look.

"You okay, kid?"

"Yeah, just thinking about how crazy Aunt Dellah is." He nods his head.

"Completely understand."

"Viiiiiiiiper. Where's ya go? *Hiccup.*"

"Shit, time to go. Over here, Bunny. Come say goodbye to your niece." He meets her halfway, and they walk back to me.

"My favorite neecy weecy." She flings her arms around my neck. It's a good thing I had just put my fishbowl down.

"Aunt Dells, you can't say stuff like that anymore. I'm not your only niece."

"Hush, you'll always be my favorite. Where's your hunky barman? Is he taking you home and ravishing you until—"

"Okay, Bunny, that's enough." Covering my eyes in embarrassment, I thank Uncle Collin for saving me, and they head out. He texts me to let me know my bag will be in the back of Scotty's truck and he'd see me Sunday for my birthday dinner.

As Uncle Collin practically carries Aunt Dellah out the door, Elliot walks my way with a shit-eating grin.

"You have a good night, Pinky. Don't do anything I wouldn't do." I roll my eyes at him and he wraps his giant arms around me.

"That leaves basically everything open."

"Exactly. And take notes. I'll expect a full report in the morning." Elliot kisses my cheek and leaves to drive his parents home.

I sit back and watch Scotty work for a while from the corner of the room. I know he sees me. He always sees me, just like I always see him.

I'm lost reading my book on my phone when a hand touches my shoulder. I squeak in surprise and see Scotty standing above me. Looking at the time, I see it's already one forty-five a.m.

"Sorry, Pinky. Are you ready to go home?" I stand and look around us, seeing the bar is mostly empty, before wrapping my arms around him.

"Hey there, handsome. I'm more than ready." Scotty kisses the top of my head, inhaling.

"I love the way you smell. How about a shower when we get home?" A shower sounds nice, but the word home sounds even nicer.

"Sounds perfect."

When we get to his house, he helps me out of the truck like he always does. As Scotty kisses me up against the side of it, I get an eerie feeling and shutter.

"Everything okay, Pinky?"

"Um, yeah, I just got a weird feeling. I had it that night when I was here alone a few weeks back. It just feels like someone is watching me." He seems to pull me closer and looks around behind him.

"It's after two in the morning. There shouldn't be anyone out here. Are you afraid of the dark?" I slap his shoulder.

"Jerk. Don't pick on me." He chuckles and puts his arm around my shoulder.

"Let's get you inside. I have an early present for you."

"Oh, I like presents."

246

34

Scotty

There were so many close calls tonight. Too many. When Jude walked in on us, my heart dropped to my stomach. I can't believe I forgot to lock the door. That's how wild this woman drives me.

I've never taken a woman in my office before. That's a first that goes to Wynnie. And last.

I wanted to kiss Hazel when she offered to take Tori for a sleepover. I watched Wynnie all night. I know she watched me, too. She sat quietly in the corner reading on her phone, and when it was time to leave, I accidentally startled her.

I downplayed her suspicious feeling outside, but I've felt it, too. It's just something that you feel when there are eyes on you. As we walk in the front door, I tap the keylock button on my truck an extra time to ensure it's locked and turn the deadbolt and the doorknob lock once we're in.

I love seeing Wynnie in my space. She makes it feel like a home just by her presence. But now that we're here, I have other things on my mind.

"This fucking dress." I wrap my arms around her waist

from behind and growl into her ear.

"You like?"

"No. It's sinful and tempting. I want it on my floor. Now." She spins and dips out from under my arms.

"Good things come to those who wait." She walks backward and darts behind a chair, using it as a shield.

"Bad things happen to brats." I smirk at her. If only she could see the things I'm imagining.

"Maybe I want to be a brat?" *Oh, please, please be a brat.*

I stop in my tracks. She wants me to chase her. Let's play a game.

"You have two options. Surrender now, and we can have a fun evening of whatever you want. Or, if you make me catch you, and I will catch you, I get to have whatever I want."

"What is it you want, Scotty?" I'm so glad she asked.

"I want your tight ass, Pinky." Her face shows a bit of shock, but she's also intrigued by the idea. "I know your limits, and you know your safeword. Keep both of those things in mind." Heat flashed in her eyes. She's going to run so I can chase her. She knows the consequences, and she's still going to do it.

She darts behind the couch, putting another layer of furniture between us.

"You think you can catch me?" She picks up a throw pillow and tosses it at me. I easily deflect it.

"I know I can catch you. The question is, how hard are you going to make it on yourself?" She tosses a stuffed unicorn at me from the couch.

"Give it your best shot, big guy." She runs down the hall to the bedrooms. There's only four options back there: three bedrooms and the main bathroom. I guess technically, five if you include my bathroom.

I take my time and peek into the bathroom, then Tori's room. The guest bedroom door at the end of the hall is still closed, but she could have quietly closed it behind her.

I check my room and bathroom first and don't see her. When I come out to the hall to check the guest room, there's a pile of red fabric in front of my bedroom door.

"You sneaky little thing. I said I wanted this dress on my bedroom floor. Now you're in real trouble." I wanted nothing more than to peel this dress off of her. Now I'm disappointed.

Opening the guest room door I see it's just as empty as the others. How did she get past me? I walk back into the living room and see her black lacy bra hanging on the back of the couch.

"My Rowyn is somewhere in here, and when I find her, she's in deep trouble." My voice is teasing, but this little game of hers is turning me on.

I remove my shirt and lay it on the back of the couch next to her bra. Toeing off my shoes, I work on the rest of my clothes until I'm in only my boxers.

I wander back into the kitchen, the laundry room, and the front foyer. Where is she?

"Oh, Pinky. Where are you?" Walking back into the living room, I notice all my clothes are gone. *How the fuck?*

I make my way back down the hallway, checking all the rooms again. I notice my bedroom door is almost closed, and I know I left it open. When I push it open, there is a very naked Wynnie lying on my bed with her hands between her legs.

"Took you long enough." I feel the growl in my chest before I hear it.

"Where the fuck were you?"

"You forget Finn is the master of hide and seek. Tori has nothing on him." I stalk over to the bed and stand at her feet, watching her fingers.

"What are you doing?" The movement of her fingers making languid circles around her clit is mesmerizing. She drops her knees wider, fully exposing her glistening pussy to me.

"Waiting for you to find me. I got bored and horny. I was promised something, and it doesn't look like you're going to deliver." Before her next breath, I have her flipped over, ass in the air, and I land a quick smack.

"Fuck." She moans as I rub a soothing palm over the handprint blooming on her ass cheek.

I smack her opposite cheek harder, and she moans louder. Now that I know she loves them, I need to figure out where her pain threshold is. Based on her reaction, I haven't found it yet.

"Keep playing with that pussy while I redden this ass for your little stunt."

"Yes, *Sir.*" Fuck. I know she said it as a joke, but I fucking loved it. "Say that again." She wiggles her ass in my hands.

"Yes, Sir." This time her voice is low and sultry.

"That. Fucking that. That is exactly how I want you to address me when we're like this. My beautiful little slut calls me Sir when her body is at my mercy. Do you understand, Rowyn?" She answers without hesitation.

"Yes, Sir."

"Fucking perfection."

I crack a hand on her ass. And another. And another. I alternate hands until her breathing is labored and my palms are tingling.

"Fuck me, please. Please, Sir."

"Where? Where do you want me to fuck you? Should I fuck this needy cunt?" I swipe my finger through her dripping folds and slide two inside without any resistance. "Or should I fuck you here?" Sliding my fingers out, they're coated in her arousal. I rim her tight hole, and she inhales sharply. I push the tip of my finger with the slightest pressure against her hole, and she moans.

"Is that your answer? Are you going to let me take your ass, Rowyn?" *Please say fucking yes.*

"Will you go slow?" I run my fingers up the bumps of her spine, and her back breaks out in goosebumps.

"I promise I will go as slow as you need. I can talk you through everything if you'd like. I won't do anything you don't want. Just use your safeword. Does that sound good?"

"I'd like all of that...Sir." It's fucking on. I crawl up her body, kissing her spine, then her shoulders, until I come to her ear.

"I more than puppy love you, Rowyn." I know those words sound so ridiculous coming from a man closer to forty than her twenty, but I need her to know as much as she can. I know she understands the meaning behind the silly statement.

She turns her head, and I capture her lips in mine. We kiss a slow, sensual kiss until I feel her hips wiggling under mine.

"Okay, okay. Eager little thing." I reach over and grab the lube from the top drawer of the nightstand. "We should get some toys. Or you can bring some here if you'd like." Oh. That thought intrigues or embarrasses her. Either way, she's turning pink, and I love it.

"Can we buy new?"

251

"Abso-fucking-lutely. We can look online and pick some out together." I crawl back between her legs and admire my handy work. Her cheeks are red and shiny. When I run a hand over one, she hisses before she hums from the touch.

"There will be a lot of pressure, possibly a little bit of pain, and then pleasure. Talk to me, and I'll talk you through it. I'm going to put lube on my fingers and start with one."

"Thank you. And Scotty, I more than puppy love you, too." There's a hummingbird in my chest attempting to escape. I want to flip her over and make love to her, but exploring is just as important, and she's put her trust in me right now.

Rimming her with a lubed finger, I circle until she relaxes.

"I know it's hard, but you need to relax and not clamp down. Play with your clit again as a distraction." Her finger slide between her folds, and after only a few strokes of her clit, she visibly relaxes, and I'm able to put the tip of my finger in.

"That feels…weird."

"Weird isn't bad. Take a deep breath for me." She inhales, and I slide my finger in further. "Shhh. This is where it might feel a little painful, but like your orgasm, it's a small pain before the pleasure. How close are you?"

"I can be closer."

"Play with my messy clit and tell me when you're about to orgasm." I flex my finger up and down, making the muscle stretch slightly as her breathing increases.

"Almost there." I feel her inner walls starting to contract, and when she lets out the first moan of her orgasm, I slide my finger all the way in and back out several times. Just before she comes completely down, I ease in a second finger.

"Fuck, Scotty. That feels…I don't even know."

"Good or bad? Do you need to use your safeword?"

"No. No. I feel...full."

"Full is a good thing." She's doing so well. I try for a third finger, and she hisses.

"Talk to me."

"I'm okay. Keep going."

"I'm adding a third finger. That's the least you have to take if I'm going to fit inside you."

"I can take it." Yes, she fucking can.

"I know you can, Rowyn. Because you're my incredible, gorgeous, little slut who's going to take my big cock up your ass like a good girl." I hear her mutter fuck under her breath, and I wonder if it's because of what I said or the fact that my third finger slid inside her.

I work her up as much as I can until she's writhing under me. "Your ass is ready for me, are you?"

"Yes fucking, Sir." I laugh to myself at her eagerness. When I remove my fingers, she jolts back. I quickly line my engorged head up to her beautiful puckered hole and push in.

"Holy fuck. You're huge."

"Well, thank you, but I'm barely in."

"Scotty, are you going to fit?"

"Trust me, Pinky, your body was made for me. I'll fit." We rock back and forth together, and I sink a little further each time. I groan loudly when my hips meet her ass cheeks.

"How are you, Rowyn? You've been quiet."

"Why does this feel weird and good and wrong?"

"Yes to all of the above." She laughs, causing both of us to moan. "Are you ready for me to move?"

"Please...Sir." I pull out slowly and back in, holding her hips steady. She is so fucking tight. When I pull out again, I drizzle a little more lube on my cock to make sure she's completely comfortable, and I pick up my pace. Wynnie moans while I grunt with pleasure.

"You're a fucking goddess under me, Rowyn. I want you to come for me again, and then I want to fill your ass and watch it drip out of you. Then, I'm going to take you to the shower and clean you up, and when you're clean, I'm going to pin you to the shower wall and make you dirty again."

"Oh, Scotty…Please…Yes, Sir." Her words come out in breathless spurts. Grabbing her hips, I pull her back onto me, pushing myself deeper. Her moans become guttural.

"Are you gonna give me one more?"

"Y-yes, Sir." She can keep calling me Sir. I fucking love it.

Reaching around her chest, I pull her up to me and slide my hand between her legs.

"Fucking strangle my cock, Rowyn. Do it. Come for me." I flick my fingers faster over her swollen clit. Her panting is out of control. My hand wraps around her neck, putting slight pressure exactly where I need it.

"Relax and breathe. Feel and let go." She instantly relaxes, and her breathing slows. Her inner walls flutter and clamp down, and I release the pressure on her neck. She screams, and I feel the tears hit my hand. I bury my face in her hair and come deep in her ass.

When our bodies have stopped convulsing, I gently ease out of her, cradle her into my arms bridal style, and walk us to the bathroom.

She squeals when I place her bare ass on the cold tile counter to turn the shower on.

"That actually feels nice. Just a little shocking at first." I laugh and squeeze between her legs to kiss her.

I wish every night could be like this. We need to tell her

parents so we don't have to hide our relationship anymore. I want everyone to know she's mine.

35

Wynnie

What a fucking night. I wiggle around on the stool as Scotty makes us breakfast. He turns around and hands me my perfectly made cup of coffee and ibuprofen.

"How did you know?"

"How are you feeling?" He gives me a knowing glance as I shift again in the seat.

"A little sore, but not bad." He leans over the counter and kisses the top of my head.

"You did incredible."

"You weren't so bad yourself." He squints his eyes at me when he turns around with a plate of scrambled eggs, sausage, and toast.

"I didn't know you could cook anything besides pancakes." I can't help but tease him. It's the only food Tori allows him to make when she knows I'm here.

"I don't think your ass is ready for the sass your mouth is dishing out right now, Pinky." Shit, he's definitely right.

"Hey, I wondered if I could take Tori on a girl's day today.

I'm already picking up Delilah. We're going to get our nails done and probably some ice cream. I'd love to invite her too."

"Of course. I'll let Mrs. Peterson know, and you can drop her off whenever you're done."

"Or you could pick her up from my house after your shift."

"Are you inviting me over for a booty call, Ms. Harmon?" I roll my eyes and shrug. But he's not half wrong.

"The apartment is almost done. Tori has been asking to see it."

"Nice. Use the kid as an excuse. But, sure, I'll pick her up after my shift."

"I'll grab some clothes and get her from my mom's."

"Sounds great. But would you like to go for a ride first before you go?" We haven't ridden together in a while.

"I don't have my bike here?" I give myself a mental forehead slap. Of course, he knows my bike isn't here, and the look he's giving me tells me he knows I know my bike isn't here.

"I meant together. I enjoyed having a Backpack. But I understand if you're too sore." The corner of his lip twitches with a smile he's trying to hide. Am I sore? Hell yes. Would I give up an opportunity to plaster myself behind this hunk of a man from hips to shoulders? Hell no.

"What am I going to wear?" I don't have any of my protective gear here.

"I have some old jackets and gloves that we can make work."

This time, when I climb onto the back of the bike, I don't hesitate to wrap my arms around his waist. His warmth instantly permeates through our clothing, and I lean my head on him.

"Good girl," he purrs through the headphones, and my clit

betrays me by pulsing. After the beating it took last night, you'd think it would be DOA. Unfortunately, my libido seems to have a mind of its own whenever Scotty is around.

He takes us to the mountain so we can ride the scenic route. I've relaxed my hands from his waist, resting on his hip bones.

We haven't been talking, just riding and enjoying the view. We hit a bump, and my hand shifts down Scotty's thigh before I put it back in place. He reaches back and squeezes my thigh, and once again, my clit pulses. The things this man does to my body.

"Hey, Scotty?"

"Pinky?"

"How well can you handle this thing?"

"What do you—" He stops talking when I slide my hand further down his thigh. "Pinky?" There's a warning in my name. I don't have a long arm stretch, but it's enough to graze the side of him.

His cock is already stirring to attention. I slide my hand down the inside of his thigh and back up.

"Rowyn, your ass is sore enough. Don't start something you can't finish." His voice is lower now. It's another warning but filled with lust.

"What if I want to finish?" He takes my hand, puts it back on his waist, and speeds up the bike. He doesn't let go until we reach a small rest area, only big enough for one car.

He follows a path through the trees until we come to a small clearing at the mountain's edge. It's breathtaking. You can see the entire town from here.

"Get off the bike," he growls as he's taking his helmet off. I jump off and remove mine. He unzips his jacket, throwing it off his shoulders, and his hands quickly move to do the same to mine.

His kiss is hot and needy when he slams into me, taking my head in his hands.

"You think you can be a dirty girl and tease me while I'm trying to drive? I should spank you for that, but I know you're sore. Instead, I'm going to make you finish what you started. You wanted my cock so badly, get on your knees and show me." His words are so dirty, but I don't even question them. I'm on my knees, undoing his pants, and I feel feral until I get him in my mouth. His moan when my lips finally wrap around him is music to my ears. It's exactly what I wanted to hear, and I squirm, rubbing my thighs together.

"Don't do that. Be a good Backpack and wait your turn to come. So I do. I take him into my mouth as far as I can and use my hand for the rest. I'm learning what drives him wild, and I do it to hear his reactions.

When I flick my tongue through the slit at his tip, his hips buck. My favorite reactions are when he can't control his body. I hollow my cheeks and squeeze tighter at his base, and he curses.

His hand grabs a chunk of hair at the top of my head and pulls at my roots.

"Fuck, Rowyn. Your mouth is magic. How did I get so lucky?" He tugs on my hair. "Stand up." I stand but don't remove my hand and continue to stroke him as he undoes my pants and drops them to the ground. I kick off my shoes and step out of my pants.

"Sit on the bike backward."

"What?"

"I said, sit on the fucking bike backward. I want to worship your pussy, and then I'm going to bend you over her and fuck you while you stare out at the view. Now get on." I look up at him and bat my eyelashes.

"Yes, Sir." He growls and lifts me onto the bike, resting my back on the handlebars. It's not the most comfortable, but when his finger slides over my clit and pushes inside me, I could care less if I was lying on a bed of nails.

"You're already dripping for me. Was it the ride, the blowjob, or the anticipation of being fucked over my bike?"

"Yes. All of it," I moan out as his fingers pump. One leg dangles down the side, and he lifts the other to rest on the seat. He pushes my knee down to give him full access.

"You're going to soak my leather seats, and I'll get to ride her knowing you've marked her with your come." That should probably gross me out, but he removes his fingers and bends down, sucking my clit into his mouth. The world around me disappears, and it's just me and Scotty's tongue that exist.

It doesn't take long before I'm coming hard. His fingers sweeping across my G-spot, combined with his relentless sucking on my clit have my screams echoing off the mountain.

"Fuck I need in you right now. I'm not going to last long. Between your mouth and your moans, you've done me in." He lifts me like a doll and positions me with my chest on the seat. His hands rub my ass cheeks, and he moans. "You have some bruising from last night. When we get home, I'll put some arnica gel on it before you leave."

"Yes, Sir."

"The things that you fucking do to me." He pushes inside, and we both let out a sigh as if we needed this to breathe. I'm beginning to feel that way, which scares the shit out of me.

His thrusts are long and deep. He's careful not to push too

hard and knock the bike over. The angle has another orgasm creeping up quickly, and my body is ready for it. I willingly take everything he gives me. It feels wild how easily my body has become in tune with his, but when he tells me he's close and commands me to come with him, my body does. We fall over the edge together, panting and moaning.

As our breathing settles, I close my eyes and think about how this is too good to be true. This man is way out of my league, but I'm going to savor every second of it.

Scotty kisses the side of my neck and helps me stand.

"I think you have a girl's day to get to, Pinky."

36

Wynnie

"I'm here for my girls!" My parents' house seems eerily quiet for the three normal kids plus three extra kids who are supposed to be here. I volunteered to take Finn and Paige back to Aunt Dellah's since I was already coming to get Tori and DJ.

The last time I walked into the house, and it was this quiet, there was a war happening. I don't see any grown man-children crawling around the floor this time, so that's a plus. But where could everyone be?

"Hey, Sweetheart." My dad walks in the back door and kisses me on the forehead.

"Hey, Dad. Where is everyone?"

"Hide and seek. Tori and Finn are both here, so it's like being in the witness protection program. Once they hide, it's impossible to find them. Phoenix and I are in the garage working on our bikes. Jude and your mom are seeking out the kids." He looks over my shoulder and huffs a laugh. "At least that's what they're *supposed* to be doing."

I look over my shoulder just in time to hear my mom giggle

262

as she walks towards me. Jude is right behind her with his face buried in her neck.

"Hi and eww." Jude pops up with a sheepish smile.

"How's the seeking going?" My dad smiles back at them.

"It's going great. The kids are amazing hiders." Jude wraps his arms tighter around my mom's waist.

"Well, I'm here to collect them all from you. Think we could make them appear?"

"Oh, easily. Watch this." Jude turns around and makes a microphone with his hand over his mouth. "Kids, Wynnie is here!" His voice booms through the quiet house, and giggles and squeals are heard all around us.

My name is shouted from several places around the house, including the pantry behind us, where an excited Tori jumps out of.

"Hey, Sunshine." When I crouch to greet her, she throws her arms around my neck. Her face suddenly turns very stern.

"Did you have pancakes without me this morning? I told Uncle Jude that he had to make us waffles because pancakes were our special breakfast." I nervously giggle and catch Jude eyeing us. I bring my hand to my chest.

"I would never cheat on our special breakfast. I had eggs and toast." She smiles brightly.

"Yeah, Daddy makes good eggs, too." I look around the room and notice everyone else is preoccupied except Jude, who's still watching us.

As the rest of the kids file into the room and greet me, I can't shake the feeling that Jude knows. I tell the girls to get packed up and ready, and I hand Tori the bag Scotty and I packed for her to change her clothes.

263

"Hey Dad J. Can we talk for a minute?"

"Of course. Library?" I nod and follow him.

We walk in and I close the door behind us. This was a room built for Jude, Mom, and me. The three of us have a love for books, and a library was on our must-list when building this house.

I close my eyes and take a deep breath.

"What do you know?"

"I *know* nothing. Would you like me to tell you what I've observed?" Opening my eyes, I see the softness in his. If I'm going to tell someone in this house about Scotty and me, Jude is the best person to start with.

"Yes, but I think that's even worse." He gestures toward the armchairs, and we sit facing each other.

"Are you happy?" That seems to be the first thing everyone keeps asking me. I love that they're concerned with my happiness.

"Uncle Collin asked me the same thing last night." Jude huffs a laugh.

"He's a smart man. Are you?" My lip curls up.

"I am." He reaches over and grabs my hand.

"Do you know what you're getting yourself into? That little girl down there is a package deal, and she already thinks the world of you."

"I think the world of her, Jude. She's my main concern."

"Does she know?" When I don't answer, he clarifies. "Does she know you're in a relationship with her father? Does she know about you and Scotty?" It's both a relief and a boulder on my chest that he said those words. One of my parents knows. Jude knows I'm dating Scotty. Most people only have to tell two parents, but I have to tell four.

264

"She doesn't exactly know, but I'm there a lot of mornings, and she's smart. Has anyone else figured it out?" He must hear the panic in my voice and shakes his head.

"I don't think anyone else has figured it out, at least not that they've told me. You need to tell them soon, though. I'll keep this to myself, but not for too much longer. I don't like secrets. The whole Dellah and Mac thing has made us talk more and be as honest as possible." I nod in understanding. It was a shock to us all to find out that Aunt Dellah knew who my dad was when my mom was still pregnant with me. It put a strain on their relationship when she accidentally let it spill one night while they were drinking.

"I know I need to tell them. But I'm scared of telling my dad and Phoenix, both for completely different reasons. The age difference being the main one." He squeezes my hand in reassurance.

"I can understand that, but we all know what a good man Scotty is. He's always been good to you since you were little. It's going to be a shock for them. I've seen it for a while, building between the two of you. Tori has been the bridge between you both."

"I love that little girl. I…I think I love him too." No, who am I kidding? I shake my head. "I do love him. I know it." Jude smiles warmly at me.

"He loves you too. I can't believe none of them have seen the dopey look he gives you. He tracked your every move at the bar last night." My hands fly to my mouth.

"Last night. Did you know we were in the office together?" He shakes his head and smiles.

"I actually didn't. You might want to get better at locking doors. Especially with spunky Tori in that house." I can't help but groan.

"He's Phoenix's best friend. My *dad's* best friend. It's like I'm living inside a romance novel. They all have happily ever afters, right?" I know Jude will understand my comparison.

"All good romance stories do." We have a good laugh together.

"Thank you, Dad J. I love you."

"Love you too, kiddo. Come here." We stand and hug, and it feels good to have a small weight off my shoulders. One down, three to go.

37

Wynnie

P aige, Delilah Jane, Tori, and I went to the nail salon after dropping Finn off at home. Aunt Dellah joined us for ice cream at the local ice cream and candy shoppe, Twistee Sweets.

The five of us happily eat our ice cream while the little girls chit-chat and Aunt Dellah and I people watch.

"Look at that hat. It looks like a seagull attacked it. The feathers are flying everywhere."

"Aunt Dellah, admit it. You want to go over and ask her where she got it from, don't you?" She scoffs at me.

"Only if it comes in bright red." I roll my eyes at her. "Speaking of bright red. How's everything going?" I know she's referring to the color I turn every time Scotty walks into a room, or maybe the red dress she forced me to buy for him.

"I told Jude. I got the impression he knew something already, and he confirmed it."

"And? Don't leave me hanging. Spill the tea."

"And he was fine. I wouldn't expect anything else from

267

him, though."

I turn my head when I hear a small commotion. There's a group of young teenage boys being rowdy at the table next to us.

"Yeah, Jude is the least of your worries. Do you think Phoenix should hear it from you or Scotty?" I've been wondering the same thing.

"I think maybe we should divide and conquer. I tell my dad, and he tells Phoenix. But then, sometimes, I think we need to be a united front. You know, safety in numbers and all that stuff."

"I think you can't go wrong either way. It might be easier to sit them all down and tell them all at once. You might have an easier time calming everyone down if Hazel is with them."

"Oh. You've got a good point there. Hmm."

"Heeeeey!" I look over to see Tori in tears. One of the teenage boys knocked her ice cream out of her hand, and it spilled all over the ground. Big fat tears stream down her face.

"That's not okay." I'm off my feet, comforting Tori in seconds.

"What are you going to do about it, bitch." Excuse me?

"Are you talking to me?"

"I don't see any other bitches here, bitch." I pass a crying Tori off to Aunt Dellah and stand in front of this kid, eyeing him. He can't be more than sixteen. His clothes are baggy and black. He's trying to look tough with a chain hanging around his hip. He may be slightly taller than me, but I couldn't care less.

"You need to apologize to her right now." He chuckles and looks back at his friends.

"Not a chance. What are you going to do about it?" He dismisses me like Tori's ice cream on the ground.

"What am I going to do about it? I'm going to—"

"Wynnie, calm down." I can hear the warning in her voice.

"Aunt Dellah, I've got this."

"Listen to that old bitch and back down."

"Is that your favorite word? The only word in your vocabulary that you can think of to insult me with?" He looks at me dumbfounded. "My five year old could come up with better words. You know, the one you just picked on. Does it make you feel good to pick on a child? Do you feel like a big man?" I watch the kid cower with each word out of my mouth. His dark, shaggy hair falls farther into his face as he dips his head lower and lower. His baggy clothes are dirty, and looking at the other kids in his group, they all look similar.

"I'll tell you what. I'm going inside to replace her ice cream. What can I get for all of you?"

"What?" His head snaps up, and several of the other kids look as well.

"I'm going to buy you ice cream. If you don't tell me what kind you want, you're all getting vanilla."

"Mint chocolate." One of the kids at the table speaks up with a smile on his face. "Please."

"Mint Chocolate. Got it. Anyone else?"

"Strawberry." Another kid says, then gets punched, and his friend laughs at him for ordering pink ice cream. I point at the laughing kid and tell him he's getting vanilla for making fun of his friend. He replies with a disheartened "yes, ma'am."

"Apologize if you'd like a real flavor."

"Sorry, man." He turns back to me, "Chocolate, please. And

thank you."

"Thank you." I smile at him warmly. "I have a Mint chocolate, Strawberry, and a Chocolate. Anyone else?" I collect the orders from all the boys except the instigator. He seems to be holding out. He gazes off to the corner of the building, looking uneasy, before asking for cookies and cream ice cream. I go back into the ice cream shoppe to get everyone's orders.

When I return, I see Aunt Dellah has everyone but Tori loaded into her car, and she's waiting outside mine. The boys apologize and thank me, and I give them a small lecture about kindness, before leaving them to eat their ice cream.

Aunt Dellah is smiling at me with pride when I walk over to them.

"Okay, Mama Bear, Wynnie. I see what you did there. That was awesome." I hand Tori her new ice cream, and she jumps with joy.

"Hey Sunshine, sometimes, even when people are mean, all they need is some kindness to turn them around." She looks over my shoulder at the boys happily eating their ice cream with smiles on their faces.

"Can we go home to my house?" She knew we had plans to go back to mine, but I'm glad she felt comfortable enough to ask to go home.

"Of course. I'll let Daddy know." I help get Tori in her car seat and close the door.

I suddenly get that eerie feeling like I'm being watched again and look around me, not seeing anything out of the ordinary. I swear I'm going crazy.

"You okay?" Aunt Dellah must see the uneasiness in my expression.

270

"Yeah. I've been getting this weird feeling lately. Almost like someone is watching me."

"Are you watching late night scary movies without me, little niece?"

"Shut up." She's probably right.

"Okay, scaredy cat. I've got mine and your mom's girls, and you've got yours. Thank you for taking Paige with you. She had fun."

"Any time."

Tori talks my ear off the entire ride back to Scotty's house about how brave I was for standing up to those big boys. I'm apparently now her hero.

I send a text to Scotty to call me whenever he gets a chance. I want to hear her tell Scotty that I'm her new hero.

He calls me just before dinner, and I put the phone on speaker as she tells him about the meanie big boy who spilled her ice cream.

"Can I talk to Wynnie alone, Little Princess?"

"Sure, Daddy." She hands me the phone and I take it off speaker.

"Pinky, did you stick up for my daughter?"

"Of course. Why wouldn't I? I won't let anything or anyone hurt her. Even if it's just her feelings." I hear him growl, wondering if I've done something wrong. Did I cross a boundary?

"I fucking more than puppy love you, Rowyn Juniper Harmon. I hope you know that."

"I…I know. And I more than puppy love you too, Scotty."

271

"I have to get back to the bar. I'll see you in a few hours."

Eventually, the real words are going to have to come out, but for now, I think we understand the meaning of our bizarre play on words.

After dinner and a bath, I get Tori all tucked into bed and sit on the couch with my e-reader. I don't know how long I sit there getting lost in a world of morally gray men when there's a knock at the door. It startles me because it's late, after eight o'clock.

When I open the door, there's a woman who looks worse for the wear with graying hair, glasses, and a fake smile on her face staring back at me.

"Can I help you?"

"Yes, I'm looking for Mr. Langford. Is he home?"

"He's not here right now, but I'm happy to message him."

"Is this also the home of Victoria Langford?" Warning bells go off in my head. I look beyond the woman to the street and see a police car sitting at the curb. I turn my phone over in my hand and hit the speed dial for my dad. I see the line connect and know he's there.

"What is this about?"

"My name is Kathy Fischer. I'm with the Georgia DFCS, the Division of Family and Child Services. It's important that I speak with Mr. Langford. Could you reach him on the phone?" My phone buzzes in my hand, and it's a text from my mom.

Mom: Your dad's on his way.

A wave of relief rushes through me. It will still take my dad at least fifteen minutes to get here, though.

"Do you have a badge I can see? And do you know the name of the officer assisting you?"

"Yes, ma'am. May I ask who you are?" She hands me a badge confirming all the information she just told me.

I see movement and notice the officer has gotten out of his car and is walking up the driveway towards us. His face changes from stern to happy to concerned when he sees me.

"Officer Taylor." I nod at Little Beau. His dad, Big Beau, is also on the police force. I've spent my fair share of time at officer related functions and events and know many of the guys on the force. My dad was proud to show me off once he found me.

"Wynnie. What are you doing at Scotty's house?" I look over my shoulder into the house, and he mouths, "Oh," and nods.

"Ms. Fischer doesn't want any trouble. She just needs to talk to Scotty." He looks a little uneasy to be here now that he's seen me.

"It's a Saturday night, Beau. You know where he is right now."

"Yes, ma'am. Ms. Fischer needs to follow protocol and start here first." I hear sirens down the road and drop my head, knowing it's my dad. Beau looks over his shoulder and back at me.

"Is that—?"

"Probably. He's so dramatic. I'm sorry." Moments later, my dad's unmarked car whips into the driveway. He barely puts it into park before he's bounding towards us.

"Taylor." My dad walks past both people standing in the door to reach me. "Ms. Fischer, my daughter has nothing to do with Mr. Langford. He's at his bar, Tipsy Penny if you need to speak with him."

"Of course, Detective Harmon. I had no idea she was your daughter. I need to confirm Victoria is safe."

"I assure you she is." My dad puts his arm around my shoulder.

"Is there a way I could see her?"

"What is this in reference to?" I feel relief that my dad is here to take over for me.

"Officer—"

"It's Detective now, remember." He's proud of the promotion he got a few years ago.

"I'm sorry, Detective Harmon. You know I can't discuss anything without Mr. Langford present."

"Understood. Taylor, have you seen the paperwork?" He nods. "Is there immediate reason to believe that Tori is in danger?"

"No, Sir."

"Alright. Why don't you escort Ms. Fischer to Tipsy Penny and I'll be right behind you."

"Yes, Sir. Ma'am?" Taylor extends his hand for Ms. Fischer to walk toward their cars first. She looks between the three of us and reluctantly walks down the steps.

"I'll be right behind you, Little Beau," my dad reminds him as he closes the door. He pulls me in for a hug.

"You did the right thing by calling me, Sweetheart. I'll find out what's going on and let you know." The adrenaline of the situation falls away, and I sob into his shoulder.

"It's going to be alright. Shhh. You're okay, and Tori is safe here with you. Do you want me to call one of the guys to come hang out with you until Scotty gets home?" I want to say yes, but I know the moment Scotty gets here, I'll have to leave and won't get the comfort or answers I need.

"Elliot. I'll call El to come hang out with me."

"Are you sure? Jude or Phoenix would be happy to come." Jude. He knows.

"Okay. Can you ask Jude to come? He's a little more level-headed." I laugh to lighten the situation, and he joins me. He takes his phone out of his pocket and sends a text. There's almost an immediate response.

"He's on his way. I should go follow them, but I'm happy to wait if you'd like." He puts his phone back in his pocket and pulls me close.

"No, I'm okay. Give Scotty a heads-up, please. He doesn't need a scene at the bar."

"Already planning on it. Call me if you need me. I love you, Sweetheart." He kisses the top of my head and leaves. I have so many questions and need answers.

38

Scotty

I feel my phone buzzing in my back pocket, but we're too busy for me to answer. If it's Wynnie and there's something wrong, she'll call the bar.

The call I got earlier from Tori ripped my heart into pieces in a good way. Wynnie is the thread that's sewing it back together. She's binding us piece by piece.

She stuck up for Tori. It was just some stupid punk kids, but if I had any doubts about Wynnie's role in our relationship, they are now non-existent. Not that I ever had any.

The bar phone rings, and Aimee picks it up.

"Bossman, it's for you."

"Take a message." I'm too busy for social calls. There's a joint bachelor and bachelorette party here, and they're keeping us all on our toes.

"It's Matt." Matt who?

"Who?"

"It's Matt. M-A-C. Mac." *Oh shit.* Wynnie. Tori.

"Office." I serve the drink I was making and run to my office picking up the phone as soon as I reach it."

"Mac, wha—"

"The girls are fine." *Thank fuck.*

"Why are you calling then? You about gave me a fucking heart attack."

"You've got trouble coming your way. I'm a few minutes behind them but I'm coming to you. It's Georgia DFCS. They came by the house asking about Tori, and Wynnie called me. I got to your place as quick as I could. We didn't let her in. Little Beau is with her." I fall back into my desk chair. Breath asshole. You've always known this was a possibility,

"What do you know, Mac?"

"Not much. The paperwork is vague. Someone is contesting Tori's birth certificate. There's no legitimacy paperwork filed. Did you not get that done?"

Fuck. Georgia has some stupid ass law that I never thought would be an issue.

"No." I hang my head over my desk. "Becky just disappeared, and life got busy. She's mine, Mac. I know it."

"I know she is Scotty, but anyone can contest it without that stupid piece of paper. I had to do it when Wynnie changed her name to mine, and I was added to her birth certificate."

"Fuck, Mac. What do I do?"

"You have to go through the process. They have no reason to take Tori from you. Just get the paperwork done. I'll be there in five." He hangs up, and I hear a knock on my door.

"Come in." Kristina peeks her head in the door. "There's an officer and a lady here to see you."

"Yeah, I know. Send them back, please. Thanks, Kristina."
"Sure thing."

"Oh, Kristina." She pops back in. "Mac should be coming in a few minutes. Send him right back here."

"Got it." I sit and wait, rubbing my fingers across my forehead, wondering how I let myself get into this mess over a piece of paper and a simple blood test. There's another knock at the door, and I stand and yell for them to come in.

"Hey, Scotty. Sorry to bother you. I see you're busy out there." Little Beau sticks his hand out, and I shake it. "This is Ms. Fischer from DFCS. She just needs to ask you a few questions." I shake her hand and gesture for us all to sit down.

"Mr. Langford, are you the father of Victoria Langford, daughter of Rebecca Roseman?"

"Yes, Victoria is my daughter." There's another knock at the door, and before I can open my mouth, Mac walks in and closes the door behind him.

"Carry on." His gruff cop voice leaves no room for question.

"Alright." Ms. Fischer shifts nervously in her seat. Mac obviously makes her uncomfortable.

"Well, Mr. Langford—"

"Scotty, please."

"Scotty. We got a call into our office contesting Victoria's birth certificate. There is another man claiming he's Victoria's father and has provided proof that he was in a relationship with Ms. Roseman around the time of conception. Since there's no legitimacy paperwork on file we need to follow up with the complaint."

"I don't know anything about another man, but I know Tori is my daughter. What does Becky have to say about all of this? I assume you've contacted her as well?" She shifts in her seat again.

"Oh. Um. I'm sorry, Mr—Scotty. I assumed you knew. Ms. Roseman passed away about two weeks ago from an overdose." My eyebrows hit my hairline. "Well, the overdose

278

was about a month ago, but she was in the hospital before she passed away."

"I had no idea." I wish I could say this surprised me. I've expected to get this kind of information for years. Or really any information to know that Tori was all mine. Knowing Becky was out there and could show up at any point and try to take Tori away from me has always been at the back of my mind. Now she's all mine. Well, she will be once I get this stupid paperwork cleared up.

"Now what?" All attention turns to Mac at the back of the room. He's looming like a bodyguard, leaning against the wall.

"Now, we need to do a home study and make sure Victoria is in a stable environment, and both men need to take a paternity test."

"Who's the other man?" I feel like I didn't know Becky at all, which is probably true since I had no idea she was on drugs when we were together.

"I can't give you that information." She turns to Mac. "And it isn't in the available paperwork to the police department." Smart woman. She's already realized I have connections with the department.

"What's involved with the home study?"

"Dellah and Collin went through one with the kids." Ms. Fischer eyes Mac again. She really doesn't like him.

"We need to schedule an appointment to see your home, and the court will set up a time for your blood test."

"Court? Can't I just take the test and send you the results."

"Unfortunately, not now that it's being contested. Everything has to be documented." Fuck. I've had five years to get this shit done.

"Okay. Whenever you want to come by, I'll make sure I'm there."

"And Ms. Harmon? Is she your regular babysitter? If so, I'd like to speak with her as well."

"She's been cleared by DFCS before to watch children." I'm glad Mac spoke up about Wynnie. I assume she went through it for Dellah and Collin during their adoption.

"Mrs. Peterson, a neighbor, also watches Tori. She's a registered foster parent."

"Yes, I know Mrs. Peterson well. I'll look up Ms. Harmon's information and make sure everything is current. I can come by Tuesday morning if that works."

"We'll be there. I'm supposed to be here at twelve-thirty if it could be earlier than that. If not, I'll make arrangements."

By the time we get everything settled, it's almost time for me to leave and let the girls take over. The crowd has thinned since the bachelor and bachelorette party moved on to another bar.

I need to get home to Wynnie and make sure my girls are okay.

I'm so focused on getting to her that I don't even notice Jude's SUV parked in front of my house until it's too late.

I walk in the front door, and my eyes immediately land on Wynnie pouring herself a glass of wine in the kitchen.

"Pinky." I rush in and spin her around into my arms, locking our lips together. I thread a hand through her hair and the other under her shirt, needing to feel her soft skin in my hands. I've been on edge since Mac's call, and I feel my body releasing tension with each second that passes.

A throat clears, and I pull Wynnie closer to my chest, not knowing who the sound came from. My eyes connect with

Jude sitting on my living room couch, and I freeze.

I should let her go. Jude just saw me kissing his daughter. His much younger than me, daughter. His lover and best friend's daughter.

"Jude." I hear Wynnie mumble something into my chest, and I lean back so she can speak.

"It's okay. He knows." *He knows.*

"You know? You're here, and you know?"

"I know, and I'm here. Wynnie needed me." I look down at Wynnie in my arms, and she smiles up at me.

"He knows." My voice is barely a whisper. She reaches up on her tippy toes and grabs my cheeks.

"It's okay."

"But Mac, I just saw him." Jude shakes his head.

"I'm the only one that knows so far."

"Jude…"

"Treat her right, Scotty, and we'll have no problems." Jude smiles, but I hear the slight threat in his tone.

"I wouldn't dream of treating her like anything but a Queen." Wynnie snuggles into my chest. "How's our girl?"

"She's been asleep the entire time. She has no idea what's going on. And neither do I."

"I'll take that as my cue to leave the two of you to talk. Will we see you tomorrow evening?" Jude looks at me, questioning.

Wynnie looks up at me again. "Are you coming to my birthday dinner?"

"I wouldn't miss it for the world." I stare into her eyes, thanking whoever is up above that this woman has found her way into my life and protects my daughter as fiercely as I do.

Pointing between us, "You two might want to tone that

down a bit for tomorrow night." Wynnie giggles and steps away from me to say goodbye to Jude.

"Thank you for staying with me." They hug, and Jude kisses her forehead.

"Always. See you tomorrow, Wynnie." Jude extends a hand to me, and we shake. "Take care of her." I give him a curt nod. In reality, it's humorous to me because I'm a few months older than Jude.

39

Wynnie

What a whirlwind of a day yesterday was. After Jude left, Scotty and I took a bath together, and he told me everything the DFCS worker told him. I wish there was something more that I could do, but I know everything is out of our hands.

After our shower, we cuddled and caressed and simply explored each other's bodies. It was as intimate as if we had sex. We fell asleep embracing and slept peacefully for several hours.

"Daddy!" I bolt up from my sleep at the panicked sound of Tori's yell. Before I have time to process what's happening, a tear-filled Tori comes stumbling into the room.

Jumping out of bed, I scoop her up and curl her into me on the floor.

"Sunshine, what's wrong." Her body is trembling in my arms. Scotty finally wakes up and comes over to us on the floor. He tries to take her from me, and she shakes her head.

"Okay, Little Princess. Wynnie can hold you. Did you have a bad dream?" Scotty rubs his hand soothingly over her back as she clings to me.

"I saw someone."

"In your dream?" She shakes her head at Scotty's question.

"In my window!" His body stiffens, and he stands and leaves the room. A moment later, he comes back and sits down next to us again.

"There's no one there, baby. Are you sure it wasn't a dream?"

"No. He was there. I saw a scary man."

"We believe you, Sunshine. There's no one there now. Daddy checked. Do you want me to tuck you back into bed?" She shakes her head on my chest.

"Can I sleep in here with you?"

"You want to sleep with Daddy?"

"No, with both of you." *Oh.* I look at Scotty, whose shocked expression matches mine.

"Of course you can. Let's put you in the middle."

"I'll grab her blankie." Scotty kisses us both on the forehead, and I climb into bed and get Tori comfortable. Scotty returns and cuddles up to the other side of Tori.

"Thank you, Daddy. I love you. Love you, Wynnie."

"Love you, Sunshine. Close your eyes and go back to sleep. You're safe." Scotty's arm reaches over Tori and rests on my hip.

"I love you. Goodnight, girls." I think I just stopped breathing. I know he made it as a blanket statement to us both and didn't specify me, but he also didn't say Tori.

Shit. Tori, who's lying between us. She didn't even question me being in here when she stumbled in and then said she wanted to sleep with both of us. How long has she known I don't actually sleep in the guest room? And thank god we had some clothes on. It may only be a t-shirt for me and boxers for him but it's better than being naked.

A hand squeezes on my hip. "Shhh. I can hear you overthinking, Pinky. Just go back to sleep." He knows me so well.

I tuck Tori closer to me, and we all fall asleep until the morning.

When I wake up, there's the cutest little snoring in my ear. Tori is still curled up next to me, but Scotty is gone. I swear this man never sleeps.

I try to slowly roll out from under the sleeping beauty in my arms, and she hugs me tighter.

"Five more minutes." Her little lips pout, and I laugh at her adorableness.

"Morning, Sunshine. It smells like Daddy is already making us pancakes. Should we go see?"

"Still sleepy." I poke at her belly, and she giggles and squirms.

"Come on, silly girl. Let's go fill our bellies." She perks up.

"Is today your birthday?" I raise up two fingers.

"Two more days until my birthday. But today is my birthday dinner at Aunt Hazel's house, and you and Daddy are coming." She throws her arms around my neck and squeezes with all her strength.

"Thank you for helping me from the scary man in my window."

"I'll always be here to protect you, Sunshine."

When we walk into the kitchen, Scotty has the biggest smile on his face.

"Good morning, my beautiful girls. How'd you sleep?" Tori runs up to him and hugs his legs. He bends down to rub her back, and when I walk into the kitchen, he pulls me into him and kisses me.

"Scotty," I whisper through our kiss.

"Shhh. No more hiding, Pinky." He pulls away and looks down to a giggling Tori below us.

"Do it again." Tori's face lights up with excitement. Scotty pulls me in and plants a big goofy kiss on my lips to hear her giggle even more then leans down and gives her the same kiss on the cheek.

The room fills with our laughter, and everything feels perfect.

Tori and I sit at the counter, and Scotty presents us with coffee and juice, then two heaping plates of not chocolate chip pancakes.

"What are these?" Tori pokes her finger at her stack.

"These are special pancakes. They have rainbow sprinkles in them because I know how much my girls love rainbows." He can keep calling us "his girls" because it does something fluttery to my belly, and I like it.

He joins us at the counter, and we happily eat our weight in Scotty's special rainbow pancakes. When Tori runs off to get ready for the day, I walk over to the sink to help him clean up.

"What did you mean when you said you were done hiding?" He hands me a towel and a plate to dry.

"I called your dad this morning and asked him if we could go for a ride before dinner tonight." He hands me a mug to dry.

"You did? I assume you're talking about Mac…and that means I have to tell Phoenix. But I thought we were doing that the other way around." He turns and takes the towel from me to dry off his hands.

"I want to tell them both myself. Seeing Tori last night accept you so openly changed something in my thought process." He pulls me in close and wraps his arms around me. "I need to stop worrying about what they're going to think. I need to man up, and I'm diving in head first. I plan to tell him first and talk to Phoenix tonight…if I survive telling Mac."

"You don't have to do it alone. We can be a united front."

"I know, Pinky. But they will have more respect for me if I talk to them alone. You can handle your mom, though." He gives me a devilish smirk, knowing that my mom will probably be just as bad to tell. "Do you want to hang out with Tori while I go? We're planning for eleven, so there's plenty of time before your party at four."

"Oh nooo. You're gonna stick me with the crazy, colorful, five year old. Whatever will I do?"

I heard Tori walk into the room behind me, and I said my sentences in the most dramatic way. I hear her huff and pretend to gasp in shock that she caught me.

Her arms are crossed over her chest, and she's scowling at me. "I'm not crazy."

"You sure are. Crazy talented. Crazy beautiful. Crazy awesome. And Crazy about ME!" I charge at her with tickle fingers, and she giggles and runs around the couch.

"No running in the house." We both freeze and turn to Scotty. We look at each other and then back at Scotty. As if we planned it, "Yes, Daddy" comes from our mouths in unison. Tori and I giggle, and Scotty groans.

"I'm going to get ready for my ride with Mac." Scotty walks down the hall, shaking his head, and Tori and I continue our little game of chase around the couch.

Scotty left the house around ten thirty to meet with my dad. To say I'm nervous is an understatement. He said he plans to be back around one o'clock unless Mac kills him and hides his body.

Tori and I choose the perfect dress for her to wear to my birthday dinner. We color and watch cartoons.

When one-thirty rolls around, I can't help but laugh at the thought of my dad hiding Scotty's body. Then I remember back to the day I ran away and Aunt Dellah making an offhand comment about my dad knowing where to hide a body if my mom ever needed him to.

When two o'clock comes and goes without a word from Scotty, I start to get a little nervous.

"Hey, kiddo. How's it going? We can't wait to see you tonight." My mom sounds so excited to hear from me, which calms my nerves a bit.

"Is my dad home?"

"Mac? I haven't seen him. Didn't he go out riding with Scotty this morning?"

"They did, but Scotty said he'd be back by one, and it's after two. He's not usually a late kind of person."

"Hmm, let me check with the other guys. Hold on." I hear a door open and her yelling. They must be outside. "He isn't out in the garage with Phoenix, and Jude hasn't heard from him either. Have you tried calling?"

"Not yet. I try not to bother him when I know he's riding."

"I understand. Maybe give it a little more time, and if I hear from your dad, I'll let you know."

"Thanks, mom. I'll see you soon." As I hang up the phone, I don't feel any better. Staring at the clock isn't helping my nerves either.

When there's a knock at the door, and I'm greeted with a frantic-looking Aunt Dellah, my heart drops.

"Aunt Dellah...don't tell me."

40

Scotty

You're a fucking grown-ass man, and you can talk to the father of the woman you love.

"Mac, I'm in love with your daughter." No, that's too direct. "Mac, your daughter is the best thing to ever happen to me." True, but not the point. "Mac, your daughter is my entire fucking world next to my daughter and…" Shit, this isn't getting me anywhere.

I pull up to their driveway and wait for someone to open the gate. The motion sensors alert everyone in the house whenever someone pulls up. I don't wait long before I hear the metal of the gate creaking.

I ride my bike up the rest of their driveway and park next to Mac's, sitting outside waiting for me. Jude steps out the back door with a smile on his face.

"Are you doing it?" I'm not surprised he knows why I'm here.

"Yeah. One at a time. I'll talk to Phoenix when I get back…if I get back. Unless you want to break that news to him?" Jude throws his hands up in surrender.

"I don't have a death wish."

"Gee, thanks." Jude grips my shoulder.

"Just be honest with them about how you feel about her. We all know you're a good guy and a great father."

"You accepted us so easily."

"I saw it coming a mile away, Scotty. Probably before either of you did. Wynnie's had eyes for you since Tori came into your life."

"No shit. That fucking long?" I rub the back of my neck, thinking about Wynnie pining for me for the last five years. "Anyway. I'm ready to get this over with. Tori climbed into bed with us last night. She had a bad dream or something. She slipped between us like it was the most natural thing to find us in bed together. If my five year old can accept us, then a thirty-seven and forty-three year old can do it too."

"Good luck, man. I'll let him know you're here."

Mac comes out a few minutes later and we get on the road and decide to ride up and down the mountain and then head back—just a quick ride for today. My plan is to tell him as soon as we get back and then decide about Phoenix based on Mac's reaction.

The ride has been beautiful. It's the middle of summer, and everything is in full bloom. The trees surround us in their greenery, and it's freeing to let loose and ride.

As we're coming down the mountain, a car speeds by us going up, flashing its lights. This road is a big attraction for motorcycles because of its turns and the locals constantly warn people to slow down.

We're approaching a significant turn when we see a car stopped ahead of us in the opposite lane. Mac and I exchange a look, and we both shrug.

"Must be tourists." Mac's gruff voice comes through my speakers. People stop to take pictures all the time. It's dangerous as fuck, but they don't seem to care.

We continue to ride. As we get closer, a deer runs in front of us.

"Shit. That was clos—"

Everything happens in slow motion. Mac's front tire gets hit by a second deer jumping over the guard rail. I have no time to react as his tire twists directly into mine.

Mac lands on my bike as we continue to skid down the mountain. When they become entangled together, the force ejects my body, and I fly directly towards the car that stopped in the road.

All I can hear in my ear is Mac's screaming and cursing. As my body flies in the air towards the parked car, I have one thought in my mind, and I need to tell him.

"Mac, I fucking love your daughter."

41

Hazel

Jude has been wandering the house for the last several hours, looking like the cat that got the canary. I walk into the kitchen to find him working at the counter, humming.

"What's up with you? Why are you so smiley?" He wraps his arms around my back and pulls me to his chest.

"Something good is happening. Well, *I* think it's good. You'll find out soon enough." He pecks my nose and lets me go, humming to himself as he continues to work on Wynnie's lasagna for tonight.

"What time did the guys say they were coming back?"

"Sorry, Little Dove, I forgot to ask. Soon, I'm sure." They haven't been gone for too long, but there's still a ton to complete before everyone arrives at four.

I get lost in cleaning and decorating when my phone rings. I answer when I see it's Wynnie.

"Hey, kiddo. How's it going? We can't wait to see you tonight."

My mom instincts kick in when I hear the worry in her

voice that the guys aren't back yet, but I try to soothe her nerves and mine by reassuring her they'll be home soon.

A little while later, my phone rings again, and it's the police station. Mac must have stopped on his ride back.

"Hey, Big Guy. Did you get lost and end up at the station?"

"Hazel. It's Big Beau." *Fuck.* I don't like the tone in his voice. I cover the phone and yell around the corner.

"Jude, get Phoenix," I yell through the house knowing Jude is in the kitchen. "Big Beau. What's wrong? Why are you calling?"

"Hazel. There's been an accident." I fall to the floor and drop the phone. I don't even want to hear what he has to say next.

Phoenix and Jude rush into the room and find me sitting on the floor, staring at my phone. It's still connected, and I can hear Beau's muffled voice, but I can't make anything out.

"Angel, what's wrong?" I point to my phone with a shaky hand, and Jude picks it up while Phoenix sits beside me.

"Mac?" Jude must see the caller ID and assume what I did. His face pales, and he puts the phone on speaker.

"…Mac and Scotty are at Mountain Pines General Hospital." I fall into Phoenix, and he wraps his arms around me.

"Fuck. What happened? How are they?" I feel Phoenix's voice rumble in his chest.

"Mac, at the very least, has a broken leg. Scotty…"

"Beau? What about Scotty." Jude's voice goes raspy.

"It's bad. A deer hit Mac's bike, and it toppled onto Scotty's, and he flew into a car. His helmet flew off in the crash, and he's pretty banged up. I heard he was heading straight to surgery."

"We-we have to go. Let's go. Call Dellah. She'll take the

294

kids. We have to go. Why aren't either of you moving? LET'S GO!"

"Shhh. Little Dove, okay. I'll get the kids and take them to Dellah's. Phoenix, take her to the hospital, and I'll meet you there. Whatever happens, we will get through this. Always."

"Together," I whisper back.

Jude

"I know, I know. We're running late. I promise I'm bringing the cake—"

"Dellah." I hear her gasp at my sharp tone.

"Oh shit. What's wrong, Jude?"

"Is Collin home?"

"Yes. Fuck. Why?" She's already panicking and I haven't told her anything yet.

"I'm coming your way with the kids. Mac and Scotty were in a motorcycle accident. Wynnie doesn't know yet. You need to get her and bring her to the hospital. Collin is going to have to man up and watch our herds."

"Elliot's here—"

"No. Bring Elliot with you. Wynnie is going to need him. Go now and bring Tori back. I'll order pizza to your house."

"Jude. How bad?"

"From what we know, Mac has a broken leg, but Scotty isn't good. Don't say much to Wynnie yet. We don't want to freak out Tori or the other kids."

"Jude."

"I know. Everyone is about to find out about them really quickly. Their relationship isn't the priority right now. Mac and Scotty are hurt. We have to be strong because emotions are going to be high. We have to Dellah."

"Okay. Okay. I'm leaving now."

42

Wynnie

"Aunt Dellah...don't tell me."

"Wynnie, there's been an accident." She grabs my forearms and looks into my eyes. "We have to get Tori to my house. I need you to keep it together for your little girl. Mac was involved, too, and all the kids are at my house with Collin. As soon as we drop Tori off, Elliot will come with us to the hospital. Nod if you understand." I nod because, at the moment, there are so many things going on in my head I couldn't form words if I wanted to.

"Tori, who wants a playdate?" Aunt Dellah squeezes my arms before letting me go and walking inside.

"Wynnie, go get in the car. I'll be right there with Tori." I nod again and grab my cell phone before walking to Aunt Dellah's car.

Getting in the front seat, I buckle on autopilot as all of the terrible images run through my head. All she said was an accident. No other details. Are they dead, alive, hurt? Why didn't she tell me anything else?

I look over when I hear the front door close and see a

smiling Tori bouncing towards the car. Aunt Dellah opens the back door and Tori instantly starts chatting.

"Aunt Dellah says we're having a pizza party at her house. Just us kids. I love pizza!" There's so much glee in her voice. I try to answer her but choke on my words.

Aunt Dellah buckles her into a car seat, and when she gets in the driver's seat, she takes my hand. She mouths, "It's okay," and leaves the driveway.

It feels like hours to get to their house. Tori hugs me around the headrest of the seat, and I manage to tell her to have fun. Elliot pulls my door open and crouches at my feet as soon as Tori is in the house.

"Elliot." The dam bursts, and my tears start to flow. "What do you know? Aunt Dellah didn't tell me anything. Is he okay? Is he…is he dead?"

"No. No, Scotty isn't dead, but it's not good. From what we know, he's in surgery, and your dad's leg is broken. There haven't been any other updates." I collapse onto his shoulder, sobbing.

"Get in Elliot. Let's go." I stare out the window blankly. Everything goes by in a blur. Aunt Dellah holds my hand, and Elliot rubs my arm. I can see their hands, but I don't feel them. I feel nothing. I'm numb. I need information.

"They don't know yet. How do I tell them?"

"Baby, it's not going to matter." Aunt Dellah smiles at me weakly. "We'll be there in a few minutes and find out what's going on. We're almost there. I promise."

Aunt Dellah drops Elliot and me off at the emergency room exit so she can park the car. We go to the reception desk, and a tired-looking woman wearing too much eyeliner looks up at us, bored.

"My dad and boyfriend were brought in for a motorcycle accident. Malcolm Harmon and Scott Langford. Can you tell us where to go?" My fingers tap anxiously on the desk. I have too much adrenaline coursing through my body and can't contain it.

"Malcolm Harmon is on the fourth floor; take a left off the elevator—" I don't even listen to the room number. I know I'll find them as soon as I get up there.

We rush to the elevator and I jam my finger into the button. I hit it several times before Elliot grabs my hand.

"I'm texting my mom where to go, but you need to relax. They're in the hospital, and there isn't anything more we can do right now."

Logically, I know he's right, but I'm not thinking logically. I feel split in two. I have to see my dad and Scotty. They're all going to find out, and I'm nervous, but I also don't care.

"Elliot." I can't help it, but I whine like a three year old. This elevator is taking forever. My entire body is bouncing as I watch the red digital numbers descend. It finally dings, and I jump in and hit the four button more times than needed. Elliot takes me in his arms, pulling me away from the panel, and I bury my face in his chest.

"I wish for them to be okay. I wish for them to be okay. I wish for them to be okay." I'm squeezing my eyes so tight it's making my head hurt.

The elevator dings for our floor, and I can't peel myself away from Elliot. He huddles me under his arm and walks us down the hall.

"Wynnie." I hear my mom's voice and her footsteps running down the hall. She crashes into us, and I turn to her, crying into her shoulder.

"Mom." My voice cracks on her name.

"He's okay. Wynnie, your dad's okay. It's just a broken leg that doesn't need surgery, and lots of road rash." I hear someone come up behind us, and Jude rubs my back. When I look up at him, he opens his arms, and I accept the hug.

"How-how…" I can't even get the words out.

"They won't talk to us because we aren't his next of kin. Do you want to try?" I nod into his chest. "Do you want to talk to them first?" This time, I shake my head. "I'll take you. Little Dove, Dellah is coming down the hall. You should go get her." I see my mom's confused look, but she doesn't question us.

"Do they know anything about…"

"I don't think he had a chance to tell Mac anything before the accident. But he's on some pain meds, and he's a little loopy. He'll be happy to see you."

We walk up to the nurse's desk, and this nurse looks much more pleasant than the one in the ER.

"Hi, I'm hoping to get an update on Scott Langford. I'm-I'm his girlfriend." The nurse sighs and looks at Jude.

"I'm sorry, I've already told you I can't—"

"I know I look young, but I'm truly his girlfriend. Please…" The tears burst from my eyes. I can't take much more. "Please. I need to know if he's okay. He has a little girl at home."

"I know this is hard, but we have protocols in place. I can tell you your friend is in surgery." She reaches up and places her hand over mine on the desk. "He has a dislocated shoulder and a head injury. He'll be in surgery for a while. I can let you know when he's out. I'm so sorry I can't tell you more right now."

"I understand. Thank you." I collapse back into Jude, and

we walk down the hall.

"Are you ready to see your dad?"

"I don't know. How bad does he look?" This already feels like too much and I haven't seen either of them yet.

"He's not too bad. His jacket took most of the beating. His hands and legs have road rash, and his leg is in a boot for now. I know he wants to see you."

"Okay. Take me to him."

We walk into the room, and my mom is sitting at his bedside, holding his hand. Phoenix is behind her, rubbing her shoulders, and Aunt Dellah sits in a chair on the other side of the bed. Everyone looks so somber, and my dad is asleep.

"Did you find anything out?" Aunt Dellah stands up from her chair and comes to me. I shake my head.

"Nothing new, but she said she'd let me know when he's out of surgery."

"He'll be okay, Wynnie." She rubs my arms soothingly.

"He has to be, Aunt Dellah. She'll be devastated. He's all she has." I can't stop the tears at this point. They keep coming.

"She has you, Wynnie. She has you." Aunt Dellah pulls me into her, and I cry on her shoulder.

"What's going on?" My mom's voice cuts through my crying. It's time to face my judgment. I pull away from Aunt Dellah, and she stops and looks deep into my eyes, giving me her strength. I nod, and she steps aside.

"Mom, Phoenix, I need you to know something." I can do this. I can do this. "Scotty and I—"

"Are in love." My dad's gravelly voice cuts through the room. My eyes snap to him. He's staring right at me.

"What?" I know there are others talking in the room, but I

301

can only stare at my dad. "Did-did he say something to you."
He clears his throat, and Phoenix hands him a cup of water.
My mom helps him with the straw before he speaks again.

"The last thing I heard from him before the speaker cut out
was him telling me he loves you. How long?" There's an edge
to his question.

"What?" I don't understand what he's asking.

"How long has it been going on, Wynnie?" This isn't how I
wanted this conversation to go.

"Since I graduated college."

"What exactly is going on?" Phoenix sounds angry, and I
take a step back and bump into Jude. He runs his hands up
and down my arms and whispers, "It's okay" into my ear.

I square my shoulders and look Phoenix in the eyes. I won't
be afraid. I can do this for Scotty.

"Scotty and I are dating. We're...in love." The last words
sound as unbelievable out loud as they do in my head. He
loves me, and I love him. That's just the plain truth.

"I don't understand. Scotty is my age. We went to school
together. I've known him since before puberty. You can't be
in love with him. I'm sure it's just a crush."

"Phoenix," Jude warns. "Don't whitewash her feelings." The
air is thickening with the heightened emotions.

"Wait. You knew?" We shift our eyes to my mom who's
now standing, staring at Jude incredulously.

"I knew, too." Oh, Aunt Dellah. A secret almost ruined
their friendship once before. I hope this doesn't do the same.

"So Phoenix and I are the last to know? You've all just been
keeping secrets." My mom is mad and hurt. Her eyes war
with her emotions. She scowls at Aunt Dellah. "Again."

"I didn't know until the crash." Mac grabs her hand for

support.

"Let's all keep a level head. Wynnie is a grown adult who can make her own life choices." I know Jude is trying to help, but I also know his words are going to fall short on the elevated emotions swirling in the room.

"Are you kidding me?" Phoenix's voice raises as his frustration grows. "Jude, he's our age. He's a single dad. She's out of her damn mind if she thinks I'm going to be okay with this." All points I knew would be an issue. He turns to me. "You're out of your mind."

"Phoenix, Hazel is older than us and was a single mom when we met her."

"Not fifteen years older. It's not the same thing." I don't think I've ever seen Phoenix and Jude argue, and I don't like it.

"Why didn't you tell us?" My heart breaks for the hurt in my mom's voice.

"For this exact reason. He's not a random stranger. You all know him. He's a good man. He treats me like a Queen. I love Tori, and I love Scotty."

"How did we end up in this situation again?" My mother looks between her lover and her best friend. Betrayal etched in her forehead.

"It's not the same, Little Dove." Jude lets go of me and walks over to stand beside my mom, taking her free hand. She pulls it away.

"We agreed no more secrets." He takes her hand again.

"I've watched them from afar for a while now. I didn't know exactly when it happened, but I saw the shift in them. If I had thought for a second that Scotty had ill intentions towards Wynnie, I would have stepped in. They didn't keep this from us because they were hiding. They kept it to themselves for them. Listen to how you're trying to already condemn them without even knowing their relationship."

I'm sobbing harder now, hearing Jude, Dad J, stick up for me and my relationship with Scotty.

The room is silent as my mom soaks up Jude's words and the information she's just learned. Finally, she takes his cheek in her hands and kisses him. "Why didn't you come to me with your suspicions?"

"Because it wasn't mine to tell. Their relationship is beautiful like ours." Jude reaches out for Phoenix's hand and waits. When he doesn't move, Jude releases my mother and steps in front of Phoenix.

"Phoenix." Jude tries to take his hand, and he steps back, shaking his head.

"I'm sorry. I can't." Phoenix glances at my mom, then back at Jude, and walks out. I turn to chase after him but Jude grabs my wrist.

"Give him a moment to process." Elliot reaches for me and I melt into him. This is all too much.

Jude smiles softly and turns back to my mom, lacing his fingers through hers. "Love doesn't have an age attached to it, Little Dove. I know it's hard to see our little girl all grown up, but she is."

"Why the fuck didn't he tell us sooner?" *He.* He's asking about Scotty. My dad is still mad, and I can understand.

"Because I asked him not to. I asked him to keep it a secret for me, and he agreed. I was afraid of this exact conversation. I'm sorry that it had to happen this way, but I'm not sorry it's finally out. He was planning to tell you today, and I was telling Mom. He was tired of hiding, and I wanted you all to finally know. I don't know what more can be said. You either accept it or you don't, but I want you to remember something. There are three of you. THREE. I may have had a small meltdown when I found out, but I was twelve, and it lasted half a day. I accepted my mother dating my two softball coaches and my father, whom I didn't even know at the time. You *know* him, and you know me. I'm not an irrational preteen who makes decisions without thinking. Maybe we shouldn't have kept it from you, but I stand by my feelings for him and for Tori." With the small amount of willpower I have left, I put my foot down. I drew my line in the sand. There really isn't any more to be said. Elliot whispers "good job" in my ear, but I don't want to hear it. I pull myself away from him and walk out.

I walk through the halls, eventually finding a bench and sitting. That went about as bad as I ever imagined it would go. I'm so emotionally exhausted. Elliot finds me and sits next to me.

"That was quite a show." I lean on his shoulder, and he puts his arm around me.

"It was, but on my quest to find you I bought snacks." He digs into his pocket and starts placing items on our laps.

"It looks like you robbed the vending machine." There's at least one of everything sitting between us.

"Only the best for my best girl."

43

Wynnie

Scotty had a six-hour surgery. After he was out, the nurse came and got me and brought me to his room. I almost fell to the floor when I saw him.

His left shoulder is in a sling, and he has road rash everywhere. I know he had his leather jacket on, but the witness told us he rolled several times, and it came off, along with his helmet. His head is completely bandaged. He had a brain bleed from hitting the front of a car.

"Hey, kiddo." I turn my head to look at the door. I'm sitting in the same spot I've been in for two days—holding Scotty's hand next to his bed. I see my mom standing in the doorway with a brown paper bag. "I brought you breakfast."

"I'm not hungry." She pulls up a chair next to me and strokes my hair.

"Wynnie. I'm putting my foot down. You need to get Tori and take her home. She needs some stability, and right now, that's you."

"Mom—"

"No. I'll stay with him. He won't be alone. Tori needs you

306

more than he does right now." The doctors have him sedated to help alleviate the stress on his body so the swelling will go down. They won't know the extent of his injuries until they feel it's safe to wake him up.

I know she's right. I've Facetimed with Tori since I've been here, but she needs more.

"What do I tell her?"

"The same thing we've been telling her. She's seen Mac. She knows they were in an accident and that the doctors are still taking care of her Daddy."

My dad got to go home yesterday morning with a brace on his leg. He was lucky. Scotty's bike saved him from worse injuries.

When he left the hospital, he went straight to Aunt Dellah's house and picked up Dean, Alex, and DJ. Tori was given the option to stay or go with them. She chose to stay, and Elliot said she's been glued to him.

"I can't lie to her." She smooths a hand down my back.

"It's not a lie. The doctors are doing their best to take care of him."

"I can't do this without him."

"You'll be strong for that little girl. But you also need to let her know it's okay to be scared. Bring Elliot with you. I know Dellah won't mind. Let him be your strength so you can be hers."

She's right. I lean into her, and she wraps her arms around me, pulling me in close.

"Phoenix?" I haven't seen him since he stormed out of the hospital room two days ago. Whenever I've asked about him, I'm told he's still processing.

"Give him time. I think he needs to talk to Scotty."

307

"But Mom—"

"I know, kiddo. It's not fair to you, but it also wasn't fair to him. Scotty and Phoenix were friends long before you and I came around. They need to work it out."

"And if he doesn't wake up?" I don't even want to consider that a possibility, but it is.

"Don't think like that. Scotty will wake up, and they'll have some kind of macho chest-pounding arm wrestling match or something, and they'll be fine. It will all be fine."

"I love you, Mom. And I love him."

"I know you do. I love you, too."

I've never been so excited to see Scotty's house. Elliot said he would drive Tori over and stay with us. I wanted to get here first to make sure nothing needed to be cleaned up. We left in a hurry on Sunday.

They should be here in less than thirty minutes, and I haven't showered since Sunday, either. As I'm getting dressed, feeling a little more human, I hear the sweetest voice on earth.

"Wynnie?"

"Back here, Sunshine." I walk out of the bedroom and a blur of yellow crashes into me. Tori's tiny arms wrap around my legs and I scoop her up into my arms.

"Wynnie. I missed you. How's my Daddy?" I brush the hair out of her eyes to see her red-rimmed silver eyes.

"Oh, Sunshine. I've missed you so much. The doctors are taking good care of Daddy. He should be home soon." I tuck her head under my chin and lock eyes with Elliot. He gives me a sad smile and I nod for him to follow me. I walk back into Scotty's room and lay down on the bed with her curled into me. Elliot walks around the bed and lies on her other side.

The three of us lay there in various states of despair, holding each other together.

I must doze off because I'm startled awake by the doorbell. Thankfully, Tori is still asleep, and I'm able to slide out from under her. Elliot opens his eyes, and I mouth "front door." He nods and closes his eyes.

The doorbell rings again, followed by a knock. Someone is impatient.

When I open the door, my heart drops again.

"Oh, Ms. Harmon. I wasn't expecting to see you. Your background information came out all clear. I left a message for Mr. Langford yesterday. Is he here?" She tries to look into the house around me, then looks me up and down. I probably look like a disheveled mess. I fell asleep with wet hair and no makeup.

"Oh, um, no." I'm so tired.

"No? We have an appointment for right now."

"He…he was…He's in the hospital. He was in an accident on Sunday."

"Accident? Where is the child." Child? She has a name.

"Tori is here. She's asleep."

"Which hospital? Can you get Mr. Langford on the phone?" She pulls out her phone, and starts typing furiously.

"He's unable to talk right now. He's sedated. There was swelling on his brain." She looks up at me from her phone, then quickly looks back down before bringing it to her ear.

"Hello, yes. This is Kathy Fischer with DFCS. I need an officer at the address I left at dispatch…I need to remove a child from the home…"

"What!" I startle myself with the volume of my tone. I pat my pockets and look around for my phone. It must still be in the bedroom.

"Oh, your Daddy can't help you this time, so don't even bother." I see red and slam the door in her face.

"I'll be right here when the officer shows up."

When I turn around, Elliot is standing in the hallway holding Tori.

"What's going on, Wynnie? Who was that?"

I walk past him to the bedroom, looking for my phone. I find it and immediately call my dad.

"Hey, Sweethear—"

"Dad, that woman is back, and she said she's here to take Tori. She said you can't help me this time."

"You're at Scotty's?"

"Yeah. She's outside. I slammed the door in her face. She called the station requesting an officer." I hear him chuckle and cover it with a cough.

"That wasn't very nice, but don't let anyone in until I make some calls. If I could drive right now, I'd be there in a heartbeat. Stupid fucking cast."

"Dad."

"Sorry, Sweetheart. Don't open the door for anyone until you hear back from me. Understand?"

"I understand. I won't let them take her."

"Who's going to take me?" *Shit.* I close my eyes and take a deep breath before turning to face Tori.

"No one, Sunshine. You aren't going anywhere without me. I promise." I pick her up and hold her to me like she's my lifeline.

310

Fifteen minutes later, the doorbell rings again.

"Wynnie, it's Little Beau. I need you to open the door, honey."

"I'm waiting for a phone call. You're going to have to wait, Beau." I hear the audible sigh from Ms. Fischer.

A few minutes later, I hear a phone ring outside moments before mine does.

"Dad." I pass Tori, who's sitting in my lap, to Elliot and go to Scotty's room, closing the door behind me.

"Wynnie, I need you to listen to me. You're going to have to give Tori over to Ms. Fischer and Beau."

"No," I say firmly.

"Listen to me, Sweetheart. Because of the contested birth certificate and Scotty being out of commission right now, it puts her in imminent danger in the eyes of the state."

"Dad, NO!" I whisper-shout, not wanting my voice to carry down the hall.

"Just listen, please. Dellah and Collin have a home study on file, but it expired last year. We're getting emergency custody transferred over to them, but we have to get special permission to extend the home study. If Scotty had any family around, this wouldn't matter."

"But I'm her family, and I'm certified to babysit." I feel like I'm spiraling. I just promised Tori I wouldn't leave her, and he's telling me I have to give her up.

"Rowyn. In the eyes of the law, you don't have any rights to her right now, and the only parent that does isn't physically able to do it. This is the best-case scenario. It should only take a few hours. Beau will stay with them at the police department while we settle everything. We're waiting on one paper to be signed and she can stay with Dellah and Collin.

311

I know it's not her home, but it's still with family. You can stay with her there."

"Dad." My voice is barely a whisper. I can't process this.

"It's a lot, and you're already going through a lot right now, but please trust me. We are doing everything we can for them both."

I hang up and immediately call Aunt Dellah. She's talking the moment the lines connect.

"It won't be long. We're already talking with our case worker. She assured us it's just a few hours." I sob into the phone. "Shhh. I know, Wynnie. I know. This isn't ideal, but I promise you she will be here before dinner."

"Aunt Dellah, I just promised her I wouldn't leave her alone, and now I have to break that promise and hand her over to a stranger because some unknown man is claiming Tori is his. This is total bullshit."

"I agree, but you're going to have to let it happen. Mac said she will have someone with her the entire time. If I know your dad, he'll hobble down there himself to sit with her so she sees a familiar face. She'll be safe and back with us soon. Have Elliot bring you home as soon as they leave."

"I feel like my world is crumbling around me."

"We're all here for you."

"Can I wait at the hospital until you hear something? I can't sit around and do nothing. At least I can be with Scotty."

"Go be with him. We'll keep you updated."

44

Elliot

Wynnie hands Tori over to me and leaves the room to pick up the call from her dad. I don't know what's going to happen, but I don't have a good feeling.

"Elliot, I'm scared." I hug Tori closer to me, resting her head on my shoulder.

"Me too, sweet girl, but you have the best people on your side to help you. We all love you and won't let anything bad happen to you." She sniffles, and my heart shatters.

It's hard not to compare my situation to hers. Paige was around this age when we lost our dad in a car accident, and Aunt Dellah and Uncle Collin took us in. We don't know Scotty's fate at the moment, but hearing bits and pieces of the social worker talk on the other side of the door doesn't give me hope.

Wynnie walks back into the room, and Tori jumps off my lap to go to her. Wynnie meets her with open arms, and I instantly know something's wrong.

When she looks up at me, she shakes her head, and her eyes

fill with tears. She sits on the floor with Tori in her lap and pulls her far enough away so they can see each other.

"Sunshine, you're going on a short trip to the police department." *Fuck*. What's going on? I must have made a noise because Wynnie looks up and quickly shakes her head. I sink back into the couch and listen as the tears prickle my eyes.

"Officer Beau and Ms. Fischer are going to take you there, feed you lunch, and hang out for just a little while. And then—"

"Are you coming too?" This is going to hurt.

"No baby, I can't come."

"Then I'm not going." If a person could physically fall to pieces, the look on Wynnie's face would be it.

"It won't be for long—"

"No. You promised you'd stay with me." Tori pushes on Wynnie's shoulders to try and get away, but Wynnie holds on to her.

"Tori, Daddy is hurt and—"

"You said the doctors were making him all better." I don't know which one of them is crying harder, but Wynnie lets Tori get up this time when she pushes away.

"Sunshine—"

"You're a liar, and Daddy said we don't like people who lie."

"Tori." Wynnie reaches out, and Tori backs away.

"No. I don't want you. I want my Daddy. I want my Daddy. I WANT MY DADDY!"

My best friend is a shell of herself, sitting on the floor listening to a piece of her heart reject her. I know this can't end well. They aren't going to come to an agreement. Someone has to be the bad guy, and I can't let that be Wynnie in Tori's eyes.

I get up from the couch and walk to the front door. Ms. Fischer and Officer Taylor look shocked to see me and even more shocked to see Tori and Wynnie crying behind me.

"She's not going to go willingly. Either of them. She loves pancakes. You might try bribing her with them." I'll give it to Ms. Fischer. At least there's remorse on her face this time.

"Could you pack her a bag with some of her favorite things? I'll be with her the entire time." Officer Taylor doesn't look happy about this situation either.

I hear a door slam behind me and see Wynnie lying on the floor, her body convulsing with the force of her sobs. I run to her side and look down the hall to see Tori's bedroom door is closed.

"Wynnie. Shhh. I've got you." I pull her into my lap and hold her. She's falling apart. I can hear Tori sobbing in her room behind the door.

"Elliot, I can't...I can't..." She's struggling to get any words out. All I can do is hold her and stroke her hair.

Ms. Fischer and Officer Taylor walk past us to knock on Tori's door. When they open the door to her room, Tori screams, and a stuffed animal comes flying past them.

"Go away. I want my Daddy. I want my Daaaaaddy!" Wynnie sobs harder, listening to Tori, and I pull her as close to me as she can go.

"Victoria, my name is Ms—"

"My name is Tori. It's T.O.R.I, Tori! Go away. I don't want you." I flinch when another stuffed animal hits the wall. I've never heard her this angry before.

"Okay, Tori. I'm a friend of your Uncle Mac. My name is Beau. We're going to take a fun trip to the police department."

"No. I'm not going with you. You're a stranger."

"How about we call Uncle Mac? He can tell you about me, so I'm not a stranger." I can hear the compassion in Officer Taylor's voice, and I gain so much respect for him.

"Uncle M-Mac?" She hiccups his name.

"Yes, Tori. Should we call Uncle Mac?"

"Y-yes." For the first time in the last several minutes, she stops screaming. I stroke Wynnie's hair in my lap, trying to soothe her, but she continues to cry.

I see Officer Taylor pull his phone out of his pocket. Neither of them has attempted to enter Tori's room yet; they're standing in the hall watching her.

"Beau? What's going on?" Wynnie stiffens at her dad's voice.

"Uncle Mac, Tori is having a hard time trusting me to bring her to the police department. She's being a smart little girl and doesn't want to leave the house with strangers. She's being so brave. Could you tell her a little about me so we aren't strangers anymore?" There's a pause before Uncle Mac speaks again.

"Tori, sweetie. Can you hear me?"

"Yes." Her voice is small and mousie, and it causes Wynnie to burrow farther into me.

"Sweetie, Officer Taylor, Little Beau, is my friend. We work together at the police department. He likes to eat stinky tuna fish sandwiches, and he's terrible at baseball." I hear her giggle, and it warms my heart slightly.

"Uncle Mac, I want my Daddy."

"I know, Baby, but the doctors are taking good care of him. He has to get better before he can come home. Where's Wynnie?"

"I don't want Wynnie. She lied to me."

"Fuck. I can't…" Wynnie stands and runs out the front door. I follow her and she stops at my car.

"Wynnie. Where are you going?" She sinks to the ground, curling her knees into her chest.

"She's never going to forgive me, Elliot. She hates me." I crouch down and curl my body around her as much as possible.

"She's just upset right now." There's nothing I can say to make this better. This is all fucked up.

"I broke a promise. I broke her trust."

"She'll forgive you in a few hours when you're both home at my house. It won't be long."

We look up when we hear noise at the front of the house. Tori holds Officer Taylor's hand with her rainbow unicorn bookbag on her back. Her face is red and tear-stained. They walk down the stairs, and Tori looks over and sees us. She tugs on Taylor's hand, and when he sees her line of sight, he lets go.

"Wynnie." Her little legs run to us as fast as she can. She throws her arms around Wynnie, who pulls her in and surrounds her. "Wynnie."

"I know, Sunshine. I'm so sorry. I'm so, so sorry. I'll see you super soon. Okay?"

"Uncle Mac is gonna come play with me at the police department. He said you're gonna go be with my Daddy, and I'll be with yours."

"Oh yeah? That sounds like an amazing idea. Uncle Mac is the best."

"He told me not to be mad at you." Tori hangs her head and Wynnie kisses her forehead.

"It's okay, Sunshine. Don't be upset. I'll see you again really soon, okay? You need to go with Beau now. I'm jealous you'll get Uncle Mac all to yourself for a few hours. I'll go see Daddy and tell him how brave you are and how much you love him, and I'll meet you back at Aunt Dellah's tonight. I love you, Sunshine."

"I love you too, Wynnie." The girls embrace again, and Tori hugs me before she walks off with Ms. Fischer and Officer Taylor.

"Can I use your phone to call my dad?" I hand it to her and Mac picks up quickly.

"Elliot?"

"Dad, it's me."

"Sweetheart. It's going to be okay. I'm going down there to stay with her. Broken leg and all. If she can't have you, I guess I'm a good substitute."

"Thank you so much, Dad."

"Your mother will be mad at me, and probably Jude, since he's driving me. Go relieve her from the hospital. I'll let you know as soon as I hear something. I love you, Sweetheart."

"Love you too, Dad."

"El, will you take me to Scotty?"

45

Wynnie

"Hey, Mom." She looks down at the phone in her hand, surprised to see me at the hospital. "I didn't call." She stands from her seat and walks towards me, seeing my state.

"What's going on? What happened? All your dad said was you were on your way?"

"Social Services took Tori."

"Wynnie." She pulls me in for a hug, and I embrace her.

"I think Dad pulled some strings, but he said Aunt Dellah and Uncle Collin can take her after some paperwork gets completed."

"I'm sure he did everything he could."

"Did he tell you where he was going?" Judging by her face, the answer is no. "He's heading to the police department to stay with Tori until she can go to Aunt Dellah's."

"Stupid man with his heart of gold. I'm not surprised." I laugh because it's true.

"Has there been any change?" I pull away from my mom and take the seat she was occupying next to Scotty's bed.

"No. He's still stable, though. That's a good thing." I rub Scotty's arm and hold his hand.

"Thank you. You can head home if you'd like. I have my e-reader and several books. Dad will let me know as soon as he hears something." I run a finger down Scotty's bruised and battered face. "Tori needs to see him soon."

"He doesn't look the greatest." That's an understatement.

"I know, but you should have heard her today. She's in this weird limbo where she doesn't know who to trust. She needs to see her dad, even if he looks like this."

"Have you eaten?" I shake my head. "I'll go grab us some food. We can eat and talk, and then I'll head home." She rubs my back, and it soothes me in the way only a mother's touch can.

A mother's touch. That's something that Tori will never feel. She asked me to be her mother the day I took her for ice cream. Does she see me as a mother figure? Tori has been mine for years. I love her like she's my own. She is mine.

"That sounds great. Thank you, Mom. I love you."

When she returns with food, we eat and chat about nothing in general.

"Spill it, Mom. I know you have questions that are eating you alive. Go ahead and ask." She looks to Scotty and back to me.

"Just one."

"Yes," I say flatly. She tilts her head to the side, confused by my answer.

"Yes, what?"

"You're either going to ask me if he makes me happy or if I really love him. The answer is yes to both questions." She smiles and huffs a laugh.

320

"Okay."

"Okay? That's it? No lecture?" She comes over to me and crouches at my feet.

"Baby girl, like you reminded me, I shoved three men in your face. One was your long-lost father, and the other two were your softball coaches. Do you remember what you asked me?" I try and think back to the weekend I ran away and can't come up with anything.

"I don't."

"At the ripe old age of twelve, you asked me if they made me happy. That's all you cared about. Two of them are younger than me, and did I mention there was three of them?" I answer through a laugh.

"You might have."

"You just wanted me to be happy. That's all I want for you. Your happiness. Now, if that ever changes, I'm pretty sure Mac still knows how to hide a body." I groan and drop my forehead to hers.

"And Phoenix? How good is he at hiding a body?" She looks at Scotty and back at me, her eyes filled with sorrow.

"Soon." She stands and brushes my hair behind my ear. "I have to go relieve the guys. Call me if you need me, and I'll be back in a heartbeat."

After she leaves, I carefully crawl into bed with Scotty. I'm emotionally exhausted and couldn't concentrate on my book. I cuddle next to him and close my eyes.

"I need you to be okay. Tori needs you to be okay." My tears are silent as they fall down my cheeks. I've cried so much in the last few days. I'm surprised I have anymore left.

"Scotty. Please be okay. You can't do this to us. We're just getting started." My fear and sadness weigh heavy on my chest, and my breath becomes labored. I'm mad. Mad that I have no control over what's happening around me. Mad that if something happens to him, he'll never know how much he means to me. How much I love him.

"Avocado. Do you hear me, Scotty? Fucking avocado. That's our safeword. You have to come back to me. This pain has to stop. You promised no questions asked. Avocado."

I bury my head into his neck, sobbing. It hurts my heart when he doesn't instantly wrap his arms around me like he does in his bed at home.

I close my eyes a little tighter and wish harder than I've ever wished for anything.

"Please bring him back to me. I want us to be a family. I wish I could be Tori's mother and show her what a real mother's love can be like."

46

Wynnie

Why is the room shaking?

"Wynnie, wake up." Something warm rubs my arm. "Come on, Wynnie. Tori is coming home soon."

"Tori." I sit up and hands grab my shoulder.

"Careful of Scotty." My head whips to the side, and I see him lying in the same spot on the hospital bed that he's been for the past three days.

"Uncle Collin. What are you doing here? What time is it?" I feel disoriented.

"It's early morning. Around six a.m."

"Morning? Where's Tori? Someone should have woken me up." I carefully climb off the bed and frantically collect my things.

"Wynnie, relax. It will still be a few hours."

"What do you mean by *hours*? It was only supposed to be a few hours to begin with. Now it's tomorrow. Where is she?"

"She's still at the police department. We found out late last night that we had to wait until the judge could sign the paperwork at nine this morning."

"Why didn't anyone call me?" I pick my phone up from the table next to the bed, and see the battery has died. I was listening to music, and it must have drained after I fell asleep.

"We tried." I flop in the chair, feeling defeated once more by life.

"We called up to the nurse's station, and she told us you were asleep, and we left a message to call if you woke up. I came in early because I thought you'd want to go home and shower. I know yesterday was exhausting." Exhausting. Draining. Heartbreaking. Pick one, or all.

"How soon will she be home? I miss her so freaking much."

"The judge will sign the paperwork first thing at nine. Dellah will be there waiting."

"Can I go with her? I don't want to wait a minute longer than I have to. I need to see her. I can't imagine how scared she is."

"Of course you can." He pulls me in and hugs me. It feels like there's been so many embraces lately, and while I love it in general, the reasoning behind them is hard. "I'll stay with Scotty. Hazel said you were thinking of bringing Tori by to see him. Did you want to do that today?"

"Let's play it by ear. It's been two…well, I guess three days now since she's seen him. I'm sure she would love it." He reaches into his pocket and pulls out his keys. "I'm in Lot G, row 7. I'll stay until someone comes to get me."

"Thanks, Uncle C." I turn back to Scotty and caress the small part of his cheek that isn't scraped up.

"I'm going to get our girl Scotty. I'll be back soon." I kiss the same spot I just caressed and thank Uncle Collin again before going in search of his car.

★ ★ ★ ★ ★

My shower felt incredible, but the ride to the courthouse felt long and ominous. I'm convinced it can't be this simple.

"You and your mom are so similar." Aunt Dellah's comment pulls me out of my worry bubble.

"What do you mean?"

"Your leg hasn't stopped shaking since we got in the car. It's Hazel's nervous tell, too." I didn't even realize I was doing it. I stop, and Aunt Dellah reaches over and takes my hand.

My mind is a jumbled mess as I look out the window, watching the houses and stores go by in a blur.

"We will have her back in less than twenty minutes. Your dad hasn't left her side. I brought them dinner last night and Tori some pajamas since Mac told me she was wearing a dress. I thought it might be easier for her to sleep."

"This has to be almost over, right?"

"We'll talk to the judge about the next step. Hopefully, Scotty being in the hospital will expedite things. He doesn't need to be awake for them to take blood for the paternity test."

"Who would do this?" Scotty and I hadn't had time to discuss who he thought Becky could have been hanging around. No one even tried to claim Tori until Becky passed away.

"I have no clue, little niece." I need to stop thinking about it. Tori belongs to Scotty, and there's no reason to worry.

If I thought the car ride felt long, the wait in the waiting room was torturous. I had to sit outside the courtroom while everyone else went in.

The hallway is eerily empty except for a man all the way at

the other end. He's dressed in all black, and his hair is a dark auburn similar to my mom's, but he's too far away to tell any other features, and he's giving me the creeps.

I mentally tick down the minutes while singing *You Are My Sunshine* in my head. It's the only thing that comforts me until I hear the heavy courtroom doors open.

I'm on my feet and have Tori in my arms before I even realize what I've done.

"I've missed you so much, Sunshine. I love you. I'm so sorry. Please don't hate me." Her tiny hands cup my cheeks.

"I love you, Wynnie." It's like my heart implodes, and all of the shattered pieces are put back together. I hear a door slam and look down the hall toward the sound. The creepy guy is gone.

"Are you ready to go to Aunt Dellah's house?"

"I want to go home."

"Sunshine, we can't go home until Daddy is all better, but I'm going to be there with you at Aunt Dellah's everyday." She hugs me tightly.

"I want to see Daddy."

"How about we go home, take a bath, and have lunch? We can go see Daddy after that." She nods and cuddles into my neck.

Tori falls asleep on the ride back to Aunt Dellah's, and her little snores are comforting. Aunt Dellah takes the opportunity to talk before the chaos of her house.

"The judge is going to send an order for Scotty's blood to be DNA tested. We should hopefully have the results back at the beginning of next week."

"That feels so long. I want to take her home to her house."

"I know you do, kiddo, but we have to follow the rules. Are

you sure she's ready to see him?" I peek back at her again, and her lips pout in her sleep. She's too little for so many worries.

"Tori asked, and I can't deny her. I'll talk to her before we go and explain how he looks so she's prepared." Aunt Dellah sighs.

"I'm not sure there's any way to prepare for that. I'll have Elliot drive you girls to the hospital. He's offered to stay the night with Scotty so that you can stay here with Tori."

"I—"

"Don't argue. I'm pulling the 'I'm older than you' card. Tori needs you more than Scotty does. He's in good hands, and there's nothing you can do for him." All of her points are valid. A good night's sleep in an actual bed does sound amazing.

"Okay."

"Elliot said you girls can have his room, and he'll bunk with Finny. Unless you think Tori wants to sleep with Paige. Wherever she wants to sleep, we can work it out."

"I'd rather we stay in El's room. I'm not sure I'm going to be willing to separate from her anytime soon."

"I completely understand. I want to assure you that Tori being with us is a formality for the courts. As far as I'm concerned, she's under your care. She's yours, Wynnie."

★ ★ ★ ★ ★

"She's yours, Wynnie. She's yours, Wynnie."

That thought is on repeat as Elliot and I walk hand in hand with Tori down the hospital hallway to Scotty's room.

I sit on the bench outside his room and pull her into my lap. Elliot sits next to me and rubs her back.

"Do you remember what I told you about Daddy?"

"I think so." She nods.

"Daddy is asleep. His head is wrapped in a bandage, he kind of looks like a mummy." She smiles. "He has a holder on his arm because he hurt his shoulder, and he has lots of booboos on his face. Some look pretty gross." I scrunch my nose to make light of the situation, and she giggles. "It's okay to touch him and sit on the bed with him, but you can't jump around."

"Can we wake him up to talk to me?"

"No, Sunshine. Daddy's brain still has a booboo, and he needs lots of sleep so he can heal. Are you ready?" She shakes her head.

"I'm scared," she whispers. Tears well in her eyes, and I pull her in close to my chest.

"Me, too. But Daddy is getting better every day. Come on. You can talk to him, and even though he can't answer, I know he can hear us in his brain. And you know what I have?" I reach into my bag, take out a pack of washable markers, and show her. Tori's face lifts a little. "I'll carry you into his room, and when you're ready, you can look. Okay?" She nods into my neck.

When we walk in, there's a nurse at his side checking his chart.

"Oh, we're sorry. We can come back." The tall woman with beautiful ebony skin and fun pink-framed glasses looks at us and smiles. Uncle Collin is sitting in the corner playing on his phone and he smiles and gives us a nod.

"He's all yours. I was just leaving." The nurse gives us a warm smile.

"Is my Daddy all better?" Tori turns her head to look at the nurse, but not enough to see Scotty.

Sheila, as her name tag says, walks over to us and looks Tori in the eyes with a smile.

"Baby child, your Daddy is doing wonderfully. He isn't all better yet, but he will be soon. Do you want to hear how strong his heart is?" Tori nods and Sheila motions for me to come closer.

I sit on the bed next to Scotty's chest, and Tori looks at him for the first time. Her body instantly trembles with tears.

"Here, little one, listen." Sheila hands me the top of the stethoscope. I carefully place the earpieces into her ears, and Sheila moves the other end over Scotty's heart. "Do you hear it? Thump-thump. Thump-thump. It's nice and strong." Tori's face softens, and a smile creeps across her cheeks.

"I hear it. Bump-bump. Bump-bump. That's his heart-beep?" I seal my lips together to not laugh at her misuse of the word heartbeat. Elliot put his forehead on my shoulder, his body vibrating with his attempt not to laugh. I hear a snicker from the corner and know Uncle Collin is just as amused by her misuse of the word.

"It sure is. Your Daddy is doing well. Tomorrow, we'll try to wake him up from his long nap to see if his booboos have healed yet."

"You are?"

"Yay, Daddy." Sheila must have heard the shock in my words.

"We are. But, sweet child, he may not be ready to wake up yet. He may still be sleepy and need a longer nap. Do you ever wake up from a nap and still feel sleepy?"

"Every morning for school." We all laugh, and for that temporary moment, I feel lighter.

"Well, it's a good thing it's summer then, huh? I'll let you all visit. Push the button if you need anything."

"Thank you, Sheila." I smile at this saint of a woman, and she smiles back. She leans in close to my ear so Tori can't hear.

"Tomorrow around ten a.m. if you'd like to be here." I nod my thanks, and she leaves.

Putting the markers on the bed next to Scotty, I look at Tori and smile. Uncle Collin walks over and puts his hand on my shoulder.

"I'm going to head out. I've called for a ride." He kisses Tori and me on the head.

"Love you, Uncle Collin. Thank you for staying." His returning smile is warm.

"I'll walk you out, Dad." Elliot and Uncle Collin leave, and I turn back to Tori.

"Are you ready to color Daddy?"

"Hey, Wynnie? How many more days till your birthday?"

"Oh, there's…" Shit. My birthday was yesterday. What a shitty fucking day. "Well, Sunshine, my birthday was yesterday." She looks at me and pouts. Turning to Scotty, she puts her hand on his chest.

"Daddy, you have to wake up soon. I have to give Wynnie her present. It's late, but I don't know wheres you put it." My heart can't take her sincerity. She turns back to me. "Do you think he heard me?"

Smiling, I nod my head. "Yeah, Sunshine. I think he did. Let's color."

47

Dellah

I'm stirring the pot of spaghetti on the stove when Collin walks in the back door.

"How is everything? And how did you get home?" He walks over and kisses me on the cheek before wrapping his arms around me from behind.

"I took a rideshare so the girls could leave whenever they wanted to. Scotty is the same. They're talking about pulling back on his sedatives tomorrow to see how he's doing." Collin's hips sway us back and forth to a tune in his head. I lean back into him and let him lead.

"That's a good thing, right?"

"Nothing has changed except the reduction of his brain swelling. It could be good or bad. They need to test his cognitive skills before making more decisions."

As soon as our temporary guardianship papers were signed this morning, we had them faxed to the hospital. Because Tori is Scotty's next of kin, we can now get updates on his status. It's a relief to be able to know what's going on.

"Will you call the kids while I grab the garlic bread?"

"In a minute. Dance with me." Collin takes my hand off the spoon and spins me around. We sway in the kitchen for a few minutes before we hear a groan.

"Can you two not be so gross?"

"Oh, Finny. I can't wait until you have your first girl crush.

"Mooooom." That word never gets old.

"Go find your sister and tell her dinner is ready."

"Ugh. Anything to get away from this." I laugh into Collin's chest.

"Oh to be twelve again. I love them."

"And I love you, Bunny."

After dinner, as Collin and I wash dishes, Wynnie and Tori come in through the back door.

"Hey ladies, we saved you some dinner. Are you hungry?" Wynnie looks drained.

"We grabbed food on the way home. Those yellow arches called our names."

"I understand. It's always tempting. What do you need? How can we help?"

"Sleep. We're exhausted."

"Wynnie?" Tori looks up at her with sad puppy dog eyes, and she picks her up.

"I know, Sunshine. Let's get to bed."

"I'll get them settled. Be right back." Collin pecks my lips, and they walk upstairs. I feel so helpless. I wish there was more I could do.

A few minutes later, Collin comes back into the kitchen, phone to his ear, looking concerned.

"What's wrong?" Collin holds up a finger, gesturing for me to give him a minute.

"Okay, son. Thanks for the update. We'll let her know. One of us will come by and relieve you in the morning. Love you."

Collin turns to me with a solemn face. "That was Elliot. Scotty just spiked a fever. They want him to be fever-free for twenty-four hours before they try to take him off the sedatives, so it won't be tomorrow."

I look up the stairs because I know the news will devastate Wynnie. "Can we tell her in the morning? She needs a good night's sleep."

"I couldn't agree more, Bunny."

"Yesterday was her birthday, and she hasn't even mentioned it. What a shit show these last few days have been." Collin nods and pulls me into him.

"We'll follow her lead. If she wants to celebrate, we will. If she'd rather not think about it, then it's just another day that's passed."

I wake up to giggling outside my bedroom door.

"I told you my dad snores loud." I silently laugh as the bear next to me snores. Paige has always made fun of Collin for his snoring, and apparently, she's trying to get Tori to join along with it.

"Good morning, girls." They squeak and run down the hallway. I smell fresh coffee, which tells me Wynnie must be up since Elliot is still at the hospital. There were no more calls last night, so I hope that means everything is still stable with Scotty.

As I walk downstairs, I find Wynnie at the stove making piles of pancakes.

"You didn't have to cook." She turns and smiles and I pour

myself a cup of coffee.

"It's Tori's favorite. I thought some normalcy would be good, and I needed something to pass the time." I walk up to her and place my hand on her shoulder.

"I have some news." She freezes. "Scotty spiked a fever last night, so they can't reduce the sedation until at least tomorrow." Her head hangs down, and she takes several deep breaths.

"Okay. One more day is good. It's more time for him to heal." She's speaking out loud, but I know she's talking to herself.

"Can I help with anything?"

"I'd still like to see him today. Will you come with me?"

"Actually, I was going to ask if I could come with you anyway. We can take two cars and leave one there so no one feels stranded. Phoenix said he would take a shift today, so whenever you're ready to come back, you can call Dad P. to relieve you." She freezes at Phoenix's name. He still hasn't spoken to her, but knowing he's offered to stay with Scotty must be a good sign.

"He's coming around." I run a hand down her back in comfort.

"Thank you. That sounds good. Is it okay for Tori to stay?"

"You never have to ask. I'll make plates for everyone. Oh, and Wynnie?" She turns and looks over her shoulder at me. I mouth "Happy Belated Birthday," and she turns back around and shakes her head.

Ignore the day it is.

"How is he, El?" Elliot looks tired, slumped in the hospital recliner.

"Hey Mom, Wynnie. His fever never came back, and there hasn't been any changes." Wynnie walks to his bed, carefully climbs up, and curls into him. Her hand rubs the beard that's grown over the last several days.

"That beard is making him look like a badass." Wynnie smiles at Elliot, but it's weak.

"Hey Elliot, how about we go raid the vending machine and get Wynnie some snacks before we head back."

"Peanut M&M's, please." Elliot rubs her legs.

"I got you, bestie." I love their friendship and I'm so glad they have each other.

We walk toward the cafeteria to get coffee and snacks in silence. It feels like everything around us has been in a constant state of chaos for over a week.

"How is she really, Elliot?"

"I don't know, Mom. She isn't talking to me. I want to help her, but I don't know how." I put my arm around his waist and pull him into my side.

"You're doing great. She'll talk when she's ready. Just keep reminding her you're here for her."

Hands and pockets full of chocolates, salty snacks, and carbonated drinks, we head back to Scotty's room. As we come down the hall I see someone standing outside his door. He's tall, dressed in black, and his dark auburn hair is slicked back to his head.

We stop when we get to the door, but he doesn't seem to notice our presence. Inside, Wynnie has fallen asleep next to Scotty on the bed.

"Hi, are you a friend of Scotty's?" He turns his head further away so we can't see his face.

"Just visiting."

"Would you like to come in and see him?" He's giving me the creeps, but I don't want to be rude to someone Scotty knows. His patrons have been sending cards and gifts to the bar, and Kristina and Aimee have stopped by several times to drop things off.

"No, thank you, Dellah." Warning bells go off in my head. He doesn't look familiar but I haven't gotten a good look at him.

"I'm sorry. Do I know you?" He turns his head slightly over his shoulder, and I see his profile. He looks vaguely familiar, but I still can't place him.

"Not yet. But you will. She's mine, and I'll have her." He turns away from us and walks down the hall.

"What the hell was that, Mom?"

"I have no idea. I don't think I know him."

"Was he talking about Wynnie? Who is he?"

"I have no idea, but I'm going to ensure the nurses know what's happening."

48

Wynnie

"Can I help with dinner?" Aunt Dellah smiles at me from the stove where she's cooking ground beef for tacos.

"Of course. Can you grab the cheese and sour cream from the fridge?"

I spent most of the day with Scotty at the hospital. I texted Phoenix to spend the night with Scotty. There was awkwardness when he came and we exchanged polite conversation before I left for Aunt Dellah's house.

The rest of my mom's household is all here, and we're making tacos for dinner. It's nice to have some normalcy right now, even if I'd rather curl up under the covers and sleep until Scotty wakes up.

"Wynnie, Tori is cheating." I look up to see a sour-faced Finn. He's grown into such a handsome teenager. His bright blue eyes are mesmerizing.

"How is a five year old cheating?" They're playing with the foam guns, and I've had several bullets wizz past my head.

"She's smaller than everyone, hides where no one can see

337

her, and then sneak attacks us." Aunt Dellah and I both burst into laughter.

"Says the teenager whining about a kindergartner."

"Moooom. It's not a fair fight."

"Finny, I believe you have Jude on your team. That means all of the little kids and Elliot are together. It seems very fair to me." He throws his hands up in frustration.

"You women wouldn't understand." He stomps away, and Tori pops up from the armchair and shoots him in the back.

He spins on us when we burst into hysterics. "See. Not fair!"

"You two are going to cause trouble." My dad's gruff voice interrupts our laughing.

"Dad, don't be grumpy because you can't play." He's been sitting on the couch with his leg propped on the table, dodging bullets all night.

"They should be happy I'm out of commission."

"Hey, Dad. Would you like to come to the hospital with me tomorrow? They're planning to try and wake Scotty up." He didn't have a fever all day. They think it was just a random spike last night and are going ahead tomorrow morning with their plans.

"If you want me there, Sweetheart, I'll be there."

"Do you promise not to kick a man while he's down?" His deep laugh is soothing to my nerves. I feel like I'm constantly on edge.

"Can I go see Daddy, too?" I open my arms for Tori to come to me and scoop her up.

"They're going to wake Daddy from his nap tomorrow. If he isn't too sleepy, maybe someone can bring you to see him tomorrow night."

"Yay." She bounces in excitement in my arms.

"I said maybe, Sunshine. If he's too tired, we have to let him nap some more."

"Okay." She starts to pout, and I whisper in her ear.

"Finn is trying to sneak up behind you." She grins and spins in my arms, popping him in the shoulder with a bullet.

"Oh, come ON! You're all a bunch of cheaters. Uncle Mac, is any of this fair?"

"All's fair in love and foam gun wars, Finny."

As the adults sit down to dinner after serving the kids, we're all engrossed in conversation when a shrill scream pierces the air.

"Tori, what's wrong?" I jump from my seat and run to her.

"Th-the man. He was in the window?"

"The man from your nightmare?" Is she seeing things?

"He was real. He's here!"

"I'll go look outside and check." Uncle Collin stands from his seat and walks towards the back door.

"I'll go with you."

"Be careful, Jude." My mom looks concerned, and Uncle Collin and Jude walk out the back door

"Stupid fucking broken leg." My mom rubs my dad's arm. Being in a cast is torture for him.

"What the fuck!" Everyone looks to the back door as more shouting continues. Tori clings to me, and Mac growls for all the kids to get upstairs. He already has his phone to his ear calling the police station.

Tori and I are at the bottom of the stairs because she won't leave me to go up with everyone else. Elliot is making sure the little kids are safe at the top of the stairs.

The back door swings open, and Jude and Uncle Collin walk in with someone between them.

"My guys are on their way. They'll be here in five." Tori screams again.

"That's him. The scary man from my window." She buries her head in my neck, and I can feel her body shaking with her tears.

When I look up at the man, I realize it's the same one from the courthouse. Elliot gasps, and Aunt Dellah looks at us then back at the man they're holding. Realization and shock crosses her face. Who is this man?

Uncle Collin throws him to the ground, and he grunts.

"Jesus fuck, Collin." Aunt Dellah's jaw drops when the unknown man uses her husband's name.

"What the fuck? Nicholas?"

"Collin, do you know him?" Mac looks between the two men. His brows furrow and it seems like he's seeing something the rest of us haven't yet.

"It's my fucking brother. Get up, asshole." Uncle Collin and Jude grab Nicholas by the forearms and haul him to his feet. My dad picks up the phone, and I hear him tell his men to roll easy.

"Collin, what's going on?" Aunt Dellah keeps looking back at Tori and me with concern.

"I don't know. Let's ask him." They sit him down on one of the bar stools at the kitchen counter. His eyes drift to me, and I get the feeling like I'm being watched again, only this time I know I'm being stared at by Nicholas.

"What are you doing here, Nicholas?"

"Ask your wife. I told her." All eyes turn to Aunt Dellah. My mom comes to sit next to me, also noticing that Nicholas is staring in my direction.

"What is he talking about?" She looks back at Uncle Collin with confusion in her eyes.

"I-We saw him outside Scotty's hospital room earlier. He was watching Wynnie and Scotty sleep. He said 'She's mine' when I asked him who he was. We notified the hospital staff in case he came back. Collin, I didn't know. I've only ever seen him in pictures from when you were younger. I swear I had no idea he was your brother." He walks up to her and pulls Aunt Dellah to his chest.

"It's okay, Bunny. I wouldn't have expected you to know."

There's a knock at the back door, and two uniformed officers walk in. One is Little Beau, and the other I haven't seen often.

"Detective Harmon. Is everything okay here?" Beau walks over to shake my dad's hand.

"Taylor. Creed. I'm not sure yet."

"Don't let him take me. Please, Wynnie. I don't want to go. I want to stay with you. Please keep me. Please. Please, Wynnie. I'll be good, I promise." Tori hysterically rambles through her tears, trying to crawl into my skin.

"Sunshine, Beau isn't here for you. Shhh. It's okay. You're mine." She pulls her head out of my neck and looks up at me.

"I'm yours?"

"Oh, Sunshine. There was never any question. You are mine."

"She's mine, you bitch." Nicholas snarls and tries to stand up from his seat, but the officers push him back down.

"Ugh, what is it with men and that word?"

"What's going on here?" Beau stands in front of Nicholas, so he's blocking his line of sight to Tori and me.

"That snotty little kid is mine. The stupid druggie cunt, Becky, told me she belonged to me. She's my meal ticket."

I cover Tori's one ear and whisper in the other.

"Sunshine, I need you to go upstairs with Elliot and the other kids. This is important adult stuff, and I want you to be safe."

"But—"

"Please. You're mine, forever and always. I super promise this time. Go upstairs, please." I look up at Elliot, and he nods, opening his arms for Tori. Once she's upstairs and I know she's safe, I put on my new mama bear persona and turn towards the room.

"I don't know who the fuck you think you are, and I don't care that you're related to Uncle Collin, but TORI doesn't belong to you."

"I guess we'll see what the DNA test says in a few days." The room falls silent for several heartbeats.

"What are you talking about?" Aunt Dellah is wide-eyed as she stares at her brother-in-law.

"That's why I was at the hospital earlier, to get my blood drawn. I'm the one contesting the birth certificate. Becky said she was mine, not Scotty's."

"No." It's him.

"Is that why you were at the courthouse?"

"Yeah, I wanted to know where she was going to be. Wasn't I pleasantly surprised to see my sister-in-law and brother get custody of my daughter?"

"She's not yours," I growl out.

"Too bad the bitch is dead, or she'd tell you herself. Who do you think she was with before she went crawling back to him? She thought he could give her a better life. All it took

342

was a call after she gave birth to the brat to get my claws back into her. Except she left without the baby. I'm here to claim her now that Becky isn't in the way to stop me."

"Officer Taylor, get him the fuck out of my house." I've never seen Uncle Collin so mad.

"It's fine. I'll go. Enjoy your last few days with her. Come next week, she'll be where she belongs. With me."

"Don't come back, Nicholas. You aren't welcome here. If I ever see you on my property again, I'll have you arrested for trespassing."

Taylor and Creed escort him out of the house, and I run to my dad.

"What can we do? She belongs to Scotty, Dad. He's not even awake to defend himself." The new information is swirling through my head, and I feel completely overwhelmed.

"Sweetheart, we just have to wait. Dellah and Collin have temporary guardianship. Until Scotty is deemed capable of caring for her and gets released from the hospital, she's safe here. My guys heard Collin tell him not to come back, and I'll make sure they are on high alert."

"Thank you, Dad." I hug him and feel comfort in his embrace for a moment. "I feel so torn. I want to see Scotty but can't leave Tori right now." My mom comes over and joins our hug.

"How about I go stay with Phoenix and Scotty at the hospital, and you go upstairs and take care of your little girl? I'll let you know if he even flinches. You can come in the morning whenever you wake up." It seems like the closest I'm going to get to being there for both of them.

"That sounds perfect. Thank you."

"Hey, Dellah. Mind if we stay, too? Jude can take the kids

343

back. I might be in a cast, but I'm not useless, and I don't trust that asshole not to come back with Tori and Wynnie still here." Before Aunt Dellah can answer, Jude puts his hand on my dad's shoulder.

"We'll all stay. I'll make breakfast in the morning."

"Paige and DJ can stay with Tori and me. Dean and Alex can have Paige's room. Elliot is already with Finn."

"Mac, are you going to be okay with your leg if you sleep on a couch?" asks Uncle Collin.

"I'll use the recliner and prop my leg up. It will be the most comfortable anyway. Sleeping with this thing is a bitch."

49

Wynnie

Thirty minutes. It's been thirty minutes since they reduced Scotty's sedation. It could be hours until he wakes up, though—if he wakes up.

No. Scotty is waking up. Period. I have to think positive. Before I came in, I threw several pennies into the well in front of the hospital. Every one of them was the same wish. *I wish that Scotty wakes up and we can be a family.* Dream big, right?

I have my e-reader, snacks, and my emotional support best friend with me. Elliot and I have gotten each other through a lot over the years, and I'm so grateful to have him. I know I asked my Dad to come, but he alerted the hospital security about Nicholas and felt it was best for him to stay at Aunt Dellah's house to keep everyone there safe.

"Go Fish." Elliot scoffs at me.

"How do you seriously have no threes?" I shrug.

"Why are we playing a kid's game anyway?"

"Because Tori said it was your favorite. She snuck it into my pocket as we were leaving." This is *her* favorite card game, so we play it often. It makes sense now.

"Bestie, are you doing okay? I'm worried about you." I know he is. I can tell by the looks and glances he's been giving me. I'm surprised it took him so long to ask.

"I'm surviving. I need today to go well. I need Scotty to wake up and everything to be fine. I need that blood test to come back proving Tori is Scotty's."

"Wynnie, you know as well as the rest of us that there's no denying who Tori belongs to."

"I know. But how ass backward is it that anyone can just say, 'Hey, I think that kid belongs to me' and turn everyone's lives upside down."

"It's definitely not ideal." I huff.

"That's the understatement of the year."

"Well, if you ever need to kick any more kids' asses at ice cream shops, I'm your gay for it."

"What does that even mean, weirdo?" We laugh together for longer than necessary because it feels good to laugh. I pull him into me and hug him. I really appreciate his friendship.

"Have I told you lately that I love you?"

"No."

"What?" I tell him all the time. He knows I love his goofy ass.

"I didn't say that." I pull away and look at Elliot. My brows knit together, trying to decipher what he's saying, when I hear rustling fabric behind us.

"Oh my god. Scotty." A beautiful, scraped-up, very groggy face is staring back at me. "Call the nurse, El." He runs from the room, and all I can do is stare. I'm afraid to move or even breathe. What if it isn't real?

"Pinky. Come here." His voice is scratchy from not being

used, and he clears his throat.

"Scotty. Oh god. You're awake." Tears well in my eyes, and I can't do anything to contain them as they spill over. I sit on the bed next to his good shoulder, and he grabs my leg, while I try and get him a cup of water.

He takes a few pulls from the straw before speaking again. "Fuck, Pinky. You're here."

"Where else would I be?" Elliot walks in with Sheila behind him. Today, her glasses are purple and sparkly. Tori would love them.

"Well, hello, Mr. Langford. You've been missed."

"Scotty, please. How-how long have I been out?"

"The accident was Sunday morning. It's been five days." He shifts his shoulder around.

"You dislocated it. We can probably take that sling off now that you're awake. Just don't go playing any softball in the hallway. Okay?" Scotty smiles but hasn't taken his eyes off of me.

"How's your pain, Scotty? Does anything hurt?" He closes his eyes, I assume, to assess his body. Various parts of him wiggle around me.

"My shoulder feels okay. My left side hurts, and my head."

"Glad to hear about your shoulder. You have a lot of road rash on your left side, but I can examine you for any other injuries. You had a few holes drilled in your head to relieve some of the pressure. I can get you some medication to help with the headache. Anything else?"

"Where's Tori?" I fumble for my phone on the side table and Facetime Aunt Dellah.

"Hey, little niec—Tori!" I didn't have to say anything. She saw Scotty's face on the screen and knew.

"I'll be back with the meds." Sheila smiles and walks out.

"I'll give you some time. Glad you're awake, Scotty. Your girls missed you." I can feel the blush creeping up, and Scotty's fingers caress my cheek as Elliot walks out.

"Someone special is on the phone for you." Aunt Dellah's voice is distant as she looks for Tori in the house. When Tori's face appears on the screen, the love between Scotty and Tori is palpable.

"Daddy! I wanna go. Let's go." The screen bounces around, and we hear keys jingling. "I gots the keys. Let's go." Aunt Dellah is laughing in the background.

"Little Princess?" A close-up of Tori's face appears on the screen.

"Daddy, naptime is over. No more sleeping. I miss you."

"Okay. Okay. I'm here. No more nap time. Can you give the phone back to Aunt Dellah?" There's more blurred screen before Aunt Dellah is smiling at us.

"She might be a little excited to see you. We're leaving in about five minutes, and we'll see you soon."

"I love you, Daddy." Tori appears above Aunt Dellah's head in the background of the screen.

"Love you too, Little Princess." The screen goes black, and I put it back on the table.

"Pinky, I—"

"I love you, Scotty. I love you, and I love Tori, and I want us to be a family. She's my little girl, too. So much has gone on in the last several days. DFCS took her away from me, and Uncle Collin's brother is the one trying to take her away from you and—" Lips crash into mine, and I instantly melt. He smells different, and his lips are dry, but it's him. It's fucking him. I want to wrap my arms around him and never let go,

348

but I'm afraid to hurt him.

I pull away before the kiss gets out of hand and put my forehead to his.

"I love you too, Rowyn. So fucking much. I don't know if your dad heard it, but it's the last thing I remember saying before I blacked out from the crash."

"He heard you. He told me."

"Okay, well, you just word-vomited a ton of things that I don't understand. And I'm sure we have a lot to talk about. Let's start at the beginning."

50

Scotty

S o much has happened in only five days. I feel like a lifetime has gone by. Wynnie gave me a quick version of what happened while I was sedated.

We couldn't get into too much detail knowing that Dellah was on her way with Tori, but hearing the bits and pieces about how she handled everything with Tori makes me fall even deeper in love with her.

I hear her feet running down the hall before I see her. Tori comes running into the room, and Wynnie scoops her up before she can jump on me.

"Hey, Sunshine. Daddy still has booboos that we need to be careful of."

"Daddy, are you all better? When can we go home?"

"Hopefully tomorrow, Little Princess. The doctors are still taking pictures of my brain to make sure it didn't fall out." Tori's face morphs from confusion to sadness to joy until I pull her into me with my good arm. "I'm just joking. It's still in there."

"You're so silly, Daddy."

"I've missed you so much. Have you been having fun at Aunt Dellah's house?"

"Yeah, but the scary man from my window came over, and Wynnie was my hero. She yelled at him and told me I was hers. Is she yours too, Daddy?" Her question is so innocent, but she has no idea the power behind it.

"No, Tori. She isn't mine." Wynnie's face falls, and Tori's lips pouts out the farthest I've ever seen. "She's ours, Little Princess. Should we keep her?" Tori bounces, and the entire bed shakes. Her excitement is infectious.

"Yes, yes, yes. Wait. Daddy, does that mean Wynnie is going to sleep in your bed every bedtime? Because I could eat pancakes for breakfast every day." I think my beautiful, nosey, blabbermouth of a little girl just asked Wynnie to move in with us.

"Hmm. I don't know. Girls have a lot of stuff. Do we have room?" She exaggerates her movements and taps her lips with a finger.

"You have lots of stuff in your closet. We can get rid of some of it." I'm doing my best to keep a straight face because Tori is taking this conversation very seriously.

"Good point. But what about in the bathroom?"

"I can share. Your bathroom is boring and looks like a boy."

"Another good point. What about all the extra pillows and blankets? Girls usually like a bunch of those. Do we have room?"

"Daddy." Her tone is stern, and her face is no-nonsense. "You like big fluffy blankets."

"I do." A small chuckle escapes from my lips, but I try to hide it. "So what should we do about all of that?" She huffs and rolls her eyes, and I almost burst out laughing.

"Daddy, you should ask her to be my mommy." She says it so matter of factly, having no idea, she just skipped the moving-in step and went right to marriage and adoption.

"What if we ask Wynnie to move in first?"

"Oh, good idea. Wynnie, do you want to live with Daddy and me?" I realize that question is where this entire conversation was going, but she still looks to me for confirmation before answering Tori. I smile and nod at her, and my heart swells at the smile she gives Tori.

"Sunshine, I would love to live with you and Daddy." She's bouncing on the bed again.

"Yay. When?"

"Little Princess, as soon as I get out of this hospital, we can *all* go home together. How does that sound, Pinky?"

"It sounds wonderful."

"Can you kiss now because that's what people who love each other do?"

"Gladly." I pull Wynnie into me and kiss her lips chastely for Tori.

"Aunt Dellah said there's a candy place here. Can we go?"

"Sunshine, there's a gift shop here that sells candy. That's probably what she meant."

"It is." Dellah pops her head into the doorway. "Sorry, I stayed out here. I figured you'd want some privacy. Hey Scotty, how are you feeling?"

"Feeling okay. Wynnie, why don't you take Tori to the gift shop so Dellah and I can talk." She nods in understanding.

"Let's go see if we can find a balloon for Daddy." I kiss both girls on the cheek and smile as they walk out of the room, hand in hand.

"What's going on, Dellah? Collin's brother? What the

352

fuck?" She sits on the chair beside my bed, looking just as confused and defeated.

"Did you know him, Scotty? I had never met him until he showed up at my house last night. Well, I guess technically, I met him here earlier."

"Here? Wynnie didn't get to tell me much before you arrived." She sighs.

"He was standing outside your room watching Wynnie sleep next to you."

"And Tori said he was the same guy that looked in her window. I thought for sure it was a bad dream. Now I feel like shit. Has he been stalking us? Wynnie mentioned feeling like someone's been watching her. Fuck, I've failed them both. I have to get out of this hospital bed."

"Scotty." Dellah places her hands on mine, seeing my panic. "We've got the girls covered. We'll keep them safe. Your first job right now is to recover so you can come home to them. Hazel having spare men has come in handy with all the extra kids and Scotty babysitting duty that we've needed the past few days."

"How's Mac? I heard he broke his leg."

"He's miserable. You know him. He's dying to do anything but sit and heal. Falling on your bike saved him from worst injuries. You had us scared there for a while."

"Dellah, I don't know exactly how it happened but thank you for stepping up for Tori. I can't imagine what everyone has gone through the last few days, but you all made my little girl your priority, and I'll never be able to thank you enough." She swipes her hand under her eyes.

"Well fuck, Scotty. Why you gotta make a bitch cry? I'm gonna lose my street cred." She grabs a tissue from the table and blots at her eyes. "But in all seriousness, you don't need to thank me. You were already family, but your relationship with Wynnie has brought you farther into our inner circle. We take care of our family, Scotty."

51

Wynnie

Scotty is coming home today. Home. *Our* home. Except he isn't. We aren't actually going home.

Because of the open DFCS case and the temporary guardianship, Tori has to stay in Aunt Dellah and Uncle Collin's custody until the DNA results. It's a minor speed bump, but we'll get to be together, and that's all that counts right now.

Scotty stayed in the hospital for two more days after he woke up. They wanted to monitor his head injury and run a few more tests. Phoenix and Jude went to pick him up and are on their way back now. Scotty texted me to say he had a long, emotion filled talk with Phoenix and things are good.

We're all staying at Aunt Dellah's until Tori can go home. Thank goodness Elliot has a queen-sized bed in his room for the three of us to share. Although he gave us strict instructions of no hanky panky in his bed, not that we could with a five year old between us.

"Honey, I'm home."

"Daddy!" Tori runs toward the guys at the back door

and stops short just before she crashes into Scotty. She remembered that she can't jump on him, but her excitement is about to boil over. Her entire body vibrates, wanting to hug him.

"Let me sit down first, Little Princess. I'm not supposed to be doing any lifting but I want to give you a great big hug."

His body is still weak, and he's putting on a brave face while walking to the couch as fast as his body will allow. He sits, and Scotty opens his good arm for her to crawl in his lap.

"I missed you so much, Daddy."

"Not more than I missed you, Little Princess."

"Wynnie said we could go get ice cream if you're good enough." He arches a brow and looks my way.

"Good enough, huh?" I see the heat flash in his eyes, and it warms something in my stomach.

"I said if Daddy was *feeling* good enough." I correct her.

"I think ice cream sounds great, and I'm definitely good enough *and* feeling good."

"Come on, Mr. Feelgood, let's go get ice cream."

"Wynnie, can we talk before you go." I close my eyes at Phoenix's voice, holding my breath. I feel a hand on my back and hear Aunt Dellah's soft voice.

"You can use the library." I nod in a silent response to both of them and walk down the hall. I hear footsteps behind me and assume Phoenix is following. My mouth is dry from nerves as the library door closes.

Walking further into the room, I hug my arms close to my chest, feeling raw with emotions. There is long moments of silence, and the air thickens around us.

"I have no excuse other than I'm a giant asshole." That's not an apology for his actions. My stomach is in knots, thinking about how he walked out of the hospital room when he found out.

I hear him getting closer, but I still can't turn around. His rejection hurt me when I was at my lowest point. His hand touches my shoulder, and I fight every instinct in my body to turn around.

"What I did was unforgivable. I realized it almost immediately when I walked out, but I was embarrassed and knew how much my actions hurt you when you were already hurting so much. I wanted to apologize to Scotty first because I knew my words to you would be hollow if I didn't. Without having seen the two of you together, I had no idea that what you had could even be possible. Scotty loves you—" I spin in his arms and bury my face in his chest. His strong arms wrap around me, and I feel his cheek rest on my head.

"He loves you. I could tell the minute he started talking about you, and his eyes lit up. I have no idea how I've missed it the last couple of months. How any of us have missed it." He lifts his head and takes a deep breath.

"Wynnie?" I look up at him and see the sincerity in his eyes. "Please forgive me. I don't deserve it, but I truly am sorry." The tears finally spill from my eyes.

"I forgive you, Dad." He hugs me tighter, and I know we're okay.

As we pull up to Tastee Sweets, Tori excitedly points at a table out front.

"Look, Wynnie, it's the mean boys you made nice with ice cream. Maybe you can make them even nicer if you buy them more." Sometimes, her innocence is so endearing.

"We can always ask." She waves at them when we get close and they smile and wave back.

The ice cream shoppe is crowded, which surprises me for a Monday afternoon, but summer is coming to an end, and I'm sure people are trying to soak up the last few weeks before school starts. We discuss the flavors, and each pick out what we want so we can order quickly when it's our turn. Tori collected the orders for the boys' ice cream outside.

"Daddy, can I go look at the candy?" She points to the other side of the small store, where there are barrels filled with individual pieces of candy and wall-to-floor candy dispensers.

"Sure, but don't go far. We're almost to the front." I watch her bounce away in her navy blue 'twirly dress,' as she calls it. The full skirt swirls around her knees as she skips.

A warm hand runs across my lower back, and I look up to see Scotty smiling at me. "I don't think I've thanked you for everything you did. And I definitely know I haven't thanked you properly." He nibbles the shell of my ear, and I curl into his side.

"You're not supposed to do anything strenuous for at least another two weeks. And have I mentioned how your bandaged head looks so sexy with your new beard?" I tug on the bottom of his chin and he mockingly scowls at me.

"Brat." He rubs his beard on my cheek and I scrunch my shoulders at the scruffy feeling. "I'm okay if you do all the work, and I'll just lay back and reap all the rewards." His hot breath on my neck sends a shiver down my spine and a bolt of electricity straight to my clit.

"Oh, is that right? You'll *allow* me to do that for you?" A loud crash sounds from behind us, and we spin around to see a display of candy littered across the floor. My eyes dart all around the small store.

"Where's Tori?" I scan the room over and over looking through the crowd of people and don't see her.

"Tori? Victoria?" Scotty's voice is forceful with an edge of panic.

The front door flings open, and one of the boys from outside steps in. He's breathing heavily from exertion while searching the room. His eyes lock with mine, and I fill with dread.

"The guy...took her...in the trunk." He's bent over, bracing his hands on his knees. He points outside, and I see a car taking off as some of the boys on their bikes chase after it.

We rush outside, and I grab my phone out of my pocket. I call my dad and tell Scotty to call 9-1-1 while we get in my car.

"It was a black four door car. The first four of the license plate are PGP-7." I look back and smile at the teenager with greasy dark hair standing behind my car.

"Next ice cream is on me. Thank you." He waves as we take off in the direction of the car and the kids on bikes.

Scotty's voice is tense as he relays the information to the dispatcher on the phone. I reach over, grab his hand, and squeeze it. He gives me a tight smile, and I can see the fear in his eyes.

"Hey, Sweethear-"

"Dad. Nicholas took Tori."

"Where are you?" I hear the phone muffle as he moves it away from his mouth, and he's asking for keys and someone else's phone to call the station.

"He took her from Tastee Sweets, but Dad, you can't drive." Scotty waves as the boys on their bikes slow down when they see us behind them. They point and flail their arms to make sure we know which car she's in.

"Fucking cast. Phoenix, let's go. Now!" My eyes are laser-focused on the car three ahead of us.

"Dad, Scotty called 9-1-1. He's keeping them updated with our location." Tastee Sweets is downtown by other small shops and surrounded by residential subdivisions. We've taken several turns since leaving the area, and he seems to be going in circles because we're back near downtown.

"Wynnie, are you safe?" I'm gripping the steering wheel so tightly my knuckles are white.

"Yeah, Dad. We aren't going too fast. There were kids following him on their bikes, but they stopped a while back. We're keeping our distance, but I can't stop following. I need to make sure she's safe."

"I understand, Sweetheart, but when my men get there, you need to let them do their job. We're on our way." He's talking to me, but I can also hear a speakerphone in the background with someone updating their location. They're close. I can hear the sirens coming from different directions.

"Wynnie, I need you to hang back now and let my guys take over."

"Dad." My eyes start to prickle as I see flashing lights in my rearview. I hear Scotty in the passenger seat, still talking on the phone. "Yeah…I see them… Okay." He looks behind him and then at me.

"Pull over, Pinky." *No.*

"I can't. I can't let her go, Dad. I promised Tori. I won't break another promise."

"Wynnie. Pull. Over." My dad's gruff voice bellows through the speaker, but I can't listen. I have to get my girl.

Scotty's hand wraps over mine on the steering wheel as a police car flies by me on the left.

"Wynnie. It's okay." Scotty sounds so calm, which only ramps up my anxiety.

"It's not!" I feel my patience snap. "I can't fail her again. I won't be able to handle it if she hates me. I have to keep going." Another police car passes us, lights and sirens blazing. I wipe away the tears that are blurring my vision.

"She won't hate you."

"I have to get to her. I have to save her." He doesn't understand. He didn't see her. Hear the betrayal in her voice when DFCS took her.

"Rowyn." Scotty's voice is stern and sharp. "Pull over." I instantly obey him and pull to the side of the road. My chest is heaving with the adrenaline coursing through my body. Scotty takes the phone from me.

"She's okay, Mac. We pulled ov—"

The sound of screeching tires and crunching metal stops time. Nicholas tried to run a red light and was hit on the driver's side by opposing traffic.

"TORI!" I jump out of my car and run full speed towards the black sedan. There's no damage to the rear of the vehicle, but the entire thing is still shaking from the impact. I can hear Scotty yelling behind me, but I have tunnel vision on the trunk and can't hear what he's saying.

I rush to the car, push an officer aside, and start banging on the trunk. I can hear Tori screaming inside, and I begin to panic. Scotty steps up next to the passenger door and looks inside.

361

"He's breathing, but he's out cold," another officer tells Scotty. "There's an ambulance on its way." Scotty glares at him.

"I don't fucking care about this asshole. I need my daughter out of the trunk now."

Scotty reaches into the car and comes back out with the keys. We try to unlock the trunk, but it won't budge.

"We hear you, Sunshine. We're going to get you out. Just hold on." Every ounce of my body is in survival mode and I try to uselessly pry the trunk open with my fingers.

Phoenix pulls up, and steps out. Seeing us struggling he grabs a crowbar from the bed of his truck, and comes to help. There's no visible damage, but the frame is bent, and it's not budging.

I hear my dad barking orders at his fellow officers to stop traffic and clear the road. He's standing in the middle of the intersection with his crutches pointing at people.

"Phoenix," I whine. My impatience is pouring out of me. Tori is banging on the trunk, crying. I have to get her out. I need to get to her. "Let me try from the inside." I rush around to the passenger side door, and it won't budge either. Phoenix comes over, puts one foot on the back of the car, and pulls on the handle with all his strength. It slowly creeks open, and an officer helps him pull it the rest of the way. When it's wide enough for me, I slip in.

I feel around the top of the back seats for a lever to fold them down while more officers arrive to pry the door fully open. My heart is breaking every second I hear her pleading cries.

"I'm right here, Sunshine. I'm not going anywhere until you're in my arms. Be strong for me. I'm here for you. I'm

362

not leaving." I finally locate the button and shift to the side to allow the seat to fold in on itself.

Tori flings herself at me, wrapping her arms around my neck so tight I instantly cough from the lack of airflow.

"Sunshine. Shhh. I've got you. Relax. You're safe now." As the words leave my mouth, my head whips back. A hand yanks my hair from the front seat, causing me to scream.

"She's mine, you fucking bitc—" I swing my elbow back and hit him on the side of the head hard enough that he releases my hair.

Scotty grabs Nicholas by the collar and yanks him out of the car. His arm cocks back, and he's about to punch him.

"Let me. Your shoulder is injured." I turn my head farther to see Phoenix mimicking Scotty's last position. He rears back, and punches Nicholas across the cheek so hard he's knocked out again.

Scotty looks on the ground where Dad P. dropped Nicholas' limp body and spits on him as an officer steps in with handcuffs.

"Don't touch our fucking girls, asshole." Scotty offers me his hand to help me get out of the car with a clinging Tori.

"Oh, thank fuck you're both safe." He examines Tori and notices a small cut at the hairline on her forehead that's barely bleeding. Determining that nothing life-threatening is wrong, he pulls us closer to him.

"I love you. I love you both." I can hear the emotions in his voice as he tries to hold back tears.

52

Scotty

I 've been a father for over five years, had best friends for decades, but the fierce protectiveness that radiated off of Wynnie is unmatched to anything I've ever felt for another person.

Her desire and determination to make sure my daughter was safe made my heart swell with pride that I get to call her mine, and she considers my daughter hers.

The EMTs checked over Tori at the accident scene. Her cut was minor and only required a small bandage.

Everyone is now congregated at Dellah's house, decompressing from yet another day of high anxiety. The exhaustion in the room is palpable. The adults are lounging around the living room and kitchen and the kids are on the floor, some asleep and some watching the animated movie on the TV. There are several boxes of pizza laid out on the counters.

Dellah comes over to where Wynnie and I are cuddling after a nap and smiles sweetly at us. She looks at Tori, who's still asleep on the couch next to us, and gestures toward the back door.

"If you guys would like some alone time, you're welcome to sneak up to the apartment. I'll watch her for you, and I don't think anyone would blame you for escaping for a little while. It's been a rough week." I look at Tori and then at Wynnie.

"What do you say?"

"That sounds nice." We gently stand from the couch and head across the driveway. I haven't been inside the apartment since last summer when Wynnie was nannying Tori.

"I haven't been here in a while, and it's still a bit under construction. Please don't judge." She takes my hand and opens the door.

I step into the room and pause. The light blues and corals are gone, replaced with burgundy and teals. The walls, once decorated with scenes of the beaches and seashells, are now lined with tapestries in bright colors and patterns. The room is rich and inviting.

"You did all this?" I pull her into my chest, and I continue to look around the room. The coffee table looks like an old door with intricate patterns painted on it. Everywhere I look, I see something different in design or pattern, but it flows together so seamlessly.

"I did."

"Did your favorite coffee shop happen to inspire this?" All of the mismatches remind me of the tables and chairs at the Book Beanery.

"How did you guess?" She laughs lightly and buries her face into my chest. Turning her head she presses her ear over my heart and sighs. "I wasn't sure I'd get to hold you ever again. I layed with you in that hospital bed for hours, listening to this exact sound—your beating heart."

I rest my cheek on the top of her head and breathe her in.

Her familiar apple scent invades my senses.

"I don't remember being away from you for those days, but my body does. I missed you so much. What a fucking week." She chuckles.

"Yeah, what a fucking week." I slowly walk her backward in the direction of her bedroom.

"What are you up to?"

"Just want to see what you've updated in your bedroom." Tipping her chin up with my fingers I gently brush my lips against hers. Her fingers weave into the hair at the nape of my neck, deepening the kiss. I feel her moan vibrate through my chest. When I lean down to grab the back of her thighs she pulls away, stopping me before I try to pick her up.

"You can't lift me. You'll hurt yourself."

"Well, then you better get your ass onto the bed." She steps backward into her room, and I look up for the first time. She's really outdone herself. The entire wall behind the headboard is made up of various textures and colors of fabric. The bedspread is a sage green, with assorted throw pillows covering half of the bed. I laugh, and she gives me a look as she climbs on.

"What's so funny?"

"All the throw pillows. I told Tori girls have a lot of pillows." She looks around and laughs before throwing herself amongst the colors and patterns behind her.

Wynnie looks so stunning and carefree. When we got back she showered, threw her hair up on top of her head, and left her face makeup free. She's breathtaking. And she's mine.

I lean down on the bed and attempt to crawl towards her. When I put too much weight on my bad shoulder, I wince from the pain, forgetting that I'm injured. Wynnie instantly sits up, concern on her face.

"Hey, are you okay? You have to be careful. You're not a spring chicken anymore. You need to let your injuries heal." I sit and scoot myself to the top of the bed, tossing pillows to the ground.

"Are you calling me old, Pinky?" She bites her lips, trying to suppress a smile.

"I would never." Her hand flies to her chest, feigning horror. "I'm just trying to respect my elders." I throw a pillow at her head, and she ducks.

"I think I remember someone offering to do all the work while I get all of the benefits."

"I think I remember someone *thinking* they were going to get all the benefits, but this is a quid pro quo exchange." She reaches for the hem of her shirt and removes it, revealing a lacy white bra. I look down at my shirt and back at her, realizing that I won't be able to remove mine without help.

"Let me help you." She smiles, and together, we're able to take off my shirt with minimal pain.

"If this is quid pro quo, you need to lose another layer." She shrugs and looks at her bra.

"Hmm. I suppose you're right." She reaches behind her and unclips her bra, slowly allowing the straps to fall down her arms. My fingers twitch to reach out and touch her, but I'll let her determine the pace of our interaction.

Her throat clears, and I look up to her eyes.

"Like what you see?" I've been caught staring at her hard, pink nipples. My tongue darts out and trails over my bottom lip.

"I'd like it even more if they were in my mouth." I watch as her eyes glaze over. Her breathing increases, and I can tell

367

she's feeling the effects of our slow pace as much as I am.

"You're so fucking gorgeous." She moves closer and sits on my lap, straddling my legs. Her hands roam over my chest, and light fingers trace some of the scratches and bruises still healing. My body breaks out in goosebumps from her gentle touch.

"I almost lost you," she whispers. The lust in her eyes dims with fear, and I grab one of her hands, placing it over my heart.

"But you didn't, and we need to think about that. I'm here, and you're here. Nicholas is in jail. Tori is safely asleep across the driveway, and in a few days, the results will come back, proving what we already know. She's mine." I watch her mouth move, repeating the word 'mine'. Cupping her cheek, I grab her attention. "She's ours, Pinky. I'm yours too if you want us to be." Her forehead dips to mine.

"So fucking much. I want us to be an *us*. You, me and Tori. The thought of losing either of you was terrifying. When Aunt Dellah showed up at my door to tell me about your accident, then watching that car get hit, knowing Tori was in the trunk…" She shakes her head, and I know exactly how she's feeling without words.

I tilt my head up to lock my lips with hers. I know I wanted to let her dictate where this was going, but I need to feel her. To touch her and know she's in my arms. She must need it too, because her body melts into mine when I wrap my arms around her back.

"I need to be inside you. I want to make love to you, Rowyn." She nods her head into my lips, and our hands go to our pants. We make quick work of our bottoms, only parting to remove them entirely.

Laying on my back, she climbs over me. Her hand grabs my cock to line up with her entrance and I'm already dripping pre-cum.

"You're so wet for me already, Pinky." Her thumb slides over my tip, and I hiss.

"So are you." As she sinks onto my cock the instant relief my body feels is jarring. Every nerve in my body is on overdrive. I grab her hips, encouraging her to move. I want to feel all of her.

"Relax, Mr. Eager. Let me do it. You can't do any physical activities, remember." I smirk and remove my hands from her hips. I give her my best serious face as I place my hands on the bed.

"My body is all yours." She rolls her eyes and leans in to kiss my lips.

"It always has been." Damn if she isn't right. Her hips move in a circle, and I close my eyes and feel. She feels so fucking good. I can't handle it any longer, and my hands gravitate back to her hips. She gives me a warning look.

"I just need to feel you. The floor is all yours." She kisses me again and our tongues tangle together. Her hips continue to rotate over me, and I let my hands roam wherever they want on her body. There's nothing rushed or heated about it. This is true lovemaking. Exploring each other.

I wish my body wasn't broken so I could worship her the way I want. Instead, I'll savor the slow, rhythmic swirl of her hips. The way her body tastes on my tongue. The weight of her breast in my hands and the shallow breaths she takes when my thumbs graze her peaked nipples.

Our minds and bodies are connecting in a way that's binding our souls together. My tongue licks and my mouth sucks from one side of her collarbone to the other, up her neck to her ear.

"Marry me." Her breath hitches, and her body stills. I continue kissing her neck and use my hands to encourage her to move again. "Marry *us*. But don't answer right now. I don't want an answer until we have confirmation that Tori is ours. And she *is* ours. Not just mine. Yours too. You belong with us. I want to make you Rowyn Juniper Langford. Think about it."

I pull back to look into her eyes, and tears stream down her cheeks. She grabs my face and kisses me. It's full of passion and love and the yes I know she'll give me when I have a ring and truly ask her.

"I'm yours," she whispers between kisses. "Both of yours." My patience snaps, and pain be damned, I roll us over. Supporting my weight on the elbow of my good arm, Wynnie looks up at me in shock.

"Your shoulder?"

"I'm fine. I promise. Let me have you, and you can nurse me back to health once you've come all over my cock." She laughs.

"Ah, there's the pervert I know and love." I playfully kiss her nose.

"And this pervert loves you too. Now give me what I want, Rowyn." She smiles sweetly up at me with defiance in her eyes.

"Yes." Three little letters. I know she's being a brat, and I know exactly what her answer means, but I let it slide and grind my hips into her harder.

When we come, we come together, and it isn't explosive or toe-curling. It's perfect. It's passion and love. It's us.

53

Scotty

ollectively, we decide we still want to celebrate Wynnie's birthday and proceed with our dinner at Hazel's house on Friday.

I made the decision that there's no time like the present, and although I already asked, well, told Wynnie to marry me, I want to do it properly. I also haven't had an official conversation with any of her parents about our relationship, except for Phoenix.

I talked to Dellah and Collin before I left about my plan, and they agreed to watch all the little kids while I spoke to them.

As I sit in their library, waiting for everyone to arrive, I try not to think about the fact that Phoenix is about to become my father-in-law. The irony of that is running through my head when he enters the room and catches me laughing at myself.

"Penny, for your thought, Scotty?"

"You probably wouldn't find it as funny. At least not yet." He's about to ask more when Hazel walks in the room looking a little pale. He rushes over to her and guides her to the nearest chair.

"What's wrong, Angel?"

"I'm okay. I'm just tired. I think the last week is just weighing on me. I'm okay."

"Want me to get you some water?" It's still strange to see the guy I would get drunk in the woods with now being a supportive, loving father...and I'm about to ask his permission to marry his daughter. What kind of strange universe are we living in?

"I'm fine. I promise. The kids probably brought a bug home again from a friend's house or something."

"Ugh. Don't remind me, Little Dove." Jude walks in and kisses Hazel on the forehead. "That stomach bug we all had a few weeks ago was something I'd rather not relive." He runs his fingers across her forehead. "You aren't warm. Let us know if you need anything."

Mac is the last to arrive. He closes the doors behind him and takes a seat. I stand and start pacing, not knowing what to say despite preparing about a dozen different speeches.

"Okay. I'm sure you all have questions, concerns, or hell, probably even itchy palms wanting to punch me. I'll accept any and all of that, but first, I need you to know I love her." Phoenix's hands close into fists. Even though we spoke it's still new and raw. I don't know who I expect the worst reaction from, him or Mac.

"I don't just love her, I'm in love with her. I want to marry her." Hazel gasps and all eyes turn toward her. Tears instantly well in her eyes. "Please tell me those are tears of happiness because your answer is about to determine my fate with these guys." She nods as Jude hands her a tissue.

"I know all of the negative marks against me. Single dad. Slightly older." Phoenix raises an eyebrow at me. "Okay, decently older."

"Fifteen years older." Mac stands and walks towards me. I do my best not to step back. I have to show Mac I can stand up for his daughter in the face of any potential danger. Even him.

"Are you asking to marry my daughter Scotty? *Our* daughter." I hear movement behind him, but I refuse to break eye contact first.

Out of my peripheral vision, I see Jude and Phoenix come to stand next to Mac. This is the moment of truth. I know these men, and they know me. We've formed a friendship over the last several years, two decades with Phoenix. But they aren't looking at me as a friend. They're looking at me as a future for their daughter—a man to love, support and protect her. I'll do every single one of those things for her and so much more.

The tension is thick, and my confidence wanes the longer the silence extends.

"Are you done measuring your dick sizes? Put the poor guy out of his misery and welcome him to the family." I finally break eye contact to look at Hazel over Mac's shoulder.

Mac shoves his hand out to shake, and I flinch at the quick movement, causing the guys to laugh. I take Mac's hand, and his grip is firm.

"I won't welcome you until she says yes."

"Fair enough." He gives my hand a vice-grip squeeze before letting go. Jude is next.

"We've already talked, and you know how I feel." I give him a curt nod and shake his hand. I turn to Phoenix, who looks me up and down, sizing me up.

"Really? You already know you can kick my ass if you want. And if I ever give you a reason to, I'll happily accept it."

"That's exactly what I wanted to hear." He pulls me in for a hug and slaps my back twice. "Care to share what you were laughing to yourself about earlier?" Do I tempt my luck? Fuck it.

"Not sure you'd find it so amusing, *Dad*."

"Holy shit." Hazel bursts into hysterical laughter as tears stream down her face. She looks between Phoenix and me several times and then a quick glance at Jude. "Oh my god. This is too good." She stands from the chair and walks toward the doors.

"Oh my god, Dellah. You have to hear this!" She's gone, and all eyes are back on me.

"Don't ever fucking call me that again, asshole." There's a very stern finger in my face, and I almost crack a smile because he just used his Dad voice on me. I can tell by the slowly dwindling composure on Jude's face that he noticed it, too.

"Yes, Sir."

"Don't call me that shit either. I'd rather be called Nix again over that stupid shit."

"Sure thing, Nix." Phoenix throws his hands up in the air and huffs.

"What the fuck ever. Don't fuck up dickhead, and we'll be good." He walks out, and Jude loses it.

"I'm going to pay for that later." Jude doesn't look the least bit ashamed. He leaves the room, and it's just Mac left.

"I don't want to wait, Mac. As soon as we get the official documents that Tori is mine and no one can take her away again, I want to ask Wynnie to marry me, and I want her to be Tori's mother. Are you okay with that?"

"Scotty, I don't think she'd listen even if I wasn't. The way she took care of you and Tori is everything I could have hoped for my daughter. Like Phoenix said, don't fuck up dickhead."

Waiting day in and day out to find out the result of the DNA test this past week has been agony. This process can take weeks to months, but my accident sped things up, and Mac has assured me he's used every favor he possibly has.

Friday was Wynnie's birthday celebration, and I've spent a lot of time at the bar this weekend trying to stay busy. Kristina is a miracle worker and managed to keep everything under control while I was away. I've never been more thankful for faithful employees.

"Is it burning a hole in your pocket, Boss?"

"What?" Kristina steps into the doorway behind me, finding me staring off, lost in thought. She laughs when I turn around in my office to face her.

"I've seen the bulge you're walking around with in your pocket, and it's not because you're happy to see me."

"Shit. Is it that obvious?" My hand slides down to the black velvet box in my pocket that I've been carrying for several days.

"No, but the constant tapping of your pocket is. When are you going to ask her?" I sit down in my chair. That's the magic question, isn't it?

"Just waiting for the courts to get off their asses and tell me what I already know." Kristina has been with me long

375

enough to know Becky when we were together, before and during her pregnancy.

"No one doubts that she's yours. I hate that you're in this situation, but I can't wait to hear about the proposal. And you might want to keep that somewhere else besides your pocket." She winks at me and walks out of the office.

I pull the box out and look at it for the hundredth time.

It's a simple square princess-cut diamond ring with three small yellow diamonds on each side of the band to represent Tori and the nickname Wynnie gave her-Sunshine. Hazel helped me pick it out and assures me she will love that little detail.

I hear giggling coming down the hall and quickly put the box back in my pocket.

"Daddy, where are you?" I stand from my desk smiling and greet my beautiful little girl at the door, crouching to hug her.

"Hey, Little Princess. What are you doing here?" She looks behind her as Wynnie walks towards us. I stare into her gorgeous blue eyes and, for a moment, forget all of my worries. She will be mine soon.

"Hey, Pinky." I walk around my desk and pull her into my arms to kiss her. The smell of apples engulfs me.

"Where is it Daddy?" I pull myself away from Wynnie's mesmerizing lips and smile down at Tori.

"Where's what?" She cups her hand around her mouth and whispers, but it's really more of a quiet talking voice.

"Wynnie's present. You said you left it in here, and I'm here." I chuckle as I turn towards my desk.

"Oh, right." I reach into my top drawer and pull out an envelope, handing it to Tori. She excitedly takes it and hands it to Wynnie.

"Open it. Open it." Her face lights up with excitement.

"Don't forget, Tori, it's up to Wynnie what she wants to do with it."

"She's gonna love it!" Wynnie slowly opens the seal and pulls out the piece of paper. Unfolding it, I see her eyes dart around everything Tori has created.

"It's a tattoo for me to color, for you." Tori had me look up fairy outlines one day until she found the perfect one. I printed it along with the outline of a heart and a sun. She colored the heart with rainbow colors and said she wanted to give the paper to Wynnie for her birthday and ask her to get it as a tattoo like mine.

I loved that she had the idea but explained to her that tattoos are permanent and Wynnie might not want permanent art on her body. Tori was excited to give it to her no matter what Wynnie's decision was.

"Did you pick this out for me, Sunshine?"

"And I colored the heart rainbow just like we like. Rainbows are our favorite!"

"And you want me to get this tattooed so you can color the fairy like Daddy's tattoos?"

"Don't forget the sunshine because that's what you call me. Will you do it?" Wynnie's eyes glisten with tears and she crouches down next to Tori.

"Where should I get it?" Is she considering getting them tattooed?

Tori lifts the sleeve of Wynnie's left arm and points. "Right here, just like Daddy's." My girls smile the brightest smiles I've ever seen, and Wynnie embraces Tori.

"I can't wait until you can color my arm just like Daddy's.

Thank you, Sunshine. Should we tell Daddy our surprise?"

"A surprise for me?" Tori nods. Wynnie looks at me and smiles. "It's time."

"It's time? Now?" She nods vigorously at me.

"My dad has pulled every last favor that he could. The paperwork has been sitting in a file, waiting for its turn. He finally convinced the judge to look it over."

"It's time." The words come out in a whooshing breath. I've never doubted my love or paternity of Tori, but a situation like this can make even the strongest man think twice. I want to get this over with and move on to my forever with Wynnie.

"Let's go, Sunshine. We're taking you to Aunt Hazel's house for a playdate with Delilah Jane."

Every minute that has ticked by since leaving the bar, dropping off Tori, and walking into the front doors of the courthouse has felt like a deep breath that I need but can't take. My heart is racing like a runaway train. Wynnie's hand hasn't left mine unless absolutely necessary.

As we sit in the judge's chambers, the door opens behind us. We expect to see the judge but are surprised when Mac walks in with him.

"Mr. Langford, Scotty. Thank you for coming. I'm Judge Moss." I stand, and we shake hands. "You know some powerful, pushy people, Scotty." He hooks his thumb over his shoulder at Mac. "This asshole hasn't left me alone all week about your case." He sits in his chair and turns his computer on.

"Are we waiting for the other party?" As far as I know,

Nicholas is still in jail. He has several charges against him and no one to bail him out. Collin's father couldn't believe it when he heard what his son did and washed his hands of everything related to Nicholas.

"Mr. McLain is still incarcerated. The results of today won't change anything for him. He'll get a letter of the findings." I can feel the relief from Wynnie. I'm sure she wasn't looking forward to seeing him, and now she doesn't have to.

The copy machine behind the judge comes to life, and several pieces of paper print out. Turning, he grabs the papers and places them on the desk in front of me with a pen.

"I'll need you to initial at the bottom of each page and sign and date on the last one." I pick up the pen and start skimming what he handed me. My head snaps up.

"So this means…" Judge Moss closes his eyes and shakes his head with a smile.

"I'm sorry. Usually, I do everything in the courtroom, and then we come back here to sign all the paperwork. Victoria Langford is your biological daughter." I hear the sob that instantly comes from Wynnie. She sits forward in her chair and wraps her arms around me. I hug her back and attempt to wipe away some of her tears.

"I didn't have a doubt, Scotty."

"Neither did I, Pinky. Let's get this over with and get our girl."

54

Wynnie

I t feels like a million butterflies are floating around me as we head to my parent's house to pick up Tori. Scotty said he had a surprise for me, but we needed her. His leg has been bouncing the entire ride, and I can't tell if he's excited about the news or nervous about something.

He made us wait in the parking lot until my dad and Jude, who had brought my dad to the courthouse, left. He's taken the scenic route to their house. A route we only take when we're on our bikes. It feels different in the car, but I have the windows down and feel the breeze in my hair—something I can't do on my bike.

The gate opens almost immediately when we pull in front of it as if someone was watching for us. My family knew we were coming, so it makes sense.

As we pull up to the house, I see Aunt Dellah and Elliot's cars in the driveway. What's everyone doing here? I look at Scotty, who's wearing a shit-eating grin.

"What's going on?" He shrugs, but it's a complete lie.

"Let's go inside and find out. Don't move." I remove my

hand from the door handle. Scotty walks around the car and opens my door, offering me his hand.

He opens the back door and motions for me to step inside first. The house is quiet, too quiet for the dozen people I know are in here.

Scotty's hand touches my lower back, encouraging me to walk in farther. I walk to the middle of the living room and still don't see or hear anyone. When I turn to question Scotty, he's gone. I'm completely alone.

The silence in the room is deafening. I think I hear a giggle from upstairs, and I walk that way. Before I can reach the stairs, a foam bullet hits the back of my leg.

"Okay. I get it now. Very funny, everyone." Another bullet hits my leg, followed by several more bullets hitting the refrigerator. I walk over and see a note with my name on it. Opening it, I read the few sentences in what I know is Scotty's handwriting.

They may be crushed, but my heart isn't.
Look in the place where I'd be stored.

Crushed? Stored? I feel like there's an obvious answer to this, but I'm confused by what's happening. A bullet hits the door leading back to the driveway, and it dawns on me. *Crushed.* Their motorcycles.

I walk out to the detached garage. It's heated and cooled at my dad and Phoenix's request during the home build. Opening the door, a feeling of anxiety washes over me. My dad's motorcycle is there, next to Phoenix's. I hadn't seen it until now. It's pretty banged up, but they've already started taking it apart to fix it. The accident totaled Scotty's bike, and I know he's upset about it.

Attached to a handlebar, I see another pink piece of paper with my name on it. This must be my next clue because it seems like I'm going on a scavenger hunt.

Just like these bikes, there will be bumps in the road,
but dents and dings can always be fixed.
Sometimes, we might need some assistance from a good book.

Book. Well, that's easy enough. I guess I'm heading to the library.

The house is still quiet when I return, which is eerie. There's always noise coming from somewhere in this house.

Inside the library I find a sketchbook and colored pencils with another note.

Pinky, my Pinky. I never knew an innocent nickname could hold so much meaning. From a silly sketch to the blush on your cheeks.
And now, you have me wrapped around your pinky finger, intertwined with our little girl's. She has a surprise for you in her favorite room.

I can't help but smile. Tori's favorite room is my bedroom. I brought her back here recently and we played together with DJ. I have a bay window that faces the backyard with a view of the trees and mountains. The lighting is perfect, and I would paint and draw for hours. When she was old enough to hold the crayons and paint brushes, we would come here and be creative together.

I make my way upstairs, and when I walk into my old bedroom, it's filled with balloons of every color. There's a balloon arch shaped like a rainbow hung in front of the window, and at least a dozen crystals catching the afternoon light, casting rainbows all around the room. It's beautiful.

"Wow." I hear a squeal of joy and turn around to see Tori standing in my favorite rainbow dress.

"Hey, Sunshine. Did you do this? It's incredible." Her smile is radiant.

"Daddy helped, but I picked out all the colors. It's our favorite. We need to make lots of wishes. Look at all the rainbows." I pick her up, kiss her on the cheek, and pull her into me. I almost lost both of them, and I don't ever want to let go.

"How about we think really hard and make one big wish?"

"I already know mine."

"You do? Okay, let's close our eyes and wish." Before I can even finish closing my eyes, they pop back open at her words. Her eyes squint so hard, and on a whispered breath, I hear her, and my heart explodes.

"I wish that Wynnie would be my Mommy." I quickly close my eyes so she doesn't catch me looking at her and silently echo her wish, willing the tears building up not to spill over my lashes. Her hands wrap around my neck, and she says, "I have your next clue."

"Alright, Sunshine, where to?"

"The kitchen." Interesting. I've passed the kitchen several times and haven't noticed anything. She wiggles in my arms to let her down and takes my hand, leading me out of my room.

Walking down the stairs, I see the living room now filled with more rainbow-colored balloons. I know my mom had a hand in this. She loves balloons.

We take a left toward the kitchen, and I see everyone standing around the island, but I'm focused on the handsome man standing in the middle wearing a suit—a navy suit with a crisp white shirt open at the collar. I just saw him thirty minutes ago in jeans and a T-shirt.

"Scotty." He extends his hand for me to come to him, and Tori leaves me to stand with DJ and Paige by Aunt Dellah.

"Hey, Pinky."

"What's going on?" His smile lights up the room. His eyes are full of love, and I melt into him when his lips graze mine.

"I think you know." I'm not stupid. I know what's going on. It doesn't mean I believe it's real.

"Do you remember the question I asked you not that long ago? The one I told you I didn't want an answer to yet?" He releases me and steps back, dropping to one knee. I hear someone crying around me, and I'd bet money it's my mom. "It's time for that answer now, Pinky. Rowyn Juniper Harmon, will you complete my life and be my forever Backpack? Will you wake up every morning with me and kiss our little girl every night before bed? Will you make silly wishes with me and color my arm with obnoxious glitter pens with Tori? Will you be ours, Pinky? Will you marry me? Marry us?" I can barely see him through the tears streaming down my face. The word sticks in my throat.

"Wynnie, you gotta say yes." I look to my right and see Tori jumping, waiting for my answer. I motion for her to come to me and pick her up, whispering in her ear. She flings herself around my neck.

"Yes, Daddy. She said yes!" Scotty stands and joins in on our hug. He kisses me with all the passion and fire I know we are both feeling. Everyone around us is cheering or crying

384

or both.

I pull away from our kiss and look into Scotty's brown eyes, knowing their mismatched colors.

"My yes was to Tori's question upstairs, but I'm saying yes to you as well." He looks at me, confused. Was her wish not planned? I assumed it was something they had talked about.

"Little Princess, what did you ask Wynnie upstairs?"

"I made a wish, Daddy. I can't tell you, or it won't come true." He looks between the two of us, still not knowing what's going on.

"It's okay to tell him because it's definitely going to come true." She beams at him and whispers into his ear. Scotty's eyes glaze over as he listens to her wish.

"Are you sure, Pinky?"

"As sure as I am that I want to share the rest of my life with both of you."

55

Wynnie

Why am I nervous? It's not like Aunt Dellah hasn't seen the apartment through all the stages of my redecorating. She left me to be as creative as I wanted, but I still got most things approved through her.

I don't live here anymore. I haven't for a couple of weeks, but it will always feel like home. It was an incredible experience to create a space from scratch. And Aunt Dellah was right; this is amazing for my portfolio.

We reach the top of the fourteen steps to the red door that I refused to change. Despite what the inside of this apartment looks like, the red door is its signature. It was never an option to change it.

"Show me what you did, little niece."

Aunt Dellah steps in and freezes, which causes my nerves to skyrocket. Her eyes widen as she slowly walks around, taking in all the colors and feeling the different textures and patterns.

"Wynnie, I don't even know what to say. It's…Wow."

"I hope that's a good wow." I took a lot of risks. I know Aunt

Dellah's style, and it's anything but this. She leans towards more neutrals and farmhouse styles. The only neutral color here is the light wood flooring, which I didn't change, but it's mostly covered in large patterned area rugs.

She spins and wraps me in her arms. "It's stunning. Absolutely magazine-worthy. We'll spend this weekend here. I'll let your mom know. Maybe it's time to invite Paige, too. She's getting older." What is she talking about?

"What's going on this weekend?"

"Period party weekend." Oh yeah. *Oh crap.* I turn my back to Aunt Dellah as I do mental calculations. I don't know what my face looks like, but I'm sure it's a mixture of panic, fear, and impossibility. I don't want her to see me.

When was my last period? Have I had one since the accident? I must have. If I didn't, it's probably just stress-related, right?

"Let's go celebrate with margaritas bigger than our heads." She flings her arm over my shoulder and walks us toward the door.

I can't drink. What if…

"I'm sorry, Aunt Dellah, I'll have to take a raincheck until tomorrow. Wouldn't want to ruin our period party weekend with a hangover."

"Fine. You and your logic. I'll tell your mom we'll be up here instead of my house. It'll make Collin happy. No whining, moaning women to dodge. I'm already crampy." She runs her hand over her lower stomach, and I give her a half smile in return.

"Tomorrow sounds perfect. I should get home and work on the next project you sent me. I can't wait to redo the lobby of the florist."

387

"You've got this, little niece. See you tomorrow evening." I nod and wave as I walk to my car.

Can this really be happening? Scotty and I just got engaged. We haven't even talked about kids. That's actually a big problem. I love Tori, but I wasn't a fan of being an only child. I'm so glad that my dads all wanted kids and Dean, Alex, and DJ all have each other. What if he doesn't want more kids? But also, what if I'm not pregnant, and I'm freaking myself out for nothing.

One thing at a time, Wynnie.

I chickened out. I chickened the fuck out. I bought a test. Well, two tests because that's how many came in the box. Now, I'm sitting in the driveway of Aunt Dellah's house, dreading going inside.

I've already decided I'm going straight to the bathroom to take it. Either I'm going to get a negative and drown my anxiety in wine, or I'll get a positive and have the two strongest women in my life there to console me.

Taking a deep breath, I finally open my car door as my mom pulls into the driveway.

"Hey, Mom. You okay? You don't look so good." She's been off lately, and it's not like her.

"Hey, Kiddo. I'm okay. Your brothers are a handful. I thought they were pains at two and four, but at seven and nine, they're even worse. I feel like I spend all day cleaning up foam bullets and pizza crusts.

"Um, there's supposed to be perks to the three extra adults in the house."

"Phoenix and Mac have been spending a lot of time working on Mac's motorcycle. It's the only thing keeping his mind off the desk duty he's been forced into."

"I get that. Ready to go drown our woes in a bottle of wine?"

"I'm not really feeling like drinking. I'm here for ice cream and moral support." I might need some of the moral support. Ask me in about ten minutes.

Today, the red door feels ominous as we climb the stairs towards it. When we walk in, I excuse myself to the bathroom as planned.

As quietly as I can, I open the package. There are two tests, one that gives a plus and one that's digital. From what I've read, the digital tests can take longer to provide you with results, and I need to be in here for the shortest amount of time possible.

I grab a paper cup from under the sink and fill it. Following the instructions to the letter, I dip the stick and place it on the counter. I stare and stare. I watch as the liquid moves from left to right on the indicator screen. The control line appears, and it switches windows. This is torture. As the darkness moves across the test circle, it darkens horizontally, and then…the vertical line appears. There was no need to wait the allotted three minutes.

"Fuck." Knock. Knock.

"You alright in there? Did you fall in?"

"Mom." My voice cracks. I hadn't realized I was crying. The door opens, and my mom sees my expression and immediately comes to me.

"Wynnie, what's wro—oh." She pulls me back and holds me at shoulder length. "Is that? Are you?" I nod and drop my chin to my chest. I'm so ashamed and scared. She pulls me back into her, crushing me with her hug.

"What's going on in here? Did we move the period party?" Aunt Dellah stands in the doorway with a large, full glass of wine, and I can't help but laugh. Hysterically. I reach down onto the counter and hand her the test. Her eyes widen and she looks between the two of us.

"Which one of you bitches is knocked up?" Um, what? Isn't it obvious it's me? My mom releases me and steps back, looking apprehensive.

"Mom?"

"I don't know anything. I've felt off, but I had that terrible stomach bug last month and haven't felt great since. I thought it just hit me harder, and then with the stress of everything going on…"

"Woman, you've had four kids. How do you not know if you're pregnant? I guess this period party is turning into a pregnancy test party. Let's go buy you a test." She turns to leave, but I stop her.

"I have another one. It was a two-pack."

"Fork it over to your mom, little niece. Let's see if I'm going to be an aunt again." Her nose scrunches and she looks at my stomach.

"What's wrong, Aunt Dells?"

"If you're pregnant, that will make me a great aunt, and I don't like the word 'great' in front of the title." I roll my eyes and push her out of the bathroom while handing my mom the extra test.

A few minutes later, she comes out with the stick in her hand and joins us in the kitchen. I put down a napkin, and she places the test on it. We all stare at the indicator screen while it flashes and flashes and flashes.

"This is torture." I look at Aunt Dellah and roll my eyes.

"You aren't the one wondering about your future."

"Like hell, I'm not. My bestie makes the cutest babies, and I need to live vicariously through you crazy bitches. I have all I've ever wanted and more. It doesn't mean I can't cheer you on from the sidelines."

"Oh fuck." My mom drops her head in her hands, and Aunt Dellah laughs hysterically. The screen says "Pregnant 3+" and my mom looks like she's crying. Her shoulders are shaking. I rub her back to comfort her, and her hands fall from her face. She's crying, but she's also laughing.

"Are you okay?" She places a hand on her belly and one on mine.

"My grandchild and your child. My child and your sibling. This is an interesting turn of events." I roll those words around in my head before I join them in their laughter. This situation is ridiculous and hilarious, and no matter what, everything will be great.

"Well, preggos, let's get our ice cream on!"

56

Scotty

Hazel invited us all over for dinner. It's usually my night at the bar, but Wynnie worked it out with Kristina and Rachel behind my back. She said it's a special dinner.

She dressed Tori in a pretty pink dress, braided her hair, and put on a dress in a similar color. They both look beautiful, and I feel like the luckiest man alive. I'm not sure why we had to dress up for dinner at Hazel's house, but I do what I'm told. Happy wife, happy life. I'll live by that motto now, and it will feel even sweeter when she officially becomes my wife.

The driveway is already packed with everyone's cars when we pull up.

"Are we late?"

"No, everyone else was just early, I guess."

As we walk into the house, Tori squeals. Pink, white, and blue balloons decorate the living room and surrounding areas. Tori loves balloons, but I wonder what we're celebrating.

I walk up to the guys, and everyone looks clueless except

Collin. He has more knowledge than we do based on the smirk he's trying terribly to hide.

"Collin, what's going on?" Phoenix shakes his head.

"Don't bother. We already tried, and he isn't talking. I don't know why he gets to be in the know, and we don't." Collin's smile widens and Mac curses under his breath.

"I think I know," Jude smirks until Phoenix steps in front of him and places a hand firmly at his collarbone.

"Are you looking for a punishment for keeping secrets?" Phoenix's voice is low and husky, and Jude's smile grows.

"I'll take my chances." Oh shit. Phoenix stares him down, kisses him firmly on the lips, and then stalks away, beelining for Hazel.

"Why do you have to amp him up?" Mac shakes his head.

"Because I enjoy the punishment." This time, I walk away. Phoenix and Jude have an amazing relationship, and I respect them, but I don't want to think of my best friend with his boyfriend.

"Thank you everyone for coming." I look up to see Dellah standing on a chair. "You all look very nice. I realize most of you have no idea why we're here, but we are about to change that so we can celebrate. If you'll find your seat at the dining room table, we can get the festivities started." I find Tori, get her settled at the kids' table, and find my assigned seat next to Wynnie.

"Do you know why we're here?"

"I do." She smiles, and it's laced with mischief.

"I assume you aren't going to tell me?"

"Nope." She just popped the P, and I know I won't get any further information from her.

"Alright, we're going to make this nice and simple." All

attention is to Dellah at the head of the table. "Reach under your seats and retrieve the taped box, but don't open it yet."

She waits for everyone to have their box in front of them before speaking again.

"Alright, everyone, open your boxes." Wynnie watches me as I tear the paper and lift the box lid. Inside is a keychain with the word Daddy and Tori's birth year. But there's also another year under it—next year. I look around the room at shocked and confused faces, like mine.

Wynnie opens her box and shows me her keychain. Hers says Mommy, with next year's date as well. Before I have time to register what it could mean, Tori runs over to us.

"Daddy, look." She hands me her keychain.

"This word is Big. Tell me the other word."

"It says Sister. Big Sister." Under it is next year's date, just like mine and Wynnie's.

"Are you...?" I look down at her hands cupping her stomach.

"Daddy, I'm not a sister." I look at Tori and smile with tears in my eyes. I place her tiny hands on top of Wynnie's and put my trembling hands over both of theirs.

"Not yet, but it seems you're going to be. Ask Wynnie what's in her belly?" Her head turns to Wynnie, not understanding my question.

"What's in your belly, Wynnie?"

"My sweet Sunshine. There's a baby in here. Your little brother or sister is growing in my belly."

"A baby? Are you the Daddy, Daddy?" Wynnie and I both laugh.

"Alice." We turn towards Mac's voice, which sounds panicked. Wynnie is smiling ear to ear. "Why are there five years on this keychain? Why is the last date next year?"

"I want to know why it says grandpa on the back of the keychain." Phoenix shows Mac the back, and his eyes flash to us.

"Scotty." I raise my hands in surrender.

"I just found out myself."

"Guys, look at the dates on both sides." Jude's face is calm, and his smile is wide. He's put something together that the other two haven't.

"No fucking way. Angel, the dates are the same. Why are the dates the same? Are you…And Wynnie…"

"Alice, are you and Wynnie *both* pregnant?" Mac is in complete shock based on his tone. Hazel nods her head, and so does Wynnie.

"No shit," I whisper, only loud enough for Wynnie to hear.

"One of you is in trouble." Hazel's smile is wide. Everyone in the room is actually smiling to some degree. I kiss Wynnie on the head, tell her I love her, and motion for her to join her parents on the other side of the table.

"Nice job with the recreation of the keychains, Little Dove." I look at Jude and back to Wynnie.

"Recreation?" She smiles.

"When Mom got pregnant with Dean, she told them by giving them Daddy keychains just like these. We thought it was fun and fitting. Especially since now, they say grandpa as well." I nod and smile, realization dawning on me.

"Hey, Phoenix. If I can't call you Dad, can I call you Grandpa?"

"F-off Scotty. My threat still stands."

"I would expect nothing less."

After several rounds of hugs and congratulations, Wynnie

returns to me.

"So I didn't get to ask. Are you okay with this?" She looks scared and apprehensive as she rubs her belly.

"This? You mean our baby? The life we created? Yeah. I'm very okay. I know we haven't talked about it yet, but I want nothing more than to build a family with you. Do you know when it happened? I thought you were on the pill?"

"With everything going on, I forgot to take it for a few days. You were in the hospital, so I didn't think it was that big of a deal. But then we had that day in the apartment..."

"The day I asked you to marry me, the first time."

"Yeah, I think that was it."

I pull her in for a kiss and can't wait to build this future with her. "I love you, Wynnie Juniper, soon to be Langford. We'll have to add Tori's date to your keychain when you adopt her and officially become her mother, too. And I'd like that to happen as soon as possible." She smiles, and tears well in her eyes.

"I'd love that, and I love you too, Scotty Too Hottie Langford, soon-to-be Daddy of two."

Epilogue Elliot

Four years of college, six boyfriends, two girlfriends, a best friend with three beautiful babies, amazing parents, determination, and perseverance that I had to push through every day. All of that has gotten me to this point.

I stare up, up and up even more. The building in front of me towers over all the others. All around me, the sidewalks are busy, filled with early morning people heading to work.

I look down at the fountain beside me and place my hand on the plaque.

Griffin Woodlyn
Beloved Husband and Father
"There's no expiration date on the love of a father."

A petite hand with a beautiful wedding band and a diamond ring lined with yellow stones wraps over mine.

"Are you ready for orientation?" Wynnie leans her head on my shoulder.

"Am I ready to follow in both my fathers' footsteps and conquer the business world? Yes." I turn and pull her into a hug. "Am I ready to live eleven hours away from my best friend, nieces, and nephew? Absolutely fucking not. Doesn't Scotty want to franchise and open a Tipsy Penny here? I can fund it."

"This is hard on me, too."

"I know. I can't thank you enough for coming out here with me. I know it's hard to be away from your littles for so long." She scoffs in my chest.

"Trust me, Scotty has it under control. And if he doesn't, Tori's favorite pastime is bossing around her brother and sister."

"Or anyone at the mini compound you live on, for that matter." When Wynnie got pregnant with her second child, Mac insisted their house was too small. He cleared several acres of land, and they all built Wynnie's family a house. Hazel is trying to wear my Dad down to build another house so Mom and my siblings can also live there.

"You're going to be late if you don't go in." I hug her close again.

"Are you sure you'll be okay alone until I'm done with orientation?"

"El, I'm a big girl, and it's only four hours. I'll be fine. I looked up coffee shops online, and there's this one nearby called S'morgasm. I *have* to check it out."

I touch the plaque one more time.

"Uncle Griffin and Aunt Zoey are proud of you. I just know it." I sniff and blink away the tears threatening to form.

"Dammit, woman. You're gonna make my eyes leak, and I have to look fabulous on my first day. Stop it. Tell me you love me, and go get your orgasmic coffee. If you're a good girl, maybe I'll take you to the aquarium to see the fishies when I'm done." I pat her head, and she reaches up and kisses my cheek.

"I love having a best friend, sugar daddy. Be good, El, or be good at it." She blows me a kiss as she walks away. I'm going to miss the hell out of that woman.

I take one last look up at the sign for MAD Gaming Inc. and walk towards the building. Ready or not, my future is on the other side of those revolving doors.

THE END

Continue reading for the beginning of Elliot's book, Elliot's Empowerment.

If you enjoyed Wynnie's book or any of my other works I'd be ecstatic if you'd leave me a review on the platform of your choice. Thank you for taking a chance on an indie author and I hope you continue to read my other works.

Elliot Chapter 1

As I walk through the revolving doors for only the second time, I try not to look like a tourist and swivel my head, looking at the incredible architecture of the building. The beautiful young woman at the front desk asks for my ID, and I hand it to her. She smiles at me while printing my temporary sticker for the day and directs me to the human resource office.

When I came a month ago for my interview, I got the same sticker, but instead of the word 'visitor,' it now says 'employee' under my name. Elliot McLain, employee of MAD Gaming Inc.

Towards the end of orientation, which included a tour, taking my picture for a permanent ID, and several videos on sexual harassment and proper workplace behavior, I was handed a note.

Please come to the top floor when orientation is over.
Annie

I've been a nervous wreck since reading the note. I've never met Ms. Poulsen, or does she go by McGrath? I know she's married now. I've googled her more times than is probably acceptable over the years.

I shake the hand of the generic-looking businessman who

led my orientation and make a mental note to never look
that bland.

"I have a note to see Ms… Mrs… Pouls… Annie?" He looks
at me awkwardly like the stumbling idiot I'm acting like.

"Ms. Poulsen is on the top floor. It requires special access.
You'll have to go back down to the lobby and get clearance.

"Oh, okay. Thank you."

The pretty lady at the front desk smiles when she sees me
again.

"How can I help you, Mr. McLain." *Whoa.*

"You remember my name already?"

"It's my job to remember." Her smile brightens. Is it your
job to flirt too, front desk lady? "What can I do for you, Mr.
McLain? Was everything alright with orientation?" She's
not just pretty. Fuck, she's gorgeous. Bright brown doe eyes,
wavy brown hair halfway down her back. Her navy dress
disappears under her desk, but I can still see her petite figure
that I would wreck if—

"Mr. McLain?" *Shit.*

"Sorry. I'm supposed to see Ms. Poulsen. The guy who ran
my orientation told me I had to start here again."

"Lucky me." She winks at me. Definitely flirting…with
a ring on. Dammit. The prettiest ones are always married.
"But you didn't need to come down here. You have full access
to the top floor with your new ID card."

"I do?" I look at my ID attached to my suit jacket pocket and
read it carefully. In the bottom corner is a green check mark
and the words "Full Access" written in bold letters. "Um, I
had no idea. Thank you. Do I need to do anything special?"

"When you enter the elevator and press the top floor, it
won't move until it scans your card. Just swipe it over the

scanner and you'll be good to go."

"Thank you..." I try to peer over and read her name tag.

"It's Alaina, but you can call me Lainey." Her smile goes straight to my dick. *Calm down, boy.*

"Thank you for your help, Lainey. I'll see you again soon." I walk away before I jump over the counter and take her under her desk. Shit. I need to get laid.

I follow her instructions once in the elevator and take it to the top floor. The doors open and I immediately step off.

"Holy fuck." My loud curse echoes through the room as I'm blinded by the floors. "What the hell?" I look up at the ceiling, hoping to regain my eyesight and hear a laugh. No, there are two laughs.

"Walk forward about six feet. There's nothing in front of you to bump into." I do as I'm told, and when I look down, I feel like I'm blinded again. Why is every woman in this building stunningly gorgeous?

I hear more laughing.

"I highly agree with you, Mr. McLain." The brunette smiles at me and looks at the blonde beside her. *What? Oh shit.* Did I say that last part out loud?

"Please call me Elliot."

"Alright, Elliot. Yes, in case you're wondering, you said that out loud. Do you usually have issues with your internal monologue?" The brunette is giggling at me at this point, and I want a hole to open up in the floor so I can step into it and disappear from this entirely embarrassing encounter.

As my vision finally comes into full focus, I recognize the blonde as Ms. Poulsen.

"Shit. I mean. Sorry. No. I don't usually have trouble. I'm normally much better at—" I stop my rambling because the more I talk, the more I sound like an idiot.

"I'm not sure I've heard anyone stumble over their words this terribly since Cole." I know who Cole is. That's who Ms. Poulsen married. I'm not entirely sure who the brunette woman beside her is, though. I've seen her in a few pictures online, but there's never any mention of her name.

"I'm BlakeLynn Rogers, you can call me Blake." She extends her hand for me to shake. "This is Danika Poulsen, but please call her Annie, despite what she might tell you." Blake turns to Annie. "I'm grabbing coffee at S'morgasm, and I'll be back. Would you like your usual?"

"Yes please. Thank you, *Mijn Diamant*."

"Oh, my best friend just went there. Brown hair and the brightest blue eyes you've ever seen, They're hard to miss. Her name is Wynnie."

"If I see her, I'll say hi. Would you like anything, Elliot?"

"No, but thank you for the offer, Blake." She kisses Annie on the lips and walks past me. I'm speechless because it was a little more than a friendly kiss.

"Elliot, BlakeLynn is my wife for all intents and purposes. This floor is part of my inner circle, and as your ID tag says, you are now a part of that. What happens on this floor stays here. You've signed several NDAs. Do you understand?"

I raise my hands in surrender. "I'm a card-carrying bisexual. And my best friend's mom has three husbands. Love is love." She nods and extends her arm to the hallway behind her.

"Glad we are on the same page. Let's continue this conversation in my office."

Coming Spring 2024

403

About the Author

Casiddie is a single mom to five amazing children who are her biggest cheerleaders. Casiddie enjoys writing contemporary romance but hopes to dive into more darker subjects in the near future.

You can connect with me on:

f https://www.facebook.com/casiddiewilliams

🔗 https://www.tiktok.com/@casiddiewilliams_author

Also by Casiddie Williams

Hazel's Harem

A new job opportunity brings curvaceous, single mom Hazel Gibson, back to her hometown where she finds her hands full with a little more than just her 12 year old daughter.

When two gorgeous men offer her a six week proposition to be with both of them together, no strings attached, Hazel decides you only live once, and why choose if you don't have to?

But life has a habit of throwing Hazel curve balls, and she finds herself having to make some major life decisions to protect her family. Curve ball #1: When you're already juggling two men, what's one more?

Dellah's Delight

Dellah Brooks is the best as far as best friends go. She lives the perfect life. She went to college. Owns her own business. Fell in love and married her college sweetheart. But there has always been something missing.

Collin McLain couldn't believe how lucky he was to win the lottery, by marrying the woman he almost ran over in a parking lot. A successful career at his family business has given him the best future for his family.

Each carry a dark secret. One from her best friend the other from his wife.

When secrets are revealed will they be able to repair the betrayal between the ones they love the most? Can a devastating tragedy heal the hole in Dellah's heart enough to forgive and be forgiven?

Annie You're Okay

Danika "Annie" Poulsen is a grumpy Billionaire and Dominatrix who has everything she could ever want out of life at the age of 34. A thriving software company, a gorgeous submissive girlfriend, and a trouble-making Doberman complete her life.

Blake Rogers is a 29 year old bubbly secretary who is willing to submit and give her body and pleasure over to her billionaire girlfriend.

Together, they're happy in their relationship and their roles within it until they meet a man who shakes up everything they know about themselves and each other.

Cole McGrath is starting over in a new town at 22. A dog walker with an Alpha personality and a side of Golden Retriever mixed in, it wasn't part of his plan to meet two beautiful women and rock their worlds in more ways than one.

When tragedy strikes and their lives and relationships are tested, will they be able to repair their shattered pieces?

Will they be okay?

Made in the USA
Middletown, DE
26 April 2025